Belinda Alexandra has been published to wide acclaim in Australia, New Zealand, the United Kingdom, France, Germany, Holland, Poland, Norway, Russia, Spain, Turkey, Hungary and the United States. She is the daughter of a Russian mother and an Australian father and has been an intrepid traveller since her youth. Her love of other cultures is matched by her passion for her home country, Australia, where she is a member of the New South Wales Wildlife Information Rescue and Education Service (WIRES). An animal lover, Belinda is also the patron of the World League for the Protection of Animals (Australia). Find out more at belinda-alexandra.com

- **f** BelindaAlexandraAuthor
- **𝕏** belinda_alexandra_author
- **⬛** belinda_alexandra_author

'*The Invitation* is a wildly entertaining and absorbing read that leaves you with a lot to think about' – *Better Reading*

'A tale of excess, depravity and hidden family secrets — there's much to love in Alexandra's latest historical drama ... Beautifully researched' – *Daily Telegraph*

Also by Belinda Alexandra

BELINDA ALEXANDRA

The INVITATION

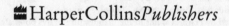
HarperCollins*Publishers*

HarperCollins*Publishers*

First published in Australia in 2018
This edition published in 2019
by HarperCollins*Publishers* Australia Pty Limited
ABN 36 009 913 517
harpercollins.com.au

HarperCollins*Publishers*
Level 13, 201 Elizabeth Street, Sydney NSW 2000, Australia
Unit D1, 63 Apollo Drive, Rosedale, Auckland 0632, New Zealand
A 53, Sector 57, Noida, UP, India
1 London Bridge Street, London SE1 9GF, United Kingdom
Bay Adelaide Centre, East Tower, 22 Adelaide Street West, 41st floor, Toronto, Ontario M5H 4E3, Canada
195 Broadway, New York NY 10007, USA

A catalogue entry for this book is available from the National Library of Australia.

ISBN: 978 0 7322 9664 3 (paperback)
ISBN: 978 1 7430 9833 2 (ebook)

Cover design by Lisa White
Cover images: Woman by Richard Jenkins; Panorama of New York river front, New York City United States, 1900. [Photograph] Retrieved from the Library of Congress, 2013647117
Author photograph by Elizabeth Allnutt
Typeset in Sabon 11/16.5 by Kirby Jones
Printed and bound in Australia by McPherson's Printing Group
The papers used by HarperCollins in the manufacture of this book are a natural, recyclable product made from wood grown in sustainable plantation forests. The fibre source and manufacturing processes meet recognised international environmental standards, and carry certification.

For 'The Girls'

ONE

Paris 1899

When I arrived at the café on Rue du Faubourg-Montmartre, my colourful friends were already there, engaged in a lively conversation. Claude was the first to see me and waved. The others turned to look at who had caught his attention. It was clear from their pleased expressions that he had shared my good news.

'Ah, here is our great literary success!' said Nicolas. He hadn't changed out of his overalls before coming to the café and his clothes and face were smeared in yellow and black paint. 'I present to you Mademoiselle Emma Lacasse, authoress of mysterious tales!'

Claude stood up and kissed me. He looked handsome in his corduroy suit with his clean-shaven face and mop of wavy brown hair. Although he was French he exuded a Mediterranean sensuality that added to his allure. Even after five years of being together I was still mesmerised by his smoky grey eyes.

'I trust you don't mind that I told them about your novella before you had a chance,' he said, squeezing my hand. 'The news is too exciting not to share it right away.'

'It gives us hope of our own ships coming in some day,' said Sophie, moving over so Claude and I could sit together. 'That's pretty by the way,' she added, casting her doll-like eyes over my navy blue dress. 'Is it new?'

I shook my head. 'No, but I added some lace to the collar and cuffs.'

'Our drinks are on you today!' said Robert, pushing back his reddish-brown hair. He was a poet but his real talent was persuading other people to pay for him.

'All right,' I said, signalling to Jean-François, the café owner, to bring us a couple of carafes of wine and some glasses. Although the advance I had received for the novella was hardly going to keep the wolves from the door, I was in a mood to celebrate. After years of submissions to literary journals, dozens of short stories and a few one-act stage plays, I'd finally written something substantial.

Belda, whose white-grey hair, high cheekbones and porcelain skin evoked a fairytale queen, leaned towards me. 'I like the premise,' she said. 'Every woman whose lover has betrayed her would like to exact her revenge the way your heroine does — although her repayment is quite unintentional. What are you writing now?'

'I'm finishing another novella called *The Mysterious Cat* as well as some more short stories,' I told her. 'After that I'll attempt my first novel.'

'Have you got an idea for the novel yet?' she asked. 'You should have a harpist as a character. It always helps to write what you know.'

While I told her about my ideas, she picked up her sketchpad and drew furiously. Belda was one of my favourite Montmartre eccentrics. She had been a promising young artist but had been exploited by her dealer. When she tried to leave him, he had crushed her right hand in an etching press. He hadn't realised that Belda was left-handed and the ensuing court case made her famous and greatly inflated the price of her work. With the proceeds she had bought a house with a garden on Rue Girardon that was large enough to rent out several rooms, and lived a good life there with her menagerie of rescued cats, dogs, geese and goats. She also ran salons for artists and from time to time wrote as a literary critic. It was Belda who had introduced me to my publisher.

When she was finished, she handed her picture to me. She had captured my snowy blondeness, my slender neck and shoulders and thin arms faithfully. Disconcertingly, she had also caught the bereft look in my eyes.

Jean-François arrived with our wine and glasses. He placed a copy of my collection of short stories, *Histoires de fantômes*, on the table for me to sign. It always gave me a thrill to see the yellow cloth cover with my name embossed in gold above the title.

'I shall place it proudly on the counter and let people know that Mademoiselle Lacasse is one of my regular customers,' he said.

'Look at them,' whispered Sophie, indicating a couple who were standing across the street and staring in our direction.

The woman's dress was bouclé silk with gigot sleeves and a collar and yoke of layered silk satin. Her companion was equally well-dressed in a striped suit with arrow-point lapels and a Homburg-style hat. They couldn't have been more out of place on the manure-strewn street but they regarded us and the café like two children gazing into the window of a sweet shop.

'Come in! Come in!' Jean-François called to them. 'Come and drink in a genuine Bohemian café where the most interesting artists, dancers and writers spend their time dreaming up wonderful ideas!'

His invitation was like dangling a carrot in front of a donkey. The couple looked at each other, then rushed across the street and eagerly sat down at the table Jean-François offered them. Claude and I exchanged a smile.

'Those gloves!' said Sophie, captivated by the rich lady's attire. 'Pale yellow — imagine that! She probably only wears them once then throws them away.' She sighed with envy. 'I bet she's never cold either. She probably doesn't get out of bed until the servants have lit the fires. I'm dreading this coming winter. Vauclain's studio is always freezing, and although he has money he puts up a fuss if I ask him to put more coals in the stove.'

'I went to dinner at Vauclain's home once,' said Belda. 'He kept his best bottle of wine for himself and served a cheaper variety to his guests.'

We all roared with laughter.

'That will be Robert one day,' said Claude. 'If he ever does invite us to dinner.'

Robert joined in the mirth. Our little group of artists ribbed each other mercilessly but we always supported each other. Despite Robert's avarice, we enjoyed his bravado and listening to his stories, especially from his time working in a circus.

While the others continued talking, I noticed Sophie's thin arm when she picked up her glass of wine. She was skin and bone, and couldn't afford to lose any more weight if she wanted to keep working as an artist's model. I ordered some mushroom soup and bread, then pretended it was too much for me and passed the rest to her.

'Thank you,' she said, taking a spoonful. 'My sister from Pont-Aven is staying with me again. I love her but she drives me crazy. She insists on cooking for me but she either over-salts the food or burns it! I don't have the money to keep going to the market.'

'Why is she staying with you?' I asked.

'She and her husband had another fight. He's a brute who becomes violent when he drinks. I told her not to marry him.'

'At least you can turn to each other in times of need,' I said. 'That's worth being driven crazy for.'

As I spoke, I sensed Claude listening. He tugged his earlobe but said nothing.

Robert began a story about Siamese twin sisters he'd known in the circus. 'One was a contralto and one was a soprano and they were beautiful to listen to ...'

Claude touched my hand and nodded to the clock on the café wall. 'We'd better get going if you want to see your publisher before he leaves for the day,' he reminded me.

We wished the others goodbye and went inside the café so I could pay Jean-François. Afterwards, he reached under the counter and handed Claude an envelope with money in it.

'I've sold nearly all your postcards this week,' he said. 'Make sure you bring me some more soon.'

Claude pushed the envelope into his pocket without a glance and gave a silent nod to Jean-François. The postcard sketches were signed 'Jolicoeur', which was Claude's equivalent of a nom de plume. He drew Paris scenes and sold them through various cafés and tourist shops to support his more serious art.

'And for you, mademoiselle,' said Jean-François, 'I have an even bigger package.' He handed me a bunch of envelopes tied together with a piece of string. 'Your admirers are increasing by the day. These all came at once.'

If only the letters were all from my admirers! I quickly tucked the package under my arm before Claude spotted the yellow envelopes from Roche & Associates, the debt collectors.

'Your publisher gave you good advice when he told you to provide an address other than your personal one for readers to write to,' Claude said as we walked out to the street. 'You'll have to hire a secretary soon.'

My smile was more of a grimace. I didn't like keeping secrets from Claude, but he was not a rich man. The last thing I wanted was for him to make some heroic effort to save me. My debts were my problem and I had to address them on my own.

◦◦◦◦◦◦◦◦

My publisher, Monsieur Plamondon, had offices on Rue Auber in the ninth arrondissement. When his clerk announced me, he welcomed me with a broad grin that showed the gap between his front teeth. I was fortunate that Belda had introduced me to Monsieur Plamondon. He took on few new writers and was exacting in his standards when it came to fiction. 'There are too many second-rate writers in your genre, Mademoiselle Lacasse,' he'd told me when I first met him. 'I'm going to push you to improve with each new piece.'

'Mademoiselle Lacasse,' he said now, 'what a pleasure to see you!' He nodded towards the letters under my arm. 'I see the correspondence we forwarded to the café reached you? The letters are increasing by the day. What a lot of happy readers you have created!'

'It appears so,' I said, taking the seat that he offered me.

Mahogany bookshelves covered every wall of his office and were crammed with novels. The air carried an intriguing combination of odours: musty old books and fresh ink from the piles of papers stacked on his desk.

'So tell me what you are working on at the moment,' he said.

I described the outline of my novella about a woman who returns to life as a cat and visits her friends and relatives to discover what they really thought of her when she was alive. 'I'm also working on ideas for a novel. For some reason the image of two sisters keeps floating up in my mind: two sisters with a secret.'

Monsieur Plamondon had a way of scrunching up his face when I was speaking and relaxing it again when I paused. It was as if he was a sponge trying to soak up every word I was saying.

'What intrigues me about you, Mademoiselle Lacasse, is that when you come to see me you look as fresh and innocent as a dandelion in a field. I am quite sure you could never harm another human being, or even hold ill will towards one. Yet your stories reveal the dark side of human nature. I find that fascinating.'

'Perhaps we are attracted to the opposite of what we are,' I told him. 'My themes of love lasting beyond the grave, gruesome deaths and bottomless grief often surprise me. I never think of myself as macabre but my writing often turns out that way.'

'Indeed we are fascinated by our opposites. It was certainly true of my late wife and me. She lived at only one volume — loud. While I have always valued tranquillity.' Monsieur Plamondon sat back and closed his eyes for a moment, as if revelling in the hushed quiet of his office. Then he smiled at me. 'I heard you played the harp for a production at the Théâtre de l'Oeuvre. I didn't know you were an accomplished harpist.'

'My grandmother taught me from an early age until her arthritis prevented her continuing,' I explained. 'Then she engaged a teacher. My grandfather was a doctor but also a gifted pianist. Apparently they fell in love playing duets.'

Monsieur Plamondon clapped his hands. 'What a perfect way to fall in love. It's a pity you don't write romantic fiction — that would make a good story.'

When it was time for me to leave, Monsieur Plamondon searched among the papers on his desk, then handed me a book written in English: *The Awakening* by Kate Chopin.

'An American colleague sent me this. It is excellent. I wondered if you would read it too and give me your opinion, as a woman? I sent him *A Tale of a Lonely House* in return, in case he feels there is an American readership for your work.'

'I hope there is,' I told him, delighted. 'To be published in English would be marvellous.'

The United States had a population of over seventy million people, double that of France. An American readership might be what I needed to save me from my financial troubles.

'It's about a woman who leaves her husband and children to find her personal freedom,' Monsieur Plamondon said, gesturing towards the Chopin novel. 'The story is set in Louisiana — you were born there, weren't you?'

'I left the United States when I was less than two years old,' I explained. 'The plantation where I was born was ruined in the Civil War, and my parents died of yellow fever. I came to live with my maternal grandmother and ... here in Paris.'

I had almost slipped and mentioned Caroline. I was careful who I told about my sister because it was too painful to explain our estrangement. Sophie's sister drove her crazy but at least they had each other. In my case, Caroline might as well have not existed.

Monsieur Plamondon rubbed his chin. 'Louisiana has an eerie atmosphere, full of ghosts and voodoo. Perhaps you will write about it one day? Although you were very young when you left, it is astounding what can lie hidden in our unconscious mind.'

❧◦❧◦❧

When I returned to my apartment on Rue Jacob in the afternoon I was surprised to find my boarders, Mrs Cutter and her daughter, Elizabeth, sitting in the parlour drinking tea. I'd expected they would still be out taking in the museums and art galleries.

'Oh, Mademoiselle Lacasse, Paris is a dream! A dream!' said Mrs Cutter, clutching her hands in her lap. 'We decided not to go to the Louvre today because every street around here is a painting. We walked to Rue de Rivoli and everywhere we turned there was something beautiful to see. Even the way the laces are arranged in the haberdashery store is a delight to the eye.'

'See here, Mademoiselle Lacasse,' Elizabeth indicated a vase of silvery pink roses on the side table, 'aren't they divine? The florist said they were Joséphine Bonaparte's favourite cultivars.'

I smiled and leaned over to inhale the sweet tea fragrance of the roses. I was sure the flowers in Boston, where Mrs Cutter and her daughter came from, were just as pretty, but like many of the American women who stayed with me they viewed French civilisation as older, richer and more elegant than their own. That was why, when their husbands started to succeed in business, they came to see me with their adult daughters, hoping I could impart the taste, intellectual wit and sophisticated charm that Parisian women were famous for. I gave them board, along with lessons in the French language and etiquette.

'And look at Mademoiselle Lacasse's pretty dress, Lizzie,' said Mrs Cutter, glancing at me with admiration. 'She certainly has that French *je ne sais quoi*. Mademoiselle Lacasse, you must introduce us to your dressmaker while we are here.'

In truth, I bought all my clothes on sale at Le Bon Marché. I was always careful to choose the simplest, best-tailored dress I could afford and then added little embellishments here and there — some embroidery, a touch of lace, an elegant brooch. But of course I couldn't tell Mrs Cutter that; or that I was born in America, like herself. As Voltaire stated: *Illusion is the first of all pleasures*. What I gave my guests was better than reality. I gave them Paris without the officialdom, chauvinism, poverty and the tainted horsemeat disguised with a rich sauce.

'I must attend to my correspondence,' I said to the women, picking up from the sideboard the post that had come directly to the apartment and adding it to the stack I already held. 'But let's get together before dinner and practise French for social occasions. Meanwhile, why don't you go over the names of the French dishes I gave you yesterday?'

Mrs Cutter and Elizabeth enthusiastically agreed to the plan. I left them to roll their tongues around *consommé de volaille à la Sévigné* and *pommes de terre à l'anglaise* and went to my room. I closed the door behind me and placed the bundle of letters on my writing desk, next to the photograph of Grand-maman.

'*Salut*, Grand-maman,' I said, gently tracing the outline of her kind face. It comforted me to see her every day but it pinched my heart too.

Underneath the frame was a folded piece of paper from the journal in which I had written down her last lucid words to me: *I am not afraid to die. I am only sorry that I am leaving you alone, Emma, because I know what a sensitive heart you have and that you will grieve deeply. Don't, my child, because I will always be with you, watching over you. My love will remain with you forever.*

I sat down at the desk and pressed my hands together. 'I will love you forever too, Grand-maman. Please help me.'

I spread the letters and postcards over my desk. The yellow envelopes paralysed me with helplessness. There were more of them than last time, and now they were being stamped *Urgent.*

I'd always known somewhere in my mind that I would lose Grand-maman one day, but I imagined she would simply fall asleep in her chair by the fire and slip from this world to the next. She was too good a person, too kind, too sweet, to suffer. At first I assumed the tenderness in her abdomen, the sudden weakness and loss of appetite were signs she was growing older. My blood turned to ice when the doctor told me it was cancer. I mortgaged the apartment to pay for the expensive X-rays, and to take Grand-maman to Germany where a doctor used localised hyperthermia to produce tumour regression in patients. Nothing helped. Grand-maman endured her pain and met her death with dignity, while I fought and fought. After that moment when her soul left her body and her chest sank and her features fell flat, I had a new companion that walked with me every day: grief.

And now the debt collectors were coming after me.

I opened the envelope from Roche & Associates with the most recent date but couldn't bring myself to unfold the letter. Instead I lifted one corner and peeked at it as if I were staring down a dangerous viper. Like the previous notices it was typewritten, which somehow imbued it with a greater sense of threat than if it had been written by hand.

I glimpsed the words: *The outstanding amount remains unpaid despite our previous reminders. We urge you to contact us immediately. If we do not hear from you within fourteen days of the receipt of this letter we will be forced to refer this matter to the courts, where your continued lack of compliance could lead to imprisonment ...*

Chills ran down my back. How was it possible that I had accrued such a formidable debt? Before Grand-maman became ill I'd been able to support us comfortably with my harp lessons and recitals and my published pieces. With careful saving, I'd even been able to take her to the spa in Vichy once a year to relieve her arthritis. But those days of happy abundance were a distant memory. When Grand-maman was in pain, I was in pain too. It was unendurable. I couldn't play the harp. I couldn't write. It would take a miracle for me to repay so much money now!

I placed the yellow envelopes in the desk drawer along with the others from Roche & Associates, and with trembling hands turned to the letters from my readers as a distraction. People who enjoyed my stories were my salvation. Maybe one day I would be a very successful writer and this dark time would be behind me. But that time wasn't coming soon enough.

TWO

On Sunday, Claude and I caught the train from Gare du Nord to Pierrefitte, the village north of Paris where his family lived. The trip was only twenty minutes by train but we may as well have travelled to another country. There wasn't much to the village besides a bakery, a bar tabac and an optician's shop with a pair of giant spectacles as its sign.

'Smell the air,' Claude said as we walked to his parents' home. He opened his arms wide and took in deep breaths.

I followed his example. The air had that special quality of freshness that braced the nostrils and caressed the lungs. I was happy to be out of Paris and escaping my troubles, even for a short while.

'I can picture you growing up here,' I said, playfully pinching his arm. 'Naughty Claude running through the village streets with his socks down.'

'A writer is always imagining things,' he said, taking my hand. 'It was a nice place for a child to grow up, but it was stifling for an adolescent with any sort of inventiveness. I once painted gold a single apple on each tree in old Madame Léger's orchard. She believed it was a miracle and told the priest. After he investigated, he suspected me immediately and informed my father who gave me a beating. Some of the old ladies here still talk about me as if I am some sort of devil. You don't know how lucky you were to grow up in Paris.'

The Tremblay family home was a three-storey house fashioned from grey stone. The roof sloped steeply and a thicket of ivy clung to the walls. It was a respectable bourgeois home for a respectable bourgeois family, headed by Claude's father who was a bookkeeper in a drapery firm.

We let go of each other's hand and walked down the path, past the pear and plum trees, which were tinged with their autumn colours, to the front door. Before we reached it, four small children burst out and circled us.

'What's the magic password?' asked Marie. At seven years of age, she was the eldest of Claude's nieces and nephews. 'You can't come inside unless you say it.'

Claude scratched his chin. 'Password? Let me see … is it … "hiccup"!'

The children covered their mouths and giggled.

'No,' said Cosme, who was four years old. With his chubby face and blond ringlets, he was a perfect model for a cherub.

'Is it "cabbage"?' I asked, trying to remember what the secret word had been last time we visited.

'No!' cried Paul and Louis, the twins.

To give us a clue Marie put her finger to her nose and twisted it.

'Ew,' said Claude, screwing up his face. 'Not snot!'

The children nodded and ran around the side of the house, giggling and pushing each other.

'Why are children always fascinated by disgusting things?' Claude said with a good-natured shrug.

'Because they haven't learned to be serious yet,' I told him.

Inside the house we were greeted by the buttery-sweet aroma of potatoes baking for Claude's mother's favourite side dish, duchess potatoes. She poked her immaculately coiffured head out of the kitchen and smiled when she saw us.

'Papa will be pleased you are on time today,' she said, kissing us both on the cheeks. 'You know he has that irritating saying: "If you are early, you are on time"!'

Although she was in her late fifties, Madame Tremblay had the pliant complexion of a young woman. She had been a singer with the Opéra-Comique in her youth, and although she was respectable in her striped brushed cotton dress and starched apron, she still radiated the magnetism and energy of a performer. Claude had inherited his charisma from her.

Madame Tremblay left the maid, Anouk, to complete the dinner preparations and ushered us into the sitting room where Claude's father and brother, Albert, were drinking crème de cassis. Albert had joined Monsieur Tremblay in the drapery business and lived with his wife, Lucie, in the house next door. The father and son could have been twins, with their round bespectacled faces and their checked suits and fob watches. They rose when they saw us.

'You look lovely, Emma, as always,' Monsieur Tremblay told me.

'What is that suit you are wearing?' Albert asked Claude, an amused smile dancing on his lips. 'You look like a dandy.'

'Thank you,' answered Claude, twisting the jab into a compliment. 'One can only try.'

Claude had left for Montmartre when he was eighteen to live the free life of an artist, so he and Albert were the opposite of each other in many ways. But despite their differences, I sensed that if something happened to either one of them, the other would drop everything to be at his brother's side.

Outside I could hear Lucie and Claude's sister, Agathe, calling in the children from the garden. 'Come and wash up before dinner,' Lucie was saying. 'Cosme, what a fright you look! How did you get so much dirt on your face?'

'Where is Franc?' Claude asked about his brother-in-law.

'Monsieur Durand's best horse has an abscess,' Monsieur Tremblay answered. 'Franc has gone to drain it.'

Claude grimaced. 'Ah, the life of a veterinarian.'

Anouk informed Madame Tremblay that dinner was on the table. Claude's mother removed her apron and directed us into the cramped dining room with its dark wooden panels and heavy First Empire table and sideboard.

The children took their places, except for Cosme who skipped past his chair and hoisted himself into my lap, resting his heavy golden head against my chest.

'I like Emma,' he said. 'She's the same colour as me.'

'Get off Emma and sit on your own chair,' Lucie gently scolded him.

Cosme smelled of Castile soap and his warm body snuggled to mine was comforting. I experienced a sense of loss when he slipped off my lap and went and pressed his head against his mother's arm.

Madame Tremblay smiled. 'You've always been his favourite, Emma. Cosme has an eye for attractive ladies.'

'As does Claude,' joked Albert.

As dinner progressed, the chatter around the table grew lively, with the subjects ranging from the preparations for the Paris Exposition Universelle to the best way to make a *bouquet garni*. I marvelled at how Claude's family could speak all at once and still understand each other. My gaze drifted over their happy faces to the family portrait that hung opposite the fireplace. In the picture, Monsieur and Madame Tremblay were seated, with Albert and Lucie, Franc and Agathe, Claude and the children surrounding them. The old family sheepdog, Bonfils, was in the picture next to Monsieur Tremblay's chair. The photograph had been taken only a year ago but I wasn't in it. Family portraits did not include fiancées let alone 'girlfriends'.

Claude and I were enjoying the company of his family so much that we lost track of time and missed the last train back to Paris. It wasn't the first time it had happened, and Madame Tremblay kept a nightdress and brush set especially for me in the guest room on the second floor.

I watched her turn back the covers on the bed and fluff the pillows. Every movement she performed exuded the elegance of someone who had trained for the stage. Did she ever regret giving up her career for a husband and a family?

As if reading my mind, she kissed me goodnight then peered into my eyes. 'I will ask my husband to have a word with Claude. Five years is too long to keep you waiting. I want you for a daughter-in-law. I want more grandchildren.'

I longed to reply that she would be the perfect mother-in-law. Even the simple things Madame Tremblay did for me — lending me books that she had enjoyed reading or collecting flowers from the garden to make a bouquet for me to put on my writing table —nurtured me. They were the kinds of things Grand-maman had done when she was well, and they meant the world to me. But, out of loyalty to Claude, I only smiled at her comment. He had expressed his views on the 'bourgeois institution of marriage' many times.

After Madame Tremblay left, I changed into my nightdress and climbed into bed. The sheets smelled deliciously of lavender water and I snuggled my face to the soft pillow, listening to the rest of the household settling down. Anouk was closing windows, and in the room above me, where Claude's parents slept, floorboards creaked. Eventually the house fell into a silence so profound that my whole body became alert. There were no noises from the street outside, and if it wasn't for the bright moon the room would have been in total darkness. It wasn't like sleeping in Montmartre when I stayed overnight with Claude. There, laughter and music drifted from the cabarets and dance halls until the early hours of the morning, and it wasn't uncommon to hear the loud grunting of a man satisfying himself with a prostitute in the laneway.

A muted tapping sounded at the door.

'What's the password?' I whispered.

'*Amour*,' Claude said softly back.

'You may enter.'

Claude, dressed in his nightshirt, closed the door behind him before lifting the bed covers and slipping in beside me. He wrapped his arm around my waist and curled up with me.

'You'll be in trouble with your father,' I said. 'We aren't married.'

'We'll be quiet,' he said. 'I was watching you all night and thinking of how I'd like to paint you naked.'

'Nude, you mean. Doesn't Vauclain always say there's a difference between nude and naked?'

Claude's fingers reached for the hem of my nightdress and tugged it up over my hips. With his other hand he undid the tie at the neckline and slid it over my shoulders, kissing my bare skin with his warm lips.

'You would make a beautiful nude,' he said.

'You want me to pose for you? Do you want to ruin my reputation completely?'

He turned my body towards him. 'It would be a painting for me only. Then, when you are busy writing, I could still admire you.'

His fingers slid gently between my legs. I surrendered myself to the pleasure of his touch, but when I moaned he pressed his lips to mine in a kiss. Then I was lost as his mouth travelled down my neck and to my breasts, and his hand continued to drive me deeper and deeper into ecstasy. I reached for him and touched his hardness, massaging him until he too was biting his lips to suppress cries of rapture. Although I longed for him to enter me and possess me completely, we pleasured each other with our hands until we were both spent. Afterwards we lay in each other's arms, listening to the silence.

'I want to marry you and have children with you,' I said.

He didn't answer. He didn't have to. We had shared this conversation many times and it always ended the same way.

'I love you, and I want a family to love as well,' I continued. 'I want to hold a little boy like Cosme, and watch a precocious little girl like Marie blossom into a beautiful young woman. I don't want to be alone any more.'

'You like my niece and nephews because you can hand them back. You wouldn't want them all the time, Emma. When would you write? When would I paint? As I've told you many times, my mother gave up a spectacular career to marry my father. I would never ask the same sacrifice of you.'

I squeezed my eyes shut to prevent my tears running down my face. It was easy for Claude to reject the idea of a family because he had one. Yes, his mother had given up her career but she looked happy and contented surrounded by her children and grandchildren. Never once had I heard her complain. A deep pain pinched my stomach: an ache born of desiring something deeply but not believing I could have it. Someone in my past had taught me that my dreams weren't as important as everybody else's.

'I love you, Emma,' Claude said, nuzzling his cheek into my neck. 'You are not alone.'

His breathing grew heavier and deeper and he was soon asleep. Despite his assurances, forlornness washed over me and I stifled a sob. I am alone, I thought. What a thing it was to have a family; but those who were born into one thought nothing of it. I'd only had Grand-maman and now she was gone. Caroline was hardly a source of love and support. Perhaps if I had parents and brothers and sisters I could depend upon, I wouldn't feel that the rug was about to be pulled from under my feet. We would work together to deal with my debts. But even if I had all that, I would still want a husband and children of my own.

Writing gave me a sense of doing something wonderful and important, but I also longed to love fully from my heart and to take care of a family in a way that was selfless. I had an inkling that if all I did with my life was to write, I might end up totally self-absorbed. I didn't want that. I didn't want to be anything like my sister.

❧

Early the next morning, Claude and I caught the train back to Paris loaded up with carrots, turnips, spinach and leeks from Madame Tremblay's garden. The aroma of the fresh produce was enlivening, making me feel like I'd lain down in a flourishing vegetable patch and become one with the earth. Although the trip was short, Madame Tremblay had also prepared us grilled cheese and tomato sandwiches wrapped in brown paper 'for the journey'. She was a woman who enjoyed taking care of people.

She had also kept her promise to encourage Claude's father to speak to him about marriage. As we were heading down the garden path for our walk to the station, he called after us, 'I expect an announcement by the end of this year. You have both just turned twenty-six — you're not spring chickens any more!'

When we reached Gare du Nord, I handed Claude the share of vegetables I'd been carrying. My maid, Paulette, was a stickler for choosing her own produce from the market.

'Give these to Sophie,' I told him. 'She has her sister staying with her and they could probably do with the extra food.'

He kissed me goodbye. 'You'll come for supper tonight? Bring me what you're working on if you like. I'm keen to hear how it's developing.'

When I returned to my apartment, Mrs Cutter and her daughter were out, and Paulette was in the kitchen making a spinach pie. Since I was a child I'd associated the aromas of pastry baking and cheese melting with our family maid.

Paulette smiled when she noticed me in the doorway, and pushed back a strand of silver hair that had escaped her neat bun.

'I'm using cottage cheese,' she said. 'It was your grandmother's favourite recipe.'

'Lovely! I'll do some writing now, and then we'll have lunch together.'

I went to my room, replaced my shoes with slippers, greeted Grand-maman's photograph, and settled down to write. I was pretending everything was normal and disaster wasn't looming over me. I had experienced so many distressing situations in the past few years that it had become increasingly difficult to face each new one squarely. My ability to attack a problem logically and efficiently had disappeared.

But I couldn't escape for long. No sooner had I begun writing than Paulette rushed into the room.

'There's a man here to see you,' she whispered. 'I left him on the doorstep. He wouldn't give his name and I didn't trust him enough to let him in.'

I frowned. Who could it be? If he was a thief or a scoundrel how had he got past the concierge? Then I remembered Paulette had reacted the same way when Nicolas had come to paint my portrait for an exhibition. She had taken one look at his paint-splattered clothes and declared him a vagrant.

But the man I found on the doorstep wasn't a thief or a vagrant. He wore a tailored black suit and gave the impression that he had been waiting a long time but wasn't in a hurry.

'Mademoiselle Lacasse? I am Monsieur Ferat of Roche & Associates.'

Perspiration broke out down my back. I was too shocked to speak.

When I didn't answer him, Monsieur Ferat regarded me with curiosity. 'I thought we might talk?'

He looked over my shoulder to where Paulette was peeking out of the kitchen with a saucepan in her hand. She was aware that I had incurred some debt after Grand-maman's illness, but she didn't know the extent. She also didn't know that I had spent the money Grand-maman had put aside for our loyal maid's old age.

I indicated for Monsieur Ferat to follow me into the drawing room. His eyes lingered over the furniture — elegant but well-worn — and the paintings — tasteful but not valuable — before returning to me.

'Paulette, bring some tea, please,' I told her.

I didn't want to encourage Monsieur Ferat to stay, but I also didn't want Paulette to hear what he said to me. While she busied herself in the kitchen, Monsieur Ferat got down to business.

'The only way for you to pay the debt you owe is to sell this apartment,' he said in an almost fatherly tone. 'You don't look like a young lady who wants to go to prison or be thrown onto the street.'

'The final letter gave me fourteen days,' I told him.

A miracle hadn't occurred in the last three years to save Grand-maman, or to pay off my debts, so it was unlikely one was going to occur anytime soon. But I clung to the hope.

Monsieur Ferat clasped his hands behind his back and sucked in a breath. 'I will not say anything further now, Mademoiselle Lacasse, but you and I both know I'll be back. You will see me again next week. Maybe by then you will have come to your senses.'

The debt collector left as Paulette came in with a tray of afternoon tea. I dropped wearily into a chair. When Grand-maman became sick my life had turned into a runaway train, and now I was sitting in the wreckage. I closed my eyes and waited for despair to wash over me.

'Emma?' I opened my eyes. Paulette was watching me with a firm expression on her face. 'You must ask Caroline to pay that debt. Your grandmother took *both* of you in when your parents died, not just you. Your sister had as much responsibility to take care of the dear lady as you did. The money you owe is nothing more than a new hat or a pair of shoes to her. She can easily afford it.'

'I have asked her,' I said. 'Many times. She hasn't answered me once.'

'Then ask her again. And again and again. Tell that selfish sister of yours it's time to pay up.'

I returned to my room, and glanced to the top of my armoire where I kept a box of newspaper clippings and correspondence. I hadn't looked inside the box in a while, but I was drawn to it now. Did I need to sink into complete despair in order to raise myself up again?

Finally, when I could no longer resist the temptation, I took the box down and opened the lid. The newspaper articles were mainly from the social pages of *Le Petit Journal*, but some were from the *New York Times*, which I used to occasionally find discarded in the Jardin des Tuileries. They all had the same subject: Caroline.

French aristocrat marries New York millionaire in lavish ceremony.

Mrs Oliver Hopper acquires Catherine the Great's pearls at auction.

Oliver Hopper buys Hudson Valley mansion for his wife's birthday.

I stared at the articles now spread out on the floor. When I'd first started collecting them I'd kept them in strict date order, as if watching my sister's meteoric rise from afar. There were details of balls she attended, weekends at estates so enormous I gaped in amazement, and steamships she sailed on, including the RMS *Umbria*, where her first-class cabin was described as 'spacious, ornate and luxurious'.

I picked up the wedding portrait postcard of Caroline in her silk and satin dress with a double-strand of pearls around her neck. The name Mrs Oliver Gifford Hopper was engraved on the back. It was the sort of souvenir that might be sent to distant relations or to the press. Caroline had enclosed it in an envelope addressed to Grand-maman, along with the wedding notice that had appeared in the *New York Times*. Oliver's mother and sister were listed as relations, but there was no mention of Grand-maman or me.

When I was a child, Caroline, who was ten years older, used to take me to look at the stores on the Rue de la Paix that were filled with jewellery and fine porcelain, elaborate fans and Swiss clocks. Admiring the luxurious items seemed to both satiate her and displease her at the same time. One day she'd turned to me and said, 'I can't bear to go on with this sort of life, Emma. I was meant for better things. Maman said so. She implored me to do whatever it took to regain our family's position in society. She said I had the mental fortitude, the inner will, to succeed.' And she'd lifted her chin and held herself erect as if she were seeing her fabulous future before her eyes.

I was too young to know it then, but my sister was not beautiful. Her protuberant grey eyes and snub nose resembled those of a French bulldog; and although her broad shoulders and large head made her appear tall when sitting down, when she stood she was short and stocky. But she had the poise and regal air of a queen and exuded supreme confidence. I was in awe of her. I had no doubt that she could do anything she set her mind to. But what she wanted was a vague dream to me. I had no memories of our grand plantation home in Louisiana. Caroline's stories of slaves singing mysterious songs while working in the cotton fields, and peacocks strutting around a tropical garden, were nothing more than fairytales to me. We had each other and Grand-maman. Who could need more than that? But Caroline was determined to return to her rightful place, and her ability to draw to herself what she needed to do that had been nothing short of spellbinding.

THREE

Paris, 1880

Although my grandfather had died years before I was born, Grand-maman had remained in touch with a cousin of his, who Caroline and I called Tante Régina. She lived in a grand mansion on the Champs-Élysées and one Saturday a month hosted an afternoon tea for her friends and people whose acquaintance she wished to cultivate. Sometimes she invited us.

On one such occasion, Caroline spent hours crimping her dark hair into ringlets which she then rolled into an elegant topknot. She emerged from her bedroom in an olive striped dress with a bustle and ruffled skirt, her hat was perched jauntily on her head. My muslin dress wasn't as fancy as Caroline's, but Grand-maman had added a rose-pink bow to the neckline and I was exhilarated by its prettiness.

Caroline opened her lace fan and waved it at me. 'Maman used to say that in New Orleans fans have a language of their own.' She twirled the fan in her left hand and said, 'We are being watched.' She swapped hands and held the fan in front of her face, fluttering her eyelashes: 'Follow me.' Then she drew it across her cheek and whispered, 'I love you.' A touch of the fan on her left cheek indicated 'no', and on her right cheek to say 'yes'. Finally, she fanned herself rapidly to signify that she was 'engaged'.

Caroline so rarely paid me any attention that when she was playful like this it was as if someone had taken the sun from the sky and placed it in my heart.

Our hired brougham arrived, and although the leather seats were worn and the paintwork scratched in places, I imagined I was Empress Joséphine as we passed the bookshops and artist-supply stores of Rue Jacob, and eventually rolled onto the grand tree-lined Avenue des Champs-Élysées.

When the carriage came to a stop before the double bronze doors of Tante Régina's mansion, Caroline gazed at the wrought-iron balconies and curved façades and announced, 'Tante Régina married well. I will too.'

Grand-maman frowned. She had told Caroline before that commenting on other people's wealth was not in good taste. But I had a sense that Caroline wasn't uttering some wistful expression; rather she had cast a spell to draw some of Tante Régina's good fortune to herself.

I turned the ringer, then patted the heads of the stone lions that flanked the doors. A footman welcomed us into the marble foyer, and led us past potted parlour palms and Greek busts, and up the monumental double-turn staircase before opening the doors to the curved pink and gilded room that Tante Régina referred to as her *petit salon*.

A dozen or so exquisitely dressed women and distinguished men filled the space with chatter and silvery laughter. Tante Régina, tightly laced into a dove-grey dress, her hair pulled severely into a roll on top of her head, sat on a long sofa. Beside her was an older man, Monsieur Boutell, who sometimes gave Grand-maman legal advice. They were so engrossed in conversation they didn't notice us, but Tante Régina's two daughters, Margot and Félicité, greeted us.

They were always beautifully turned out, but today were exceptionally so. Margot's magenta dress with mother-of-pearl buttons flattered her pretty brunette looks, while her sister's pink silk flounced dress with cream lace trimmings, along with her blonde hair and rosy cheeks, gave her the appearance of a Vion et Baury porcelain figurine.

'How have you been keeping, Tante Sylvie?' Margot asked Grand-maman, taking her arm and leading her to another sofa.

'I'm well enough,' Grand-maman replied, although I knew her arthritis was troubling her. Before we came out, she had applied cold compresses on her wrists and drunk willowbark tea to ease the pain.

Caroline, Félicité and I followed and sat down on some side chairs. Although Caroline's silk and linen dress wasn't as fine as those worn by the other women in the room, her proud bearing and bright eyes made her stand out among them.

Félicité lowered her voice and said to Caroline, 'Your sister is an odd little thing, isn't she? She's like a light elf: fairer than the sun. Is she still writing stories on any piece of paper she can find?'

Caroline bristled. 'Emma is a supremely talented child. The nuns at the convent consider her quite a genius. Not to mention her harp-playing, which is sublime. No one believes she is only seven years old when they hear her play.'

I grimaced in surprise. Why was it that Caroline praised me to other people but was so critical to my face?

'Emma tells superb stories,' agreed Grand-maman. 'She has a vivid imagination and better powers of observation than most adults. She wrote me a story the other day about a cat and dog that lived at the end of a rainbow, and then another one about a haunted house. I hope she will continue with her harp-playing, but if she doesn't I am sure she will become a successful writer.'

Tante Régina turned from her conversation with Monsieur Boutell and said in a loud voice, 'Goodness me, Sylvie, I hope she doesn't. Writers are as immoral as actresses and music hall dancers!'

I thought of all the books in the library across the hall, and remembered how much pleasure Oncle Victoire had taken in reading them. Why was it immoral to write books but not to read them?

The doors opened and two male servants marched in with the afternoon tea on silver trays. They placed the trays on a low table in front of Tante Régina, and the rest of us drew up our chairs so we were sitting in a semi-circle facing our hostess. My mouth watered at the sight of the three sponge cakes, one of which was layered with chocolate buttercream.

When tea was served, the tinkling of silver spoons in the china cups was so musical that I reached into my pocket for my notebook so I could record my description of it. A frown from Caroline stopped me mid-action and I slipped the book back.

'Where is Philippe this afternoon?' Monsieur Boutell asked Tante Régina with a gravely polite air.

'I expect he will be here soon,' replied Tante Régina. 'He's bringing a business acquaintance with him. An American.'

A titter went around the room as if Tante Régina had announced Philippe was bringing along a baboon.

'You can't be serious,' said a woman with a flabby, colourless face. 'Another transatlantic invader, here in your esteemed salon?'

'They aren't all bad,' Félicité said. 'My brother describes this one as "larger than life" and says he's among the richest men in America. He came to Paris so his mother and sister could buy their clothes at Worth. I heard they spent a fortune in one afternoon!'

'Philippe said his acquaintance has interests in railroads, textile factories and real estate,' elaborated Tante Régina. 'He also has mining rights on the land his railways run through.'

The guests' disapproving expressions turned to awe, except for one fine-featured young man named René.

'He sounds like a typical Wall Street leech,' he sniffed, his voice tinged with irritation at the curiosity everyone was showing in the American. 'I don't know why Philippe thought to bring him. Perhaps for our amusement?'

I was dying to see the visitor. What did 'larger than life' mean? How big was life, and what could be larger than it?

The murmur of voices came from the hall, then the doors opened and Philippe burst in with a tall ginger-haired man at his side. The women touched their fans to their chins, as if they needed a moment to collect themselves. This man was larger than almost everything! He had to stoop to move under the doorway, and dwarfed Philippe and the footman who closed the doors behind the men. The American was older than Philippe and his face was round-cheeked and he had a slight spread about his middle. I was sure that if I were to poke his stomach it would wobble like a blancmange.

'Mother,' said Philippe, 'allow me to introduce to you Monsieur Oliver Hopper.'

Tante Régina tried to keep her attention on Oliver's face but her eyes kept dropping to his clothes. His suit was of fine black wool, his waistcoat was gold brocade with diamond buttons, and he wore an enormous diamond-studded belt buckle. His necktie pin was dotted with red rubies, his watch chain was embellished with emeralds, and on his right hand was a black opal ring as big as a walnut. He glittered like the Mississippi riverboat Caroline had a painting of in her bedroom.

Tante Régina had barely welcomed him before Félicité leaped out of her seat and held her manicured fingers out. 'Do come and sit with us, Monsieur Hopper,' she said, indicating for the rest of us to move along so she could place Oliver in a chair between herself and Philippe.

Félicité was behaving strangely. It was discourteous to make us change our seats like that. And besides, she was usually only interested in people who were as impeccably attired as herself.

Oliver wore his suit badly: it puckered at the buttons when he sat and wrinkled around his ankles. But I liked the way he looked at everybody with a grin on his face. He even smiled at René, who was squaring his shoulders and puffing out his chest.

I turned to Caroline to see what she thought, but her eyes were downcast and her hands were stretched out on her lap. At first I feared she might be fuming at Félicité, but the depth of her breathing, slow and controlled, indicated she was concentrating on something.

'Will you accept a cup of tea, Monsieur Hopper?' Félicité asked, smiling charmingly.

The chair Oliver sat in looked as though it could barely support his weight, and when he took the delicate Limoges teacup from Félicité, I feared it was in danger of shattering in his large hand. He was a giant among us. I imagined him as a colossal gingerbread man for my next story.

As hostess, Tante Régina had the privilege of commencing the conversation. 'What brings you to Paris, Monsieur Hopper? I believe you have brought your mother and sister with you for shopping? You must allow my daughters to advise you on the art galleries and amusements you should take them to see. We have a box at the Opéra de Paris and would be delighted to invite you all to join us.'

I stifled a yawn. What boring questions to ask the gingerbread man. I would have asked him if he'd eaten the old lady who baked him before running away?

Oliver sat in his chair sideways, trying to get comfortable, as he answered Tante Régina. 'I must confess, Madame Tolbert, that I have little appetite for shopping, sightseeing or music. While I am inclined to indulge my mother and sister, I am a man of business and keen to return to New York as soon as possible to attend to my interests there.'

Tante Régina stiffened but managed a smile. 'Well then, you are a most admirable son. But I thought perhaps you were in

Paris to find a wife? Then you would not have to worry about shopping, decorating or entertaining at all.' Her gaze dropped to his clothes again. 'You know that French women have exquisite taste ... and they are the most beautiful in the world.'

She glanced at her two daughters, who had come out into society the previous year. Was Tante Régina contemplating marrying one of them off to Oliver? Why? I giggled, but a reproachful glance from Grand-maman stopped me.

Oliver missed the subtlety of Tante Régina's hint and answered matter-of-factly. 'Indeed that may be so, Madame Tolbert, but the French seem to lack energy to me. Perhaps they are worn out by all the beauty and art around them. Business in New York is a cut-throat occupation and a delicate woman would not make a suitable wife for a businessman like me. To be truthful, discipline and ambition in a woman are more important to me than beauty.'

The guests glanced nervously at each other. I had once heard Grand-maman say that to the French beauty was everything, and had assumed that people wanted money so they could buy books and have pets and music lessons. Shoes for walking in the park, delicious cheeses and fresh strawberries in summer would be nice too. 'A cut-throat occupation' sounded intriguing, however. Was Oliver Hopper a pirate?

'I was born in New Orleans,' Caroline said, finally lifting her eyes to meet Oliver's. 'We combined the best of both cultures there: the French love of beauty and the American appreciation of hard work.'

Félicité sniffed and Tante Régina frowned in Caroline's direction. Was my sister being what Grand-maman always warned her against: 'too forward'? Caroline laughed when people described her as impatient, arrogant or opinionated. She took all those descriptions as compliments.

'Didn't the plantation owners have Negroes to do all the hard work?' asked Tante Régina.

But Oliver paid her no attention. He fixed his eyes on my sister as if there was no one else in the room. 'New Orleans?'

'Yes, that's right,' Caroline answered. 'My parents had a townhouse in New Orleans and a cotton plantation on the Mississippi. Until everything was destroyed in the war.'

He nodded sympathetically. 'Foolish business that war. I have a fondness for the people of Louisiana. I got my start running cotton clandestinely from the south to the north. The south had cotton it needed to sell and the northern factories were short of it.'

'So while the north and south were fighting, you were selling southern cotton to their enemies?' asked René, gloating as if he had scored a remarkable *touché* in a fencing match.

Oliver glanced at him. 'Why yes. When war breaks out you can sell anything at any price you are bold enough to ask.'

René lifted his nose in the air. Defeating this giant was going to take more than a gentlemanly jab. 'Isn't that immoral, Monsieur Hopper? While your countrymen were dying for their ideals, you were turning a profit!'

The room fell silent. It was as if everyone was holding their breath. Oliver was twice René's size. The span of his hand was bigger than the Frenchman's face. I secretly hoped he would punch him.

But Oliver only raised his ginger eyebrows in a world-weary way. 'Where I come from we have a saying: "If someone sings out of tune in the choir, should you sing out of tune too?" Those young men were nothing but pawns, I'm afraid. Their ideals were noble but they had believed a pack of lies. A businessman can't afford to be noble. He has to see things as they are, not as he wishes them to be.'

The guests exchanged glances, uncertain whether to side with Oliver or support René. Oliver appeared unperturbed whether people agreed with him or not.

Philippe's face had flushed at the antagonistic turn of the conversation and he came to his companion's defence.

'Monsieur Hopper has used his profits to invest in railroads. Which in turn has greatly helped with rebuilding after the war.'

But Oliver was regarding Caroline again with fascination. 'You're a southerner,' he said. 'What's your opinion?'

Caroline matched his scrutiny glance for glance, her eyes alive and attentive. 'I am haunted by the stench of the cotton burning on our plantation. It was destroyed at the order of the plantation manager so it wouldn't fall into Yankee hands. If I'd been older and had a choice, I would have asked you to sell the cotton to save my family and the remainder of our slaves from starvation.'

Voicing an opinion so vehemently was not considered ladylike. Tante Régina shuddered and glanced at Félicité, who hid a grin behind her fan. She seemed pleased that Caroline had shown herself as ill-bred.

'Perhaps Monsieur Hopper would like to hear my sister and me sing a duet?' she said. 'If you don't have time to go to the Paris Opera, we shall bring the music to you.'

Félicité's smile vanished when Oliver nodded to her politely but sent Caroline a significant look. My sister's face shone with triumph. She had captured the rich American's attention, if only for a few minutes. I remembered her intense expression earlier and was convinced that she had drawn Oliver to her by the sheer force of her will.

Tante Régina was terse with us when she wished us goodbye and I had a feeling it would be a long time before she invited us to one of her afternoon teas again.

◦◦◦◦◦◦

When we returned from church the following day, Grand-maman asked me to go to my room to practise my harp. She wanted to speak with Caroline alone. I worked on my glissandos and phrasing, but my sharp ears picked up every word that Grand-maman said to Caroline.

'Darling Caroline, I love you and I admire you,' she began, 'and there is no doubt in my mind that you will create a great destiny for yourself. But in regard to men like Oliver Hopper, you mustn't get ideas —'

'Above my situation?' Caroline finished for her. She didn't sound angry or hurt, just amused.

Grand-maman sighed. 'When you lost your parents I welcomed you and Emma into my home. I gave you everything in my heart and shared all I have with you both. But I cannot offer a dowry, and that is always going to be a hindrance to a rich man. Marriage among the very wealthy is as much a business transaction as it is a union of souls.'

'What I have to offer is worth much more than a dowry,' Caroline replied, with such absolute conviction that a chill ran down my spine. 'I have the impression Oliver Hopper wants an ambitious woman by his side. Someone he can confide in.'

'And how could you possibly know that?' Grand-maman asked. 'Yesterday was the first time you'd met him and you spoke for only a short time.'

I imagined the exasperated expression on Grand-maman's face. She'd once told me that my heart was as clear as a summer sky, but Caroline's was a mystery. I'd known exactly what she'd meant. It was impossible to guess what my sister was thinking most of the time.

'Even if a man like Oliver Hopper did marry for those reasons,' Grand-maman continued, 'his family, friends and associates would snub a woman who was not an equal match for him. Apart from that, he is twice your age …'

I became distracted from the conversation by something happening in the street. A black brougham with a liveried coachman and footman had stopped in front of our apartment building. The footman jumped down and helped two women out of the carriage, one elderly and one middle-aged. I couldn't see their features clearly due to their extravagant hats, but their clothes were magnificent. The older woman's skirt was trimmed with tassels and fringing, while the younger woman's bustle dress was brocaded floral silk. Both wore velvet dolman sleeves trimmed with marabou feathers. I was wondering who they could be when a tall gentleman stepped out of the carriage after them. I recognised Oliver Hopper immediately.

Our building's elderly concierge greeted the party on the street, bowing and nodding as if royalty had arrived.

'Grand-maman! Caroline! He's here!' I said, running excitedly into the drawing room. 'And he's brought two ladies with him.'

'Who?' asked Grand-maman. While she had many friends who might call on us on Sunday afternoons, there were few men among them.

Caroline guessed who I was talking about. She calmly stood up and checked her appearance in the mirror above the fireplace. It was as if she had rehearsed this moment and was now readying herself for the performance. Her eyes darted me a warning, as if commanding me to leave the room. But I pretended not to notice. I wasn't going to miss this visit.

The ringer on the apartment door jangled and Paulette answered it. Grand-maman started as if she couldn't believe what she was seeing when Oliver Hopper materialised in our drawing room flanked by the two finely dressed women.

'My dear Madame Mercier,' he began, 'it was such a pleasure to meet you and your daughters yesterday at Madame Tolbert's home that I wanted to bring my mother, Mrs Mary Hopper, and sister, Miss Anne Hopper, to see you.' His cheeks were a high colour and he twisted the opal ring on his finger incessantly, as if he were trying to undo a screw.

Mrs Hopper and Anne were not what I had been expecting. Although their clothes were of the finest fabrics, their faces were care-worn and far from beautiful. Mrs Hopper's skin was dry and wrinkled, and Anne's sandy-grey hair was matched by sandy eyelashes and eyebrows. She appeared to have no colour at all about her. I had to blink my eyes a few times at Mrs Hopper's hat. Attached to its high crown was a stuffed hummingbird. The sight of a lifeless pigeon in the street filled me with pity and I couldn't imagine why anyone would want to wear a dead bird on their head. I stared at it with morbid fascination until Caroline stepped on my foot to stop me.

Mrs Hopper's severe mouth pursed into the faintest of smiles when she accepted Grand-maman's offer of a chair. Anne seemed reluctant to sit and looked about the room with a frown on her face, until Oliver took her hand and almost forced her onto the sofa next to him.

Grand-maman did her best to put the women at ease, asking them how they were enjoying Paris. Mrs Hopper only gave the slightest inclination of her head in response to the questions, while Anne fidgeted with her sleeves and glanced at the clock on the mantelpiece as if she couldn't wait to get out of our apartment.

For the first time since arriving, Oliver looked directly at Caroline and smiled. Her face lit up and then she checked herself, returning his smile with a nod of her head.

I wanted to rush back to my room and collect my writing pad and pencil so I could record in detail this strangest of scenes, but as Paulette had arrived with a tray of tea and madeleines, I had no choice but to commit it to memory.

'Will you accept a cup of tea?' Caroline asked the women, trying to save a conversation that seemed in danger of lapsing into silence. 'Or do New Yorkers prefer coffee at this time of day?'

Mrs Hopper lifted her eyes, surprised by Caroline's perfect English. She shook her head and glanced at Oliver. 'Tea, thank you.'

Her reluctance to be drawn into conversation was obvious. Why had Oliver brought his mother and sister to see us if they were so unhappy to be here? Grand-maman valiantly continued to attempt to entertain the guests by telling them about the Exposition Universelle that had taken place in Paris two years previously, and how the head of the Statue of Liberty was showcased in the garden of the Trocadéro Palace. But after several awkward pauses, she left it to Caroline and Oliver to keep the conversation going.

'I believe Bartholdi, the sculptor, modelled the face on his mother, and that the seven spikes on the crown represent the seven oceans and continents of the world,' Caroline said, holding the plate of madeleines out to the women.

Anne gingerly accepted one, but Mrs Hopper stared at the small cakes as if she'd been offered poison before shaking her head.

Caroline put down the plate with a good-natured smile. Oliver sent her an admiring glance, as if grateful for her ability to persevere in the face of difficulty.

'I've heard that when it's erected it will be the tallest iron structure ever built,' he said. 'I wish I could recall the civil engineer's name ...'

'Gustave Eiffel,' Caroline told him. 'I do hope one day he will build something magnificent for Paris too.'

Although Oliver and Caroline were enjoying each other's company, Anne's attention kept returning to the clock as if she was mentally trying to manipulate the hands to move faster.

Oliver noticed and, with a resigned expression of obligation, stood up and brought the gathering to an end. 'Thank you very much for your kind hospitality, Madame Mercier, but we must not take up any more of your time.'

'Not at all,' replied Grand-maman graciously. 'It has been a pleasure to have you in our home.'

࿇࿇࿇

From the way his mother and sister behaved, I assumed that we wouldn't hear from Oliver again. So I was taken aback when a week later I returned from school to find his brougham parked in front of our house and the footman and coachman in conversation beside it. I couldn't imagine why he had returned. Had his mother or sister left something behind?

I slipped through the front door and heard Oliver talking with Grand-maman and Caroline in the drawing room. Their tone was serious and I was sure that if they saw me they would send me away. So I hid behind the coat stand and peered into the room through a gap in the door.

Oliver was seated in a chair opposite Grand-maman and Caroline, who were on the sofa. My sister had styled her hair in fashionable loops piled on top of her head and she was wearing her best silk tea dress. Had she expected Oliver to call? She had an uncanny ability to predict events.

'My mother and sister found you both charming,' Oliver said. He sounded more at ease than during his previous visit.

'But they were so quiet,' replied Grand-maman, unable to keep the astonishment out of her voice. 'I had the impression they were unhappy to be here.'

Oliver looked sheepish for a moment before regaining his confident demeanour. 'Yes, indeed.' Then, glancing at Caroline, he added, 'That is their manner and you mustn't be disturbed by it. Paris has its charms but they are overawed by it, and were intimidated by your social ease. They prefer to be in their own home with each other for company.'

I replayed the visit in my head. What we had taken for disapproval had merely been timidity. But how could two women from New York — so big and frenetic from the pictures I'd seen — be overawed by Paris?

'So they are shy?' asked Grand-maman, rubbing her eyebrow.

Oliver grinned. 'Unlike me, Madame Mercier. We are originally from the Midwest. My father died when I was nine and life on our farm was a struggle for my mother and sister. We lived in a single-room log cabin that was freezing in winter. I left for New York when I was fourteen to make something of myself so I could help them.'

'How extraordinary,' said Grand-maman, 'and how admirable too.'

Caroline leaned forward in her seat. 'You have my sympathy, Mr Hopper. As you know, I lost my parents and our plantation home as a child. I understand how difficult life can be, and how strong one must be not to give in to despair.'

My sister was a kinder person around Oliver. If I had told her about something unfortunate that had happened to me, she would have replied, 'Too bad for you!'

Oliver shrugged. 'Unfortunately my father was a violent drunkard, Miss Caroline. His death was the result of a foolish accident with a plough. I do the best I can for my mother and sister, but they have never recovered from the harshness of their early life.'

Caroline took a moment to consider what Oliver had said. Then she straightened her back and replied with an air of unruffled strength, 'I am certain that confidence will come in time … and with the right kind of encouragement.'

I watched their exchange with fascination. There was another conversation taking place beneath the surface. It was as if they could read each other's minds.

Oliver's eyes dwelled on Caroline for a moment before he turned back to Grand-maman. 'Well, I think Miss Caroline and I understand each other,' he declared. 'Madame Tolbert asked if I was looking for a wife, Madame Mercier. I didn't want to say it in her company, but indeed I am. I need a practical and ambitious woman, not a frivolous one. Someone who can charm the wives of the men I must do business with.'

'I see,' said Grand-maman, looking taken aback. She glanced uncertainly at Caroline.

'I didn't expect to find such a wife in Paris, but as fortune has turned out I have,' continued Oliver. 'I ask your permission to marry your granddaughter.'

My hand flew to my mouth. I'd heard that New Yorkers were always in a hurry, but this seemed to be moving especially fast. I wished I could see inside Caroline's head to know what she was thinking. But from the flash of victory in her eyes, this was the outcome she had expected all along.

'Asking my permission is gallant of you, Mr Hopper,' replied Grand-maman, her voice trembling. 'But in this case it is up to Caroline to decide for herself what is in her heart. You haven't had a chance to get to know each other. You certainly have my approval to court Caroline if she is agreeable to it.'

'There is no time for courting, unfortunately,' said Oliver in a tone of apology. 'I must depart for New York in three days' time, so I need a decision today.'

Grand-maman stared at him incredulously. 'But, Mr Hopper, this is not Wall Street and you are not making a decision about buying stocks! How do you know you and Caroline will be compatible? Marriage is for life.'

'I'm not taking this lightly,' replied Oliver, 'but I am a man who knows what he wants when he sees it. And I think Miss Caroline is a woman who knows her own mind too.'

Grand-maman was about to protest again when Caroline placed her hand on her arm to stop her.

'I would like to hear what Mr Hopper has to say,' she said firmly.

Oliver nodded. 'I have amassed a fortune of twenty-five million dollars, starting from nothing, but my investments are quickly rising. I intend to be the King of New York by the time I'm forty, and I want you to be my queen. You will not lack for any material comfort you desire, Miss Caroline. I am not after a trophy, a mere decoration. You will be in charge of organising my social affairs and I will not withhold from you whatever amount of money you need to accomplish that. I only ask that you be kind to my mother and sister and help them along where you can.'

Grand-maman fixed her eyes searchingly on Caroline. But my sister paid her no attention. She was pursuing her own train of thought.

I remembered what Grand-maman had said about marriage between the wealthy being like a business transaction and that was certainly the way Oliver's proposal came across. But then his gaze softened and a smile came to his face and for a few seconds I imagined he was a romantic prince serenading my sister beneath her window.

'What do you say to that, Miss Caroline?'

My sister's face was glowing and she lifted her chin regally. 'The Queen of New York,' she repeated. Then, ignoring Grand-maman's imploring expression, she looked directly into Oliver's eyes and said, 'My reply to your proposal, Mr Hopper, is yes. A most certain yes!'

FOUR

'But why can't you marry here in Paris?' Grand-maman asked Caroline while we watched her pack the steamer trunks and hatboxes that had arrived from the Moynat store that morning.

The bed was covered in furs, hats and gloves and there was nowhere to sit. Grand-maman stood in the doorway, while I crouched near the armchair and fingered the lace on one of the gold-embroidered silk petticoats draped over it.

Oliver had returned to New York three weeks previously and Caroline was due to follow him in one week's time. He had opened accounts at all the exclusive stores on the Rue de la Paix for Caroline to purchase her trousseau. I had seen the receipt for the silk corset she was now folding into a satin bag. It had cost five hundred francs! When Oliver had promised Caroline she would not lack for any material comfort she desired, he had been true to his word.

I picked up one of the new parasols. Its jade handle was encrusted with rubies. Apart from the clothes Caroline was packing, she had ordered a full wardrobe of morning dresses, dinner dresses, visiting dresses, tea gowns, ball gowns and opera cloaks from Worth. The three hundred seamstresses employed by the couture designer would be working overtime to fulfil the order, but the exorbitant amount of money Caroline was spending made it worth their while. My attention turned to a fan of mother-of-pearl sticks and leaves of Belgian lace decorated with flowers and birds, and I remembered all the times Caroline and I had stood on the Rue de la Paix and gazed in the store windows. It was as if all she had willed was coming to pass.

'Do you even know what religion your future husband is?' Grand-maman continued.

'I believe he attends the Episcopalian church, but what does it matter? He is not particularly religious and neither am I,' replied Caroline.

Grand-maman winced. In her eyes, a life without God was unimaginable. She believed that God was slow to anger, kind and loving, and she strived to emulate those characteristics in her life and encouraged us to do the same.

'But Emma and I will not see you married!' she protested.

Caroline clamped shut the steamer trunk. 'Oliver insists we wed quickly and so I must marry in New York. You know your health will not allow a long trip across the ocean, and Emma has school and her harp lessons. But I shall return every year to Paris to refresh my wardrobe and will visit you both then.'

Grand-maman pursed her lips and a troubled look came into her eyes. 'You will help Emma, won't you?' she said, her voice containing a trace of panic. 'If something should happen to me ... you will act as her guardian and help her finish her studies?'

Caroline gave a sharp laugh. 'You do worry so, Grand-maman. Nothing is going to happen to you.'

Grand-maman shrank back, her face stricken. She did not look at Caroline again, but said in a strained tone, 'Please take Emma with you this afternoon when you go for the final fitting of your wedding dress. So at least your sister can be part of the marriage ceremony in some way.'

When we arrived at the House of Worth that afternoon, Caroline stepped from the carriage and swept towards the doors with her head held erect. I imagined a crown on her head and a sceptre in her hand: Caroline, Queen of New York.

A clean-shaven young man in a frock coat opened the door for us and bowed deeply while two of the black-clad shop assistants curtsied. It was as if all who gazed upon Caroline recognised her pre-eminence.

A woman in a black velvet dress with her silver hair fashioned into a magnificent pompadour greeted us. 'Good afternoon, Mademoiselle Lacasse. Monsieur Worth will receive you immediately.'

The woman led us up a grand staircase covered in crimson carpet so plush that my feet sank into it. When Caroline wasn't watching I allowed my fingers to brush the vanilla orchids, parlour maples and other exotic plants that bordered the stairs.

We were shown into a drawing room with walls lined in pearl satin and a bronze and crystal chandelier hanging from the ceiling like a cluster of icicles. The air was fragrant with the scent of fresh-cut lilies. A middle-aged man was standing waiting for us, along with a young woman in a high-necked white blouse and black skirt. The woman was pretty with porcelain skin and her hair perfectly coiled on top of her delicate head, but her good looks were overshadowed by the extraordinary man. He could have stepped out of a Flemish baroque painting with his medieval velvet hat, walrus moustache and a floppy cravat tied in a bow. I bit my lip, wishing I had brought my notebook with me despite Caroline's warning not to do so.

'It is a pleasure to see you again, Mademoiselle Lacasse,' he said, taking Caroline's hand and paying no attention to me. 'Mademoiselle Cagnat will help you with the final fitting today. The dress is truly enchanting. It is everything we dreamed it would be.'

He bowed and left the room, and Mademoiselle Cagnat tugged aside a heavy silk curtain and ushered Caroline into a fitting room. I sat outside on a settee and resisted the urge to pull faces in the mirror opposite. Half an hour later the curtain opened and there stood Caroline in an ivory satin and silk damask dress with a long train. I caught my breath. The skirt was embroidered with silver roses, and on her head she wore a diamond tiara with a delicate tulle veil.

Caroline smiled radiantly and my heart swelled with pride, then suddenly my joy became tinged with sadness. I now understood the gravity of the conversation between Grand-maman and Caroline that morning. I would not be with my sister on her wedding day. She would be far away and marrying a stranger. I was seized by an impulse to get down on my knees and beg her to take me with her. I could please her guests by playing the harp.

Caroline frowned at me because I hadn't said anything yet. I didn't want to incur her wrath so I held back my tears and told her, 'You are more beautiful than a *Boule de Neige* rose!'

Mademoiselle Cagnat smiled and pinched my chin. 'What a charming young girl you are. You have a face like an angel.' Turning to Caroline she asked, 'Will your sister be your flower girl? Would you like us to keep some of the silk for her dress?'

Caroline's attention was on her reflection in the mirror. She posed with her eyes sparkling and her lips softly moving, as if she was standing before a circle of admirers.

'No, my sister won't be there,' she said, smoothing the skirt of her dress and not looking at us. 'Now let's discuss my gloves.'

Mademoiselle Cagnat seemed taken aback by Caroline's frosty tone but quickly turned to business. 'Certainly, Mademoiselle Lacasse. Won't you step this way?'

They went into an adjoining room, and I sat back down on the settee, overcome with foreboding that part of my life was coming to an end.

My sense of unease grew worse the morning Caroline departed for New York. She insisted that it wasn't necessary for us to accompany her to the port, but acquiesced that we could go with her as far as the train station.

'You don't have to tire yourself, Grand-maman,' she said when we arrived at the bustling Gare Saint-Lazare, where three porters were required to take charge of her assortment of luggage. 'You really shouldn't be out in a crowd like this.'

Her words sounded kind, but as we waited on the platform together she kept glancing over our heads as if imagining a better place somewhere in the distance. Her unconcealed eagerness to leave us made my heart sink. Perhaps she was caught up in the excitement of the future that was unfolding so brilliantly before her. I hoped that once she settled in New York she would remember us fondly and regret the offhand way she had treated us on leaving Paris.

I was roused from my thoughts by the screech of wheels on the track. The train for Le Havre pulled into the station. The porters directed Caroline to the first-class doors.

Before she boarded Grand-maman pleaded one more time on my behalf. 'You will write to Emma, won't you, Caroline? *Often*. You know how much she idolises you.'

'I shall come back to Paris every year, and Emma and I can go to the House of Worth together. When she is old enough I will buy her a beautiful gown of her own. How about that?' Caroline leaned towards me and straightened the collar of my coat. 'But in the meantime, Emma, you must take good care of your grandmother, and you must keep up your writing and harp-playing because you are a very clever little girl.'

My jaw dropped. They were the warmest words Caroline had ever spoken to me and I would treasure them. I resolved that each year she came back to Paris she would find me more grown-up and accomplished. I would make her proud of me yet.

'Goodbye, Caroline!' I said, as she entered the compartment and took her seat.

She opened the window and waved at us as the train slowly moved out of the station. 'Goodbye, Grand-maman! Goodbye, Emma!' she called.

After the train disappeared, I imagined the kind of dress from Worth that I would have when I was old enough. Maybe something in sapphire blue silk trimmed with beads and sequins. Everyone would tell Caroline that she had a very pretty sister and she would be pleased.

I was lost in my daydream when Grand-maman squeezed my hand. I looked up to see her face was filled with pity. Maybe she had already sensed the truth.

'Keep praying for your sister,' she said to me. 'Pray every day for her soul. That's all you can do, Emma. That's all either of us can do.'

⌾⌾⌾ ⌾⌾⌾

I browsed the newspaper cuttings I had spread out in my room. What Paulette had said was true: my debts were less than Caroline would spend on hats for the races or a new horse for one of her fine carriages. They were laughable for her and crippling for me.

Caroline might be the only person who could help me, but I couldn't forget how she had responded when Grand-maman was suffering and I'd appealed to her for help with the cost of the treatments. I'd torn up the letter containing her reply but the words burned in my memory: *You need to stop persisting with this foolishness that Grand-maman's illness can be treated or her pain relieved and accept that she is going to die. She is an old woman, Emma. You are only ruining yourself …*

If it wasn't for Claude and Paulette, I would be utterly alone in the world. I may as well not have had a sister at all. Caroline hadn't even come to Grand-maman's funeral let alone helped with the burial costs.

During her annual trips to Paris, she was usually too busy with dress fittings and social events to find time to visit Grand-maman and me. We sometimes received invitations to teas or musical events that were cancelled at the last minute. The last time I had seen my sister was five years earlier, when she had invited me to dine with her at the elegant restaurant Voisin's. Although Grand-maman was already too frail then to join us, Caroline didn't ask after her. Her self-absorption was tedious and I'd never cared to repeat the experience, although we did keep up a sporadic correspondence — until Grand-maman's condition became grave.

When Caroline failed to visit Grand-maman in her last days, or to help with any of the doctors' bills, I would have cut her off entirely if Grand-maman hadn't implored me otherwise.

'My darling,' she'd whispered on the last morning she was able to say anything at all. 'Don't hate your sister. She is the only family you have. I never had any siblings, and a life without the support and bond of a family is a lonely one.'

Caroline was my only chance now. Perhaps another attempt would miraculously stir an inkling of compassion in my sister. I returned to my desk and wrote my appeal to her.

I am not asking for charity; I fully intend to pay the money back. I am asking for a loan until I can get myself on my feet again. This last year since Grand-maman died has been the hardest I have ever known ...

After completing the letter and signing it, I was filled with a sense of relief — quickly followed by a dark foreboding.

I glanced at the photograph of Grand-maman, then tossed the letter into the drawer with the demands from Roche & Associates and slammed it shut.

FIVE

The following day, the weather was warm with a kiss of autumn in the breeze but it could not lift my downcast spirits. I walked to Montmartre instead of taking the omnibus, although it was a false economy. The centimes I saved weren't going to change my situation, and my shoes were already worn at the heel.

Paris was preparing itself for the Exposition Universelle and my journey was interrupted by construction sites and the deep holes and dust that were part of building the new Métro underground system. *Le style Mucha* had blossomed in the city and I stopped to admire a tea shop's sinuously carved cabinets and the stylised leaf pattern of the mosaic tiles on the floor. 'So beautiful, so feminine, so charming,' I sighed as I gazed at lamps in a shop window whose bases were long-tressed maidens in flowing gowns.

Montmartre remained untouched by all the industrious activity. Its narrow streets and tree-lined squares, windmills and vineyards gave it the atmosphere of a place where time had stood still; and its steep slopes, and the craggy-faced men who sat on benches and watched the passers-by, were a stand against modernity. It was ironic then that the place should be a magnet for artists, writers, dancers and performers who were constantly reaching for the new and exciting, and through that pursuit had created a wild and vibrant nightlife.

As I approached our usual café, Claude and Nicolas arrived from their studios at the same time. Claude kissed me as if he hadn't seen me in years.

'Don't you have a pretty sister, Emma, who you could introduce me to?' Nicolas said wistfully. 'Why should Claude have all the luck?'

I bit my lip and exchanged a smile with Claude. I was sure Nicolas would not appreciate me introducing him to Caroline.

As well as Belda, Sophie and Robert, two friends we hadn't seen for over a year were in the café: Julie and Marcel. Both talented artists, they had been away in Italy. Julie had been one of the first women accepted into the École des Beaux-Arts and Claude was constantly praising her work for its originality. It wasn't only their talent that made the couple memorable but also their dress sense. Marcel wore his hair *à la victime*, cut very short at the back as if he had been prepared for the guillotine. Julie was dressed in a frilly puce frock with a red choker ribbon around her neck: her parody of Marie Antoinette.

'I'm sure Jean-François is happy to have you back,' I said, kissing their cheeks. 'I don't think we are eccentric enough to attract high-paying customers to the café.'

Julie laughed good-naturedly. Her face was fuller than I remembered and her arms were plump. It must have been all that delicious Italian food she'd eaten while away.

'We have some news for you!' said Marcel, throwing his arm around Julie and looking at each of our faces in turn. 'We got married in Rome.'

For a moment you could have heard a pin drop. Julie and Marcel had never expressed the slightest interest in getting married.

'Well, you've surprised us all with that news,' said Nicolas. 'But let's have a drink to your health and happiness.'

'Yes,' agreed Sophie. She called over Jean-François and told him the news.

'Tch-tch!' he said, shaking his head. 'I was married once. Marriage is sealed with rings and ends with drawn knives.'

Julie and Marcel just laughed at Jean-François's rendering of the old French proverb.

'How are your paintings coming along for the salon?' Claude asked Julie, changing the subject. 'You must have been inspired by the great artists of Italy.'

'There will be no more of that,' said Marcel, tightening his grip on Julie's waist. 'Two artists cannot live together happily. She cannot be my wife and my colleague. Imagine what would happen if she became "inspired" when I needed my dinner or a clean shirt? It is the role of the woman to spare her man from petty daily cares.'

Claude's face fell. I knew he was thinking about his mother. I couldn't bring myself to look at Marcel. Julie was a superior artist to him. Why was it always the woman who had to sacrifice herself?

'Are you so happy to give up all that you've worked so hard to attain?' Claude asked Julie. 'You know Vauclain had never taken a female artist into his studio before you.'

Julie's eyes misted and she touched her belly. 'I'm going to have a baby. That is more important to me than painting.'

My head spun. Marriage and a baby! Julie was getting what I most wanted, but she had to give up her art for it. I had an enlightened man who valued my talent and intellect and demanded no sacrifice from me. But then he didn't want to be married and have a family.

Marcel, sensing he was being viewed narrowly by Claude, quickly added, 'Of course bringing a child into the world is more important. No artist can produce life. We can only imitate it!'

Claude did not shy away from expressing his opinion, and I sensed an argument brewing.

'I won't be able to stay long. I have to get back to my writing,' I whispered to him. 'I'm at a crucial point in my new story.'

Claude nodded, relieved that I'd come up with an excuse to leave. 'Yes, I have to get back to a portrait.'

We shared a drink with our friends, keeping the conversation to the designs for the new Métro stations and Toulouse-Lautrec's poster art. Then we went inside to see Jean-François. Claude collected his payment for the postcards, and Jean-François handed me some more letters.

'I'll accompany you to the omnibus stop,' Claude told me.

We walked down the hill in silence, each lost in our own thoughts. Julie and Marcel's news couldn't have been worse for my case that marriage between two artists could work.

Claude stopped and turned to me. 'Do you think Julie and Marcel are doing the right thing? I have a feeling Marcel is purposely sabotaging Julie's career out of jealousy. I can't believe he managed to persuade her to give up her art. She always struck me as headstrong.'

I shivered at his suggestion. But if I was honest, Julie and Marcel's marriage did seem too spontaneous, as if neither truly cared about the long-term meaning of it. They were the type of people who could happily drift apart if it didn't work out. That was different to how I felt about Claude. I wanted us to be married for life.

'To have an illegitimate child is a terrible burden for a woman and the child,' I said. 'If Marcel cares about Julie at all, he did the right thing by marrying her.'

Claude kicked the ground thoughtfully. 'That's why we must always be careful. I never want to put you in that situation.'

His words drilled right into my brain. Sometimes it was as if Claude and I were speaking two different languages. I loved him, but I resented him too. Why did he have to be so stubborn about something that I was sure would bring more happiness for us?

When we had stayed at Belda's country home in Normandy over the summer, she'd taken me aside and told me, 'Be patient with Claude. You two are so happy together, and I know you want a family. But he is struggling as all artists do to develop his own style. Let him establish himself. Otherwise his fear is that he will have to paint conventionally to support a family. If he does that, he will feel forever disappointed with himself.'

There was much truth in what she'd said, but there was a problem too. Claude acted like we would be young forever, but we would not. I had witnessed Grand-maman die, and it had brought home to me that we would die one day too. I did not want to walk the path of my life alone.

Grand-maman had been the one constant in my life. Now she was gone, and I was on the brink of losing the only place I had ever known as home. If Claude didn't want me for a wife, there would be nowhere I truly belonged.

ᘰᘰᘰ ᘰᘰᘰ

The apartment was quiet when I returned. Paulette was out running errands and Mrs Cutter and Elizabeth were having dinner with friends. I collected the letters that had been delivered directly to the apartment and went to my room.

'*Salut*, Grand-maman,' I said to her picture before sitting down at my writing desk. My shoulders slumped with exhaustion. Smiling and pretending all was normal at the café had drained me.

I inhaled a couple of deep breaths and sat back. I was too discouraged to work on my story so I turned to the letters and spread them like a deck of cards. One of the envelopes had a picture of a familiar-looking Beaux-Arts building in the corner. Time came to a stop when I read the words 'Le Grand Hôtel, Paris' next to it. There was only one person I knew who ever stayed in that luxurious hotel. My fingers trembled as I opened the envelope.

Dear Emma,
I am in Paris at present. I have a spare hour in the
afternoon tomorrow. I will meet you in the Café de la
Paix at four o'clock. I expect you to be there.
Your Faithful Sister,
Caroline

I dropped the note, as stunned as if I'd received a blow to the head. I hadn't heard from Caroline since I'd written to her about Grand-maman's funeral, but she didn't express any remorse about not corresponding at all during the darkest time of my life.

I expect you to be there. Her patronising tone rankled me. Was I really such a worthless person in her eyes that she expected me to be at her beck and call?

I was about to tear up the note when I remembered the letter I had written to Caroline the previous day. I opened the desk drawer and stared at it sitting on top of the yellow envelopes. Ripples of gooseflesh prickled my arms. Writing was a mysterious process. Had penning that letter to Caroline drawn her to me again?

I looked from the note to the envelope in the drawer several times, as if I was being lured by something beyond my control.

'All right, Caroline,' I said, 'I will obey your summons. But only because I need something from you.'

෯ල෯ඁ෯ඁ෯෯

Watch over me, Grand-maman, I prayed as I sat on the omnibus on my way to Le Grand Hôtel. My stomach churned with the uneasy feeling that came whenever I was to meet Caroline. I'd gone to our last engagement at Voisin's with high hopes, and left irritated at myself for not accepting that Caroline would never change, and that we could never be close. This time I couldn't imagine not getting angry with her for not coming to see Grand-maman in her final days, or even sending flowers for the funeral. But I knew that getting into an argument with my sister was futile. She wasn't afraid to punch below the belt, and I was the sort of person who was easily hurt. If she repeated her sentiment that I shouldn't have spent so much money on Grand-maman because she was old, I didn't know what I'd do.

The café was full of rich Americans and European royalty decked out in pearls and expensive silks. I was conspicuous in my Le Bon Marché dress and the hat I'd decorated with silk roses and velvet fern leaves, but I threw back my shoulders and steeled myself when I explained to the maître d' that I was meeting my sister, Mrs Oliver Hopper.

Think of the money, Emma. Think of yourself for once.

Caroline was waiting at a table under the red awning. She was wearing a lemon-yellow silk dress with lace at the collar and cuffs, and an enormous hat with a band of mink wrapped around the crown and an upstanding peacock feather secured by a jewelled medal. Her dark hair was now peppered with grey and her mouth had deep grooves either side, but her eyes still shone with the intensity of someone ready to take on the world. Hers wasn't the sort of ageing that came through being gradually crushed by life's blows and losses. It was an idle, self-satisfied decline that resulted from a routine of rich meals and sipping champagne on yachts.

'Hello, Caroline.'

My voice squeaked. It was terrifying how quickly I reverted to my child-self in the presence of my sister. I thought of Grand-maman, and reminded myself that I'd be safe as long as I didn't let anything hurtful Caroline said into my heart. I had to let it flow over me like water flowing over a river stone.

She rose and grabbed my shoulders, planting firm kisses on my cheeks. 'Oh, Emma, what a joy it is to see you again!' she cried, then held me at arm's length. 'And how lovely you look! Every time we meet, you are exactly the same.'

My mind turned with confusion. Was that a compliment or an insult? I'd been prepared for Caroline to be stand-offish and cold. Now I found myself wondering why she wanted to see me. But then my sister had a way of picking me up and discarding me that never made any sense. It wasn't the Paris season, so perhaps she was simply bored and I was somebody she knew in the city.

We sat down, and she ordered *café crème*, *petits fours glacés* and tartlets for both of us without asking me what I would like.

'So tell me, what have you been doing with yourself since I saw you last?' she asked.

I flinched. Although I should have been used to it, her insensitivity always caught me off guard. *What have I been doing? Well, let me see … I nursed Grand-maman through the last stages of a horrible illness, and although I'm no longer wearing black I am still in deep mourning. Since then I've been busy writing, giving harp lessons and recitals and taking in boarders to pay off debts that you refused to share, despite them being far less than what you're paying to stay in this hotel or even for that ridiculous hat!*

But Grand-maman's dying plea for me to get along with my sister, as well as a sense of self-preservation that warned me to stay calm and get the money from her, made me bite my tongue. Instead, I took from my bag the signed copy of *Histoires de fantômes* I had brought with me and handed it to her.

'This is a collection of my short stories. It's rare for a publisher to accept stories that have been previously printed in literary journals.'

Caroline glanced at the book and placed it at the edge of the table. Then she smiled condescendingly, as if I were a child who had brought her a dead insect from the garden as a gift. A familiar tide of heat and shame swept across my skin. I was sorry I'd given the book to her. I imagined it would be thrown in the fire, or 'accidentally' left behind in her hotel room.

'I've also had a novella accepted for publication,' I added. Her eyes glazed over and I saw no point in continuing. 'How about you?' I said. 'What have you been up to since we last met?'

Her face lit up and she clasped her hands to her chest. 'My new house on Fifth Avenue has been completed! The façade is Indiana limestone and the grand hall is Caen marble. The architect is a genius and a master of interior design. There are no reproductions in the house; every item of furniture, every vase and painting has come from an ancient European castle or mansion.'

My annoyance at Caroline's self-centredness was growing by the minute. She didn't see anything wrong with plundering the historic homes of Europe? Before I could say something sarcastic, the waiter brought us more coffee and I resolved to raise the subject of money before I lost my patience completely.

'Caroline, you must have received my letters about Grand-maman's funeral and the expenses I've incurred?'

She sliced one of the *petits fours* in half and put a piece in her mouth, savouring the marzipan before swallowing it. 'Where is she buried?'

It was an odd question and it threw me off my train of thought. 'In Père-Lachaise, of course, in the family tomb. Would you like to visit her grave? We could go together tomorrow.'

She shook her head and said, 'I don't like cemeteries,' before finishing off the rest of the sweet.

I would have assumed the blunt statement was intended to turn me off my objective, but I'd seen something deeper flash in her eyes when she spoke. Was it possible she was actually sad about Grand-maman's death? Or was she remembering how our parents had died? I had been too young to experience the horror, but Caroline had lived through the war and their deaths.

It would have been a terrible ordeal. An ache of compassion for my sister overcame me despite her behaviour, but I had to persist.

'Caroline, there is no way I can pay all those debts in time. I need your help or I will lose the apartment.'

She glanced over her shoulder and around the café as if searching for someone.

I sighed and repeated the line from the letter I had written to her but not sent. 'I'm not asking for charity. I'm asking for a loan. I intend to pay you back.'

'You worried too much about Grand-maman,' she said, her face still turned away from me. 'You always did. Even when you were a child you were always worried she was going to die. She got old, Emma. You should be thankful she lived as long as she did, considering all her health problems.'

Her words hit me like a blow. Despite my attempted defences she'd struck me where I was most vulnerable. *Again!* All hope of help from her withered away. If one good thing had come from this meeting it was that I'd never waste my time asking for her assistance again.

Caroline waved to someone: a young woman, barely seventeen, who had just walked into the café. She was wearing an elegant dress in the palest shade of rose, with cream appliqué on the collar and three ornamental buttons down the front.

'Here she is at last,' said Caroline when the young woman reached our table. 'Emma, you remember my daughter, Isadora?'

Isadora? I hadn't seen the girl since she was four years old. Caroline had never mentioned her daughter in letters or brought her to visit me and Grand-maman. I'd met her by accident one day in the Jardin des Tuileries. She hadn't spoken a word to me, and I remembered the way she had clung to her mother's skirt and Caroline had kept pushing her off. Isadora was the only secret I'd ever kept from Grand-maman. It would have broken her heart to know she had a great-granddaughter who would never be part of her life.

'Hello, Isadora,' I said, taking the young woman's hand before she sat down. I had always imagined my niece would grow up to be a replica of her mother. But there was nothing of Caroline in her. She was tall and svelte like me, but while I was blonde she was ebony-haired. Her doe-like eyes had circles beneath them; an unusual blemish in such a young woman.

The waiter approached and Isadora glanced at the cup in front of me. 'A coffee with cream, please,' she said to him in English.

'Oh no,' Caroline told him. 'She'll have a camomile tea, thank you.' Frowning at Isadora, she added, 'You know coffee will only upset your stomach.'

Caroline turned back to me. 'Isadora and I have been fully occupied these past few weeks having dresses made at the House of Worth for the coming winter season. Isadora is to make her debut in January. Dear Monsieur Worth passed away a while ago, but his sons, Gaston-Lucien and Jean-Philippe, have maintained their father's high standards. Most of the clients are catered for by a *vendeuse*, but Jean-Philippe looks after us personally.'

Did it even occur to her, I wondered, that she was boasting of her great wealth to someone who sewed her own underwear and had a patch on the sole of one of her shoes? Someone she had just refused to help with debts that should have been shared equally between Grand-maman's two granddaughters?

Isadora smiled at me and looked away again. She was lovely and graceful but had none of the poise and self-confidence a young woman of her position would normally exhibit. She certainly didn't seem very excited by the subject of her debut.

She picked up the book Caroline had laid aside and stared at the cover. Her eyes opened wide. 'Did you write these, Aunt Emma? Are you an authoress?'

'Yes, I am,' I replied, wondering if Caroline had spoken of me at all to my niece. 'Do you like to read?'

'Indeed I do! I am currently reading Baudelaire in translation. Do you like him?'

'Look at your aunt when you are speaking, Isadora,' interrupted Caroline.

I frowned, embarrassed for Isadora. Why did Caroline speak to her as if she were a child?

Isadora blushed but met my gaze. 'I shall read your stories with great pleasure, Aunt Emma,' she said, clasping the book to her heart in a way that left no doubt as to her sincerity.

'I don't see how,' said Caroline, cutting up a tartlet. 'They are in French, and you haven't worked as hard at the language as you should have. Let alone the other skills a debutante has usually mastered by this time.'

Isadora blushed deeper. She turned to me and said in broken but not terrible French, 'I would have worked harder if I had known I had such a lovely Parisian aunt to correspond with.' She gazed at the book again. 'Even if I have to sit up night after night with a dictionary I am determined to understand these stories.'

I smiled, happy that my book wasn't going to be tossed away after all. 'I'm sure your French will improve very quickly that way,' I told her. And then, with daring, added, 'And should you wish to write to me to practise your French, I would be happy to receive your letters and correct them.'

I touched Isadora's hand, feeling an affinity with her that I had never shared with her mother. It seemed Caroline was not my only remaining family after all.

Caroline, unnaturally quiet, looked between us with an intense expression, no doubt plotting how to break the bond Isadora and I were forming before it could go any further. I wasn't even sure why she had allowed us to meet today. My niece existed in a different milieu. She was one of the richest heiresses in New York and would be expected to marry a man of equal rank and take her role in society. I was a writer who associated with the shabby artists of Montmartre. Caroline wouldn't like someone like me influencing her daughter.

When it was time for me to leave, Isadora kissed my cheeks with an affection that warmed my heart. 'I will write to you every day, Aunt Emma.'

I squeezed her hand, fighting the tears that were prickling my eyes. How I wished she had known Grand-maman!

I turned to Caroline, careful to hide my fury. We had grown so far apart, and she was so unsympathetic to me, there seemed little point keeping up the relationship at all now. Grand-maman would surely have understood that I had tried my best. I was on my own regarding my debts, that much was clear.

'Goodbye, Caroline,' I said. 'I wish you both every success for the coming season.'

She raised her bejewelled hand to her throat. 'Thank you, Emma. It's sure to be an exciting one!'

❧

On my way home, I soberly reflected on the events of the afternoon. I had failed miserably in my attempt to arouse any sense of duty in Caroline. Tears filled my eyes as I surrendered to the consequences of that failure. I had fought and fought during the last few years: firstly to save Grand-maman; then to make her last days as comfortable as I could; then to hold on to my home and pay back my debts. But I was beaten. Monsieur Ferat was right: my only option was to sell.

I slipped quietly into the apartment and the first thing I saw was Grand-maman's wedding portrait on the hall table. My gaze drifted to the parlour, where my harp stood next to the pink bergère armchair that Grand-maman used to sit in when she gave me my first lessons. How could I give up this place? It was the only home I'd ever known and held so many memories of Grand-maman.

Pots and pans clanged in the kitchen as Paulette went about making dinner but I couldn't face her yet. I went to my room and sank down on the bed.

It wasn't that I couldn't be happy in a little rented room in Montmartre, but this apartment was a sanctuary. In the absence of a family of my own, it gave me a sense of comfort and continuity.

A memory appeared before my eyes as vividly as if I were watching the scene unfold in the room. Grand-maman was tucking me into bed when I was very young and calming me during a thunderstorm. 'Don't worry, my little darling, it is only God and the angels rearranging their furniture. Like when Madame Bellamy's maid does the dusting upstairs.'

My tears fell harder and I turned to her photograph on my desk. 'What do you think, Grand-maman? Have I done something terrible to displease God? First he takes you from me, and now our home. And what shall I do about dearest Paulette? She's too old to find work anywhere else. Without you here she has been such a comfort to me.'

I took several deep breaths. I couldn't give up like this, but every avenue had closed before me. I imagined Claude scolding me for being so attached to 'some walls and floors'. But he was self-reliant and could make a home anywhere. That wasn't my nature. I needed the familiar. I needed to feel safe.

I stared up at the ceiling. *I can't help anybody. Not myself, and not Paulette. I am a useless human being.*

SIX

After a restless night, a vestige of courage returned to me. My situation was desperate and I would have to write to Monsieur Ferat, but having fought daily for so long I wasn't able to stop. I rose at dawn and sat at my writing desk to finish my novella *The Mysterious Cat*. I would send it to Monsieur Plamondon right away; and then write a short story in the afternoon. Perhaps I could dig my way out of my prison a spoonful of dirt at a time.

Paulette knocked on my door mid-morning. 'A letter has arrived for you registered mail,' she called.

My blood froze. Registered mail? It must be a summons to court. My day of reckoning was here.

I opened the door and Paulette handed me the envelope, but it didn't look like an official notice. It was the finest cream vellum with gilt scrolls around the edges. It looked like an invitation to a ball.

I opened the envelope gingerly and took out the letter inside.

Dear Emma,
I am returning with Isadora to New York today, but
I have given some deliberation to your request and I
have a proposal. In exchange for me paying the debts
you owe, you are to present yourself in New York

*by 1 October to assist Isadora in preparing for her
debut. She was clearly impressed by you when we saw
you yesterday, and responded to your encouragement
in a way she never has with the many governesses
and tutors I have employed to help her overcome her
affliction, which you could not have failed to notice.
Her condition requires great discretion, and because you
are my sister I trust your ability to keep family matters
to yourself.*

*If you contact Monsieur Depaul at the address
enclosed, he will organise your passage and other
arrangements. I will also instruct him to pay a deposit to
your debtors to demonstrate good faith. The rest of the
money shall be forwarded when Isadora is successfully
married to a suitable companion. To that end, I anticipate
you will need to stay in New York until at least May.*

*During this time you will be a guest in our home and I
expect you to conduct yourself with decorum. Under no
circumstances are you to reveal that you are an authoress.
I will give you further instructions when you arrive.*

Your Faithful Sister,
Caroline

I took my handkerchief from my sleeve and patted my cheeks
and neck, then had to read the letter through slowly twice more
to assure myself that I wasn't dreaming.

Caroline's condescending tone both irritated and amused me.
Conduct yourself with decorum — what did she think I was? A
savage? Her insinuation that my career was shameful infuriated
me, as did her assumption that I could simply drop my own life
to be at her beck and call.

But the point that most confounded me was her reference
to Isadora having an 'affliction'. The only thing wrong with
Isadora that I could detect was that she was acutely shy. It

could have been a family trait because Oliver's mother and sister had also been that way. But I suspected the condition had another cause: Caroline's formidable personality would terrify any sensitive soul. If my sister hadn't gone away to New York while I was still young I might have ended up as tongue-tied and lacking in confidence as Isadora.

Then I smiled. Perhaps God hadn't deserted me after all. Two extraordinary avenues had opened up before me. Firstly, I would be able to keep my beloved home and give Paulette a decent pension. Secondly, I would have a chance to get to know my sweet niece, and perhaps to help her in some way. What potential lay behind those beautiful, sad eyes? Although I had only seen Isadora for a few fleeting moments, she had affected me greatly. The age gap between us was almost the same as the age gap between Caroline and me, but how differently I would treat Isadora from the way my sister had treated me. I would be her friend, her confidante, her protector and guide.

❧

'Tell me again your reasons for going to New York,' asked Claude, studying me across the table. From the frown on his face it was clear he thought I was about to do something foolish. 'Your sister seems to only use you or else completely disregard you. Why would you willingly continue with such abuse?'

I tore off a piece of bread from the loaf in front of me and dipped it into my *café au lait*. We were eating our supper at the table in the corner of Claude's studio. He had a small two-room apartment down the hall where he slept and kept his books and household items. The white-painted studio and its bare wooden floors were clear of anything except artwork and supplies. During the day the space was filled with light from the three large windows, but in the lamplight shadows danced about the walls and ceilings like magical beings.

'It's got nothing to do with Caroline and everything to do with my niece, Isadora,' I said. 'She's the only blood relation I have besides my sister and I want to get to know her.'

Claude grimaced, unconvinced.

I stared at my hands. I hated keeping secrets from the people I loved: firstly, Grand-maman about Isadora; and now Claude about my debts. While it was true I was keen to get to know Isadora, he had no idea of my other motive. Caroline wasn't offering me a loan as I'd requested. *She was willing to pay my debts in full!* I would be able to keep the apartment I loved, and Claude and I would have a more secure future. We'd never have to worry about rent, and he could focus on his painting and I could concentrate on my writing. And perhaps he wouldn't be so reluctant then to start a family.

Claude tried again. 'Seeing Caroline occasionally is one thing ... but staying in her house in New York for months? You can't trust her. She might be trying to trap you in some way.'

'Trap me?'

It was true that Caroline's erratic nature meant I could never trust her. Every decision she made was stacked heavily in her favour. But in reality she had nothing to gain from me except a sense of being superior. She would enjoy making me jump when she said 'jump' because she knew I was desperate for money.

'I can bear it for a little while,' I said. 'Besides, I'm no longer a child. Now I can observe her with a writer's keen eye. And being in New York might fuel some story ideas.'

Claude didn't answer. Instead, he picked up our cups and saucers and took them to the sink. While he washed them, I leaned back in my chair and cast my eyes over the series of paintings he was completing. They showed milliners and their beaus picnicking in the forest of Fontainebleau. The setting and the people were so alive and natural it was as if I could reach out and touch them and laugh along with them. How I longed to share their carefree spontaneity.

'If I end up staying in New York longer than planned, you will have to come and join me,' I told Claude. 'The city might offer artistic inspiration for both of us. Besides, the only thing that I'm truly concerned about regarding this trip is being away from you.'

He laughed. 'If you aren't back by spring, I will come and rescue you! I'm worried about you, Emma. I don't like this situation at all. You will be in a city where you have no friends and with someone who doesn't have your best interests in mind.'

It warmed my heart when Claude was caring and protective of me. I stood up and put my arms around his waist. He pressed my head to his chest and kissed my hair.

'Let's sleep on it,' I said. 'And see what answers we find in the morning.'

The following afternoon, I stepped off the omnibus in Montmartre to find Claude waiting for me at the stop.

'I have someone I want you to meet,' he said. 'She's an American artist and something of a radical.'

Curious, I walked with him uphill to Rue Rodier, past the vegetable-sellers with their cane baskets overflowing with cauliflowers and potatoes, and past a rag-and-bone man hauling a cart stinking of fatty grease from the scraps he'd collected. Claude stopped in front of a ramshackle building above a cane furniture store. One of the windows upstairs was open and somebody was whistling 'J'ai du bon tabac'.

'Don't be deceived by appearances,' said Claude with a grin. 'Florence Garrett is the daughter of a wealthy congressman but she has lived in Paris for the past ten years as an independent woman. She has made a great success with her art.'

He directed me up the building's narrow staircase ahead of him, and when we reached the second floor he knocked on the bright blue door of an apartment. A pair of cat's eyes and whiskers had been painted on it. The sharp odours of linseed oil and turpentine from a painter's studio wafted in the air.

'The door's open,' called a female voice from inside. 'Come in.'

We entered a room that was the opposite of the monastic atmosphere of Claude's studio. Every wall was covered in canvases from the ceiling to the floor. Stacks of books were piled on a faded Persian rug, a chaise longue and an upright piano. Near the window a painting of a King Charles spaniel leaned against a potted red hypericum, over which were draped a dog leash and collar. But the most extraordinary feature was a washing line strung wall to wall, with used envelopes, leaflets and torn pieces of newspaper pegged to it instead of clothes.

In the middle of this muddle sat a woman at an easel, applying the finishing touches to a painting of street musicians. A white cat was asleep in her lap. The woman wore a tailored dress with skilfully placed darts and seams that gave shape to her tall, narrow body. Her dark blonde hair was neatly pinned, and her skin was smooth and unblemished. Despite the fact she was working, there wasn't a smear of paint anywhere on her clothing. As for the cat, its coat had been brushed to silky smoothness and around its neck was a pink velvet ribbon with three bells. An elastic glove-fastener had been ingeniously added to create an expandable clasp.

'Claude!' the woman cried, standing and placing the cat on top of the piano stool. She quickly cleaned her brush, then came over to greet us.

After kissing Claude's cheeks in greeting, she took my hand. 'You must be the talented Mademoiselle Emma Lacasse that Claude has been telling me about.' She stared deeply into my eyes with her intense blue ones, giving me the impression she was trying to assess what kind of person I was. Then she smiled as if she had found something remarkable in me. 'I'm Florence Garrett.'

She was perhaps thirty-five years of age, and on the collar of her dress I noticed the pin of the Société Protectrice des Animaux. Its symbol was an angel preventing a man from beating a fallen horse.

'You know, I read your short story collection in one night and didn't sleep a wink,' she added. 'It was very atmospheric and breathtakingly original.'

I blushed at her compliment and turned to her paintings to hide my embarrassment. 'These are magnificent!'

Her style was impressionist, but her women weren't sitting in gardens or at the piano or taking tea. Florence's women were working with their sleeves rolled up — laundresses, merchants, grape-pickers. There were also many paintings of dogs, cats, chickens and horses.

I turned my attention to the washing line with the pieces of paper pegged to it. There were sentences scribbled over them.

Florence let out a bright, crystal-clear laugh when she caught me looking at them. 'I wish my ideas for articles or a painting would come when I'm ready to receive them. But I never seem to be near my desk or my notebook when my muse starts talking, so I jot my ideas down on whatever I find, then try to put them in some order.'

'So you are a writer too?' I asked her.

'Not of novels, but I do write for several journals here in Paris and New York. My topic is social reform.'

'It certainly is an exciting time in France,' I told her, 'with the government about to pass legislation to limit the working day and to make arbitration of labour disputes compulsory.'

Claude picked up the cat and cradled it in his arms. 'Florence is planning to return to New York soon,' he told me. 'She's giving an exhibition to raise funds for a school for immigrant children. She's also been commissioned to paint a mural.'

'I've enjoyed my stay in Paris,' Florence explained, 'but it's time for me to return home. Claude tells me you are intending to go to New York for a while? He asked me to travel across with you on the ship. If you have to be in New York by 1 October, that means taking the French line from Le Havre on 22 September.'

I glanced at Claude and the penny dropped. This was why he was introducing me to Florence: so I would have a companion to travel with. Part of me was touched that he cared enough to find someone for me to travel with to New York; the other part wished he wasn't quite so understanding about being separated from me for several months.

'I am visiting my sister and niece,' I said, feeling too self-conscious to elaborate. 'My sister is paying my fare as a gift.'

'You'll like New York,' Florence said. 'It will give you a fresh eye on things. I'm tired of not being able to walk around in Paris on my own without being harassed by someone of the male sex. I'm sure that's why women have traditionally painted flowers and fruit — so they don't have to deal with all the obstacles of leaving the house.'

Claude lowered the cat to the floor and it scampered off to drink from a bowl of water with the name *Minette* painted on the side. 'If you go to New York to develop yourself as a writer, I can feel better about it,' he said, but he had trouble meeting my eye. 'Knowing that Florence will be there if you need a friend reassures me that you will be fine.'

'Of course she'll be fine,' said Florence. 'She's not a child, Claude!' Turning to me she added, 'American readers are having a love affair with Gothic and fantastic fiction. Europe has its history, but New York will soon be the cultural capital of the world. Everything is happening there. It's an exciting place to be.'

Florence offered us some tea and we accepted. She put the kettle on the stove, and cleared the chaise longue and an armchair of books so we had somewhere to sit. As we sipped our tea, she chatted about the shows and plays we could see together on Broadway.

Claude interrupted her to ask if she was staying in New York for a while or whether she intended to travel around.

'No, my exhibition and the mural will keep me in the city,' she said, and smiled at me over the rim of her teacup. 'It sounds to me, Emma, that Claude is nervous you might find somebody else and he wants me to keep an eye on you. Well, do you remember what the serpent tempted Eve with? It wasn't fine jewels or fancy clothes. It was knowledge. For centuries men have been terrified of what might happen to women if they gain the knowledge that comes with freedom.'

Florence was wrong about what was really bothering Claude, but he smiled good-naturedly at her. 'Yes, you are right, Florence. Goodness knows what Emma will get up to if I let her go free.'

⋘⋙

Monsieur Depaul, the lawyer who was to organise my passage to New York and pay a goodwill bond to my debtors, had an office on the Île de la Cité. When I entered it the air was heavy with the spiciness of tobacco, although no one was smoking.

A clerk directed me to Monsieur Depaul's desk and introduced me, but the lawyer — a small man with a receding hairline and a salt-and-pepper beard — gave me only a cursory glance through his rimless glasses. He indicated for me to sit down, and took a sheet of blank paper from a pile on his desk and began to write a note.

I sat awkwardly, listening to his pen creak and his noisy breathing. It hissed in and out of his body with a sound that reminded me of fire bellows.

'I've never been to New York,' I said. 'Have you ever visited the city, Monsieur Depaul?'

He ignored my remark, folded the note and placed it in a box behind him. Then he pushed a piece of ledger paper in front of me and pointed to some figures. 'Fifteen per cent of your debts will be paid to Roche & Associates upon your departure for the United States. The firm has agreed to accept the final amount, plus interest, by 30 May 1900. If for any reason you cancel your agreement with Mrs Oliver Hopper, you will be responsible for the full amount immediately, including the initial deposit.' He indicated a line at the bottom of the page. 'Sign here if you agree.'

A stirring of anxiety tingled in my veins. The ledger paper brought home how much Caroline viewed my visit as a business transaction. It didn't seem that Monsieur Depaul was even aware that I was her sister. But what choice did I have? I signed the paper and passed it back to him.

Monsieur Depaul opened the drawer of his desk, took out an envelope and handed it to me.

'I wish you a safe voyage, Mademoiselle Lacasse.'

It was an abrupt dismissal. I stood and waited for him to see me to the door but he showed no sign of moving. I might be an independent woman but that didn't mean I couldn't give and receive common courtesies.

'Well,' I said to the clerk on my way out, 'I hope the men in New York have better manners.'

Outside on the street, I took a couple of breaths to regain my composure before checking inside the envelope that Monsieur Depaul had given me. I took out the one-way ticket for my journey by steamship and perused the cursive script.

This ticket entitles the bearer, Emma Virginie Lacasse, passage from Le Havre to New York on 22 September 1899 on board the …

Despite my trepidation about leaving Paris, my blood began to stir with a sense of adventure. Weren't the steamships that crossed the Atlantic beautifully appointed? Did elegant dinners in a saloon with a domed skylight and walls papered in white and gold lincrusta await me? Would I be writing about my journey at a mahogany desk in a cabin furnished with velvet carpet and a canopied bed?

I was lost in my visions of a luxurious ocean voyage until my eyes fell on the last words on the ticket: *second-class passage*.

∽∽∾❀∾∽∽

'Well, at least we can say that a leopard doesn't change its spots,' said Claude when I showed him the ticket at his studio later.

I leaned against the wall and stared out the window at the treetops. 'I can't believe my sister, one of the richest women in New York, would send me a second-class fare when she herself always travels first class. If I was going to New York of my own volition of course I would travel second class. But when she summons me to New York and buys me a second-class passage it is an insult. Does she think I'm going to be a governess to my niece?'

Claude tossed the ticket onto the table and put his arm around me. 'Second class on the French line is still going to be very comfortable,' he said, a grin on his face. 'Now if she was sending you *steerage* on an immigrant ship, I would not let you go.'

My mouth twitched and I tried to suppress a smile. 'I don't know whether to laugh or cry. She's outrageous!'

Claude's eyes darkened and he turned serious again. 'You'd better keep a sense of humour about your sister — I believe she will have plenty more slights for you yet. But if you're still determined to go, you must stick to your intention of viewing everything from a writer's perspective.'

'How will I tell Florence I'm travelling second class?' I asked him. 'It will be humiliating. I won't see her on the ship at all.'

Claude picked up the ticket and handed it to me. 'I think you'll find Florence much more accommodating than you give her credit for. Why don't you go and tell her now?'

SEVEN

On my way to Florence's studio, I pondered all the ways I could explain my situation to her. The best I could come up with was that the booking agent had made a mistake and it was too late for me to change it now. I was too embarrassed to explain that my wealthy sister was a penny-pincher when it came to me.

When I arrived at the apartment on Rue Rodier, I found Florence on her way out. She was carrying a basket filled with an assortment of yellow flowers: sunflowers, chrysanthemums and daisies. When I showed her my ticket and gave her my excuse, she was unperturbed.

'To tell you the truth, I'd much rather go second class,' she said. 'You meet more interesting people. The people in first class are insufferable bores.' She made a note of my cabin number and handed me back the ticket. 'I'll write to my booking agent and make sure we're in the same cabin. I'm sure you don't want to make your first Atlantic crossing with a stranger.'

I thanked her for her understanding and pointed to her basket of flowers. 'They look lovely. Where are you going?'

She tilted her head and smiled. 'Why don't you come with me and find out?'

I was surprised when we took the omnibus to Asnières-sur-Seine, which was on the outskirts of the city. I wanted to ask

Florence where we were headed, but we were surrounded by a group of chattering young women loaded up with parasols and picnic paraphernalia and it was impossible to have a conversation. When we got off the omnibus, Florence led me towards a trail along the river. The picnickers, to my relief, strolled off in the other direction.

'It's good to have peace again,' I said, enjoying the cushioned sensation of walking on grass. 'At least my ears have stopped ringing.'

Florence laughed. 'Claude told me that you've played the harp for shows at the Théâtre de l'Oeuvre and that you've written a few stage plays. I'll give you a letter of introduction to my friend Marguerite Durand for when you come back to Paris. I have a feeling you will like each other.'

I was flattered. Marguerite Durand was a celebrated actress and a woman of elegance and style. She was famous for walking her pet lion on a lead along the Champs-Élysées, but was also editor of the feminist daily paper *La Fronde*, which I suspected was how Florence knew her.

'I agree with a lot of feminist ideals,' I said, 'but not the ones about marriage. I'm a romantic at heart.'

Florence raised her eyebrows at me. 'Marriage and love are not synonymous, Emma. In fact, they are antagonistic to each other. Love can only truly be love if it is given freely. French marriage laws are draconian — they turn women into powerless and property-less slaves. Nothing undermines a woman's spirit or destroys her health faster than marriage.'

All of Claude's and Florence's philosophising about the subject of marriage and commitment meant nothing if you died alone, I thought. 'But wouldn't marriage to a good man keep a woman safe?'

Florence shook her head. 'Marriage is a dreadful insurance policy! One of the greatest social problems among poor women is being deserted by their husbands. Rather than being shackled to a man, it would be much better for women if they had more choices about how to live their lives and received equal pay for their work.'

We came to a stretch of land near the river and walked on through a set of stone gates that were still being constructed. Inside the park, adjacent to a gravel path lined with oak and plane tree saplings, were a dozen or so small headstones. A garden of hawthorns and lilacs had also been started.

'Le Cimetière des Chiens,' explained Florence. 'It has only recently been opened; the statuary and the sign are yet to be placed. It was founded by Marguerite and another friend of mine, Georges Harmois, a lawyer and animal advocate. My little dog, Babou, was among the first to be buried here.'

Now I understood the picture of the King Charles spaniel in Florence's studio and the pot of flowers next to it.

'How touching,' I said surveying the miniature graves. 'A cemetery for pets.'

An epitaph on one of the stones caught my attention: *The more I know people, the more I love my dog.* I remembered Grand-maman's dog, Léon, and cat, Bisou, who had been my childhood companions. When they passed away, we were too grief-stricken to consider putting their bodies in the garbage, which was what the City of Paris expected residents to do if they had nowhere to bury them. Fortunately for us, one of Grand-maman's friends allowed us to make graves for them in her country garden.

Florence crouched down near one of the tombstones and placed a bunch of yellow chrysanthemums on it. 'I saved Babou from a vivisector the first year I came to Paris. He travelled with me back and forth across the Atlantic several times. I was ready to leave Paris a couple of years ago, but Babou was already old and I didn't want to take him away from his home in his last years. He was a true Parisian dog.'

My gaze drifted to the epitaph on the tomb next to Babou's: *One would have thought he was human … but he was faithful!*

The loyalty of animals and the untrustworthiness of humans seemed to be a theme in the cemetery. Could there be some truth to it? With another human you could never be sure that what they were saying was actually what they were thinking. Animals were transparent in their sentiments.

Florence sighed and brushed her fingers over Babou's headstone. Then she placed the remaining flowers from her basket on the surrounding graves.

'I've often agonised over what might have been Babou's fate if I hadn't rescued him from the vivisector,' she said. 'I can't fathom how an intelligent, educated man is able to torture innocent animals in the name of research. I cry when I imagine all those poor dogs begging for mercy and licking the hands of those so-called men of science.'

I shuddered. I hated walking past slaughterhouses and hearing the bone-chilling cries of the cattle and pigs inside. Once I'd seen a beautiful old mare being dragged into a knackery, her legs trembling in terror and her hooves covered in the blood of the horse that had been slaughtered before her. The sight still haunted me.

Florence shook her head. 'I'd like to believe that with enlightenment all of us can become finer human beings, but I'm convinced that some people are born ... *empty*. As if their soul is missing.'

'It would be very frightening to look into the eyes of someone like that,' I said. 'It would be like staring into an abyss.'

A nagging doubt rose in my mind as I recalled Caroline and a particularly terrible argument between her and Grand-maman.

I'd known since childhood that my sister resented the fact that I had survived the yellow fever that had killed our parents. 'Maman wasn't weak like you, Emma,' she told me. 'But you were sick all the time and you sapped the life from her. It was you who gave her the yellow fever, you know. You were the first one to catch it.'

When I told Grand-maman that I was to blame for my parents' deaths, she was furious with Caroline. 'How can you say that to your sister!' she scolded her. 'What a thing to tell a child!'

She'd stared at my sister as if mystified by her nature, but if she'd hoped to reach Caroline's heart, she'd failed.

I shook off the strange feeling. No, Caroline was selfish and not very compassionate, but she was nothing like the men Florence was talking about. Caroline wasn't evil. She would never take deliberate pleasure in destroying another living creature.

⌘

The day before my departure, my friends gathered in the café to wish me farewell. I would miss them over the coming months, and was grateful again for Claude's kindness in introducing me to Florence. A pleasant rapport had sprung up between me and the American artist, and at least I would know someone in New York other than my sister and her family. Florence was already in Le Havre, visiting a friend, and would meet us on the ship the following morning. I had an inkling that crossing the Atlantic with her would be anything but boring.

'Have you heard about Marcel and Julie?' Sophie said. 'It seems things aren't working out as Marcel planned. He's finding it difficult to sell his work now that they are back in Paris. Julie is going to get as big as a whale and still be sitting at her easel.'

Nicolas tittered. 'Perhaps Marcel will take care of the child after it is born so Julie can concentrate on her painting!'

'Why not?' said Belda. 'Do we have to base our relationships on convention or public opinion? Why can't we arrange ourselves as we are most suited?'

'I agree,' said Claude, glancing at me. 'My parents are happy together despite marriage, not because of it.'

His comment irritated me. On the train to Le Havre later that afternoon I asked him what he'd meant by it.

He rolled his eyes. 'Not this again? How many times can I tell you that I love you and I'm here for you? How will marriage make that any different? Marriage makes people rigid. Love is a plant. It can't grow if you stifle it.'

'I don't want to be lonely all the time, Claude. It's tiring always relying on myself. I don't even know if you will be waiting for me when I get back from New York. What if you find someone else while I'm away?'

He folded his arms across his chest. 'What if *you* find someone else in New York? Is it marriage you want — or me? If you are lonely with me now, marriage will not help, Emma. Nor will having children. You are asking me to fix something only you can solve.'

We spent our last night together in a quaint pension near the port, but instead of making passionate love we turned away from each other and lay in bed in obstinate silence.

Perhaps Claude was right. There was an emptiness deep inside me that only I could fill. Despite all the things I told myself about accepting the fact that Caroline, my blood sister, had never cared for me, the pain of her rejection had left a scar. Perhaps I didn't believe that anyone would be faithful to me unless they were tied to me in some way. On my own I wasn't enough to keep them by my side.

And what would happen if Claude never changed his mind about marriage? What would I do then? Resign myself to an insecure, childless existence the way I'd resigned myself to the fact of Caroline's selfishness and abandonment of me?

⚜

Florence met us in the steamship's great saloon, which had the atmosphere of a hotel lobby. Businessmen lounged at tables smoking and reading the daily papers, while in another corner a middle-aged woman wearing a hat that was a mix of feathers, flowers and frills drank champagne with a group of younger women. Mothers pushed babies in perambulators, and nurses assisted elderly people in wheelchairs. Florence was the only person in the second-class saloon accompanied by an animal, but I had seen some of the first-class passengers boarding earlier with French bulldogs and Pomeranians.

Minette sat in her cane carrier and regarded the goings-on around her with a nonchalant air.

'I wish I had her confidence,' I said, sticking my finger through the carrier front to stroke her chin.

Florence put her hand on my shoulder. 'This ship is solid. It is built for the heaviest of seas and we will all be quite safe. Look, here comes the captain now.'

A grey-haired man in a tailored double-breasted blue coat with gilt buttons and a cap with gold laurel leaves on the peak was walking up the gangway accompanied by his equally smartly dressed officers. The distinguished, efficient air of the men inspired confidence that we were in capable hands, but I hadn't been worried about the safety of the voyage.

Claude understood. He took my hand and smiled. 'Write to me often, Emma. That way you'll know I'm always there with you in spirit.'

He took a package wrapped in brown paper from his coat pocket and handed it to me. I opened it and found a red journal with gold-edged cream paper. Claude had written an inscription from Thomas Browne on the inside cover: *All the wonders you seek are within yourself.*

'Thank you, my love.' I was even sorrier now that our last night together had been wasted in an argument. 'Before we know it, I'll be returning to you, and I'll have many stories to tell.'

He embraced me and whispered in my ear, 'My greatest wish is that you discover who you are without me, Emma. So that when you return, you will know whether a life with me is what you truly want.'

The ship's bell rang. 'All ashore!' the steward called. The guests stood up and began farewelling the passengers.

Claude turned from me to Florence. 'I wish you both a safe and happy voyage. You'll look after Emma, won't you, Florence?'

'Of course I will,' she told him.

My heart tore as I watched Claude disappear with the others down the gangway. Perhaps going to New York would bolster my self-reliance and help me face my insecurities once and for all. Maybe then I would be able to accept that what Claude and I had was complete.

The ship's engines burst to life; the vibrations hummed through the floor. The passengers in the saloon moved out to the promenade deck to wave goodbye to the crowd of well-wishers on the port.

I scanned the hundreds of people onshore, all waving their handkerchiefs and hats. How would I ever spot Claude among them? Then I saw him, hoisting himself up a post and raising his hand in farewell. The parting gun fired, giving me a start, and the ship glided away, slowly and ponderously at first, then gradually gaining speed.

I fixed my eyes on Claude for as long as I could. Rather than being excited that I was setting out on an adventure, I was overcome by sadness.

EIGHT

I had been angry that Caroline hadn't arranged a first-class passage for me, but when I entered the second-class library later that afternoon my indignation subsided at the sight of the varnished mahogany tables and velvet-upholstered chairs. The bookshelves were well supplied with works by American writers, including Emily Dickinson, Henry James and Mark Twain.

Later, when Florence and I went down to the dining room, we were served a delicious mushroom soup and potato and leek pie, followed by peach compote.

'I'm sure they're not eating better than this in first class,' said the man sitting opposite to us to his wife. 'All that green turtle soup and *pâté de foie gras* won't help their stomachs tomorrow when the seasickness sets in.'

The man turned out to be an engineer on his way to New York to work for an electricity company. When he learned I was making my first trip to the city, he was quick to reassure me: 'New York is the hub of invention and ingenuity. It never stops evolving. The streets are lit with electric lamps; and while it's costly now, I believe that soon every household will have a telephone.'

Florence introduced me as a writer and I was flattered that the woman next to me, a music teacher, had read some of my short stories.

'Emma Lacasse!' she said. 'I'll have to write to my sister and tell her that I met you. Are you going to write more stories? Is that why you're going to New York?'

'In a way,' I answered.

'Oh, good,' she said. 'I look forward to many more tales from you.'

I had been gradually building up a body of work but I was hardly famous. To meet someone who treated me like a luminary sent a wave of pleasurable excitement through me. Perhaps Caroline hadn't been trying to belittle me by sending me a second-class ticket; perhaps she'd anticipated I would enjoy myself more among educators and musicians?

Then the man next to Florence explained that he was a valet on his way to serve in a wealthy household and I cringed at my naïve optimism. Why did I keep trying to find excuses for Caroline?

❧

Florence and I had begun an affinity of friendship in Paris, and it was to be cemented by the challenges of travelling by sea. Our cabin was narrow, with a built-in bench on one side, a double bunk on the other, and a washstand with a mirror in-between. Along with Minette and her sand tray it was a cramped space, but something about Florence made it easy to be cheerful in her company despite the circumstances.

'I'll take the bottom bunk,' she offered when we returned from dinner and changed into our nightclothes. 'I sometimes get an idea for an article in the middle of the night and I have to get up and write it down. That way I won't disturb you; nor will Minette when she jumps up and down from the bunk.'

It amused me that despite our limited space, one of the first things Florence did was hang up her washing line ready to receive her inspirational notes.

'Does that system work for you?' I asked, watching her from the top bunk. Minette jumped up next to me and curled against my side.

'I've used it for years and it keeps me productive,' she answered, picking up Minette and placing her back on the bottom bunk. 'If I don't pay attention when the muse strikes, she might move on to someone else.'

Florence switched off the electric light and we settled down to sleep. My body was still swaying with the movement of the ocean. A few moments later Minette leaped back up next to me and snuggled into the crook of my arm. I nuzzled my head against hers and caught a whiff of her fishy, but not unpleasant, breath.

'Is she with you again?' asked Florence. 'That cat has a mind of her own. She doesn't appreciate that I had to pay for a ticket for her to cross with us.'

'I don't mind,' I said, rubbing Minette's cheek. 'I like a cat's nature. They're loving and graceful but they don't give in to anyone else's control.'

'Well, as long as you're sure you don't mind,' said Florence, making the bunks shake as she rolled over. 'I've always said only someone with a sensitive nature can appreciate a cat. That's why artists and writers adore them!'

When Florence said that her washing line technique worked for her, she was telling the truth. I soon learned that no matter what we were doing, she could plonk herself in a deckchair and scribble down a few sentences. On top of that, she talked to everybody, and somehow arranged it so we were given a tour of the bridge, where we met the captain, engineer and the navigating officer. Then, when we returned to our cabin, she wrote a piece about it in half an hour that flowed beautifully: *For the days we are at sea, the captain is the ruler of a small city ...*

But it was her story of the stokers that I liked best. The piece had me tugging at my collar as I read about the claustrophobic working conditions in the bowels of the ship: *While my companions and I travel in comfort, let us not forget we do so thanks to the backbreaking work of the stokers whose conditions are hot, dirty and dangerous* ... Her description of the heat — *like being boiled alive* — had me squirming. The details were too real for her to have obtained them second-hand.

'Florence,' I asked, 'did you get someone to show you the engine room?'

'Of course,' she answered, not looking up from her current piece.

I shook my head in admiration and wondered when she had gone down there. Perhaps while I was in the library writing letters to Claude; or napping on the promenade deck? Florence was a genius. She seemed able to write solidly while using only snatches of time. A writer who wrote in the midst of life, not separated from it. It usually took me a while to settle into my writing. Often when I came home in the evening, I needed to wash my face and hands, change into my slippers and have a cup of tea before I could re-engage with my work.

I hadn't heard from Monsieur Plamondon yet about whether he would publish *The Mysterious Cat*. I remembered the excitement I'd felt when the woman at dinner had recognised my name. If only I could become as well-known as she'd assumed, I could earn a decent living and wouldn't be beholden to Caroline. I wouldn't be beholden to anyone.

⚬⚬⚬⚬⚬⚬⚬

It was on the last day of our trip that things turned awkward between Florence and me. We were packing our trunks in preparation for arriving in New York the following morning when she turned to me.

'I've been so excited to have met such a talented writer that it's only just occurred to me that I haven't asked you a thing about your family. You mentioned you are visiting your sister and niece in New York; and Claude told me you are originally from New Orleans? I never would have guessed it. You are as French as a piano accordion. What is your sister's married name? I might know her.'

I was searching through my papers for the ticket for my harp, which had travelled in the baggage storage as there was no room in our cabin for it. If my mind hadn't been so preoccupied with that I might have thought more carefully before answering.

'Mrs Oliver Hopper. She and my niece live on Fifth Avenue.'

The ticket had slipped between the pages of the book I had brought for the journey: *The Strange Case of Dr Jekyll and Mr Hyde*. I looked up to find Florence staring at me. Her face had turned grey as if from shock.

'Your sister is married to Oliver Hopper?' she asked. 'You mean your sister is Caroline Hopper?'

I thought she must be surprised that the sister of such a wealthy woman was living on limited means and travelling in second class like a servant, and resolved to tell her the whole story at dinner. But once we were seated at our table, it was as if a gulf had opened up between us. While Florence remained polite, she avoided meeting my eye, which made it difficult to engage her in a personal conversation without drawing the attention of the others.

When we returned to the cabin, she went immediately to bed and seemed to instantly fall asleep, so there was no chance to talk to her then either.

The following morning when I awoke, Florence's packed trunk stood in the hall but she and Minette were gone. Had she gone somewhere to write? Was she investigating another of her stories before we disembarked?

I dressed and went to the promenade deck. It was crowded with passengers braving the biting cold and eager to catch their first glimpse of New York Harbor. I couldn't see Florence among the scarf-wrapped faces and coated figures.

A loud cheer rose from the group when the Statue of Liberty emerged through the mist. Some of the passengers burst into tears at the symbol of their homeland. The statue was an impressive sight: an enormous goddess raising a torch in her right hand and holding tablets of law in her left. She looked as though nothing could daunt her. But I couldn't participate in the excitement. I had expected that Florence and I would be sharing this moment together.

Even when the doctor boarded the ship to check the passengers before disembarkation, I couldn't find her. Was she going to leave without saying goodbye? It was such an odd way for her to behave.

Finally, after the first- and second-class passengers had been herded through the perfunctory customs inspection on the dock, I spotted her. She'd already acquired a porter and was directing him towards a line of hansom cabs.

'Florence, please stop!' I called to her.

She turned but didn't smile, regarding me as if I were a stranger. My stomach sank and I wondered if our friendship was fated to end with our journey.

'I thought we might travel into the city together,' I said.

She pointed towards an elegant carriage with a coachman and footman in frock coats and black silk hats. Two black horses stood in front of it, their coats groomed to gleaming perfection. On the door was a family crest with a falcon at the centre of it.

'That's your carriage,' Florence said.

I gasped in genuine surprise. After Caroline's treatment of me so far I had expected to make my own way to her address.

'May I take you to your aunt's home then?' I asked Florence. 'At least after making you travel second class I can offer you comfortable transportation for this part of the trip.'

She shook her head. 'No, I'll make my own arrangements. I'm only questioning why you didn't tell me. Were you playing a game with me?'

I burned with shame. I had never set out to deceive Florence. 'If you're wondering why my sister only arranged a second-class cabin for me, I can assure you I don't know the reason for it myself. Her treatment of me has always been unpredictable. Since she married and came to live in New York nearly twenty years ago, she hasn't really been part of my life. I don't know much about her, her husband or even my niece. I didn't tell you about it because, frankly, I'm ashamed. I'm hoping this trip will allow me to get to know my niece better.'

Florence frowned. Then her eyes widened as understanding dawned. 'So you don't know much about your sister's life in New York?'

'The barest of information. She practically disowned me and my grandmother when she left Paris. She didn't even return for Grand-maman's funeral.'

Florence rubbed her chin. 'Now I know why Claude was so concerned about you.' She reached into her purse and took out a card from a silver holder, then pressed it into my hand. 'This is my address in New York. Emma, if you need anything, any help at all, please come and see me.'

Most of the passengers had dispersed by now. The footman stepped down from the carriage and walked towards us, clearly assuming that one of us must be the person he was waiting for.

'Please, Florence,' I begged her, 'let me make up for the misunderstanding.'

She glowered at the carriage as if it was the most disgusting thing she'd ever looked upon. 'No, thank you.' She sent me a final worried glance before directing the porter towards the line of hansom cabs.

The footman approached me and bowed. He cast a striking figure with his clean-shaven face and thick eyebrows. He was as handsome as the horses.

'Miss Lacasse?'

I nodded, and he directed the porter to lift my battered trunk and harp case onto the carriage. Then he opened the door and assisted me into the blue silk-upholstered interior. As he closed the door, a huddle of people stared in my direction as if speculating who I must be to be getting into such a grand vehicle. I stifled an urge to giggle. The carriage, the footman and horses, the curious onlookers — none of these things were part of my world.

By the time we passed the rank of hansom cabs, Florence had already departed. It struck me how desperate her parting words had sounded. *Emma, if you need anything, any help at all, please come and see me.* From the way she had acted it was as if I was Jonathan Harker off to see Count Dracula; I could almost picture her pressing a crucifix into my hand rather than the card with her address. An unsettling notion that she was warning me about my sister and her husband prickled me.

NINE

I soon forgot my misgivings when I laid eyes on New York. At first the streets near the port were crooked and narrow, and the air was rank with the stench of rotting fish. Women walked with their handkerchiefs to their noses, examining the goods the pushcart vendors were offering. 'Shelled nuts! Potatoes! Onions!' they cried. But soon the streets opened up and a substantial and elegant city unfolded before me. Some of the buildings were more than ten and twelve storeys high. I'd heard that New York office buildings, hotels and even some of the homes had elevators. I couldn't imagine being pulled up to the top floor in a cage attached to a cable. I promised myself that if ever I should find myself in such a building, I would use the stairs.

We passed piano-makers and mattress stores. Flower-sellers were everywhere, perhaps even more than in Paris. On every corner there seemed to be a street vendor with their wares spread out on a blanket. We passed one toy-seller demonstrating a spinning top, with a crowd of businessmen in suits crouched around to watch. The vendor pulled the top's string and sent it into motion. The men's faces lit with fascination and they handed over their money for a top of their own. Was it for a child at home, I wondered, or for themselves?

We turned into Fifth Avenue, where the cross streets had numbers instead of names and led off at regular intervals.

Commercial activities gave way to a procession of churches and row upon row of elegant brownstone mansions, their stoops, doorways and window lintels all identical. The further along the street we travelled, the brownstone houses gradually became interspersed with mansions of marble and light stone.

Up ahead an expansive park came into view, its trees showing their bronze and gold autumn colours. A number of sightseers stood on the pavement next to the park, staring at something across the street. One man was sitting on a box and sketching what he saw. I turned to the other window to see what the people were looking at, not noticing that the carriage had come to a stop, and found myself face to face with the footman who had opened the door and was offering his hand to assist me down the step.

I alighted before a grand French Renaissance-style palace that could have been plucked straight from the Loire Valley. It was enormous, spanning almost the entire block, with a three-storey tower dominating the entrance, and gargoyles, flying buttresses and oriel windows. From the gleaming limestone walls and the untarnished blue slate roof trimmed with copper, it was obvious that the building had only recently been finished.

'Is this a hotel?' I asked the footman.

'No, Miss Lacasse,' he answered, a smile twitching at the corners of his mouth. 'It is the residence of Mr and Mrs Oliver Hopper. It was completed only a few months ago and is the grandest home in all of New York.'

So this was the house Caroline had told me about in Paris. It had sounded lofty but I hadn't imagined something so like a palace.

The footman directed me to the front door, where we were greeted by a butler in a high-buttoned black waistcoat and tailcoat. The footman jumped back on the carriage and it started to move off.

'Oh,' I said, panicked. 'My trunk and harp are still on it!'

'Do not worry, Miss Lacasse,' the butler said in a well-articulated British accent. 'They are taking your luggage to the carriage entry, where it will be promptly delivered to your room.'

He showed me into an entry vestibule, where a maid in a black dress and white apron helped me remove my coat. From there, the three of us moved into a grand hall. I had to catch my breath because I had entered another world. The hall was at least seventy feet long and faced in Caen stone. Italian tapestries adorned the white walls; and a double fireplace, its marble mantelpiece decorated with porcelain jardinières, kept the space at a comfortable temperature despite the high ceiling. At the end of the hall, a grand stairway with bronze railings divided into two at the first floor.

The butler stopped at the foot of the stairs. 'Jennie will show you to your room, Miss Lacasse. Mrs Hopper is away with Miss Hopper at a luncheon, but they will return to greet you at five o'clock. Meanwhile, shall I have the cook fix you something to eat?'

I shook my head. 'No, thank you.' I was hungry, but I was out of my depth. I didn't know what to ask for in a house such as this. Would a soup put the cook to too much trouble? Would a sandwich seem woefully humble?

I followed Jennie up to the first floor, and along a wide corridor decorated with life-sized Greek statues and a painting of Cupid and Psyche by Boucher. Jennie opened a door and showed me into a glittering room decorated in rococo-style with white walls trimmed in gilt. The chairs, the curtains and bed canopy were all silver-blue satin. A fire was burning in the Louis XVI fireplace.

'Mrs Hopper thought you would like this room the best,' Jennie said. She indicated an escritoire near the window. 'That originally belonged to Marie Antoinette. That's why this is called the Marie Antoinette Room.'

A male servant arrived with my trunk and placed it on the bench at the foot of the bed.

'My harp?' I asked him.

'It's been put in the music room, miss,' he said with a bow before leaving the room.

Jennie looked dubiously at my battered trunk. 'May I help you unpack, Miss Lacasse?'

Considering the kinds of guests Jennie was probably used to taking care of, I didn't want to cause either of us embarrassment by making her unfold my linens. I also wanted to locate my harp as soon as possible. I hated to be separated from it. Having it travel in the baggage compartment on the steamship had been bad enough.

'That won't be necessary,' I told her. 'But please tell me where the music room is.'

'On the left of the grand hall. You go back the way we came.'

After Jennie left, I sat down in a chair near the fire, closed my eyes for a moment and thought of the sumptuous grandeur of the house. Just moving from the front door to this room had been an overwhelming experience. But this was what Caroline had always wanted and now she had it. A queer sensation ran through me. I was inside Caroline's dream. She'd gathered me in.

After unpacking my trunk, I freshened up in a bathroom that dazzled me with its gleaming white tiles, marble bath and sink, and stained-glass windows. Not only cold but *hot* running water was available from the solid gold taps.

It was only half-past two in the afternoon and it would be a while before Caroline and Isadora returned. I went in search of my harp.

A maid carrying bed linens gave me a curtsy before disappearing into a room. Further along, a male servant was standing on a stepladder fixing a clock. His eyes widened with surprise to see me but he bowed politely. How many servants did it take to run a house as large as this? Besides those I'd already met there was sure to be at least thirty others including a valet, lady's maid, housekeeper and chef. As I made my way along the corridor I was conscious of doors opening and gently closing again. Did Caroline expect her servants to be invisible? The feeling that dozens of eyes were watching me stiffened the hairs on the nape of my neck and encouraged me to hurry my step.

The music room was cooler than the rest of the house because the fire was unlit, but it wasn't uncomfortable. At the end of a cream Aubusson carpet stood a grand piano with a gilded harp next to it. It wasn't my harp; that was still in its case by the piano stool. I stepped forward to examine it. Its pillar was decorated in gold leaf with motifs of Egyptian pharaohs and winged lions. It was beautiful and must have cost a fortune. Did someone actually play it, or was it meant for decoration only?

Although two ormolu and crystal chandeliers hung from the ceiling, at this time of day there was no need for artificial light. Three full-length windows looked out to a parterre courtyard, while on the other side of the room the light was reflected in a grand Venetian mirror. The fluted Corinthian columns with bands of gilded foliage twisted around them added to the sparkling atmosphere. The overall effect was sublime. Caroline had always had extravagant taste and now she had the money to express it.

I lifted my harp from its case and, after folding down the pedals, began to tune it. It hadn't fared well on the long journey. I was so intent that it should be perfect that I didn't notice the daylight fading around me.

'Aunt Emma!'

I looked up and through the gloom saw Caroline and Isadora standing in the doorway.

'My goodness,' said Caroline, 'nobody lit a fire for you or turned on the lights? They are electric, you know.'

She tugged a cord and the chandeliers' golden light illuminated the room, making everything shimmer even more magically than it had in the early afternoon.

Isadora ran forward to embrace me. 'I wrote to you every day as I promised,' she whispered in my ear. 'But Mother said my French was too embarrassing to send the letters to you.'

'It's all right,' I told her. 'We will work on it together.'

Isadora was so warm and familiar with me that I was loathe to let go of her. But dutifully I turned to my sister.

Caroline came towards me with open arms too, but stopped short at my harp case, which was shabby compared to the ethereal beauty of everything else in the room. Then she enfolded me in an embrace so stiff that if I'd closed my eyes I could have had my arms around a statue.

She let me go and pointed to my harp case. 'I'm so glad you kept it up. Isadora needs help with her playing. I'll ask Woodford to acquire a more suitable case for you. I trust that your trip across the Atlantic was comfortable?'

I'd only been in her presence five minutes and already Caroline was riling me. But I took a breath and reminded myself why I was here. I would have to develop the fortitude of a prisoner-of-war during my stay and concentrate on working towards my freedom. 'Yes, it was very pleasant,' I replied.

Caroline studied me with those piercing eyes and smiled. 'I must apologise for sending you second class, but I knew some of the Van der Heyden family would be on that ship and I didn't want you to cross paths with them until you've been properly introduced into New York society.' She sighed. 'Things are so different here, not at all like Paris. Everything must be done correctly and no wrong step is forgiven. You must follow my instructions to the letter, Emma. We cannot put a foot wrong while we prepare Isadora for her entry into society.'

She tugged on another cord and the butler appeared.

'I would like you to give Miss Lacasse a tour of the house,' Caroline told him. Turning to me, she smiled again. 'I must attend to some matters with my lady's maid and the housekeeper, and Isadora needs to rest before dinner. Woodford will show you around. Tonight at dinner you shall meet Oliver again and some guests who you will find most interesting.'

We all moved into the hall, and Caroline headed towards the grand staircase. Isadora squeezed my hand and gave me a secret smile before hurrying after her.

'Won't you please come this way,' Woodford said, directing me to the next room. 'The library has been decorated in Italianate and Second Empire styles ...'

I barely heard him because my mind was jumping from one thought to another. Could there be two women more unlike mother and daughter than Caroline and Isadora?

◈◈◈◈◈

Dinner in my Paris apartment with my American guests had always been elegant but modest affairs. The only dress I had for more formal occasions was a lilac and white tulle gown with dots of black appliqué and balloon sleeves. I had no jewellery other than a pair of pearl earrings and a gold locket that held a picture of Grand-maman. As I descended the grand staircase of the house on Fifth Avenue, I knew I was a fish out of water.

Jennie led me to the salon where we were to gather for sherry before dinner, and when she opened the door I discovered my prediction was right. The first thing that struck me was the Florentine tapestry bearing the coat of arms of the Medici family above the marble fireplace. The second was the elaborate evening dress of the four people who turned to look at me.

'Well, here she is!' said the only man among them.

It took me a moment to recognise Oliver, so much had he changed in the intervening years. His face had been distorted by a triple jowl and his body was greatly misshapen by a bulging paunch. If it wasn't for his red-gold hair and the giant black opal ring he still wore, I may not have known him at all.

'So lovely to see you again, my dear,' he said, walking over to take my hand and kissing it.

There was something more than his figure that had changed since I had last seen him. In Paris, he had been vital and dynamic, but there was nothing optimistic in his expression now. His movements appeared lacklustre, like a man worn out by life.

Oliver led me to the divan where Caroline and Isadora were sitting with a third woman.

'Good evening, Emma,' said Caroline. She looked resplendent in a dress of Nile-green silk, and a necklace of round brilliant-cut diamonds and matching earrings that sparkled each time she moved. 'I would like you to meet my very good friend, the Duchess of Dorset.'

The Duchess was an attractive woman of an indeterminable age: she could have been thirty or she could have been forty. Her jaw and brow were heavy but there wasn't a line on her face. The deep blue of her dress flattered her cinnamon-coloured hair, and her fine eyes and small mouth gave her face the appearance of a doll. But there was too much vitality in her smile to ever mistake her for an inanimate object.

'None of this "Duchess" nonsense,' she protested. Her accent was English but the force of her voice was bold and gave me the impression she might actually be American. 'When I am in New York among my dearest friends, I insist that you all call me Lucy as you have always done.' She took my hand and squeezed it, then withdrew it to touch the gold and lapis lazuli necklace she wore. It looked as if it might have once belonged to an Egyptian queen. 'Well, at least within the walls of this house. I suppose outside you had better address me as "Duchess" otherwise what was the point of me marrying a duke?'

Her comment brought peals of laughter from Caroline. Lucy laughed too and clasped Caroline's hand. The obvious bond between them sent a twinge of envy through me. It was how I imagined sisters who were close would be together.

I glanced at Isadora. She was studying me with a pleasant expression. I smiled back, glad to have an ally in my niece at least.

Caroline checked the clock on the mantelpiece. 'We are waiting for Harland,' she said. 'Then we will proceed to the dining room.'

Footsteps echoed in the hall, and Woodford, in evening livery of a black waistcoat and white shirt, opened the door. He was about to announce the guest when a figure in a tailcoat ensemble and white bowtie pushed past him into the room.

'Hello, everyone, I'm here!' he said, smoothing back a wisp of blond hair that had fallen across his forehead. His smooth tanned face gave the impression of someone well-pleased with himself and with life. He took out a diamond and emerald pocket watch and glanced at it. 'And only fifteen minutes late tonight! I had to listen to all Marion Fisher's woes about her unmarried son.' He let out a hearty laugh that rang through the room. 'But I did manage to persuade her to buy those Scottish suits of armour I obtained from Blackness Castle last year, which have been gathering dust in my warehouse!'

'Oh, Harland, you are such a delight!' said Caroline, rising from her chair. She slipped her arm into his and led him towards me. 'I would like you to meet my sister, Miss Emma Lacasse, who arrived in New York today.' To me she said, 'Emma, this is Mr Harland Hunter, the architect who created this magnificent house.'

'Ah, Miss Lacasse,' said Harland, taking my hand and smiling at me with straight white teeth. 'So pleased to make your acquaintance.'

He greeted Lucy and Isadora with the warmth of familiarity, but his handshake with Oliver was brief and both men avoided each other's gaze.

'I trust that you received the first-class pass for the railway you requested through my wife?' said Oliver. The words were polite enough but held an undertone of resentment.

Harland hesitated a moment, then quickly recovered. 'Yes, thank you, Oliver. The pass will be convenient when I don't have the use of the Clement-Madens' private railcar.'

'So Marabel has succumbed to your charms too,' said Oliver, smiling through gritted teeth.

Harland's eyes narrowed. 'Well, she had to, my friend. She has no one else to escort her midweek. Her husband's nerves are so wrecked by Wall Street that he falls asleep in the middle of dinner.'

Oliver bristled and was about to say something else when Woodford returned to inform us that dinner was ready.

'Let us eat,' said Caroline, looking grateful for the distraction. 'Harland, won't you escort my sister to the table?'

'It will be my pleasure,' Harland said. He plucked a purple rose from a vase on a side table and handed it to me. 'Here, carry this in with you, Miss Lacasse. It goes perfectly with your dress.'

The dining room spanned almost the entire length of the house and was decorated in the English style with a panelled oak-wood ceiling and walls of deep crimson. Polished brass fittings sparkled in the Gothic fireplace. The oak dining table could have accommodated perhaps a hundred people, but we sat in a section closed off by a movable screen to create a more intimate atmosphere, if an intimate atmosphere was possible while we were waited on by Woodford and three footmen. I sighed inwardly each time a new dish was presented to us — oysters, crabs, a tureen of green turtle soup, duck, lobster, steak and a serving of terrapin. It was going to take a lot of walking around New York to work off all this food. No wonder Oliver and Caroline had grown round with age.

'Now we have conquered Fifth Avenue,' Caroline said to Harland, 'we must start talking about a new residence for Newport.'

Harland dabbed at his mouth with a napkin. 'I have some brilliant ideas —'

'Because the house we already have isn't grand enough?' interrupted Oliver.

'Well, you did promise me that I would be queen of New York society,' Caroline said, sweeping his protest away like dust. 'So the new house must eclipse all others.'

'Queen or not,' said Harland, cutting into a piece of rare steak that bled into his potatoes, 'your wife is a smart woman, Oliver. I couldn't pull the wool over her eyes if I wanted to. I have never known a woman to immerse herself in every detail of a house as Caroline did when we were building this one.'

'Yes, I believe she was up to her knees in mortar!' said Oliver with a sarcastic laugh.

Oliver was surlier than I remembered him. Although he had been welcoming to me his manner towards Harland was antagonistic. With combative parents like Caroline and Oliver, it wasn't surprising poor Isadora was so shy. I looked around the grand room. My brother-in-law had risen from poverty to amass all this wealth, which would have taken tremendous determination and perseverance as well as business acumen. For that I admired him. But what had it done to his personality?

Lucy nodded to Harland. 'Tell Caroline your story about Winthrop Carrington.'

He took a sip of wine, and grinned. 'Oh yes, Carrington wanted something different for his Newport house. I've had for some time a baroque vaulted ceiling that I bought at a steal from a palazzo in Florence. The fresco, panels and bas-reliefs are all truly exquisite but it's such an awkward shape with such unusual dimensions that I couldn't find a client's home where it would fit. So when I designed Carrington's dining room I did so in a way that only one possible ceiling could fit there, then convinced him to pay for my trip to Italy to find "the right ceiling". After a month of enjoying myself as the guest of the Countess Carraresi, I returned to New York and fitted the ceiling I already had. Carrington was none the wiser and more than happy to pay five times the price I paid for it. He's been telling everyone what a genius I am ever since!'

'Poor Carrington,' said Oliver, shaking his head.

'Oh, don't be so soft!' Caroline told him. 'You can't stand fools any more than I can. You always say anyone gullible deserves to be separated from their money.'

'Speaking of fools,' said Lucy, leaning forward with excitement, 'guess who I met the other day? May Satterfield! It seems that old husband of hers isn't any closer to dying than the day she married him. He suffered a haemorrhage last Christmas so severe that May was sure it was finally the end of him and she ordered a dozen mourning outfits from Worth, but then the old man pulled through. Now she's distraught because she's convinced that by the time he does eventually die, all her mourning clothes will be out of fashion!'

'Oh, she's jinxed herself,' said Isadora. But nobody seemed to hear her except me.

Caroline laughed into her napkin. 'What was dear old Satterfield thinking to marry a young girl like that? A shopgirl of all people!'

'I know what he was thinking,' said Harland with a sly smile.

Caroline and Lucy roared with laughter. Even Oliver allowed himself a grin, although he glanced in Isadora's direction, perhaps concerned the joke was too fresh for her young ears. It touched me that at least he seemed to have a soft spot for his daughter.

Isadora put down her knife and fork. 'I have an amusing story too,' she said.

'Pray do tell!' said Harland, turning to give her his complete attention.

'Well, when I went to call on Rebecca Clark, her aunt was there. I hadn't seen her for some time and there was something odd about her face. It was an unnatural shade of pink and didn't move at all when she spoke, nor could she smile or frown. When her aunt left the room, I asked Rebecca what was the matter with her aunt's face.' Isadora giggled. 'Do you know what she told me? Her aunt had her face *enamelled*! First the skin is prepared with an alkaline wash and any wrinkles are filled in with a paste. Then the face is painted on the same way a doll's face is painted, only using a mixture of arsenic and water. Apparently it costs twenty-five dollars a week to have it done.'

'That's called embalming!' said Harland.

'Apparently it's very popular among the royalty of Europe,' insisted Isadora.

'I very much doubt that,' replied Lucy. 'They aren't anywhere near as vain about appearance as we Americans.'

'Yes,' agreed Caroline. 'It was probably an advertising ploy to take in the gullible and the vain.'

Isadora's face dropped, disappointed that her story hadn't elicited the same delight as the others. She was on the verge of telling another when Caroline gave a nod to Woodford.

'Let's retire to the drawing room for a digestif,' she said to us. 'Emma and Isadora must rise early tomorrow to begin their lessons.'

Although Caroline had alluded to me tutoring Isadora in preparation for her debut, she hadn't discussed her exact plans with me. I wondered when she intended to do so as it was already late.

On our way to the drawing room, Lucy drew close to me. 'You have been put in charge of someone who is very undeveloped for her age and frankly a bit odd, I'm afraid,' she whispered, nodding in Isadora's direction. 'You might have observed her attempts to make conversation were … awkward. She is very naïve too. Last year a footman convinced her to take a walk with him in Central Park — a kidnap ploy of course. Oliver discovered the plan just in time. Caroline is loath to put her out into society until she matures a bit and has more poise.'

I stared at her. I didn't like her talking that way about my niece. I was about to tell her so but she continued on before I had a chance.

'Caroline said you were also rather odd as a child but you must have grown out of it because you now give etiquette lessons to young ladies from middle-class families. Apparently one of your students married the Earl of Norwich? That makes you the perfect person for Isadora. You might understand her better than we do. Lord knows, I've tried to help the girl. It's unbelievable that she is the daughter of such a glorious mother.'

I was too shocked by Lucy's lack of tact to know whether to be humiliated or furious. For a supposed duchess she could certainly do with an etiquette lesson herself.

That night, before turning out my light, I sat down to write a letter to Claude.

My arrival in New York has been full of surprises. Caroline's house has to be seen to be believed. I feel as if I'm living in a city within a city. There was a lot of laughter over dinner this evening, but her friends, Harland Hunter, an architect, and the Duchess of Dorset, have a falsity about them. It's as though nothing here is as it seems ...

Their bantering voices filled my head again. Their merriment had always been at someone else's expense. I recalled Lucy's insult to me. Had Caroline really said I'd been an odd child? Or was Lucy jealous that I might come between her and my sister so was trying to divide us from the start?

I stared at the writing paper. The situation was confusing and I didn't know how to explain it to Claude. I sighed. It would only make him worry anyway. Instead I changed tack.

*There is an original Boucher on the first floor that you
would appreciate. The house has been decorated in
a mixture of styles, and many of the original pieces
have an interesting history, including the desk I am
writing at now. Apparently, it once belonged to Marie
Antoinette ...*

TEN

It was clear the following morning that the house ran to a strict routine. Jennie entered my room at eight, opened the curtains and left me with a schedule for the day written out in Caroline's hand, starting with breakfast in the dining room at nine o'clock.

Isadora and I ate together. Oliver, I understood, had already left for his office.

'Is your mother going to join us?' I asked my niece, eyeing the spread of food. Poached apples with raisins and cranberries, eggs, pancakes and muffins were all elegantly displayed on silver platters.

Isadora shook her head. 'Mother has breakfast in her bed. Then she will meet with the housekeeper and her lady's maid to give them their instructions for the day. No matter how late we go to bed, she always begins her day early. She's never been one for sleeping late.'

I thought back to our years in Paris and recalled that Caroline had always been self-disciplined. Her clothes and toilet articles had to be perfectly laid out, so much so that she had refused to let Paulette touch them.

'Mother is meticulous,' Isadora continued. 'She keeps a card file on everyone: their birthdays, their friends, the names and ages of their children, their favourite roses, their favourite drinks, and their brand of tobacco. She's like a detective — she notices the tiniest details about everyone she meets.'

One of the two footmen who were waiting on us stepped forward to refill my coffee cup. While the female servants I had encountered had been quite ordinary-looking, the house's male staff were uniformly tall, with even features and athletic physiques. I could understand how a young girl might be tricked by one of them, but Isadora didn't come across as foolish or gullible. However, from the way her mother and Lucy so easily dismissed her, I realised her life in this household must be quite lonely.

'How are your Grandmother Hopper and Aunt Anne?' I asked her. 'Are they keeping well?'

'My grandmother died when I was a child and I don't remember much about her,' she replied. 'Aunt Anne passed away a few years ago. I miss her. I used to go and visit her every day to watch her bake — I was fascinated by how skilfully she blended ingredients and decorated her creations. Even though Father employed servants for her, she insisted on cooking everything herself. She never was one for saying much, but she expressed herself through food. Sometimes when I catch a whiff of bread baking or stewed apples, I think, "Oh, Aunt Anne is talking to me!"'

'That's a nice memory,' I said. 'But didn't your aunt ever live with you?'

Isadora shook her head. 'She and Mother couldn't get along. But I liked her place in West 52nd Street. She lived there with her three dogs: Dandie, Picco and Flash.'

How different Anne was when described by someone who loved her. I could only remember how uncomfortable she had been when she'd visited our home in Paris with Oliver and her mother.

'Your father was very devoted to your grandmother and his sister, wasn't he?'

Tears welled in Isadora's eyes. 'He was. He used to visit Aunt Anne every evening before returning home so he could talk to her about his business dealings and worries. Now he has no one to talk to about those things.'

'Not even your mother?'

My niece shook her head. 'Least of all her.'

∽◦◦◦◦∽

Our lessons were to take place in a sitting room off Isadora's bedroom. According to Caroline's instructions they were to consist of two hours of French language tuition, then one hour of deportment practice before lunch. I found it amusing that Caroline was instructing me to conduct myself with 'decorum' one minute and the next entrusting me with her daughter's behaviour and manners. There really was no consistency in how she viewed me.

She'd also assigned me to take over from one of the maids supervising Isadora while she took her art lesson with a Mr Gadley three afternoons a week, and then we were to finish with a harp lesson. I rubbed my forehead. If this was to be a regular routine, it didn't leave me much free time for writing or for exploring New York. I sighed and resigned myself to the commitment I'd undertaken: Caroline hadn't invited me to New York for my own pleasure. Besides, I was enjoying getting to know Isadora and would do everything in my power to help her. Perhaps I would have to take my cue from Florence and learn to write on the run.

Isadora's sitting room wasn't what I'd expected. Instead of being decorated with gilded mirrors and bowls of roses, it was lined with black walnut bookshelves that held volumes of books about Italian art and history. I examined them closely. Unlike the near-perfect books in the library, the wrinkled spines of these books showed they had been read many times. I picked out a copy of Goethe's *Italian Journey*. The pages were marked with copious notes and comments. 'Goodness!' I said, 'You are a meticulous scholar!'

'Mother hates me writing in books,' said Isadora, sitting down in a wingback chair, 'but I can't see the point of simply reading a book. I want to absorb the writer's knowledge and commit it to memory.'

I was seeing Isadora with fresh eyes. This was no simpleton sitting before me in her tea-rose pink dress. I scanned the bookshelves and found several volumes on the history of the Medici family. It occurred to me that the reason Caroline and Lucy might not understand Isadora was because my niece was exceptionally bright.

'If you have read all these books, Isadora, you must be an expert on Italy!'

She laughed. 'I've been passionate about Italy since I took my first trip there as a child with Mother and Father. I'm not like a typical American when I travel, always boasting everything is better at home. When I go to Italy, I feel as if I have gone home.'

'How wonderful! The greatest thing in life is to be passionate about something.'

Colour rose in Isadora's cheeks and she sat up straighter. 'Do you think so, Aunt Emma?' Then she shook her head. 'I'm afraid my passion for Italy has eclipsed other things, which is why my French is so poor although I've had tutors for years. Don't misunderstand me: I loved our annual trips to Paris, but those visits were always about shopping — while Italy was about art, about history ... about life.'

I flinched. Not because Isadora hadn't taken to my beloved Paris as well as she had Florence or Rome, but because her comment drove home that Caroline had been in Paris regularly with Isadora and hadn't once brought her to meet Grand-maman.

'I wish you'd had a chance to get to know your Great-Grandmother Sylvie,' I said. 'She was cultured and would have spent hours talking with you.'

Isadora fidgeted with her hands. 'I would have liked that. What a great pity she died before I was born.'

A chasm opened up in my heart. Was that what Caroline had told her? What other lies and deceptions would I uncover? What had she told Isadora about me?

'But how lovely to have you here, Aunt Emma,' Isadora continued. 'You will be able to tell me all about Great-Grandmother Sylvie and I will get to know her through you.'

I buried my fury as best I could and turned my attention to the bookshelves again. The bottom rows were stacked with dozens of plain-bound notebooks.

'What are those?' I asked.

'Oh, Mother refers to those as my "lunatic books". Ever since I was a child I've been mad about recording things. I write about what's inspired me, what I've thought about people I've met, things I've learned ...'

'So they're journals you've kept since childhood?' I was impressed.

'Oh no,' said Isadora with a wave of her hand. 'Those are stored in the attic. The journals on the shelves are only from the past year.'

I was dumbfounded and struggled for something to say.

Isadora giggled. 'I have a lot of ideas in my head.'

✧✧✧✧✧

After luncheon Isadora led me to a room near the stables and carriage house that had been converted into a studio for her. I was expecting her art classes to be in oil painting or sketching, but when we entered the studio it was crowded not only with stands, easels and pedestals as all artists' studios were, but also a mounted toolboard on which hung callipers, crafting knives, clamps, mallets and cutting wire. The floor-to-ceiling shelves were stacked with plaster busts and casts of horses, dogs, birds and other animals, and everything was covered with grey dust.

'You're a sculptor?' I was surprised at Isadora's choice of medium. She had such delicate, soft hands.

She lifted a cover from the bench to show me her works in progress. The figures were mainly animals but there were human busts and some angels too. Some were worked in clay, others in plaster or stone. The breadth of the works was impressive — from full-round sculptures to bas-reliefs — and all displayed excellence in line, form and style.

'These are magnificent!' I told her. 'You truly are an artist.'

'She is my most talented student,' said a male voice behind us.

I turned to see a man of about thirty years of age stepping into the studio. He was thickset with broad shoulders and a moon-like face, and wore a suit with the sleeves of the jacket short enough to reveal his cuffs. When he shook my hand and introduced himself as Isadora's modelling teacher, Mr Thomas Gadley, he left a film of plaster dust on my fingers.

'Mr Gadley teaches at the Art Students League of New York,' explained Isadora. 'But he comes here three times a week to tutor me.'

I caught the whimsical note in her voice when she mentioned the school, as if she was describing a faraway exotic land. I had heard of the Art Students League and was sure that they admitted female students on an equal footing with men. I wondered why Isadora didn't study where she would have the company of other artists to inspire her. Without our little group of artists at the café in Montmartre, I would have found writing a lonely occupation.

'Let's begin on that hare we were talking about last week,' said Mr Gadley, sitting down on a stool. 'Have you made the armature?'

Isadora nodded. She put on an artist's apron and went to the shelf, returning with a basic wire skeletal structure mounted on a board and a sketch of a hare covered in gridlines. For the

next couple of hours I watched with fascination as, under the
direction of Mr Gadley, Isadora added clay to the wire piece by
piece and the hare began to take shape under her skilful hands.
I was there as a chaperone, but from the way the teacher and
student worked together there was nothing but respect and an
excellent rapport between them. They took a great deal of time
to get the long ears perfect, clearly not content to settle for less.
As the hare's facial features came to life it was as though I was
witnessing creation itself. When Isadora etched the details of
the fur so realistically, I wanted to give her a standing ovation.

'That's unbelievable!' I said when she showed me the final
product. 'I can picture him sitting in the grass, his nose twitching.'

'Miss Hopper is equally talented in carving so I am keen to
see how she handles this in stone,' said Mr Gadley, wiping his
hands on a piece of cloth. Then he grinned as an idea came to
him. 'Why don't you do a bust of your aunt, Miss Hopper? You
have a patient model there, I can tell, and she has a graceful
neck and jawline. But we'll need to set aside a whole day to do
the basic clay model.'

'What a brilliant idea!' said Isadora, regarding me with keen
eyes. 'Please say you will, Aunt Emma. You will look beautiful in
white marble! I've never had a live model to work from before.
Mother says the servants don't have time to sit all day for me.'

I had modelled for Claude and the other artists in our
Montmartre group many times and found holding a pose
uncomfortable, but Isadora was so excited I could hardly refuse
her. As a sculptor, she needed the practice of modelling from life.

'Of course I will,' I told her.

After Mr Gadley had left, and Isadora had scrubbed her
hands and changed her clothes, we went to the music room
for her harp lesson. I tuned the gilded harp, which sounded as
though it hadn't been played in months.

After an excruciating rendition of Handel's Air in B-flat
major, it became apparent that Isadora hadn't mastered the

harp as well as she had sculpting. Thankfully it was a forgiving instrument and after going through the piece phrase by phrase, Isadora began to produce a reasonable sound.

I expected she would become tired of it after an hour but she urged me to continue. 'Oh, please let's go on, Aunt Emma. I'm getting the hang of it now.'

I sensed it wasn't so much a desire to learn the harp that was motivating Isadora, but rather that she was enjoying having my company. Before I could agree, Jennie appeared at the door.

'Mrs Hopper wishes to see you, Miss Lacasse,' she told me.

'You've been summoned,' said Isadora.

I smiled as if it was a joke between us, but that was exactly what it felt like. My whole journey to New York was about obeying Caroline's orders. As I followed Jennie to the drawing room I had to suppress my anger by thinking about my apartment in Paris with all its sentimental meaning, and about Paulette whose welfare depended on me. The satisfaction I would get from berating Caroline could mean losing the things I most treasured.

Caroline was sitting at a table that held a silver tea set and a layer cake. She dismissed Jennie with a nod and gestured for me to sit down with her.

'How have you enjoyed the company of your niece?' she asked, pouring the tea herself and smiling warmly at me.

A hollow feeling of melancholy clutched my heart. How much a smile or a kind word or gesture would have meant to me as a child. Now I crossed one arm over my chest as if to protect myself from any arrows Caroline might fire my way. I was still furious that she had told Isadora that Grand-maman had died before she was born.

'She's charming,' I answered. 'And very bright.'

Caroline sipped her tea and watched me over her cup. 'One must be careful with a girl like Isadora,' she said. 'That she doesn't get any ideas.'

'Ideas?'

'About being independent or living from her art.' Caroline's tone had a hard edge and I assumed she was alluding to me and how I earned my living. But to my surprise she qualified her statement with a compliment. 'Isadora's not strong like you, Emma. She might appear that way now because she wants to impress you. But she's been bedridden twice with nervous exhaustion and she's not yet even eighteen.'

I caught my breath. 'You mean she's suffered nervous collapses?'

In Montmartre, a beautiful, delicate dancer named Ambra had once been part of our group. I had always enjoyed speaking with her and hearing her perceptive insights into life and people. But one day she stopped coming to the café, and we found out that she had thrown herself in the Seine. If Isadora had similar melancholic tendencies, I would have to be vigilant with her.

Caroline shrugged. 'Isadora has always been fragile, so putting her out in society the right way and finding a suitable husband for her is my priority. That is why I asked you to come. I can trust you to lead her on the right path. I don't trust anyone as much as I trust you.'

'Why do you trust me?' I asked her, surprised. Her attitude towards me had always suggested the opposite.

'Because you genuinely care for her — I could see that the moment you started talking to each other in the café in Paris. And because you are selfless, Emma, and have a great sense of responsibility.'

I would have been flattered by anyone else's recognition of my positive attributes. But when Caroline cited them it sent a chill through me. Isadora had said that her mother took careful note of the tiniest details about people. I was sure that far from admiring me, Caroline was figuring out how to use those positive traits to her advantage.

'It's true that I would never hurt my niece,' I told her. 'And I have every confidence that she will pick up all the skills you wish her to before her debut. But her chief disadvantage is her sheltered life. She would benefit from spending time with people her own age.'

Caroline shuddered. 'But that's impossible, Emma! Young Americans these days don't know if they are coming or going — they're always chasing the latest fad. Isadora doesn't have the constitution for that kind of frenetic activity, which is why I keep a close watch on her. I intend to find her a husband with a sense of duty; someone who demonstrates steadiness and who she can look up to.'

I couldn't see Isadora benefiting from being married to a man who didn't view her as an equal, but given my own situation with Claude I wasn't in a position to advise others on their nuptial arrangements. Still, something inside me wanted to protect Isadora, and to do that I had to maintain Caroline's confidence in me.

'I would like to see Isadora happy in life. If I can contribute to setting her on the right course, it will be my pleasure,' I said.

Caroline nodded, pleased with my answer. She picked up a knife to slice into the cake. 'I don't know if you remember this,' she said. 'We used to eat it on the plantation. It was Maman's favourite.'

'I don't remember it, but I do remember you telling me about it. The sponge layers are light, but the filling is chopped pecans, raisins and coconut.'

Caroline smiled girlishly. 'It's silly what we keep from childhood, isn't it? Our French chef can whip up the most fanciful cakes and yet I like this old southern one the best.'

We fell into a contented silence as we enjoyed the cake. The filling was sweet and the sponge was fragrant with banana and pineapple. If only Caroline and I could be like this more often, perhaps our relationship would improve.

I breathed deeply and drew up my courage. This was a better time to raise the matters that burdened my heart than when I was angry.

'Caroline, why were you so reluctant to have anything to do with me and Grand-maman after you married? I would have so liked us to stay in regular contact. It hurt us both greatly that you didn't.'

Caroline's mouth twitched and she stared at her plate in silence for a full minute. It was as if she was trying to avoid answering me in the same way a young child thinks they become invisible by hiding their face behind their hands.

'Caroline?'

'Oh, Emma, you must know,' she said, looking up at last. 'You must have seen how much Grand-maman detested me. We could barely be in the same room.'

'What? Grand-maman loved you very much!'

That there had been tension between Caroline and Grand-maman could not be denied, but it had sprung entirely from Caroline's side. I couldn't recall any incident that would lend truth to Grand-maman being unkind towards my sister.

'Sweet Emma, of course you would think that. Grand-maman adored *you*. You were her angel who could do no wrong. But I reminded her of Maman. I was too strong-minded and had to have my own way.'

'But she loved Maman too!' I insisted. 'After all, she took us into her home after our parents died.'

Caroline pursed her lips. 'She most certainly did not love Maman! That's why Maman ran away to New Orleans. And Grand-maman didn't like my influence on you. It broke my heart the day I left you at the train station, but I knew how attached you were to her. I couldn't come between the both of you.'

What Caroline was saying couldn't be true. She was twisting reality as she always did, trying to poison my mind against Grand-maman. Well, she wouldn't succeed!

'You could have come to see her when she was dying at least. Whether you got on perfectly or not, she did take us in when we were young.'

Caroline lifted her chin defiantly. 'I was the last person Grand-maman would have wanted to see then. She would have wanted you there, Emma, and only you. I didn't intend to intrude.'

I was about to protest again but a niggling doubt stopped me. Had my childish perspective back then allowed me to miss something obvious?

'Were you so cold to me when I was a child because you were jealous?' I asked her. 'Did you truly believe Grand-maman preferred me to you?'

'I was never *jealous*.' Caroline paused for a moment, as if fighting tears. 'And I was never cold to you, Emma. I sewed you clothes, I took you for walks, I encouraged your music and your little stories.'

I winced, wishing I'd never said anything. Now I was questioning if perhaps I'd been too self-righteous to perceive that I was partly to blame for our estrangement.

Caroline tugged a lace handkerchief from her sleeve and patted her eyes although they were dry. 'Can't we put all that in the past, Emma? You're here now. Let's not speak of things we can't change. Let's begin again.'

Listening to her was like hearing the words of a fairground trickster: you knew you shouldn't trust him, but you allowed yourself to be seduced anyway. I couldn't imagine dismissing a past that had haunted me for so long. But the chance to build a bond with my sister was very tempting.

'All right,' I said, taking her hand. 'We won't speak of the past again. We'll begin afresh.'

Caroline's shoulders relaxed. She peered into my eyes and gave me one of her enigmatic smiles. 'Yes, we shall begin afresh, Emma. You and I will be the sisters I always wished we could be.'

ELEVEN

Despite the new rapport I believed I'd built with Caroline, she didn't take me out with her when she paid her afternoon calls, and showed no understanding that I might like to see something of New York. At first I assumed it was because she wanted me to keep an eye on Isadora when she wasn't home. But on Monday evening Caroline, Oliver and Isadora went to the opera with Harland and Lucy, and I was left alone to have dinner in my room.

The following morning, as Isadora set about modelling my face and shoulders in clay, she complained, 'I can't understand why we go to the opera on Monday night. Nobody is there for the music, just to see and be seen. Last night we arrived during the second act and left before the opera was over. It's quite ridiculous. It was much better when I used to go with my governess on Saturday afternoons.'

Was Caroline hiding me like some sort of shameful secret, I wondered. Was being an authoress really so *déclassée* in her social circle? Harland made his living as an architect but seemed to be accepted into New York society.

I wanted to ask Isadora about her mother's attitude towards me, but each time I went to open my mouth it was as if an invisible hand clamped itself over my lips. Caroline and I had made peace, but given my sister's volatile nature that could change in an instant. If she thought I was putting unfavourable ideas about her into Isadora's head, I would be on the ship back to Paris the next day. Besides, I was no longer confident my view of Caroline was entirely accurate. She had, after all, been clear that introductions in New York had to be done properly. Perhaps she was waiting for the right moment before presenting me to her circle.

I forgot my vexation when Isadora prepared to sculpt me. I had expected Mr Gadley would be here to supervise, but he was only coming later to check on Isadora's progress.

First she took detailed measurements of my facial features with a caliper.

'You have a beautifully shaped head,' she said, writing down the measurements in a notebook. 'But the most important part of this work is that I capture your essence. So please relax and let whatever thoughts go through your mind show on your face. This isn't like posing for a painting. You don't have to sit absolutely still or hold the same expression for hours.'

When Isadora laid out her knives and modelling tools on a piece of cloth, I flinched as if she was about to perform surgery on me.

Sensing my discomfort, she smiled and said, 'Aunt Emma, I promise you that this won't hurt at all.'

She kneaded the clay and rolled it out into a slab. 'I love the sensation of soft sticky clay under my fingers. Our hands are such beautiful instruments. You must feel that way when you play the harp.'

I watched with fascination as she rolled the slab into a cylinder and marked out the placement of my facial features with a knife. Could that primitive thing ever resemble me? But when she pressed in the eye sockets and formed the nose, I averted my gaze. It was as if the clay was coming to life.

'It must be wonderful to be a writer,' she said, looking from me to the clay model and indenting a jawline. 'I read your collection of short stories five times, and each time I marvelled at your imagination. Surely you must live within the worlds you create?'

'To a degree,' I said. 'I'm always careful what I write in first person. I find those stories can often escape from the fictional realm into real life.'

'Really?' Isadora's eyes were wide with interest. 'Do you write every day? I sculpt or sketch every day. I can't bear to go for long without engaging with my work.'

Guilt pinched me. I was usually an obsessive writer, always needing to record things I'd seen — like Isadora and her notebooks. I wrote down observations about the ways people walked, the feel of a dog's fur under my fingertips, the quality of a particular person's voice, and then enlivened those descriptions with emotions, and further enriched them with colours and sounds. But after a few days in New York, my senses had deadened and my imagination felt frozen. The writing journal Claude had given me sat untouched on the same desk where Marie Antoinette had supposedly penned her letters. Was it because I found my new circumstances overwhelming? Or had I taken on the shame Caroline had expressed at my profession?

'How is it that you never married?' Isadora asked me after a while.

She turned from the clay figure to me, waiting for an answer, but I was wary of sharing my burdens with someone younger and even more sensitive than myself. Was all hope of marriage gone? It was true I was approaching an age when women were relegated to spinsterhood. I loved Claude, and had been raised to believe that if you loved someone, you married them — but he provoked such anguish in me over the issue.

'There wasn't any need,' I said.

They were Claude's words, not my own, but I noticed how Isadora's face lit with curiosity and stopped myself explaining further. Caroline had warned me not to put any ideas in Isadora's head about being independent or living from her art. Besides, my niece had been brought up with every privilege anyone could want. I couldn't imagine her shivering in some studio in Montmartre, or wondering where her next meal was coming from.

'Mother wants to put me on the marriage market after Christmas,' Isadora said. 'But with all the building going on in New York I am sure I could make a living from sculptural commissions. Harland could help me obtain them.'

Isadora's secret desire was dangerous ground and I was relieved when Mr Gadley strode in the door. 'Be careful not to work too quickly,' he warned her, 'or the model could collapse. Let's wait for the clay to stiffen slightly.'

'I'll ask Woodford to organise some sandwiches for us,' she said. 'I'm starving.'

While Isadora was gone I questioned Mr Gadley if it would be possible for a young woman to make a reasonable living as a sculptor in New York. His eyes opened wide and his manner became lively, as if he was thrilled that someone in the family was taking an interest in Isadora's art.

'For someone of Miss Hopper's immense talent it certainly would be! But she needs to study and perfect her art in Europe. The real masters are there. After that, the world would be her oyster. I can see it all — the exhibitions, the commissions, the fame.'

Mr Gadley regarded me hopefully, as if I might be able to persuade Caroline to take her daughter's talent seriously. But I doubted I could be any influence at all. Caroline was determined to marry Isadora off next year.

After we'd eaten our Swiss cheese sandwiches, the work on the clay model continued for the rest of the afternoon and into the early evening. Mr Gadley and Isadora spent as much time perfecting my ears as they had the hare's, then they sculpted my eyes and lips. Isadora's graceful hands moved over the model, shaping the cheekbones and adding clay to fill out the features. The resemblance between it and me was unsettling. As she touched the model and smoothed the browline, I twitched as though she was caressing my skin.

She worked at the features with her wire tools and brushes as a painter does. Then she and Mr Gadley created the hair, and Isadora rubbed over the surface with a sponge to even it out.

'I'll make some more refinements over the next few days. I'm quite enjoying observing you, Aunt Emma.'

'It's wonderful,' said Mr Gadley, admiring the model from all angles. Turning to me he added, 'Most of my students could only create an impressionistic model in the amount of time it takes Miss Hopper to produce a fairly detailed one.'

A flush crept across Isadora's cheeks. 'Well, Mr Gadley, I did have you to help me,' she told him.

When I looked at the model it was as if I was staring at my reflection in the mirror. Far from being impressionistic, it was hard to believe Isadora had rendered me accurately in clay so swiftly. My eyes and mouth were serene, but my brow was slightly furrowed.

⤶⤷⤶⤷

Dearest Claude,
Although my niece, Isadora, is excellent company I feel
like a prisoner in this house …

I put down my pen, reread the words I had written, and screwed up the piece of paper. If I was a prisoner it was my own fault. What was to stop me from going out and exploring New York? Why did I have to wait for Caroline's permission before I could do anything?

Now that Isadora had completed the clay model of me she was busy in her studio, preparing to carve it in marble. She no longer required me to sit for her, and given her passion for her art, she would be content on her own for hours. I searched my purse and found the card Florence had given me when we parted ways at the dock. I would pay a call on her at her aunt's house.

I picked up my hat and gloves and went downstairs. Woodford was in the great hall supervising two maids who were dusting the jardinières. When they finished each object he ran his white-gloved hand over its surface to test they hadn't missed anything. He bowed when he saw me and the two maids curtsied.

'I'd like my coat, please,' I told him.

'Are you going out, Miss Lacasse? Perhaps for a walk in the park? I will arrange for Jennie to accompany you.'

The confidence I had summoned a few moments before wavered under his penetrating gaze, but I was determined to have my way. 'No, thank you, Woodford. I'm going to pay a call on a friend.'

His face remained composed, but he rolled back and forth on his feet. I had the impression he was searching for some excuse why I couldn't go.

'I was not aware of your need for a carriage, Miss Lacasse,' he said, his voice all politeness but with an edge to it. 'Would you like to take some tea in the drawing room while I speak to the coachman about what is available? I'm afraid that Mr Hopper is driving the Daimler today, and Mrs Hopper has taken the landau to pay her calls. Her Grace, the Duchess of Dorset, has been given the use of the barouche while her own brougham is being repaired. But perhaps there is a horse and phaeton available for you. Will you allow me a moment to check?'

Getting out of the house was becoming so difficult that I was tempted to give up on the idea. Perhaps that was the effect Woodford was hoping for.

'Truly, I don't wish to be any trouble,' I told him, maintaining an air of ease that I no longer felt. I gestured towards the wide glass panels on either side of the front door. 'I can see a hansom cab waiting by the park there. Perhaps you could ask the driver if he will take me?'

I was proud of myself for sticking to my purpose, and a hansom cab was surely a reasonable compromise. I hated to think what Woodford might say if I told him I had intended to walk, or to take the elevated train if it went in the direction of Gramercy Park.

'Oh no,' he said, lowering his voice. 'A hansom cab isn't a vehicle for a lady, Miss Lacasse. I will speak to the coachman immediately and find out what can be arranged for you.'

I waited almost an hour before Woodford appeared in the drawing room with my coat.

'The driver, Mackinnon, is awaiting you,' he said. 'I apologise for the delay. As the phaeton wasn't expected to be used today it hadn't been cleaned properly.'

He was doing his charming best to let me know that I had put him and the coachman to some trouble. I doubted he would have treated Lucy the same way.

'Thank you, Woodford,' I said as I stepped out the front door and into the open air for the first time since I arrived. My legs trembled as I walked towards the elegantly curved phaeton with its driver in his formal livery and the two white ponies standing to attention. I was like a prisoner who had made an escape, checking over my shoulder and hoping no one would catch me.

The driver stepped down to help me up into the seat, then got in beside me and took the reins. 'So we're heading to Gramercy Park, Miss Lacasse,' he said, reading the card I gave him. 'I'm Ted Mackinnon, but everyone calls me Teddy.' He was young and clean-shaven like the footmen, but seemed more earnest in his manner.

'I'm sorry if I've put you to any trouble,' I told him.

'Oh, no trouble at all, Miss Lacasse. I was free today, and it's been a while since I've taken out one of the horse carriages.

I'm Mr Hopper's chauffeur, but he wanted to drive the Daimler himself today. He's quite the motor car enthusiast.'

'Horseless carriages do seem popular here,' I said, nodding in the direction of a man driving a carriage with a steering wheel and no horses, which looked very strange. 'I've seen quite a few of them in France too.'

'Oh, those things,' said Teddy with a laugh. 'I call them park benches on wheels because that's what they feel like to drive. Mrs Hopper has a small electric car that is not much faster but Mr Hopper's Daimler is a real automobile. It runs on gasoline and has a four-cylinder engine with an output of six horsepower at seven hundred revolutions per minute.'

'That sounds impressive,' I said, although it was all Latin to me.

'He's ordered a new car that will be even faster and more powerful — a racing model.' His voice rose with excitement, then he smiled sheepishly. 'Mr Hopper is something of a speedster — that's why he gets me to drive him around the city. But Mrs Hopper wrote in the daybook this morning that the master would be taking the motor car out himself. I must say it was a little out of character. On fine days like this, Mr Hopper often likes to stroll to his office so he can see the developments that are going on in the city.'

We lapsed into a comfortable silence as we made our way down Fifth Avenue and past the rows of brownstones I'd seen when I'd first arrived.

'Is this your first time in New York?' Teddy asked me after a while.

'Yes, indeed it is.'

'Well, I'm going to make a slight detour for you.'

He turned off Fifth Avenue into a street congested with carriages of every description, from hansom cabs to broughams and coupés. Then we turned onto Sixth Avenue, where the pavements were crowded with smartly dressed women. Some were carrying packages, while others had stopped to admire the enticing window displays of the numerous stores that lined the avenue. Every item attractive to women seemed to be available, from fabrics to home furnishings, from jewellery to pet accessories.

'This area is known as the Ladies' Mile,' Teddy explained, and indicated a gigantic Beaux-Arts building of glass and cast iron with a tall central tower and grand marble entrance. 'That's the Siegel-Cooper department store — the largest in the world. When it opened three years ago it was absolute mayhem. The glass front doors were shattered in the crush, and women had their dresses torn and their hats ripped off.'

'Women like their shopping,' I said, gazing at the building in awe and imagining all the gorgeous treasures inside. It was the biggest store I had ever seen, occupying an entire block. It eclipsed Le Bon Marché in Paris.

'They sure do,' agreed Teddy. 'In fact, this is a place a lady such as yourself can come without an escort. It would be quite proper. Just ask Woodford to speak to the coachman, and one of us will drive you here and wait to collect your packages. But you'll need to set aside an entire afternoon, and even then you won't have covered half the store. It has fifteen and a half acres of selling space.'

I smiled gratefully at his suggestion. If only leaving the house was that simple!

Florence's aunt's house was one of a row that overlooked a gated private park. It was a brownstone in Italianate style, with a high stoop and cast-iron handrails leading to a recessed doorway and double-leaf wooden doors. I turned the ringer and a maid in a white apron and cap answered. I told her I was calling on Florence and she led me down a walnut-panelled hall to a parlour at the rear of the house.

'Emma!' cried Florence when she saw me. 'How splendid of you to come!'

'I'm sorry to intrude on you — and your companions,' I said, smiling in the direction of the two women sitting on a crimson sofa who were regarding me with curiosity. 'But this was my first opportunity to visit.'

'You are not intruding at all,' said the older of the two women, giving a throaty laugh. She had a plump face, ample bust and unnaturally bright red hair for a middle-aged woman. 'This house doesn't run on formality. Never has, and never will.'

Her comment amused me because the parlour's decor was highly formal. The windows were hung with lace curtains and velvet over-curtains that looped to a golden border, a heavy crimson Axminster rug covered the floor and the furniture was all rosewood. But the conservative décor highlighted the humorous painting of kittens raiding an elegantly set tea table that hung above the fireplace, and the row of porcelain cat ornaments lined up on the mantelpiece below it.

'Emma, this is my aunt, Mrs Theda Husing,' said Florence, 'who will no doubt insist that you call her Aunt Theda.' Then she indicated the younger woman, who wore a neat pinstriped dress with a small cameo brooch at her neck as her only embellishment. Her ash-blonde hair was parted in the middle and pinned in a knot on top of her head. 'And this is my good friend Miss Cecilia West.'

'I'm very pleased to meet you,' Cecilia said, standing. She was no more than five feet tall and bony, but her handshake was firm and confident. Her body seemed filled with a latent energy, as if she were a coiled wire that could spring at any moment.

'Won't you please sit down, Emma,' Aunt Theda said, indicating an armchair. She reached to a cord next to her and pulled it. 'I'll ask Nora to bring us some tea.'

I sat and stroked Minette, who was asleep by the chair, curled up on an embroidered cushion. 'I've missed her company,' I said.

'Oh yes, that's right,' said Cecilia, casting her eyes over me as if she was trying to sum me up. 'You're the friend who travelled with Florence from Paris, aren't you? The writer? Your stories are a great success in France, I believe.'

Her manner was friendly but her scrutinising gaze had me squirming in my seat. 'Hardly a great success. But I am starting to obtain some recognition.'

'Cecilia is a writer too. A journalist,' said Florence, so quickly that I got the impression she was trying to warn me in some way. 'We are working together on an essay competition for schoolchildren. The topic is why it's important to be kind to animals.'

'She is more than a mere journalist,' said Aunt Theda, raising her eyebrows at Florence. 'Cecilia is a muckraker! She doesn't report how things appear on the surface; she investigates a topic thoroughly.'

Now I understood something of Cecilia's intensity. 'I remember reading about Nellie Bly, who had herself committed to a women's lunatic asylum so she could write about the shocking conditions there,' I told her. 'She was incredibly brave. What are you working on at the moment?'

'Nellie Bly is a heroine of mine,' said Cecilia, looking impressed that I knew who she was. 'I'm writing a piece for *McClure's Magazine* about how foreign-born labour is exploited here in New York. Those workers, both men and women, are too scared to protest against the dangerous work, low wages and wretched housing they are subjected to. I want to expose the employers who are misusing them while they themselves live in luxury beyond all —' She broke off as Nora arrived noisily with a tray of tea things.

Florence jumped up and helped the maid distribute the cups, then she opened a box on a side table and took out some tobacco and began rolling it. I rarely smoked — Grand-maman hadn't considered it ladylike — but before I could refuse, Florence had handed me a cigarette and lit a match for me.

'I was arrested once in London for smoking,' said Aunt Theda, taking a slow drag of her cigarette and letting out a steady stream of smoke. 'All the men were smoking in the café where I was sitting, but as soon as I lit a cigarette the proprietor called the police.'

The room became heady with the jasmine scent of the tobacco. There was something deliciously subversive about three women smoking together, I thought, especially as it was usually an activity men did together, out of the sight of women.

'Men have smoking jackets,' said Florence. 'Someone should invent "smoking dresses" for women.'

'Oh, spare us,' said Cecilia, tapping her ash into a tray and taking a sip of tea. 'Up on Fifth Avenue they're already changing their clothes several times a day. No woman needs yet another outfit to contend with.' She put down her cup and nodded in my direction. 'Where are you staying in New York, Emma?'

'West 57th Street, isn't it?' interrupted Florence. 'Not far from where I'm having my exhibition.'

Now I was sure that Florence was protecting me against too many questions from Cecilia.

'How is that all progressing?' I asked. 'Please do make sure you send me an invitation.'

'I certainly will. I've also got the mural to paint and have several commissions for portraits, so things have taken off. Spending all that time in Paris has given me cachet.'

I glanced at the cat clock on the mantelpiece. The hour I had allotted for my visit had passed.

'I'm sorry, but I'll have to leave,' I said, rising. 'My sister is extremely punctual about dinner.'

'Please return as soon as you can, Emma,' said Aunt Theda. 'Next time we'll put a gag on Florence so she doesn't interrupt you each time you try to tell us something about yourself.'

I laughed as if it was a great joke and Florence joined in.

'Here, let me show you to the front door,' she said. Out in the hallway, she helped me with my coat and added in a lowered voice, 'I'm sorry about all that. Cecilia is a very loyal friend, but terrible to have as an enemy.'

I thanked her and promised to return as soon as I could. As I stepped towards the waiting phaeton, I mulled over Florence's warning. I couldn't fathom any reason why I should make an enemy of Cecilia, but something in her manner and the fact she was a 'muckraker', as Aunt Theda had put it, convinced me Florence was right to be careful.

⁂

When Teddy and I arrived back at the house on Fifth Avenue, Woodford rushed out to meet us, his face pale and grave. He assisted me down from the carriage and opened the door to the house, but instead of coming inside after me, he returned to speak to Teddy. The chauffeur's expression changed from perplexed to deeply troubled at whatever Woodford was telling him.

The lights in the great hall hadn't been turned on and the atmosphere was sombre. There wasn't a servant in sight until Jennie came down the staircase to take my coat.

'Do you mind going to see Miss Hopper straight away?' she whispered. 'She is distressed and has been asking after you.'

All the victory I had felt in my dash for independence drained away. I'd assumed Isadora would be happy working on her own on the sculpture, yet maybe I had upset her by disappearing without telling her where I was going. But when I entered her room and found her sitting by the window, gazing wanly out at the street, I realised her misery had nothing to do with me.

'Oh, Aunt Emma,' she said quietly, 'I'm so glad you are back. Mother and Father have been shouting at each other fiercely. Now Father has retired to his room, and I've been told by Woodford that you and I are to eat dinner in our rooms.'

'What were they arguing about?' I asked.

'Something to do with Father and his motor car. But really they have a serious row every few weeks. It's been like that ever since Mother began planning this house.'

I recalled the ill temper Oliver had displayed during my first dinner in New York; it must have been a disappointment for Caroline that she had married a cantankerous man when he had appeared quite an amicable person in Paris. After all, it was Oliver who had promised her then that she could have anything she wanted.

'Don't worry,' I told Isadora, 'I'm sure it will pass. Why don't I eat dinner with you here and you can tell me how your sculpture is progressing? Mr Gadley is delighted with you. He couldn't praise your talent highly enough.'

My mention of Mr Gadley calmed her. Her shoulders relaxed and she let out a breath. 'Until you came, Aunt Emma, Mr Gadley was one of the few people I could have a conversation with. I always feel better when he talks about art and all the great masters.'

'Is there anything I can do to make you feel better?' I asked.

She was about to say something but thought better of it. 'No, it will be too cold down there now.'

'Where?'

'I left my art notebook in the studio. I don't want to run into Mother when she's in a temper. She's likely to take it out on me and ban Mr Gadley from coming. Do you think you could get it for me? If I read over it tonight before bed I am sure it will settle me.'

'Of course. I'll fetch it now, and bring it with me when I dine with you tonight.'

The way to Isadora's studio was along a stone hallway and past the kitchen, laundry room and servants' dining room.

I hurried, hoping nobody would notice me, and was relieved to find that the door to the courtyard was still unlocked.

I opened the door to the studio and searched for the light cord with fumbling fingers. During the day the studio was a welcoming place, flooded with light from the sky dome and tall windows. Now it was bone-chillingly cold and the only illumination came from a lamp shining in the courtyard, causing the statues to cast foreboding shadows.

As the interior light came on, I saw the clay model of my head on a pedestal in the centre of the room, covered with a white gauze cloth tied with a dark ribbon around the neck. I shivered and thought of Marie Antoinette ascending the scaffold to the guillotine, a white cap on her head and her hands tied behind her back.

I quickly searched for Isadora's notebook and found it on the pedestal behind the clay model. I grabbed it, as if afraid the model might come to life and start talking to me. In my haste, the notebook slipped from my fingers and landed on the floor with the middle pages open. Large loopy writing filled every line.

A paragraph jumped out at me: *I am weak, foolish and stupid! I know it and Mother knows it too. I am only pretty in a very average way and not in the least bit entertaining. Last night at dinner nobody paid me any attention when I tried to tell them about …*

I had a strong belief that it was immoral to read someone's private diary without their permission, so stopped immediately and shut the notebook. But as I did I noticed the date of the entry: 12 May 1899. It seemed that Isadora being ignored was nothing new.

I held the notebook to my heart and sensed my niece's loneliness. It pained me that she was so full of self-loathing. She needed a friend, a steady hand to guide her. Once again I was determined to be that person for her.

I was returning across the courtyard when I heard the clang of metal coming from the carriage house. The door was open and I caught a glimpse of a motor car. Curious, I stepped closer.

Teddy, no longer wearing his livery but a pair of grey overalls, was examining the front wheel of the car. He pushed back his hair and ran his hand over his face, clearly distressed. Had he been reprimanded for taking me out without Caroline's permission?

He picked up a rag and dipped it into a bucket of water, then hesitated before wiping it over the wheel's spokes and rim. After a few moments, he threw the rag to the floor and vomited into the bucket. I shuddered when I saw the rag. It was covered in blood and what looked like shreds of black hair.

I ran back into the house and hurried down the hallway, my heart beating furiously. Had I imagined what I had seen on the rag? Had my fancy about Marie Antoinette created a hallucination?

Woodford stepped out of the kitchen and I nearly knocked him over in my hurry.

'Miss Lacasse, are you all right?' he asked, gazing over my shoulder as if trying to ascertain where I'd come from. 'You are terribly pale.'

I was too overwrought to play games. 'Has something happened?' I asked him. 'Did Mr Hopper have an accident?'

'I am afraid so, Miss Lacasse,' he said, with a deep sigh. 'A dog ran out in front of his motor car this afternoon. It came from nowhere and there was no chance for Mr Hopper to avoid hitting it. Unfortunately the dog's spine was broken and a policeman had to come and shoot it.'

'Oh,' I said, lifting my hand to my mouth. 'That's awful.'

'Indeed it is.' He guided me in the direction of the great hall. 'Mr Hopper is very fond of animals and I'm afraid the incident has upset him greatly.' When we reached the staircase, he stared into my eyes in a way that might be considered impertinent.

'Because of the distressing nature of the incident, it would be best if you didn't mention it to him. Or anyone else.'

'No, I won't,' I said.

He bowed slightly. 'Mrs Hopper has requested dinner in her room. I believe that you are to dine with Miss Hopper in her room?'

I nodded.

He reached into his pocket and took out an envelope. 'In the confusion of this afternoon I forgot to give you your mail,' he said, handing it to me.

I climbed the staircase with trembling legs. I would need a few moments to compose myself before I went to see Isadora. What an unsettling day it had been.

I closed the door to my room, took off my hat and shoes and sat by the fire, then glanced at the envelope Woodford had given me. My heart lifted when I recognised Claude's handwriting.

I unfolded the letter, smiling as I read about his progress with his paintings for his exhibition and the antics of our Montmartre friends. For a moment, I could forget the tension in this house and the poor creature that had met its end under the wheels of Oliver's car.

> Well, my lovely Emma, I'll end my letter here. I miss you
> every day and look forward to your return to Paris.
>   All my love,
>   Your Claude
>   PS. I enclose a letter from your publisher. It is late,
> I'm afraid. It slipped between the counter and the wall at
> the café and Jean-François only discovered it yesterday
> when he was retrieving a coin that had fallen into the
> same gap.

The way he had signed off with 'Your Claude' warmed my heart. It made me think about Isadora asking why I had never

married. Perhaps my answer had been more honest than I'd
realised: because there hadn't been any need to do so.

I opened the envelope from Monsieur Plamondon.

Dear Mademoiselle Lacasse,
It is my great pleasure to inform you that the translation
rights for three of your short stories from Histoires de
fantômes *have been sold to* New York City Magazine.
The stories will be published over three successive
months, with accompanying illustrations, starting with
the special Halloween edition published on 31 October.
Although the payment for the stories is not large, this
is a prestigious magazine with an expansive readership
among New York society and intellectuals alike. As the
magazine usually only publishes the most illustrious
British and American writers, it is a great achievement
for a French writer to be included. Hopefully this will
allow me to sell the translation rights for A Tale of a
Lonely House *to an American publisher on favourable*
terms …

I took a deep breath. Monsieur Plamondon had encouraged me
to become better with each piece I wrote and that advice had
paid off. *New York City Magazine*!

I turned to my writing journal on the desk next to the picture
of Grand-maman I had brought with me from Paris. I promised
myself that I would rise early the following morning to work,
and would do so every morning before breakfast no matter what
took place the night before. Isadora was a committed artist, and
I had to return to being one too.

TWELVE

Isadora greeted me cheerfully at breakfast the following morning, but I ached at knowing the inner revulsion she harboured. Ambra loomed in my mind again: the world could be harsh on gentle souls. Whatever Caroline deemed my role should be in preparing her daughter for adulthood and a place in society, I was determined to help Isadora value her unique qualities. Thinking well of herself, appreciating her resourcefulness and intelligence, would hold Isadora in good stead no matter what life threw at her.

Mrs Green, the housekeeper, appeared in the doorway. She had always given me the impression of being a frosty woman with her hollow cheeks and thin lips, but this morning her manner was decidedly grim as she said, 'Mrs Hopper has requested your presence in the morning room, Miss Lacasse.'

I was halfway through eating a slice of toast and presumed I would at least be allowed to finish my breakfast, but Mrs Green continued staring at me. I swallowed and stood up sheepishly.

My eyes met Isadora's and I saw concern flash across her face. This time she didn't make a joke about me being 'summoned'. Although I did my best to hold my head up high and remember I was an adult, I scurried after Mrs Green like a naughty schoolgirl on her way to the headmistress's office.

The morning room was on the east side of the house, across the great hall and next to the ladies' reception room. When Mrs Green opened the door and announced me, it was as if I had been granted an audience with a queen. The room was filled with sunlight that illuminated the white and gold-leaf walls, gilded furniture, and the baroque-style ceiling depicting angels in flight.

Caroline was seated at a marble-top desk with bronze eagles mounted on each corner. Rather than displaying her usual commanding bearing, she sat slumped as if she was utterly exhausted. 'Thank you, Mrs Green,' she said. 'That will be all.'

Mrs Green closed the door behind her, and Caroline indicated for me to take the chair opposite her desk. She studied me a moment before handing me a newspaper. 'We have a problem. Please read the article I've circled.'

The newspaper was essentially a gossip sheet titled *Town Topics: The Journal of Society* that listed engagements, weddings, balls, dances, receptions, teas and at homes.

At last the identity of the mysterious lady who arrived by ship from Paris last week and stepped straight from the second-class gangway into the carriage of a notable Fifth Avenue family has been discovered. She is not a governess or a lady's maid as first supposed, but an authoress of mysterious tales and a harpist. Perhaps the lady in whose house she is a guest is interested in writing her memoirs? We would not put such vanity beyond her; she is known for seeking attention with her monstrously large abodes. Or perhaps the daughter of the house needs some brushing up on her music lessons? In fact, my dear readers, the truth is far more intriguing than that! This pretty young bohemian is the sister of the lady of the house! One can only wonder what other intriguing family secrets the lady in question is hiding.

I winced at the article's nasty tone, vexed that my profession and harp-playing were treated as something disgraceful, as if I were a grave-robber or a murderess rather than a respected writer. My first thought was that Florence's friend Cecilia had become suspicious and made enquiries about me. But she seemed far above writing for a scandal sheet like this one, and I knew Florence wouldn't have said anything to her.

Caroline appeared so upset by the article that I was compelled to apologise. 'I'm so sorry. And things may get worse as I'm about to be published in *New York City Magazine*. I only found out last night.'

'It's not your fault,' said Caroline in a weary tone that implied this was only one of many problems she was addressing that morning. 'That gossip could have come from anywhere — someone on the ship; even one of our own servants. That is why I emphasised you must not speak to anyone without my permission; and why I have been hesitant to take you out into society. I wanted to wait until you were more familiar with how things are here. The editor of that piece of garbage is Colonel William d'Alton Mann, a Civil War hero. He presides at a table at Delmonico's and claims to be on a mission from God to expose the secrets and peccadilloes of New York's millionaires. In reality he's nothing more than a crook.'

'At least he doesn't mention anyone by name,' I said, trying to sound encouraging.

Caroline shook her head. 'Look at the article below.'

I turned back to the newspaper and saw an illustration of Caroline and Oliver participating in a motor car parade on Fifth Avenue. Oliver was at the wheel of the Daimler I had seen the previous night, with Caroline next to him in the passenger seat. Street vendors, office workers and mothers with small children were fleeing in all directions with expressions of terror on their faces. The caption read: *Pedestrians used to rule the streets of New York. Now Mr and Mrs Oliver*

Hopper do: New York's wealthiest abandon their horses for automobiles.

'It's a ploy of Mann's,' explained Caroline, 'to avoid being sued for defamation. He doesn't give any names in his scandal articles, but places a seemingly innocuous social note under each one so everyone can be clear who he's talking about. He's tried to blackmail us before by saying he wouldn't print a certain article if Oliver bought advertising or stocks in the news-sheet. Oliver refused, but most of the millionaires in New York give in to him.'

Before Caroline could say any more, an excited female voice burst from the great hall. The next moment Woodford showed Lucy into the room.

'Caroline!' she cried, stretching out her arms to embrace my sister. 'I came as soon as I read the article. How terrible for you, my dear! And what unfortunate timing for Isadora's debut. You were being so cautious!'

She turned to me and grimaced in a way that made me feel instantly guilty for being the subject of the article.

Lucy pulled a chair for herself closer to Caroline and took both her hands in hers. 'On my way over I racked my brain for what we can do to solve this. Of course we can't pay off the Colonel because then he'll fill that rag of his with flattering accounts of you and everyone will know you've bought him off, which will only make the whole thing worse.'

'That's what I think too,' said Caroline.

Both women turned to look at me then and I shrank back into my chair. I seemed to have opponents coming at me from every direction. Colonel Mann sounded like a truly awful person; and I couldn't forget Florence's warning that Cecilia West could be a formidable enemy. At that moment, I would have willingly boarded the first ship back to France if it didn't mean being in debt again to Roche & Associates.

'Emma is to have a short story published in *New York City Magazine*,' Caroline informed Lucy. 'So there is no hiding who she is now.'

'*New York City Magazine?*' Lucy blinked. 'The impression you gave me is that she writes penny dreadfuls and dime novels. *New York City Magazine* is quite a different thing altogether!'

I was too affronted to reply. Penny dreadfuls and dime novels? Why was Caroline always either demeaning me or greatly exaggerating my accomplishments? I went up and down in her esteem like a volatile stock on the New York Exchange.

Lucy glanced from me to Caroline as something ticked over in her mind. She released one of Caroline's hands and, to my surprise, took mine so we were sitting like three girls about to play ring-a-ring-o'roses.

'Emma being an authoress is the cause of this problem,' she said. 'And Emma being an authoress is its solution.' She closed her eyes as if savouring her own genius.

Caroline and I stared at her.

She opened her eyes again and cleared her throat. 'I have the perfect plan. Everyone will be curious about Emma now. Why has no one ever heard of this mysterious sister? Why were you separated? Who is Mademoiselle Emma Lacasse exactly and why is she here now?'

Caroline was enthralled by Lucy's theatrical manner. 'What shall we do?' she asked.

Lucy released our hands and sat back in her chair, a self-satisfied smile on her face. 'We will host a very *exclusive* luncheon for some of the best-connected ladies in New York. No more than five of them. We will dress Emma in Doucet and she will give a harp recital. Each guest will receive a copy of *New York City Magazine* signed by Emma, along with a specially designed pearl bracelet with a single gold harp charm inscribed with the date of the luncheon. They will feel like members of a privileged club.'

Caroline came to life at Lucy's idea. The vitality returned to her countenance and she laughed out loud with delight. 'Lucy, that's brilliant! The others will be kicking themselves that they weren't invited!'

They giggled like two schoolgirls as they hatched their plans. The more excited they became, the more uncomfortable I grew. Rather than being introduced into New York society with dignity as Caroline's sister, I suspected I was about to be launched as some sort of curiosity from the Continent.

'We will get Maria de Amaragi to write the invitations. Her delicate calligraphic work will add prestige to the occasion,' said Caroline, writing notes for herself on a sheet of paper. 'And we should invite Grace Hunter. She always adds sophistication to an event.'

'Oh yes, Grace for sure,' agreed Lucy.

I excused myself to return to Isadora and my breakfast, but they were so involved in their plans they barely noticed me get up to leave.

As I shut the door behind me, I heard Lucy say to Caroline, 'You know, all this time we've been thinking of your sister as a liability when in fact it might be Emma who gets you entrée into old New York society.'

When I told Isadora what had taken place, her face filled with dismay. 'Oh, you are a lamb about to be thrown to a pack of wolves.'

I cringed at the image.

Isadora took my hand and squeezed it. 'You must be bold. You must remain utterly yourself no matter what Mother and Lucy tell you.'

I looked at my niece in amazement. I was supposed to be encouraging her, but it seemed she was encouraging me.

❧❧❧

On the day of the luncheon and recital, Jennie helped me dress. When she left the room, I stared in the mirror, unable to believe my transformation. The dress Lucy had obtained for me was beautiful. The fitted bodice was red velvet with puffed shoulders and tailored sleeves. The skirt was red and gold brocade.

I touched the seven-strand pearl choker around my neck with its ruby centrepiece. It was dazzling, and I guessed more expensive than anything I could have dreamed of wearing. Woodford had brought it up from the strongroom along with an emerald-cut ruby and diamond ring.

'Wear that on your right hand,' Lucy had instructed me when we'd surveyed Caroline's impressive array of jewellery in the strongroom the previous day. 'When you play the harp nobody will miss it.'

Everything I wore, from the dress to the jewellery to the silk shoes embroidered with rosebuds, made me feel different: elevated somehow. I had always liked to dress well, but had never imagined such a sumptuous outfit could make me see myself so differently.

There was a knock at the door. Isadora stepped in, a vision of loveliness in a violet silk foulard dress with a lace yoke and high neck.

'Do you mind if we go downstairs together?' she asked. 'I don't much enjoy these social functions.'

'Of course. Truth be told, I'm feeling quite apprehensive myself.'

'At first I was worried for you,' she said. 'But you are so interesting, and all those women are so bored, and that will be your great advantage. You will be a novelty to them in their otherwise monotonous rounds of social functions. Harland's wife, Grace, is different. She's exquisite. And of course Lucy will be there to make sure everything runs smoothly.'

Harland had a wife? I was surprised: he didn't seem like the kind of man who would be married. As for Lucy, there was something about her that I couldn't put my finger on. How had she grown so close to my sister that Caroline was willing to trust her completely?

'Who is the Duchess of Dorset exactly?' I asked.

'Ah,' said Isadora, with a nod of her head, 'you might have noticed that she is the only person Mother takes advice from? The Duchess is in fact Lucy Dyer-Ripley, born right here in New York. Her father was James Dyer-Ripley, the extremely successful speculator; and her mother was a beautiful theatre actress before she married. Despite their wealth, the family wasn't welcomed by the old elite — until Lucy Dyer-Ripley married the titled heir to a prestigious but impoverished English estate. Now she is welcomed everywhere. Even Augusta Van der Heyden invites her to her exclusive dinners and balls.'

'Who is Augusta Van der Heyden?' I asked. 'Your mother has mentioned that family name before.'

As we reached the grand staircase, we heard excited voices pouring from the ladies' reception room. Isadora grabbed my arm as if to steel herself.

'Augusta Van der Heyden is Mother's arch-enemy,' she said in a low voice. 'She is a descendant of an old Knickerbocker family, one of the original Dutch inhabitants of New York, and views herself as the gatekeeper to what she calls "The Great American Aristocracy". A cut or snub from her is enough to keep you out of that exclusive club. Of course there is no real aristocracy in the United States, which is why people are so enamoured of European titles. I told you they are all extremely bored.'

For someone who had been brought up in such a sheltered environment, Isadora showed remarkable astuteness.

'If Augusta Van der Heyden has accepted Lucy, why not your mother?' I asked. 'Caroline is hardly a barbarian. Your grandparents came from respectable French families, and owned one of the finest plantations in Louisiana before the Civil War.'

Isadora shrugged. 'She senses Mother's ambition. Most of the newly rich fawn over Augusta and are grateful simply to sit next to her. But Mother wants more than that. She wants to be the queen who presides over everyone else. Augusta won't allow herself to be displaced as the arbiter of New York society, so she does all she can to keep Mother out all together.'

We had to stop our conversation as we had reached the bottom of the staircase and Lucy had slipped out of the reception room to meet us. She looked every part the elegant English duchess in a dress of lightweight blue wool with a black satin collar and insert in the square neckline.

'Everyone is here,' she said. 'They are very excited to meet you, Emma. Did you memorise the list I gave you?'

I nodded although her condescension nettled me. I had memorised eight pieces by Chopin, Bach, Handel and Mozart for the afternoon's recital; it had hardly been an onerous task to learn the names of five ladies, what their husbands did, and one or two facts about them.

Woodford opened the door to the reception room and there was a flutter of excitement as Lucy swept inside, followed by me and Isadora.

Caroline, wearing a teal dress with gold passementerie trimming on the front and sleeve cuffs, flashed me a smile that conveyed she was delighted at my transformation. Suddenly the ridiculousness I felt at allowing myself to be pulled into this farce left me.

'Ladies,' Lucy announced, 'may I present to you Mademoiselle Lacasse, who will personally sign your copies of *New York City Magazine* before we proceed to luncheon.'

She directed me to a bureau plat with a vase of sweet-scented lilacs on it. Caroline brought each guest to the table one at a time to have their magazine signed. I was glad now that Lucy had given me that list as it was difficult to distinguish one expensively dressed matron from another. But these women were somehow important to Caroline and I didn't want to let her down.

First came Bessie Graham, the wife of an oil magnate; followed by Charlotte Harper, who came from a family of successful oilcloth and linoleum manufacturers. Helen Potter's husband was a banker; and Elsie Bishop's family ran a meatpacking business. Each woman was already wearing the pearl bracelet with the harp charm that they'd been given with the magazine. How eager they were to feel they were part of something special.

The last woman to have her magazine signed was Grace Hunter, Harland's wife. She was willowy and raven-haired with almond-shaped brown eyes, skin the colour of fresh cream, and a small rosy mouth with a perfect cupid's bow. Dressed in a fitted black bodice with a gold skirt decorated in appliquéd hyacinths, she stood out among the rest of the women. I should have known Harland would have a stunning wife; but unlike him, she was softly spoken and polite.

'It is a pleasure to meet you, Mademoiselle Lacasse,' she said. 'But I must confess, I have been reading your stories for some time. A French friend sends them to me. I love a good supernatural or fantasy tale, but your stories are more than that. Many of them are poignant as well.'

'I hope you will tell me what you think of the English translation,' I replied. 'Sometimes nuances are lost, and sometimes heightened, when translating from one language to another.'

'Your stories are so good I am sure they will be wonderful whatever language they are translated into.'

Grace was charming and elegant, and it was impossible to imagine her being married to someone as loud and crass as Harland. But before we could speak further, Woodford announced luncheon was served.

In the salon, a table had been set up with a jacquard tablecloth and a centrepiece of crimson and pink roses. The service was *à la française*, so all the food was on display at once. My gaze drifted over the platters of devilled crabs, whitebait, clams, beef, vegetable fritters, artichokes and salad in jelly and I wondered if a small group of women could really consume so much food.

During the meal, I remembered to adhere to Lucy's instructions about smiling graciously and saying little. But when these wealthy women kept sneaking intrigued glances in my direction I had to bite my lip to stop myself from laughing. I had never been the centre of attention in my life, and certainly never around Caroline. However, Lucy manipulated the conversation away from questions directed at me, in the same way Florence had intercepted whenever Cecilia West had asked me anything at Aunt Theda's.

'Where did you study music, Mademoiselle Lacasse?' Bessie Graham asked me. 'Lucy says you are a skilled harpist of the highest calibre.'

'She was taught by the Comtesse de Genlis,' answered Lucy on my behalf. 'The Comtesse instructed only the finest pupils.'

I squeezed my hands together under the table to prevent a grimace from breaking out on my face. The Comtesse de Genlis had taught various members of the French royal family, but she had also died in 1830.

The only guest who seemed perplexed by Lucy's reply was Grace Hunter, who glanced at me with a puzzled expression. My eyes met hers and we exchanged a secret smile. From that moment on, I felt we were conspirators.

'I believe you come from a long line of French aristocratic writers, Mademoiselle Lacasse,' Grace said, raising her eyebrows in order to keep a straight face. 'Writing has always been considered a worthy occupation among the nobles of France, hasn't it?'

'Indeed it has,' agreed Lucy before I could answer. 'You are quite right there, Grace.'

As the luncheon went on and my fictional life grew more fantastic, I began to understand how this gathering of women was a world within a world. Although they were some of the wealthiest people in the wealthiest city in the wealthiest country, they knew very little about anything outside their circle: not of history, music, or perhaps even life. I glanced at Isadora, who was sitting quietly between Charlotte Harper and Elsie Bishop. My niece was an observer. Caroline had said Isadora would not survive outside this protected little world, but I doubted that was true if she was only given a chance.

I was roused from my thoughts by Elsie asking me a question. 'Have you been to the Ladies' Mile yet, Mademoiselle Lacasse?'

I had become so used to Lucy answering on my behalf that I hesitated, before realising that she, Caroline and Grace were engaged in a conversation of their own. At last I had a chance to speak for myself!

'I have driven through it,' I said. 'I believe the Siegel-Cooper department store requires an entire afternoon.'

'Oh, more than an afternoon!' exclaimed Charlotte, as if relieved we were finally on a topic she could understand. 'They have everything there: silverware, linens, china, even pets and hardware.'

Helen Potter nodded enthusiastically. 'I bought a *Vanda sanderiana* orchid from the conservatory on the roof. Do you know how rare they are?'

Caroline and Lucy exchanged a glance when they finally realised I was holding a conversation of my own.

'It's time we moved to the music room for dessert and a private recital by my sister,' Caroline said, signalling to Woodford to open the doors that led from the salon through the library to the music room.

I heard Lucy whisper to Bessie, 'Mademoiselle Lacasse only plays for the most exclusive audiences. She never gives public recitals.'

'Oh,' exclaimed Bessie, obviously delighted to be considered one of the esteemed few. 'Then we are privileged indeed!'

I had practised my pieces with all the dedication I would have applied if I was about to play with the Paris Opera, but I needn't have tried so hard. Usually when giving a recital I played four pieces, took a break, then played another three or four. But I could see from their drooping eyelids that the women weren't used to listening attentively to music for long periods of time, so I stopped after every second piece so they could chat and pick from the table of mince pies, *biscuits glacés*, chocolate éclairs and peaches in chartreuse jelly. Only Grace Hunter listened to my performance like someone with a passion for music. She closed her eyes as if savouring the phrases, and opened them again slowly as if waking from a dream.

Despite their lack of attention to my harp-playing, when it came time to leave it was evident that the guests had enjoyed themselves.

'Your sister is utterly charming!' Bessie told Caroline. 'We will send you a dinner invitation shortly. It's a while since we've seen Oliver — I know Newton will be happy to talk with him again.'

The other women chimed in with similar compliments and invitations.

Grace lingered behind as Caroline and Lucy farewelled their guests. 'Your performance was superb,' she told me. 'I played the harp for many years, but sadly I have neglected it since I got married. I would be delighted if you would give me some lessons while you are in New York.'

I wanted to get to know Grace Hunter better; there was something more to her and I was intrigued. Lucy was signalling me to turn down the invitation but I pretended not to see her.

'That would give me great pleasure,' I told Grace. 'Would Wednesday afternoon be convenient for you?' I was eager to confirm an exact date in case Lucy or Caroline tried to stop me.

'I'll send my carriage for you,' Grace replied, as if she

understood my position perfectly. 'Then you won't have to worry about bothering the coachman here. This household is far busier than mine.'

After she left, Lucy frowned at me. 'I should have warned you not to accept any invitation that would have you alone with anyone.'

I glanced at Caroline, but to my surprise she didn't seem perturbed.

'You needn't worry, Lucy. My sister handled herself with aplomb. Everyone was taken with her. And Grace isn't a trouble-maker.'

Lucy scrutinised me in that condescending manner of hers. 'Don't get too complacent, Emma. Those ladies were only bait. Let's hope they go out and do exactly what we want them to do: gossip. We have a much bigger fish to catch — and one that won't be so easy to impress.'

I wondered whom she was referring to, but of course Lucy and my sister weren't about to take me into their confidence. The ease between them grated on me, but I was pleased that at least my sister was starting to respect me.

✥

Isadora excused herself to carry on with her sculpture; and I returned to my room and changed into my ordinary clothes. I had started a story in the morning based on the ruby and diamond ring I had been given to wear, and I wanted to continue with it before dinner.

But first I penned a letter to Claude:

I gave my first harp recital in New York today. I know you will be proud of me. It was well received, although I don't think my audience understood too much about music …

When I'd finished, I collected the other letters to Claude I had written during the week and folded them all into an envelope. I rang the bell for Jennie, but when she didn't appear I went downstairs to look for Woodford so I could give the envelope to him for the afternoon post and also return to the strongroom the jewellery I had borrowed.

I thought he might be in the scullery or china pantry, supervising the cleaning and return of the dishes and silverware from the luncheon, but only found a kitchen maid up to her elbows in hot water. She seemed flabbergasted to see me in that part of the house.

I asked her where I could find Woodford and she pointed back to the great hall. 'You'll find him in the smoking room, miss,' she stuttered. 'Refilling the cigar box and brandy decanters.'

I went in the direction she had indicated, passing a winter garden filled with palms and lilies and other exotic plants. Woodford hadn't brought me here when he'd given me a tour of the house and I got the impression from the Turkish rugs and Moorish wallpaper in the hallway that this was the masculine wing. I opened one door and found a billiard table. I opened another, and reeled back in fright.

Stag heads hung from every wall, and zebra, tiger and giraffe skins covered the floor. By the fireplace a stuffed lion and lioness stared at the room with fixed glass eyes, while near a bookcase a grizzly bear stood at its full height with its paws raised, forever frozen in time by a hunter's gun. I moved closer to it, filled with pity and horror.

'It's a magnificent beast, isn't it?' I turned to find Woodford in the doorway. 'It was a female, extra fierce because she was defending her cubs.'

My insides turned hollow. The animals in the room must have been killed by Oliver, but what kind of man thought hunting animals for pleasure was a worthy pastime, let alone killing a female with young?

'I thought you said my brother-in-law was a lover of animals? The day he ran over a dog with his motor car, you told me he was upset because he likes animals so much.'

Woodford's face darkened, but he maintained his composure. He pointed to a painting above the fireplace of a labrador retriever with a duck in its jaws. 'I meant to say that Mr Hopper is fond of dogs.'

The butler was all politeness, but the way he stood close to me and stared into my face was intimidating, and his tone contained a warning not to question him further. There was something he wasn't saying — about the accident and about this room.

'Could you kindly add this to the afternoon's post,' I said, handing him the envelope containing my letters to Claude. I tried to keep my voice steady but it wavered. 'My sister said I should give my letters to you.'

He nodded, and I returned in the direction of the great hall. I couldn't get away from him fast enough. I reached the end of the corridor and looked back. Woodford was still watching me, my letters to Claude balanced in his white-gloved hand. I was sure that whatever I said to him would get back to Caroline. He was her eyes and ears in the house.

THIRTEEN

Two days after the luncheon, Isadora and I were on our way to her studio when Jennie caught up with us. 'Mrs Hopper would like to see you in the drawing room, Miss Lacasse. Her Grace, the Duchess of Dorset, is here.'

On my way to the great hall, I glimpsed Oliver slipping into his study. It was unusual for him to be at home during the day. Since my strange encounter with Woodford, I had only seen my brother-in-law once, at dinner. He had cut his food as if in a trance and given perfunctory answers to any questions he was asked.

'A busy day at the office, I see, my dear,' Caroline had said, nodding to Woodford to refresh the wine glasses.

Oliver had roused himself then. 'Yes, indeed. I think I will retire early tonight.' He'd looked apologetically at Isadora and me, but not at Caroline.

Being with my sister and her husband was like watching a play, I thought now, where nobody's lines indicated what they really meant.

I forgot about Oliver when I saw Lucy waving me into the drawing room. 'I didn't expect things to happen so quickly!' she said, holding up a letter and seating herself next to Caroline on the sofa.

I sat in an armchair opposite them.

'Lucy received this letter this morning,' explained Caroline, and nodded to her friend who read the note out loud.

Dear Duchess of Dorset,
It has come to my attention that a certain Mademoiselle Lacasse is in New York, and that she is a skilled harpist and a writer of some fame in her own country. For reasons you well understand, I cannot call upon her hosts in New York, and so I wanted to extend this invitation through you. I would very much like you to bring Mademoiselle Lacasse to my next Thursday night dinner. However, if you do not consider her a suitable person to be invited into my home, I trust that you will inform me of this before inviting her ...

'The old dragon!' said Caroline, hissing out a breath. 'I'm sure she's up to something, Lucy. You should reply that Emma is engaged on that night.'

Lucy rubbed her temple. 'Yes, she could be drawing us into a trap. On the other hand, her formal dinners are so boring that the younger set often search for excuses not to go. I'm guessing she's afraid of losing some of them to newcomers like Addie Fishburn. She might regard Emma as a chance to add some novelty.'

I didn't like being a pawn in the game between Caroline and Augusta Van der Heyden, and was about to say so when Caroline turned to me with a grave expression on her face.

'Everything you do will be scrutinised, Emma. Everything! For Isadora to be a successful debutante she must be welcomed by the old New York elite. It is among those families that we are likely to find a suitable husband for her: someone with good values, judgement and refined taste. You are part of the Hopper family now and you must represent yourself that way, for Isadora's sake.'

'Of course I will behave honourably,' I said. 'I wouldn't do anything to jeopardise Isadora's future.'

Lucy puffed up her shoulders. 'Then I shall accept the invitation at once.' She ran her eyes over me as if I were a charity case. 'If Emma is going to represent the Hopper family she needs a suitable wardrobe.'

Caroline nodded. 'I'll organise Madame Bertin from Fifth Avenue to come.'

When I eventually entered Isadora's studio, Mr Gadley was already there. Teacher and student looked up at the same time, their faces beaming.

'Aunt Emma! The bust is finished,' cried Isadora, indicating the object hidden under a piece of white silk. 'Please, have a seat so we can reveal it to you.'

Like a magician tugging away a cape, Isadora lifted the cloth. Goosebumps ran over my skin. My face was colder in stone than it had been in clay, and a subtle change had taken place in the expression. While the clay model had looked serene except for a slight frown, now that it was rendered in white marble my face was prouder, perhaps even a touch haughty around the eyes. I was disconcerted and delighted at the same time.

'It's magnificent!' I told Isadora. While I had been reluctant to sit for her, now I was seeing the end result I couldn't deny that its beauty appealed to my vanity.

'It's her finest work yet,' said Mr Gadley, jutting out his jaw with satisfaction as if he had carved the bust himself. 'Her artistry improves in leaps and bounds.'

There was something infinitely likeable about Mr Gadley. He had the warm, kind personality that tended to draw in children and animals; and I could imagine him discussing art with Claude and Belda, and charming everyone at the Montmartre café.

'I asked Mother if I could place the bust in the music room,' Isadora said. 'Normally she hates my art anywhere in the house. But for this she has made an exception.'

The idea that Caroline had liked a piece of art representing me was gratifying, especially after her comment about me being part of the Hopper family. Perhaps our relationship was improving more than I had realised.

'Well, I must get going,' said Mr Gadley. 'I have a class at the art school in half an hour.'

Isadora opened a drawer in the bench, took out an envelope and handed it to Mr Gadley. 'That's reimbursement for the marble as well as the lessons.'

He reached into his jacket pocket and pulled out another envelope. 'And that is your receipt.'

I had observed that Woodford handled the household money, paying for all the food and flower deliveries, and wondered why he didn't settle the fee for Isadora's lessons as well. But perhaps my niece preferred to pay for everything herself out of her allowance given the resistance Caroline showed to her art.

'Mr Gadley's students are so lucky,' said Isadora with a sigh after he'd left. 'I get him for a few hours a week, but they can have classes with him anytime.'

'Yes, but when he's here you have him completely to yourself,' I said.

Isadora's cheeks turned pink and she scooped up her artist's notebook and the receipt. 'I'd better clean up and get dressed for dinner. Mother hates us to be late.'

❦

Caroline's dressmaker, Madame Bertin, arrived the following day to measure me for a wardrobe that included outfits for different times of the day, as well as for visiting, promenading and attending the opera. She burst into the morning room where I sat awaiting my fitting, and plonked her thick style books on the table in front of me.

'You are French, yes? From Paris?' she asked me. Her oval face was accentuated by her high coiffure, which bobbed each time she moved her head.

'Well, actually ...'

'I am too,' she said, her pert nose wrinkling as she smiled. 'It is not difficult to dress a French woman well. Even when I make a beautiful gown for an American woman, she cannot seem to wear it properly. It is we Parisians who have the artistic taste.'

She indicated for me to stand up so she could take my measurements. She draped the tape around my neck and made a note in her record book, then looked around the room. 'Even this magnificent house — you can tell it belongs to a woman who lived in Paris a long time and has French blood. American houses resemble museums or hunting lodges.'

I nodded to be agreeable with a fellow Parisian, but in truth I had only seen this house and that of Florence's aunt. Aunt Theda's house was stately and graceful, and although perhaps one-twentieth the size of this one it had the atmosphere of a home. As for American women, it seemed to me that Florence, Grace Hunter and Isadora each had a style that was uniquely their own.

After recording the rest of my measurements, Madame Bertin turned to her books. 'The princess line will be most flattering for you for a dinner dress,' she said, pointing to a gown whose front extended to the feet at the centre, while a circular flounce draped down the sides and back to create a panel effect. 'A combination of plain and spangled floral satin will make this dress dazzling.'

'Oh, yes indeed!' I said. I had to pinch myself as she flipped through the style books, suggesting some of the most beautiful gowns imaginable, with no thought to cost.

'This velvet afternoon dress will look beautiful on you in marine green,' she said. Smiling, she added, 'I believe you need the visiting dress and dinner gown post-haste, so I will cut the patterns this afternoon and my girls will start on them immediately. I will return in two days' time for another fitting. Everything must be done perfectly, yes? Your sister instructed that you shall have the best.'

She gathered her things, then winked at me. 'I would not take an order as large as this or as urgent from any other woman on Fifth Avenue, no matter how rich. They are all cheats. I cannot tell you the times a woman has tried to return a dress after wearing it once and claiming she never did. Others refuse to pay when one of my girls delivers their order, making excuses that their husband or butler will settle the account, but that never happens. Their husbands have millions of dollars and they want to cheat my girls out of their eight dollars a week and me out of the cost of the materials. But Mrs Hopper always pays a deposit, then promptly settles her account.'

I was pleased to hear that Caroline was honest in her financial dealings. It reassured me that at the end of my stay in New York, and after Isadora was married, she really would pay off my debts.

Caroline herself appeared at the door, and Madame Bertin showed her pictures of the gowns she was proposing and the materials she was going to use.

'Very good,' my sister said. 'You have chosen well, as always, Madame Bertin. And I may trust your discretion? You will not reveal that my sister's clothes were not made in Paris?'

'Of course,' Madame Bertin answered, tapping the side of her nose. 'It's a secret!'

'Woodford has an envelope for you then; and we will settle everything else when the dresses are delivered.'

After she had left, Caroline turned to me. 'Are you pleased with the gowns?'

'Yes, very much so. Thank you.'

She smoothed her sleeve cuff. 'Of course the very best clothes are made by Worth or Doucet in Paris, but Madame Bertin's designs will do nicely for now. Besides, with Augusta's set, it's best not to out-dress or out-jewel anyone.'

As arranged, Grace Hunter sent her carriage to take me to East 64th Street the following Wednesday afternoon. The house she lived in with Harland was an Italian Renaissance palazzo-style mansion with gilt-iron and bronze gates and a *porte-cochère* that looked as if it had come directly from Rome.

A butler, also English like Woodford, welcomed me into the grand hall. It was no less spectacular than Caroline's, with an intricately carved and pierced foliated stair balustrade, mirrored panels and Venetian lanterns. The only incongruous piece of furniture was an antique sarcophagus planted with palms and ferns. It seemed irreverent to use a coffin as a decoration.

The butler showed me into a library that displayed further European plunder in the form of a Renaissance ceiling and marquetry panels decorated with religious imagery.

Grace, who had been tuning her harp, looked up when he announced me. 'Emma, you escaped!' she said with a laugh. She was beautiful in a cream tulle tea dress with yellow trimmings.

'Let's have a chat before we start,' she said, directing me to sit in the armchair opposite her, and indicating a book on the low table between us. 'Look at what I've started reading again.'

The book's title was *Laelius De Amicitia*, by M. Tullius Cicero.

'It's in Latin?' I said, astonished.

Grace grinned. 'It often surprises people when they learn that I read Latin and Greek. You can blame my father for that. He was a true gentleman who devoted his life to cultivating his mind and didn't see any reason why girls shouldn't be as well-educated as boys.'

I regarded Grace with renewed appreciation. She had studied the classics, and her music education had obviously not been neglected either. Grand-maman had always admired well-educated and cultured people and had instilled the importance of those qualities in me. Yet Grace was years ahead of anything I had achieved.

'You are truly a Renaissance woman,' I told her.

She picked up the book and ran her fingers over the cover and spine as if caressing a precious object. 'It is a treatise on friendship by the Roman statesman Marcus Tullius Cicero,' she explained. 'He believed friendship to be the strongest tie among human beings; that it gives hope and lifts one's spirits. A true friend is honest, outspoken and caring. There is no friendship when bonds are formed for one's own advantage, and therefore friendship is not possible when there is rivalry in love, money or politics.'

I remembered the well-meaning but inattentive women who had attended my harp recital. If they were Grace's only company, she must feel isolated. My mind drifted to Harland — I still couldn't picture them as man and wife. She was so lovely, sensitive and well-mannered, while he seemed to mock everyone.

To my surprise, the man himself appeared. 'There you are, darling,' he said to Grace, filling the room with his blustering presence and booming voice. 'I'm on my way out. Don't wait up for me. I have a lot of work to do at the office.'

'I understand, sweetheart,' she replied. 'But Miss Lacasse is here. Won't you at least stop a moment to say hello.'

'Goodness me,' said Harland, striding towards me to take my hand. 'I didn't see you there, Miss Lacasse — you are so quiet. If my wife hadn't pointed you out, I might have accidentally sat on you as I did on her ill-fated kitten.'

He chortled, and I swallowed, hoping it was just black humour.

Harland was popular with Caroline and Lucy, and he was married to the most beautiful woman I had ever seen. But when he was around, a nervous tension gripped me as if I was walking on the edge of a cliff and in constant danger of falling off.

He kissed Grace and stepped back to admire her. 'Aren't you ravishing in that dress, my darling. I knew it would suit you. You look like a beautiful magnolia.'

Grace turned to me and smiled demurely. 'My husband chooses all my clothes. He always insists on coming with me to Paris when I buy my seasonal wardrobe. The Duchess and your sister are forever trying to "borrow" him. He knows exactly how to display a woman to her best advantage.'

Harland squeezed her hand and gazed at her, by all appearances very much taken with his wife. Had I misjudged him?

'Well, I have to credit you with doing your part, Grace.' He turned to me. 'My wife looks ten years younger than she is because she works so hard at it. The New York beauty industry would go downhill if it didn't have Grace to support it!'

If a man had said that to me, I would have been humiliated. But Grace didn't seem bothered at all and laughed merrily at the comment. Perhaps this was simply the way they humoured each other.

'You'd better get going, darling,' she said. 'You have your work to do, and Caroline has only spared Miss Lacasse for a couple of hours.'

He kissed her again, then headed towards the door. Before he reached it, he stopped and turned back to me. 'I hear you've been invited to one of Augusta Van der Heyden's formal dinners, Miss Lacasse? You poor thing! I have to warn you that they are frightfully tedious. Grace and I used to be invited before we got married, but thankfully that was the end of that.'

He left the room, and I tried to regain my composure by searching for something pleasant to fix my attention on. The first item that captured my eye was a Flemish tapestry that hung between two bookshelves. It showed three women standing over the body of a fourth.

Grace caught me looking at it. 'I bought that recently — Harland was furious. The three women represent the Greek Fates: Clotho spins the thread of life; Lachesis measures it to decide how long a person will live; and Atropos cuts the thread to bring death.'

The sight of the three women holding the power of life and death over a fourth did nothing to comfort me.

'Why was Harland furious that you bought it?' I asked.

'Because it's a reproduction of course.' She stared at the tapestry for a long time as if she had discovered something new in it. 'Harland plunders Europe for its old treasures, fully believing that New York is the rightful capital of the world. He loves nothing more than to wrestle an artefact off a weeping widow.'

So Grace did have insight into Harland's behaviour. How could she stand being married to him? From the little I had seen of her, she seemed like a moral person.

I must have looked perplexed because she sighed. 'You've noticed that my husband likes to cheat people and tries to get everything for free? It's become a game with him — he doesn't need the money. He's like an overgrown child. Most people are greedy and self-seeking in some way; Harland simply isn't afraid to show it. In many aspects he is a visionary — hell-bent on converting this city from a settlement of dull brownstones into a magnificent sparkling metropolis. My fear is that he'll cheat the wrong person one day and they'll kill him for it.'

An odd, tense sensation settled in my chest. I could have understood it if Grace was blinded by love to Harland's faults; but she seemed not only to know them well but to accept them. Surely her admiration of his vision for New York wasn't enough to justify the way he went about achieving it?

'Why did Augusta Van der Heyden stop inviting you to her formal dinners after you were married?' I asked.

'There is an example of a friendship destroyed by rivalry,' she said, glancing at the book. 'An architect isn't the kind of person the old New York elite would normally have at their dinner tables, especially a young unestablished one. But Harland was born into an affluent family that lost its fortune, so he had the credentials of old money just not the wealth. Besides that, his charm was irresistible. Augusta acted like a mentor for him, introducing him to the finest families in New York, buying all his clothes and jewellery, and even setting him up in a luxurious apartment in the Fifth Avenue Hotel. But Harland has always been his own person. Your sister is his champion now — she chose him to design her home here in New York. That has put some of the old guard's noses out of joint.'

I remembered what Isadora had told me about Caroline and Augusta being in competition. It made what Grace had said sound plausible. But I suspected there was more to the story than she had revealed.

Before I could ask, she turned to her harp. 'Let's begin our lesson, shall we?'

Grace played a Mozart sonata. She was more than an accomplished student: she had flexible wrists and lightweight fingers, and tackled the markedly contrasting shifts of mood in the piece — from passionate to playful — with natural flair. With regular practice, I was certain she could achieve the level of a concert harpist, if that was what she wanted.

When she'd finished, I gave her some suggestions on improving her technique and the precise stroke needed for certain strings to produce the most elegant sounds. She grasped everything readily and eagerly, and had the discipline to work on a single phrase until it was perfect.

I lost all track of time until the clock in the grand hall struck five.

'Goodness,' I said, 'I don't know where the time went. I'll have to return soon to give Isadora her music lesson.'

'Don't go yet,' Grace said. 'There's something I want to show you.'

She led me through a pair of trompe l'oeil doors depicting an Italian garden into a drawing room with a moulded ceiling and provincial French chairs. Above the carved marble fireplace hung a portrait of a younger Grace. She was perched on a sofa and wearing a white satin ball gown with a blousy pink rose at the bustline. The striking, fluid brushstrokes had captured the expression of a young woman in love: her eyes sparkled and her rosebud smile was tender.

'My first husband commissioned Giovanni Boldini to paint it,' she said. 'When I look at it now, I can hardly believe that young woman was me.'

'Your *first* husband?' I stammered. I had never imagined that Grace had been married before.

She lowered her eyes. 'Sometimes fate sneaks up on us so quietly we don't see it coming. I thought Clarence and I would be together forever, but he died only a couple of years into our marriage, of blood poisoning. The months after his death were the worst I could imagine — blackness, gloom, fits of depression. My mother told me that my grief was a failure of self-command; that I must think away sadness, and to fail to do so was a deficiency of resolve. Then I met Harland, and gaiety and laughter seemed to return to my life.'

They *seemed* to return to her life? Hadn't that actually been the case?

The butler appeared to inform us that the carriage was ready to take me back to Fifth Avenue.

'Very good, Aston,' Grace told him. 'We'll be along shortly.' She clasped my hand as he left. 'When I met you at the luncheon last week, Emma, I knew you were different. You've inspired me to re-examine my life. But be careful: this city can give you everything and then quickly take it away again. The more you associate with the fashionable crowd, the more alienated from your soul you will become.'

A maid arrived with my coat and helped me to slip it on. After she'd left, Grace said, 'She tried to kill Harland, you know.'

'Who?'

'Augusta Van der Heyden.' She linked her arm with mine and walked me out to the great hall. 'She was madly in love with him, you see. Her husband is dead now, but in those days he was neglectful. He provided her with every material luxury anybody could want, but no love or companionship. He preferred to spend his time sailing around the world on his yacht and entertaining women of dubious reputations. Harland took up escorting Augusta everywhere and made her feel like a queen.'

Grace looked at me directly. 'Nobody understands what women desire better than my husband. Everybody is happy, so amused, so delighted! Until the game comes to an end and he moves on to someone else. Augusta couldn't believe that he would betray *her*.' Her voice took on a bitter edge. 'She went to Harland's office with a pistol she had taken from her husband's gun room. Fortunately for Harland, she was a terrible shot. She fired several times from just a few feet away but only managed to graze his arm.'

The butler was waiting to open the front door for me.

'How did she avoid the scandal?' I whispered. 'Were the police called?'

An amused smile arose on Grace's face. 'When you have money, you can always avoid a scandal in New York, Emma. Harland didn't call the police. Instead, he put Augusta into a carriage and told her never to do such a foolish thing again. My husband can be quite chivalrous when he wants to be.'

She clasped my hand and gave me a parting kiss on the cheek. I thanked her for the afternoon and we agreed to have another lesson in the near future.

But as I climbed into the carriage, an unpleasant sensation, like the touch of a cold finger, ran down my spine. No matter how she acted, Grace wasn't happy in her marriage. How could she be? Harland was unscrupulous.

FOURTEEN

Lucy and I were to go to Augusta's dinner in the grand carriage the Hopper family used for important occasions. It was drawn by four magnificent horses, two white and two black.

Caroline saw us off. 'You look like one of us now,' she told me.

The chiffon dress in pale tones of blue and cream Madame Bertin had made was glorious with its low neckline and flounced skirt, and to it Caroline had added, from her own wardrobe, a cloak of cream velvet with cascades of lace rippling down the front. Part of me was flattered by my sister's double-edged praise, while another part of me was aware I was being sent into enemy territory. I was like Madame d'Oettlinger spying for Napoleon.

The footman opened the carriage door and helped us inside, and out of the icy night air. My days of travelling by omnibus to Montmartre and buying clothes on sale at Le Bon Marché seemed years away. I thought of Claude and wondered what he would make of all this opulence. I could hardly believe it myself.

Augusta's home was Dutch Renaissance in style, with an array of elegant turrets, chimneys and red-tiled gables. Unlike my sister's imposing house it was quainter and much less ostentatious.

A red velvet carpet ran from the front door, down the steps to the pavement, where two footmen in olive-green livery, powdered wigs and white face make-up were waiting to open the guests' carriage doors as they arrived.

Another footman posted at the top of the stairs bowed and opened the door for us, showing us into a grand hall with a curving staircase and portraits covering the walls.

A maid took our coats but not our evening gloves, which Lucy had advised must be worn until we had been seated for dinner. 'Place them on your lap under your napkin,' she had instructed during one of the many drills she and Caroline put me through in preparation for the occasion. 'I like to make a fold in the napkin and tuck them into it so they don't slip off. There is nothing as unladylike as searching for your gloves under the table when it's time to move to the drawing room.' Caroline had been so pent up about my attending Augusta's dinner that I hadn't dared point out that I'd been teaching my etiquette students that trick for years.

A gathering of people waited ahead of us to be taken into the formal reception room and announced by the butler. The gentlemen were each handed an envelope and guided to a seating-arrangement diagram placed on a side table.

Lucy gave the diagram a cursory glance as we passed it. 'That's not so good,' she whispered to me. 'We've been seated away from each other. Be very careful what you say, Emma. It could be a ploy.'

The magic of the evening disappeared in an instant and I remembered why we were there.

The butler ushered us into the reception room, Lucy a few steps ahead of me because of her rank. 'Her Grace, the Duchess of Dorset, and her companion, Mademoiselle Lacasse,' he announced.

The eyes of the elegant assembly turned to us, staring and curious. Lucy was an object of envy because of her aristocratic title, and many of the guests must have known from *Town Topics* that I was Caroline Hopper's mysterious sister.

But there was one gaze that was more penetrating than the others and when our eyes met, I knew who it belonged to. Augusta Van der Heyden wasn't imposing in height but she was imposing in person. A matronly woman of about sixty years of age, she was exquisitely dressed in a black silk dress embroidered with beads and sequins. She wore a diamond tiara in her high coiffure, but her jet-black hair looked dull and lifeless. It was surely a wig, I thought.

'Good evening, Duchess,' she said, taking Lucy's fingertips. 'I'm very glad you could come.' Her voice was cool and silvery.

How different she was to my sister. Caroline was spirited and impetuous, while Augusta appeared dignified but rigid. She turned to me and I tried to read her thoughts, but her face was impeccably composed.

'Good evening, Mademoiselle Lacasse,' she said, taking my fingertips as she had Lucy's. 'I'm glad you could come.' At the moment she released my hand something flashed in her eyes, so fast and deadly it was like a scorpion's sting.

Caroline had warned me that Augusta's reason for inviting me was dubious, and I might have been terrified of the older woman if I hadn't heard Grace's story about her foolish infatuation with Harland. That folly made her human.

Augusta turned to the man standing by her side. He was tall, with a military-like posture, a cleft in his chin and tawny-coloured eyes. The grey that threaded through his thick brown hair gave him a distinguished appearance. I wondered if he was Augusta's current younger lover — another Harland.

'May I present to you my nephew, Douglas Hardenbergh,' she said.

Douglas took our hands in turn and gave us both a slight bow, although from the enquiry he made about the health of the Duke of Dorset it was clear that he'd met Lucy before.

Indicating an elderly couple standing by the fire, he said to me in French, 'Allow me to introduce you to Mr and

Mrs Williamson, Mademoiselle Lacasse. They will be seated at your table tonight.'

He spoke so perfectly and elegantly that it was a shame to make it clear that I spoke fluent English. But decorum demanded it. He would be embarrassed if he found out from someone else.

'That would be most kind of you,' I told him.

'Ah,' he said with a smile, 'my efforts to impress you have missed their mark. Never mind, perhaps some other time you will allow me to practise my language skills. I do believe French to be the most beautiful language in the world.'

He guided us through the guests towards the elderly couple, but before we reached them a woman of corpse-like paleness and wearing an emerald snake ring on her hand intercepted Lucy. Her smile revealed yellowed teeth.

'When is the Duke going to grace us with his presence?' she asked.

Lucy tilted her head. 'I'm afraid my husband travels poorly by sea and it's difficult to entice him away from his beloved Rosebery Hall.'

Her reply seemed well rehearsed and I guessed this wasn't the first time she'd given it. I had wondered myself about her husband and why he wasn't in New York with her.

'Indeed,' the woman said, her eyes narrowing as if she didn't believe a word of it, 'I've heard the English are very attached to their estates.'

When it became obvious that she intended to continue the conversation, Douglas guided me away towards the Williamsons. Mr Williamson was a stout man with flowing side whiskers, and his wife had a florid face. She was obviously near-sighted and used a lorgnette to look me up and down.

'So you are the young lady we have been hearing all about,' she said in a high, imperious voice. 'The one who plays the harp and writes stories. Well, no doubt Douglas will want to tell you all about his literary endeavours.'

I glanced at him.

'I'm rather fond of writing poetry,' he confessed. 'But I keep it largely to myself. I'm always impressed to meet a published author.'

Mrs Williamson leaned towards me as if speaking in confidence. 'It's all very well for men to while away their hours writing. But there will be no time for that once you are married, my dear. You will see.'

It seemed to be a common belief that a woman's artistic life ended with marriage. Once she had taken her wedding vows, she was viewed as a servant to her husband. Claude, too, was convinced that marriage would somehow change our relationship for the worse, even though we would both be the same people.

The butler announced that dinner was served, and Douglas excused himself to lead the guests into the dining room. My dinner companion approached me and offered his arm. He was a musky-smelling man with a bulging forehead and sharp nose.

'I'm Frank Beaker,' he said, enveloping me in his stale tobacco breath. 'And I'm afraid we are seated at the least important table tonight. Still, better to be seated at the lowest table at one of Augusta's dinners than to be at the table of honour in any other house in New York.'

I feared I might be in for a tedious night — as Harland had warned me — in the company of such an obsequious man. But my concern was overtaken by delight when we entered the dining room. Paintings by old masters covered the walls, their gilded frames arranged jigsaw-style as in a museum. There were originals by Jules Lefebvre and Édouard Detaille — how Claude would have loved to see them! I wished I had my writing journal with me so I could record all the details, and then imagined how horrified Caroline would be if I did. I reminded myself that I was here for Isadora's sake.

The room held a centre table of twenty people, and four corner tables of eight each. The tables were covered with white damask cloths and each was decorated with a candelabrum surrounded by a wreath of roses. The plates were monogrammed with the initials *BVdH*.

Mr Beaker guided me to the table in the far corner, and we were soon joined by Mr and Mrs Williamson and two other couples. Mr Williamson introduced them to me as Mr and Mrs Warburg and their daughter and son-in-law, Mr and Mrs Chaser. Our table had three footmen to attend to us; the centre table had eight.

We all stood at our places until Augusta finally entered the room with an elderly gentleman on her arm. I wondered who he was. A war hero perhaps? A former diplomat? His steps were slow and unsteady and it took some time for them to reach the centre table, but not a guest stirred or fidgeted. I sensed I was taking part in an elaborate performance that had been repeated time and again for years. Even the arrangement of the polished-to-perfection silverware and the five crystal glasses of varying shapes and sizes at each setting created a sense of ceremony.

When Augusta and her guest of honour were in their places, Douglas announced the dinner had commenced and the guests sat down in unison. We had no sooner settled into our chairs and placed our napkins and gloves on our laps when a procession of food and drink was brought before us: green turtle soup served with amontillado sherry, followed by salmon with potatoes and chicken cutlets, accompanied by glasses of Veuve Clicquot champagne.

'It's such a pity Augusta had to move from her beautiful home in Lafayette Place,' Mrs Williamson said. 'I remember that house from my childhood. But they were building around her, and if she didn't want to end up surrounded by warehouses and department stores she had to relocate.'

Mrs Chaser shook her head. 'It's much more fashionable to live uptown anyway these days —'

Her mother interrupted her. 'It's a blessing Augusta brought her old paintings and furniture with her. I can't imagine what a horror this room would be if she had employed one of those fashionable architects to design her interiors, as all those *parvenus* do these days.'

Was she aware that I was Caroline Hopper's sister? Perhaps her comment had been a deliberate jab. Her use of the term *parvenu* irked me. Caroline and I had both been brought up by a refined grandmother; and Isadora was grace personified. But as the conversation continued, it became clear to me that the old elite were more envious of the newly wealthy than they cared to let on.

'Oh, but that Rhinelander mansion on Madison Avenue is so beautiful,' Mrs Chaser exclaimed. 'I've heard that the ballroom has one hundred electric lights and can hold a thousand people. I'd be very curious to see inside. Besides, the French Renaissance style suits this city very well. It's much prettier than sombre brownstone.'

From the uncomfortable glances around the table, it seemed that Mrs Chaser had uttered a blasphemy.

'I don't believe the strange heiress has even moved into that house,' said Mr Williamson. 'I heard from my real estate man that the ballroom you so wish to see, Mrs Chaser, is occupied by crates of precious European furnishings that have never been unpacked.'

'Indeed,' chimed in Mr Beaker. 'I happen to know that Gertrude Rhinelander has chosen to live with her sister across the street in a brownstone row house! Which only proves that a grand statement does not necessarily make a home a person can live in.'

'What do you think, Mademoiselle Lacasse?' asked Mrs Williamson, pointing her lorgnette at me. 'The Europeans understand taste. They don't mistake frivolous parties and grandiose mansions for class as those arrivistes do. I heard that Mrs Fishburn hosted a dinner for toys at which everyone had to speak in baby language; and on another occasion gave a birthday party for her poodle where the guest of honour wore a diamond collar costing thousands of dollars.'

Mrs Warburg laughed, a sound like a macaw. 'We mustn't judge, my dear. Those newly rich coal miners, fur traders and share croppers don't have the breeding to know any different.'

Now I was sure the sanctimonious comments were directed at the Hopper family. As for Europeans being superior in culture and taste, one only had to look to the French royal family for a display of extravagance and vulgarity. But I remembered the warnings Caroline and Lucy had given me about not being drawn into a trap.

I gave them my most charming smile and said, 'I am a poor judge, I'm afraid. I believe what my grandmother used to tell me: When we are grateful for what we have, we don't envy other people and are content with our own lives.'

My answer seemed to mystify them, as if Grand-maman's simple wisdom was beyond their grasp.

I was relieved that any further comment on the subject was rendered impossible by the footmen serving the next course: roast beef accompanied by peas and sweet potatoes, along with four varieties of champagne. The conversation changed to horseracing and hunting — two subjects that repulsed me although I was careful not to show it. I took the opportunity to withdraw into myself and gather my wits.

The beef course was followed by terrapin served with a Château Lafite Bordeaux; and still the dishes kept arriving. A game course of quail was followed by a beetroot and potato salad, which in turn was followed by a selection of cheeses. Just as I thought there couldn't be any more food in the kitchen, a dessert of ices and fruit was set before us.

Mrs Chaser leaned towards me and touched my arm. 'You seem to have caught the attention of a certain man,' she whispered. 'I've seen him sneaking glances at you all evening.'

I followed her gaze to the centre table where Douglas Hardenbergh was indeed looking in my direction. He wasn't embarrassed and smiled in a friendly manner, not turning away until the man across the table engaged him in conversation.

'He is a fine specimen of a man,' Mrs Chaser said with a sigh. 'He dotes on his two children.'

'So he is married?' I asked.

She pursed her lips and shook her head. 'What a tragedy that poor man has suffered. His wife died only a year after the youngest child was born. Tumours everywhere apparently — they say the disease ate her away in the end. Augusta doesn't believe Douglas will ever get over his grief, although he is too much a gentleman to wallow in it around others.'

My heart ached for any human being who had watched someone they loved suffer. But to be left a widower with two small children was especially tragic.

The end of dinner was signalled with coffee, candies and cognac. When the guests seemed to have had their fill, Augusta nodded to the lady nearest her and they stood up in unison. Everyone followed suit, and Mr Beaker took my arm again. In a procession of pairs, following Douglas and Lucy, we all went into the drawing room.

The men took leave of the ladies in order to return to the dining room to smoke and drink more cognac. The women settled into small groups, and Mrs Chaser invited me to sit with her and three other women. Lucy, the female guest of honour, was required to stay with Augusta's group, and was soon deep in conversation with a dowager dripping with so many diamonds she resembled a chandelier.

Coffee and a rose-scented liqueur were served. I found it curious that although Augusta had made a point of inviting me to her dinner, she hadn't spoken a word to me apart from her initial greeting. Yet she constantly glanced in my direction as if evaluating my gestures and behaviour.

After about a quarter of an hour, she stood up and approached me. Under the electric lights of the drawing room her skin appeared mottled beneath a dusting of lavender-tinted powder. The sour-sweet scent of her bergamot fragrance filled the air as she moved.

'I'm very glad you were able to come this evening, Mademoiselle Lacasse,' she said with a stiff smile. 'It's so rare that one meets a *true artist*.' I caught the note of derision in her voice. 'I would be delighted if you would perform a reading of one of your stories for the ladies before the gentlemen return? I have a copy of the French journal in which it was published. I will send one of the servants to fetch it.'

Neither Caroline nor Lucy had warned me that this situation might arise. I wasn't an artist and didn't pretend to be. I was someone who wrote entertaining tales that were deemed of high-enough quality to be published in literary journals. My cheeks felt as if they were on fire, but if I didn't answer her quickly I'd look like a fool. The best course of action, I decided, was to refuse diplomatically.

'I am flattered, Mrs Van der Heyden, but I would not insult your guests by performing a reading unprepared. I would need to translate the story for the ladies who do not speak French fluently. But I would be more than happy to read for you on another occasion after some time to prepare.'

Augusta's eyes burned with steely determination. She raised her voice theatrically. 'I understand your perfectionism, Mademoiselle Lacasse, but I am disappointed. I am enchanted by that particular story and hoped you would read it for us tonight.'

I caught the look of horror on Lucy's face as she realised what was unfolding. She was too far away to come to my rescue. My mind raced. Which story was Augusta talking about? I'd had dozens of them published over the years. She'd caught me off guard and I stumbled straight into her snare.

'Which story is that, Mrs Van der Heyden?'

Her eyes never left my face. 'The one about the two queens: the rightful one, born to her role; and the illegitimate one who wishes to usurp her. It doesn't end very well for that second queen, does it? It's a delightfully imaginative story, Mademoiselle Lacasse, but it makes an important point. You either belong or you don't.'

Mrs Williamson and Mrs Warburg tittered, but Mrs Chaser bit her lip, embarrassed on my behalf. Some of the other women exchanged nervous glances. Not everyone in the drawing room was under Augusta's spell, it seemed, even if they were afraid to stand up to her. *What would Caroline want me to do?*

Suddenly I was seven years old and back at school at the convent in Paris. One of the older girls there was a bully and she'd once dumped the contents of a flowerpot on my head, pouring dirt into my hair and over my face. 'Now you are a normal colour,' she'd said. 'Your paleness was blinding me.'

When I'd cried to Grand-maman and Caroline about what had happened, Grand-maman told me to never stoop to the low behaviour of others and to always hold my head high.

Caroline, however, had berated me for being weak. 'An eye for an eye; a tooth for a tooth,' she'd said. 'That's how the world works, Emma.'

'Then you didn't read the second part of that story, Mrs Van der Heyden?' I said, matching her stare. 'It was published in *La Plume* the following issue. The second queen creates her own alternative realm: a thriving one, free of oppression.'

Augusta's mouth pinched.

The tension in the room was as thick as the liqueur we'd been drinking. Offending one's hostess was unthinkable, but so was offending one's guest. Everyone held their breath, waiting to see what would happen next.

The men burst into the room, laughing and merry, accompanied by a striking-looking woman with dark hair and wearing a brocaded emerald-green dress with a Spanish shawl draped over her shoulders. I recognised her immediately: she was Arlette Boulay, the famous French soprano. If she was the entertainment for the evening, her fee must have cost a fortune.

Augusta turned her attention from me and rushed to greet the diva.

The men settled into chairs, and Douglas sat next to me. He glanced around, then whispered, 'You ladies don't seem to have enjoyed yourselves quite as much as we did. Did my aunt make a scene?'

'Does she make a habit of scenes?' I asked, more sharply than I'd intended.

'Ah, so she she cut you? Don't take it to heart, Mademoiselle Lacasse. She cuts every newcomer before she accepts them. Consider it a rite of passage. She was downright hostile towards my late wife, Nancy, when we first got engaged. But Nancy could win anyone over. Her bright smile and cheerful manner were too hard to resist.'

My quarrel with Augusta had been more than a 'rite of passage' but I didn't want to make things unpleasant for Douglas. Although he'd spoken fondly of his late wife I'd caught the note of bereavement in his voice. He'd been through a terrible ordeal, and to carry on about his aunt's treatment of me seemed trivial.

'I've heard Madame Boulay perform in Paris several times,' I told him. 'She is superb.'

'Then you must make sure you go to the opera on Monday night. She is singing the lead in *Roméo et Juliette*.'

My mind calmed when Madame Boulay began to perform Violetta's aria from *La Traviata*. Her perfect technique and purity of tone were mesmerising, and the richness of her voice soothed my cares. Despite the beautiful music, I was glad when the evening came to an end and the guest of honour got up to leave. I wanted nothing more than to go home and sleep.

As we gathered in the great hall to receive our coats, Lucy whispered to me, 'You certainly didn't let Augusta Van der Heyden get the better of you. You are full of surprises, Emma. I'm sure that little bit of controversy is going to be the talk of the town.'

I forced myself to meet Augusta's gaze when our time came to farewell her and Douglas at the front door.

'Good evening, Mademoiselle Lacasse,' she said, her face taut with tension. 'I trust you enjoyed yourself.'

Douglas glanced at her, then said to me, 'I noticed you admiring my aunt's art collection during dinner, Mademoiselle Lacasse. I have quite a collection of old masters myself. My grandfather started it and I have humbly continued. Should you and the Duchess wish to see them you would be most welcome to pay me a visit.'

Augusta stared at him stonily, no doubt furious her nephew was extending an invitation to me. Could my first meeting with her have gone any worse?

Lucy answered for me. 'We would be most honoured to see your collection. I know Mademoiselle Lacasse's sister and niece are great art lovers as well. I hope they will be welcome too?'

'Of course,' he replied.

I didn't dare look at Augusta again, and hurried after Lucy towards our waiting carriage. I could only imagine the daggers the doyenne of New York society was sending in my direction.

✑✎✐ ✐✎✑

It was three in the morning when we returned, but Caroline was waiting up for us in the library. She ordered a maid to bring us tea, then urged us to recount the evening's events.

'Augusta put Emma in a spot,' Lucy said, explaining the situation. 'Emma didn't handle it the way I would have chosen, but she tried her best.'

'How dare Augusta be rude to Emma?' Caroline cried. 'My sister did exactly the right thing!' Her mouth twitched between a frown and a smile. 'So Augusta didn't know about the second part of your story?' she asked me. 'Where the rival queen created an alternative society?'

'There isn't a second part of that story,' I said.

Both women fell silent. For a moment Caroline and Lucy resembled one of the paintings I'd seen on Augusta's dining room wall: a Samuel van Hoogstraten portrait of two women caught in the middle of a conspiracy. Their expressions were both intrigued and stunned.

Caroline recovered first. 'My goodness, it has been an evening of surprises!' she said, her voice full of admiration. 'Emma, you are a little devil. You made that up?'

I nodded.

'Well, you will have to write that part of the story now! Imagine Augusta's face when she reads it in *New York City Magazine*.'

I smiled to indulge her, but I had no intention of using my writing to wage a battle between the old Knickerbockers of New York and the newly rich. I couldn't imagine a subject any less engaging.

Caroline seemed to be turning something over in her mind. At first her expression frightened me: it was angry and distorted. Then it vanished and was replaced by a wide grin.

'Why not an alternative society?' she said, a new note of excitement in her voice. 'For years I've put up with Augusta's snubs. Not once has a member of the Van der Heyden family called on me, although they have gradually accepted the Clement-Madens and the Harpers. I've not retaliated for Isadora's sake, but now I'm going to force those people to come to me. I'll do something so deliciously different that they won't be able to resist.'

'What on earth are you planning?' asked Lucy, intrigued by Caroline's tone of mischief.

My sister played with the rings on her fingers. 'You both said that the guests at Augusta's dinner were wildly curious about this house?'

'Yes,' said Lucy, tilting her head. 'Mrs de Graaf kept plying me for details. They are dying to know how Harland has decorated it.'

'Of course they would be,' replied Caroline, a glint in her eye. 'They all live in houses that are exactly like those of their neighbours. If they accidentally walked into the house next door they probably wouldn't even realise! How long can people go on doing the same repetitive things? Attending the same parties; repeating the same dreary platitudes? Every Thursday night at Augusta Van der Heyden's for a reception, a musical evening, a bridge game. Every third Thursday of the month for a formal dinner. Every day of their lives they are expected to live up to Augusta Van der Heyden's set of rules if they want to remain members of her elite society. If they so much as paint their front door an unusual colour or add a different sort of braid to their clothes, they could find themselves ostracised.'

I had been tired in the carriage but now I was wide awake. What a monotonous existence Caroline was describing. But hadn't she told me she hoped to find a husband for Isadora among the old elite? At the time I had thought the company of people who valued education and culture even more than money would be a good environment for Isadora. Now I wasn't so sure. My niece had too much vitality to be condemned to an uninspiring life. Would she be strong enough to stand up for herself if she didn't like her mother's chosen suitor?

'I shall throw a ball they will never forget,' Caroline continued. 'I will invite all of New York's old elite and they will come.'

'They may not,' said Lucy, taking a sip of tea. 'They snubbed Addie Fishburn.'

Caroline shook her head. 'This won't be some tasteless toys' party, Lucy. This will be the most elegant, the most luxurious, the most spectacular ball this city has ever seen, and I'm going to spend half a million dollars to do it!'

'Caroline, that's absurd.' Lucy sat bolt upright. Her tea splashed on the saucer when she put down her cup. 'Nobody spends that much money on a ball! Besides, it would be vulgar if you went around telling people how much money you were intending to spend.'

'That's true. But unlike the old society that does everything in secret, we're going to reveal the details to the press one enticing tidbit at a time. They will tell everyone for us.'

Lucy glanced at me as if to see if I was thinking the same thing. 'Isadora isn't out in society yet. That could be a problem.'

'I'll make it her debutante ball. Everyone's tired of the same old *bals blancs* for debutantes. If they won't accept me as the queen of New York, they will have to accept Isadora. She is the wealthiest heiress of all. The theme will be the Palace of Versailles. Everyone will have to come as aristocrats, nobles and famous contemporaries of the French court.'

Lucy twisted her sleeve thoughtfully before her face broke out into a wide smile. 'That does sound a rather splendid idea: different but still tasteful, especially if Harland does the decorations and Madame Bertin designs our costumes. What date were you thinking of?'

Caroline's gaze travelled to the ceiling and fixed on the mural depicting the Battle of Lepanto. A vicious smile appeared on her face. 'The third Thursday in January. I'll make the old elite choose between Augusta and me.'

Lucy blanched. 'Are you sure, Caroline? You are taking a terrible chance. The theme is daring enough but choosing that date is risking everything.'

'Exactly!'

A pulse beat in my ears. My sister was about to throw down the gauntlet. And whether I wanted to be or not, I was a member of a family at war.

FIFTEEN

In early November, the New York Zoological Park opened and Isadora invited me to go with her and her friend, Rebecca, to see it.

'The Central Park Menagerie is depressing,' Isadora explained. 'Those poor animals have been dumped by carnivals and circuses or private owners. At least they say the new zoo has placed the animals in groups and tried to emulate their wild habitats. I need to study them in order to do justice to the sculptures I make of them.'

I didn't like zoos. Grand-maman had taken Caroline and me to the zoo in Paris once, and never again. While Caroline had been intrigued by the animals, Grand-maman and I became distressed as we moved from cage to cage. Not only was the stench of the place an assault to the nostrils, but our hearts broke at the sight of the unfortunate creatures sitting in solitary cages with cement floors, and nothing to occupy them but the faces of the humans taunting them, trying to provoke them into some action. 'It was worse than a prison,' Grand-maman said years later. 'Because those unfortunate animals were innocent.' But Isadora's description of the new zoo gave me some faith that the animals would be treated better; and it was true that she needed to study her subjects and how they moved in order to improve her art. Besides that, I was keen to meet the young woman who appeared to be my niece's only friend.

We bundled ourselves into coats and scarves, and packed Isadora's art supplies to take with us.

'I'm so pleased to meet you, Miss Lacasse,' Rebecca told me, when we picked her up on our way. She was a stout, homely girl with round spectacles to match her round face, but her grey eyes glinted with intelligence and character. 'I've read your collection of short stories,' she told me. Then, playfully pinching Isadora's arm, she added with a smile, 'I had to read them in Isadora's sitting room. She wouldn't lend me the book.'

It was touching that my niece held me and my work in such regard. 'I hope you enjoyed them,' I said.

Rebecca nodded enthusiastically. 'Your collection was the best fiction I have read this year.'

'And Rebecca reads a lot,' chimed in Isadora.

Rebecca dipped her chin. 'I do! Quite often a book a day when Mother isn't interrupting me about some tedious social function I have to attend. I made my debut last season and she's desperate to show me off.'

'You must have quite a collection of books,' I said.

'This is the city for bookstores, Miss Lacasse. Perhaps one day the three of us can go to Fourth Avenue together. It has so many new, used and rare bookstores it's referred to as "Book Row".'

Our conversation continued pleasantly until we reached the Bronx. Unlike the rest of the city the area was rural with rustic cottages and large tracts of woodland. The carriage brought us to the wrought-iron gates of the zoological park, where a sign boasted that it was the largest of its kind in the world. Indeed the fresh air and the park's many trees, hills and rocky outcrops were heartening compared to the awful conditions I'd seen at the Paris Zoo, but the animals were still behind bars. Perhaps zoo life wasn't as tragic for the smaller animals like the beavers and turtles, who seemed contented enough with their artificial ponds and rivers. But my heart sank at the sight of a majestic lion sitting in a cage with nothing more to amuse him than a rock formation. But even in his bleak surroundings, he exuded a kingly grace with his luxurious mane, golden eyes and massive paws.

'He's a Barbary lion, from the North African plains,' said Rebecca, reading the plaque on the cage. 'There are very few of them still in the wild. They're being hunted to extinction.'

'I've heard the director of the park used to be a big-game hunter, but now he's a conservationist,' said Isadora.

Rebecca finished reading the plaque and rejoined us. 'There's a rumour that half the tropical animals died in that cold snap last month and they're simply going to replace them. He can't be that much of a conservationist.'

I enjoyed listening to Isadora and Rebecca talk together. They weren't frivolous girls consumed with petty things; and seemed to have an affinity for nature and wild creatures, despite having grown up in a city.

'I want to travel,' Isadora said with a sigh, 'but not like people in society do. I want to travel freely, to view animals in their native habitats, and experience how real people live. You're the only person I know who travels like that, Aunt Emma. Everyone else just moves from one luxurious hotel to another. They may as well stay in Manhattan.'

I brought my hand to my chest. Was that how Isadora viewed me — as some sort of adventuress? I was sorry to disappoint her. I wasn't free at all. In fact, I was not unlike the poor Barbary lion: Caroline had captured me and put me on display.

We stopped by the reptile enclosure, where Isadora and Rebecca made detailed sketches of an alligator's horny scales.

'Are you an artist too?' I asked Rebecca.

She shook her head. 'No, I'm a palaeontologist. Well, at least I pretend to be. My mother refuses to send me to university. But I've read every book on the subject at the New York Public

Library, and one day I hope to work at the American Museum of Natural History.'

My heart ached for Rebecca. If her mother was anything like Caroline, that dream of hers was unlikely to be realised. Perhaps I was freer than I had assumed. My only real restriction in life was pecuniary; if I had money, I'd be at liberty to do almost anything. That brought home the irony of the difference between my life and Isadora's and Rebecca's. Their families had more wealth than most people could ever imagine, but that wealth meant they weren't allowed to choose how to live their lives.

Our final stop for the day was the bear den, which housed a collection of grizzly, black and polar bears. A grizzly bear stood on its hind legs, leaning against the bars of its cage and watching us. Rebecca sketched it, while Isadora took a lump of clay from her bag and formed it into a bear paw.

'Until you observe a real grizzly stretching its paw, you can't appreciate how big and powerful they are,' she said excitedly. 'Look at the pad! It's as wide as a dinner plate!'

I recalled the stuffed bear and lions in Oliver's trophy room and shivered. Did Isadora even know that room existed?

While the girls worked, I conjured up a story about a sculptress who rescues a bear from a zoo by moulding a piece of him every day: first his paws; then his back and forelegs; next his rump; and finally his head. When she reassembles the model in her studio, the sculpture turns into a real bear and the bear in the zoo disappears. The zookeeper thinks it has escaped and organises a bear hunt among the wealthiest and most brutal men in New York. The sculptress has to find a way to smuggle the bear out of her house on Fifth Avenue and back into the wild. She decides to use her father's private railcar to pull off the feat —

'Aunt Emma?'

I woke from my musings to find Isadora and Rebecca looking at me.

'Where were you?' Isadora asked, laughing. 'Somewhere miles away! The zoo is about to close.'

After we'd dropped Rebecca home and returned to the house on Fifth Avenue, Isadora and I parted ways: she to her studio with her clay models, and me to my room to work further on my story. We had both been inspired by our outing.

On my way back downstairs for dinner, I met Oliver who had just arrived from his office.

'How was your day at the zoo, Emma?' he asked. 'Was it all you expected it to be? What did you think of the enclosures?'

The fact that he'd lowered his voice so no one else would hear what we were talking about gave me the impression that he was keen to know my opinions rather than simply making polite conversation.

'It was certainly a more pleasant zoo than others I've visited,' I told him. 'It inspired all of us — especially Isadora, who made some remarkable models of a *live* grizzly bear's paws.'

I hadn't intended to make the point so sharply, but Oliver didn't register my barb. Perhaps he was one of those hunters who supported a zoo's role in conservation so they could have an endless variety of animals to terrorise and destroy.

'I'm pleased to hear it,' he said. 'When they were building that zoo I made a sizeable financial contribution. This country is extraordinary in its natural beauty, and I had a chance to see it when I travelled along the routes I intended to purchase for railway lines. I've seen bison in the wild, a moose giving birth, and buffalo stampeding. In my view, the natural landscape is the only way to appreciate the true majesty of animals. But all that will be gone before long — Isadora and my grandchildren will probably never get to see it. At least the wild beasts in the zoo might give them an idea of what once made this country great.'

Oliver's speech stunned me; and also reminded me of Isadora's expression earlier that afternoon of her desire to travel to wilder parts of the world.

'Why don't you take Isadora with you when you next make
a journey for your railway lines?' I asked him. 'She would most
certainly appreciate the landscape you describe.'

A light flashed in Oliver's eyes for a moment, before his
face returned to its usual expression of discontent. 'Isadora is
Caroline's domain, and she would never allow it. It is a mother's
role to direct the life of her daughter.'

The tiny doorway of understanding that had opened up
between us was firmly closed again.

Caroline sauntered down the stairs and greeted her husband
with a stony glare. 'You're late tonight, Oliver. You haven't
even bothered to change. Don't complain to me if the food has
turned cold. You can't expect the chef to perform miracles.'

But before we entered the dining room, Oliver drew me aside
and said in a hushed tone, 'I'm glad you came to New York,
Emma. I can tell you are doing Isadora a world of good.'

~❦~❦~

Dearest Claude,
As I move deeper into my sister's world, I often ask
myself what you would make of it all. It is so different
from café life in Montmartre where our conversations are
colourful and intense. We never hesitate to discuss the
innermost workings of our minds. Here everything is on
the surface.

When I went to Le Cimetière des Chiens with Florence
to visit her little dog's grave, there was an epitaph that
read: 'One would have thought he was human … but he
was faithful!' I remember that made me think about how
with another human being you can never be sure that
what they are saying is actually what they are thinking,
while animals are transparent in their sentiments. That
feeling has increased one hundredfold here. I find that

my own thinking is becoming muddled from the sheer
inability to speak authentically in this environment.
In many ways the conversations about clothes, about
houses, about who is who in society, seem very safe —
but are not safe at all. I find myself wondering what
pent-up emotions and impulses are hidden behind those
perfect façades and all the show of wealth and pomp.
Just as the surface of the sea seems calm, but underneath
lurk all sorts of dangerous creatures.

I have nearly filled the writing journal you gave me.
I am sending you my story about a grizzly bear that
escapes from the zoo in New York in a most unusual
way. I hope you like it. I wrote the original in English
and will see if I can submit it to a journal here.

I miss our late suppers together, our sharing of ideas
and our conversations about our work.

Please give my best regards to everyone at the café and
send me news about them.

My love always,
Emma

After I'd sealed the letter, a wave of longing washed over
me. Paris was still my home: a place where I could find love,
protection and security. My Montmartre friends had been a
substitute family, especially after Grand-maman died.

Here I had a blood family, but Isadora was the only one I was
close to. Despite my wariness of Caroline, I still found myself
longing to be closer to my sister. But her love was like a carrot
on a stick that she dangled before me. Each time I reached for
the carrot, she tugged it away. It had always been like that, and
I wasn't confident she would ever change.

The distance between us was driven home to me as
Thanksgiving approached. I was anticipating an intimate
family occasion, until I learned that Caroline and Oliver were

usually invited by the Harpers to the fashionable restaurant Delmonico's, and Isadora customarily celebrated with Rebecca and her family. Caroline didn't include me in the invitation to Delmonico's, and I didn't want to intrude on my niece's friendship with Rebecca, so I was relieved when Florence invited me to join her and her aunt and a few friends for the celebration.

Caroline was occupied with ball preparations when I told her. 'Who is this friend of yours again?' she asked, her head bent over the invitation list.

'A very respectable woman from a good family in Gramercy Park,' I said. Why did I need to justify to my sister who my friends were and where they lived? I wasn't a child.

'Please yourself,' she answered. 'We shall have a family celebration for Christmas.'

Aunt Theda's dinner was to commence at five o'clock. Woodford arranged a carriage for me, but I paused awkwardly at the front door. Teddy had been assigned to drive me. The horrible memory of the night I had seen him cleaning blood and gore off the wheel of Oliver's motor car came back to me. I wouldn't mention it to him. He didn't know I had seen him and there was no need to bring up such a terrible event on Thanksgiving.

'So we're off to Gramercy Park again?' he said cheerfully as he helped me into the carriage.

'I'm eagerly anticipating my first Thanksgiving in America — or at least the first one I can remember.'

'It's my favourite celebration of the year,' he said. 'I like the idea of giving thanks, and my mother and sister make such a fuss. There's the dressing and roasting of the turkey, the cranberry sauce, and of course all the candies and pastries to be given out to the little ragamuffins who come begging at the door.'

'Where does your family live?'

'In Brooklyn.'

'So you're from New York?' I said with surprise. 'I had the impression you were from the country.'

He chuckled. 'Well, there are those in Manhattan who would consider Brooklyn the frontier. But I assure you that we're quite civilised, especially since the bridge was built between the boroughs.'

'I only meant that I'm stopping you from spending Thanksgiving with your family,' I told him. 'Couldn't someone else have taken me this evening — someone who doesn't have family so close by?'

'Mrs Hopper has given me permission to call on my folks for a few hours as long as I return to pick you up at eleven o'clock,' he said, merriment in his eyes. 'So don't worry about me when my job is to worry about you.'

He shut the door to the carriage and climbed up onto the driver's seat. The interior was luxuriously fitted out with plush seats and a reading lamp. I checked my appearance in the mirror and pinched my cheeks to give them a healthy glow, feeling every part the grand lady.

I had expected the city's population to be at home with their families but the streets were anything but quiet. Fantastically garbed young men and women, as well as children, were masquerading on the pavements, on horseback and on the backs of wagons: Uncle Sams, John Bulls, harlequins, sailors, dolls, clowns, scarecrows and mythical creatures of every description were out in full force. The festive atmosphere enhanced my mood for celebration.

At Aunt Theda's house, Teddy opened the carriage door and helped me down the step. 'Please don't hurry back on my account,' I told him. 'I promise I won't say anything to my sister.'

His face turned serious. 'I will be here to pick you up at eleven exactly.' Then, measuring his words carefully, he added,

'If I don't follow Mrs Hopper's instructions to the letter, there will be trouble.'

An awkward silence settled between us. Of course that would be the case with Caroline. I had only wished to be considerate of Teddy, but I had to remember that wasn't how things worked between employers and their servants.

'I hope you have a nice time with your family,' I said, 'and I'll expect you at eleven o'clock.'

He tipped his hat and climbed back into the driver's seat.

A young maid welcomed me into Aunt Theda's house. The air inside smelled as I imagined a Thanksgiving celebration would: a blend of cherry, mint, walnut, cardamom and toffee mixed with the oily aroma of a fowl roasting.

The maid led me to the drawing room, where Florence and her aunt and the other guests were already seated in tufted purple satin armchairs before a roaring fire. They were all engaged in a lively conversation and no one heard the maid when she announced me.

'I've never read *Vanity Fair*,' a gangly young man was saying. 'I'm always afraid that books that sell in large numbers can't be much good.'

Florence and one of the female guests groaned in unison.

'Oh, you are a snob, Edgar,' said Aunt Theda. 'You're one of those people who believe that if too many people like something it can't be art!'

Minette was perched on Florence's lap and spotted me before anybody else did. She sprang down and rubbed against my skirt.

Florence's gaze followed the cat and she gave a cry when she saw me. 'Emma!' She rose and kissed my cheek before thanking the maid. 'Come and sit down next to me, Emma, and let me pour you a glass of Dubonnet. Then I'll introduce you to these other orphans.'

The comment was made in jest but I flinched. When Grand-maman had been alive I'd never thought of myself as an orphan, but now I was in New York that old feeling of being cut adrift in the world had returned.

'This is my sister, Constance,' said Florence, indicating a young woman who was as different from Florence as fire was from ice. She was dark-haired and plump, and wearing what looked like men's trousers. 'And this is Edgar, her fiancé,' Florence continued, nodding towards the young man who had spoken out against Thackeray's novel.

The other guests were Violet, who was an artist like Florence, and Richard who was an actor.

'Where is Cecilia this evening?' Aunt Theda asked Florence. 'She's usually the first to arrive.'

'She's helping with the dinner for the true orphans at the Catholic Protectory,' Florence answered. 'They're feeding nearly three thousand little boys and girls today and she doesn't expect to make it in time for our meal.'

The maid returned and whispered something to Aunt Theda, who nodded and rose. 'The table is laid, everyone,' she announced.

We followed Aunt Theda down the hall and into a dining room that was painted Pompeian red and frescoed with a frieze of lotus leaves. In the centre of the table sat a roast turkey surrounded by a sumptuous display of mashed potatoes, baked squash, parsnip fritters, olives and pastries.

After we were seated, Aunt Theda lifted the lid of a soup tureen. 'I've given Nora and Louisa the rest of the evening off so they can be with their families. We are going to serve ourselves. No airs and graces today. Pass me your bowls one at a time.'

I'd always served myself and my guests at home in Paris, but I'd had every need taken care of by a footman or a maid for several weeks now and my old way of doing things had become strangely unfamiliar. If Caroline could have seen me passing a sauce dish to Florence, she would have been displeased.

The dinner conversation couldn't have been more different either. There was no talk of hunting, horseracing or fashion. Aunt Theda was a woman of keen intellect who took pleasure in extracting interesting facts from each of us.

'Constance, I saw you absorbed in Edvard Westermarck's *The History of Human Marriage* the other day. Do tell us what you have discovered.'

Florence's sister put down her knife and fork and considered the question. 'Well, he certainly challenges the commonly held assumption that in the past humans were promiscuous and lived in group marriages. He argues that human beings have naturally evolved into alliances of men and women, and that it is western civilisation that is having an adverse effect on marriage. More people are eschewing the institution than ever before.'

'Marriage is different these days,' said Richard. 'Men and women used to work alongside each other in the fields or in the market. Now men are expected to go out into the world and women to stay at home. In some houses in New York, the spheres are so separate that husbands and wives only see each other at breakfast and dinner.'

That described Caroline and Oliver's marriage perfectly. They didn't even see each other at breakfast and they had separate rooms. I remembered waking up in Claude's arms in the room beside his studio; one of my greatest pleasures was snuggling into his warm body before rising to face the day. Was it true that marriage might be the death of that simple intimacy?

'Constance and I shan't be like that,' said Edgar. 'I intend to take her with me when I make my anthropological studies of the primitive people of Borneo.'

'As long as you keep her safe from head-hunters!' said Aunt Theda with mock horror.

Aunt Theda's question to Violet was on evolution, and her one to Richard on the implications of the discovery of radium. When she asked Florence to explain Nietzsche's philosophy on 'eternal recurrence' I wondered if it had been written on the invitation somewhere what field we were expected to have studied before coming.

Aunt Theda glanced at the clock on the wall. 'I'm disappointed Cecilia isn't here to tell us about the legal status and property rights of women in the United States as I believe she is writing an article about them for the *New York Journal*.' She turned her keen eyes on me and I shrank back in my chair like a naughty child who hasn't done her homework. 'Now, Emma, before I bring out the pumpkin pie, I should like to know your view on the purpose of a novel. Should it encourage us that love and goodness will prevail and wrongdoers will always be punished? Can writing that is entertaining also throw light on social injustices?'

I was taken aback that my questions were so easy. Was it because Aunt Theda judged me less bright than the others?

'A novel can certainly throw light on social injustices and be entertaining at the same time,' I told her. 'Charles Dickens is an excellent example of that.'

'I couldn't agree more.' We all turned to see Cecilia standing in the doorway, her coat in her hand. Her penetrating gaze rested on me. 'I believe that all writers, no matter their genre, have a duty to society. We must improve it by exposing its faults and hypocrisies; and those faults and hypocrisies almost always originate in ourselves.'

Her eyes drifted over my bronze satin dinner dress as if taking in every detail. I could tell she'd noticed I was much more expensively dressed than when she had last seen me.

Florence jumped up. 'Let me take your coat. Are you hungry? I'll set a place for you.'

'I won't have dinner,' said Cecilia, ignoring the chair Florence pulled out for her next to Edgar and sitting beside me instead. 'I ate at the orphanage. But the pumpkin pie sounds tempting.'

After the pie, and a stimulating philosophical debate around a topic proposed by Aunt Theda — 'Can there only be one best way to solve a problem?' — we returned to the drawing room for apricot brandy, bonbons, mints, walnuts and hickory-nut cake.

'Now it's time for some games,' announced Aunt Theda, handing out cards with the name of a guest written in the top left corner. 'I want you to study the person whose name is written on your card, then write down the vegetable they most resemble.'

The game elicited giggles at first, but once we set about the task the room fell quiet as we sneaked furtive glances at each other. I'd been assigned Florence's name. I closed my eyes and imagined myself at the market in Paris, lingering over the brightly coloured baskets of tomatoes, pumpkins and green beans sitting among the fragrant basil and wildflower bouquets. At first I selected a carrot, but then chose asparagus because she was so naturally elegant and subtle.

'All right,' said Aunt Theda, holding out her hand. 'Everyone pass me their card.' When she'd collected them all, she perched her glasses on her nose. 'The first card is for Richard,' she said. 'His vegetable is a potato because "he is down to earth and smells like dirt".'

The description brought peals of laughter from the guests.

'There are worse smells than dirt,' Richard said. 'At least the scoundrel who wrote that didn't say I was a cabbage!'

Aunt Theda suppressed a smile and read out my description of Florence as asparagus, before turning to the next one. 'Oh, this one is for me.' She pursed her lips. 'Hmm, apparently I am an artichoke because I "love an entourage and to be the centre of attention".'

'It's so true!' cried Edgar. 'What an insightful game this is.'

Edgar himself was described as a leek because 'he sticks to his principles like a leek to the pan'. Constance was a bell pepper, and Violet was a cauliflower.

'A cauliflower!' she exclaimed. 'In what way am I like a cauliflower?'

Aunt Theda read the card slowly and dramatically. 'Because "she has a heart of gold".'

We all sighed in unison and another round of apricot brandy was served. Then it was time to read Cecilia's card.

'Cecilia is an onion because "she can make you laugh or she can make you cry. She divides opinion and her effect remains long after she has gone".'

Cecilia looked pleased. 'That's very perceptive, which is why I know Florence wrote it.'

Florence smoothed her hair and turned to Aunt Theda. 'One card left. What is Emma?'

Aunt Theda squinted as if she was having trouble reading the handwriting. 'An aubergine, because she is "charming yet mysterious".'

'That sounds like it was written by someone in love with Emma!' said Edgar. 'Who was it?'

The ringer at the front door tinkled and Florence went to answer it. She quickly returned. 'Emma, your carriage is here.'

'Goodness me,' I said. 'Is it eleven o'clock already? I must go!'

'Like Cinderella leaving the ball,' said Richard, raising his glass to me.

'Don't leave anything behind,' chimed in Violet, 'or we'll have to come searching for you.'

Cecilia stood up to shake my hand. 'I was the one who described you as an aubergine,' she confessed, her breath scented with the sweet brandy. 'I do find you rather fascinating, Emma. I have the distinct impression you're hiding something from me, which of course makes you all the more intriguing. There's nothing we journalists love more than unravelling a mystery.'

My face tingled under her gaze. 'I'm French; we are more reserved than Americans. There is nothing mysterious about me other than I'm much more comfortable thinking about philosophy than the nuts and bolts of life.'

'Oh, do leave Emma alone,' Florence scolded Cecilia as she helped me with my coat. 'The poor girl has only been in New York a short time. She doesn't need you pestering her.'

A slow smile came to Cecilia's face. I could hear her thoughts as loudly as if she had shouted them. 'Florence, why are you always rescuing Emma? What are you protecting her from?'

'Goodbye, Cecilia,' I said, firmly shaking her hand and hoping she wouldn't look out the window and see the carriage with the Hopper family crest on its door. 'I hope we meet again soon.'

'I'm sure we will!' she answered.

SIXTEEN

Lucy, urged by Caroline, had confirmed a date with Douglas Hardenbergh for us to view his art collection.

'Augusta will be breathing fire when she hears of the visit,' Caroline said gleefully. 'This will be the first time I have called on anyone related to her and been received.'

'It will be an historic occasion,' Lucy agreed. 'Something like Cleopatra's visit to Caesar.'

I pondered Caroline's and Lucy's words as I dressed in the visiting ensemble Madame Bertin had made for me: a carnation-pink wool jacket and skirt decorated with cream corded braids and tassels. In Paris, I had chosen to associate with people I liked and hadn't mixed with people I disliked, but here in New York society whether you liked or disliked a person had no meaning. Associations and social events were about power: gaining it or protecting it.

I paused to admire my reflection in the mirror. It exhilarated my spirit to wear an outfit that sat so perfectly on my shoulders, flattered my arms and draped elegantly over my hips. I examined the emerald and pearl navette ring Caroline had lent me, which had once belonged to Catherine the Great. Only in Caroline's world was it possible for me to wear a ring that had once belonged to a Russian empress!

My mind drifted to Isadora and her comment about envying my lifestyle and apparent freedom. She would never understand the ability of luxurious things to transform someone because she had been born into this extravagant world. Could she ever be happy living a modest life like mine in Paris? Then another thought occurred to me: could *I* be satisfied with that life once I returned to it?

Caroline gave a nod of approval when she saw how well my outfit suited me. 'What a good investment you have turned out to be. I can see why Douglas Hardenbergh has invited us.'

Rather than being flattered by Caroline's rare compliment, I felt my stomach tighten. What did she mean about me being the reason Douglas Hardenbergh had invited us? Even if I felt the faintest spark of attraction towards him, which I didn't, I wouldn't be interested. Claude had my heart completely.

Douglas's Greek Revival home in Lafayette Street with its tall parlour-floor windows and temple doorway reminded me of pictures I had seen of genteel homes in New Orleans. A butler and a footman appeared on the doorstep, but Douglas rushed past them and down the front steps to open our carriage door himself.

'What a charming delegation,' he said. 'The children are very excited to meet you.'

Inside, the walls were painted with garlands, urns and busts edged with a Greek key pattern. A grand redwood staircase wound up to the first floor, its starting newels carved with an intricate olive-vine design. The decoration of the hall gave the effect of standing in a garden.

'What a beautiful home,' exclaimed Isadora. 'So refined, so tasteful.'

Douglas brushed his hand over the unusual satinwood wainscoting. 'With all the development going on in this part of town, I've resigned myself that one day I'll have to move further uptown like my aunt. But I'll resist for as long as I can. This is the house where my children were born and it has many happy memories for me.'

It was the second time since we'd arrived that Douglas had referred to his children. They obviously held an important place in his heart.

'Where are the children?' I asked him.

'I thought I'd show you the picture gallery and then we could have some afternoon tea,' he replied. 'The children will join us then.'

He guided us to a room beyond the staircase. Before we entered it, he bent his head to me and said, 'I believe my son and daughter are working on a painting of the Eiffel Tower especially for you, Miss Lacasse.'

Caroline overheard his comment and a smile twitched at the corners of her mouth.

I blushed and took a step away from Douglas. 'How adorable!'

From its high ceiling and generous length I had the impression the picture gallery had once been a ballroom. It had no windows, but was illuminated sublimely by a domed skylight.

'What a collection!' cried Isadora, looking around her. 'How fortunate to have a room specially dedicated to it.'

There were at least two hundred paintings in the gallery, the frames so tightly fitted together that the wall behind them was invisible. In the centre of the room stood several life-sized classical sculptures: Persephone and her mother, Demeter; Flora with a garland of flowers about her head; Eve being tempted by the serpent. I turned from them to the paintings and recognised some works by Jean-Léon Gérôme of ladies lounging around in Turkish baths, and several bathing nudes by William-Adolphe Bouguereau. I glanced up and down the walls for any depictions of men but the collection was dominated by women: Venuses; odalisques; women at their toilette.

Isadora voiced what I was thinking. 'This collection is certainly centred on beautiful women.'

'Indeed,' said Douglas with a slight smile. 'But not because women are far more pleasing to behold. My maternal grandfather believed that women represented the pinnacle of civilisation and men should worship them. I've tried to continue the theme of his collection.'

After we had spent some time admiring the paintings Douglas moved us through to the music room, which was bright with golden plush draperies and chairs covered with flowered silk tapestries on a background of lemon yellow. Afternoon tea had been set out on a round table. The centrepiece was an iced orange cake that smelled deliciously fragrant. It was surrounded by platters of egg and gherkin sandwiches, shortbreads and blackcurrant buns.

'I do like your use of yellow,' said Caroline, touching one of the chairs. 'I feel like I'm standing in a field of buttercups.'

Douglas indicated for us to take seats at the table. 'Yellow was Nancy's favourite colour. This room makes me feel cheerful, as if she's still here watching over us.'

'Oh, indeed,' said Caroline, smiling pleasantly, but I could tell she was unimpressed by Douglas's reference to his deceased wife.

The door opened and in burst two small children — a boy and a girl who looked to be five and seven years old respectively — followed by a nursemaid. The little boy ran straight to his father, who hoisted him onto his lap, while the girl sidled up to me and sat the waxed doll she had been holding firmly in my arms.

'What a beautiful doll,' I said. 'Does she have a name?'

'Arabella,' answered the little girl.

Douglas laughed. 'You are privileged, Miss Lacasse. Arabella doesn't get offered to other people very often, not even me.'

The girl regarded him with wide open eyes, then laughed. 'That's because you play silly games with her. You make her dance and Arabella doesn't like to dance.'

'And do you have a name?' Isadora asked her.

She answered in a serious tone. 'My name is Mabel, and my brother's name is Auberon.'

'Where is the painting of the Eiffel Tower you promised me?' Douglas asked his children.

'It's upstairs in the nursery,' said the nursemaid. 'I thought it best to leave it to dry properly before we brought it down.'

She was middle-aged with traces of a German accent, and primly attired in a black dress and white lace apron and cap. Her eyes glanced over each of us in turn before settling on me for a moment, then she looked back to Douglas. 'Will that be all, sir? Would you like me to help the children with their meal?'

'No, thank you, Minna. We'll manage.'

She nodded and left the room.

'I'm afraid Minna doesn't enjoy the company of adults very much,' Douglas told us. 'She comes across as downright odd sometimes, but she's wonderful with the children. I don't know what I would have done without her after Nancy died.'

'They are certainly beautifully behaved,' Lucy told him. 'My two little boys are terrors.'

It was the first time Lucy had mentioned her children and it surprised me. Were they with her in New York, or back in England with their father? If so, how could she bear to be so far away from them?

'I'm sure your nursemaid does a fine job, but a nurse can't replace the touch of a mother,' said Caroline, glancing in my direction. 'Perhaps in time you will marry again, Mr Hardenbergh.'

Caroline's comment was so forward that even Lucy looked startled. I locked eyes with Caroline and shook my head, but she merely shrugged. Thankfully, Douglas was distracted by Auberon pointing to the blackcurrant buns and appeared not to have heard.

After we'd finished the tea, Minna returned to collect the children but Douglas seemed reluctant to let them go. He kissed their cheeks and watched them skip out of the room.

'The "children's hour" is my favourite time of day,' he said. 'No matter how busy I am, I never miss it.' He invited us to sit in more comfortable chairs away from the table, then indicated a harp by the window. 'I wondered if you might give us the pleasure of hearing you play something, Miss Lacasse?'

'Of course,' said Caroline before I could answer.

Isadora covered her mouth with her hand to stifle a giggle. It appeared that I still wasn't trusted to speak for myself.

Douglas moved the harp to the centre of the room and set a chair behind it. I ran my fingers over the strings and was surprised to discover the instrument was perfectly in tune. He had obviously intended my playing to be part of the afternoon's events.

I played the same étude by Chopin that I had performed at the recital for Caroline's friends.

'So the stories I've heard were not exaggerated,' said Douglas when I'd finished. 'You are most accomplished, Miss Lacasse.' He took a flute from its case and assembled it. 'I've been studying the flute since I was a child, but it's a melancholy instrument to play alone. Would you do me the honour of playing something with me?'

I didn't dare look at the others, but glimpsed Caroline out of the corner of my eye. Her face was as bright as a bonfire as she watched us.

Douglas suggested Saint-Saëns' Romance Op. 27, which fortunately I knew well. His playing was elegant and clear: his phrasing was perfect, and unlike other flautists I had performed with he didn't try to dominate my harp. Our duet was the delightful interaction of two musicians in empathy with each other, but when his gaze rested on me longer than made me comfortable I looked away.

At the end of the afternoon, Douglas thanked each of us for coming, then handed me two books. The first was a novel by Oscar Wilde: *The Picture of Dorian Gray*. The second was my short story collection in French. How had Douglas obtained it so quickly? He must have had it sent from France the day after Augusta's dinner.

'The first is for you to read; the second is for you to sign,' he explained. 'Your tales kept me awake for many nights.'

I took the pen he handed me and signed the book: *With pleasure, Emma Lacasse.* As I wrote, I was aware of Caroline peering over my shoulder, watching everything like an eagle eyeing its prey.

⚜⚜⚜

Dearest Emma,

I enjoyed the story about the escaped bear immensely. You are in your element when you write fantastical fiction. How is your novel progressing? Have you considered making your detective character female? Although women aren't officially recruited by the French police, historically they have been employed as undercover agents. A female character would create a delightful combination of subterfuge and logical deduction.

Please send me your entire draft when you complete it. The last time you gave me only the first half of one of your mystery stories, I found myself lying awake wondering who killed the maid.

I have been keeping myself busy painting but I too miss our supper talks ... among other things.

All my love,

Your Claude

PS: I have some exciting news. Maignat is talking about organising an exhibition of French artists in New York. If he does, he has promised that I will be included. So you and I may get to explore New York together after all!

Claude's letter greatly pleased me. I was glad he was missing me, and it would be wonderful to explore New York with him. I was sure the city he and I discovered would be vastly different from the one I had seen with Caroline and her friends.

In the same post, I received a note from Florence inviting me to join her for an event in Greenwich Village, which she told me was known as 'the Montmartre of New York'. I was intrigued, and asked Isadora when we were alone in her studio whether she thought Caroline would disapprove.

'Of course you should go,' said Isadora. 'Mother will be at her bridge night, and Father won't notice that you're gone; or if he does he won't say anything. Besides, if you go I can live vicariously through you. I've heard that all sorts of interesting people gather in the Village — Mr Gadley and his students from the League often go there.'

For a daring moment I was tempted to suggest Isadora come with me, but we both knew that if Woodford found out and told Caroline, the consequences could be devastating.

'Thank you, Isadora. I'll tell you all about it.'

She smiled. 'Watch out for Mother, by the way. Ever since we visited Douglas Hardenbergh's home, she's been concocting plans to marry you off to him. Not that I would mind you staying in New York permanently, or that Mr Hardenbergh isn't a nice man. But it wouldn't be the life for you.'

I had suspected Caroline was scheming something. She had ordered more clothes for me from Madame Bertin, and had started to show me off to her friends when they paid calls or came for lunch. While I was flattered that she was paying me attention, I knew it was out of self-interest rather than familial love. What revenge it would be if her sister married Augusta Van der Heyden's favourite nephew!

'I haven't told your mother this,' I said to Isadora, 'but I have someone back in Paris. His name is Claude. He's an artist.'

Isadora's eyes flew open and she let out a laugh of delight. 'Well, you're going to have to tell me all about him!' she said, putting down a lump of clay and sitting on the stool opposite me.

I told her about Claude and his studio and his family, and our little group of artists at the café. Isadora's face beamed brighter with every detail. It was good to be able to talk freely about Claude: it made me feel close to him, even though we were so far apart. The only thing I didn't tell her was that he didn't want to marry me; that still hurt me too much.

When I'd finished, Isadora shook her head in wonder. 'He sounds like the perfect man for you. If I have to marry someone, I can only imagine being happy if we're in sympathy with each other like you and Claude are. You don't know how much I envy you and your freedom, Aunt Emma! My life is so boring; and it'll get worse after my debut — one tedious formal dinner after another, visits, luncheons, balls, and more visits. It's not really living, is it? I never get to experience anything important firsthand. Not even life.'

I squeezed her wrist. 'I have faith in you, Isadora. Wherever life takes you, you will always carve out a place of your own — just as you have here. You are much stronger than you think.'

❧

That evening, I instructed Teddy to drop me outside a stately Georgian house in Washington Square as Florence had suggested on the hand-drawn map she had included with her note. It wasn't where Cecilia's apartment was located, but Washington Square was a respectable part of the Village where the heirs of the old rich lived in the residences their grandparents had built before the Civil War. Florence had probably guessed how Caroline would react if she learned I was venturing to an 'unsavoury' part of the city. The other advantage of Teddy leaving me in the square was that Cecilia's prying eyes wouldn't see me arrive in a Hopper family carriage.

I walked the short distance to Cecilia's apartment building near Waverly Place. When I knocked on the door it was opened by Violet, the artist I'd met at Aunt Theda's house at Thanksgiving.

'Hello,' she said with a chuckle. 'So Cinderella has returned!'

Florence was already there, lounging on a sofa in the pie-shaped parlour and chatting with Cecilia. The apartment walls were shamrock green and, along with the heat provided by an iron stove and the abundant ferns, palms and heliotropes that crowded the bay windows, I had the impression of having entered a tropical jungle. A slender woman, who Violet introduced as Edna, was playing a Hungarian folk song on a piano, a cigarette dangling from her lips.

'You're right on time,' Cecilia said, handing me a glass of sweet vermouth. 'Florence and I were discussing how male novelists portray women who live independently as always coming to a bad end and requiring a man to rescue them from their folly. What is needed is for women writers to create a new type of heroine for the younger generation to emulate.'

'I was thinking about that myself today,' I told her. 'I'm considering a story with a female detective and I don't want to make her the typical meddling woman that lady sleuths are often portrayed as. I want her to be intellectually rigorous, disciplined and efficient.'

'Perfect!' said Florence. 'I'm so tired of frivolous fictional women.'

While we were chatting, more women arrived. They were Jane, an editorial assistant at *The Outlook*; two proofreaders for Scribner's named Myrna and Theresa; another reporter called Edith; and a shy woman named Mary, who was employed by the US Postal Service and wrote poetry in her spare time. They were all dressed in the same tailored suit-dresses that Florence and Cecilia favoured. I felt like an overblown rose in my purple silk two-piece dress, but it was the plainest outfit I now owned. After Madame Bertin had made my new wardrobe, Caroline had instructed Jennie to get rid of the clothes I'd brought with me from Paris without asking my permission. Hence I had nothing to wear that didn't make me look as if I belonged on Fifth Avenue.

When everyone had a drink in her hand, Cecilia raised her glass. 'The Confirmed Bachelor Girls' Club social night is now underway.'

'All right, ladies,' said Florence, 'let's go enjoy our food.'

Rather than make their way to the dining room as I expected, the women undid the buttons of their jackets and took off their blouses. What was this? My mind jumped to a certain nightclub in Montmartre. Did 'bachelor girl' have a different meaning in New York?

The women slipped off their corsets and flung them onto the sofa, before redressing themselves.

'Come on, Emma,' said Cecilia, 'get rid of that garment of oppression.'

Because I had hesitated, everyone's eyes were now on me. I didn't want to take my corset off in front of a strange group of women, but it seemed I didn't have a choice. I gingerly undid my blouse, hoping the others would find something else to occupy themselves with, but they continued to watch me. To make matters more awkward, my corset was nothing like the utilitarian beige and white garments the others had discarded. Mine was a magnificent peacock blue with green contrasting trimmings and embroidered with pink roses, and had been hand-sewn by Madame Bertin's best corsetière.

'Goodness, Emma,' said Florence, helping me undo the ties, 'how can you breathe in that thing?'

The truth was: not very well. Ever since I'd started wearing the elaborate corset I'd found it difficult to exert myself, and when I sat down I had to perch on the very edge of the chair or I'd become light-headed and faint.

Once Florence had undone the garment and tossed it on the pile with the others, the relief of air moving freely in and out of my lungs and the enlivening sensation of my blood circulating properly made me giddy. At the same time, it was like losing a piece of armour and being thoroughly exposed. I quickly rebuttoned my blouse and bodice.

We filed out of the apartment and down the stairs to the ground floor.

'Why did everyone take off their corsets?' I asked Florence when we reached the street.

'Because we're going to indulge in a feast and we don't want indigestion and constipation tomorrow. Besides, if you always wear a corset your back and abdominal muscles never develop strength of their own, and your internal organs get compressed and possibly become misshapen. Those garments badly affect women's health, but if we don't wear them when we go to work we're hounded by men and women alike. It's difficult enough to move in a man's world without being accused of being a woman of loose morals.'

The Village was different from anywhere else I'd been in New York. The grid system hadn't reached here, and the maze of crooked streets and narrow alleys lined with tearooms, saloons and restaurants did indeed remind me of Montmartre.

We came to a brownstone house that had been converted to apartments, and took the stairs down to the basement level. When Florence opened the door for us, the delicious aroma of garlic and butter frying wafted out. The restaurant was a bare space with unplastered walls, curtainless windows and bare wooden floorboards, but it was crowded with people of every description. A clean-cut businessman conversed with a man with a wild beard and a Russian accent; an actor still wearing his theatre make-up shared a joke with a companion whose flat nose and muscular body resembled those of a prize fighter. When the fighter threw back his head and laughed, he revealed a mouth full of gold teeth. Workmen rubbed shoulders with artists and dancers, and everywhere there were women without male companions.

We jostled our way to a long wooden table already occupied at one end by what looked like the male equivalent of the Confirmed Bachelor Girls' Club: clean-cut young men in utilitarian suits and wearing reporter badges. One of them was a Negro. From what I'd read about the United States, this restaurant must have been one of the few places that made a virtue of cosmopolitanism. Student clubs and artists in Paris made a point of being inclusive, so racial mixing was nothing new to me, but Caroline would have been shocked.

Within minutes of taking our seats, an Italian woman placed a bowl of minestrone soup in front of each of us along with a thickly sliced piece of bread. The main course was a choice of either spaghetti bolognese or pasta mixed with olive oil, garlic and fresh parsley. The food was aromatic, flavourful and remarkably cheap. I was glad I had discarded my corset so I could fully enjoy it.

Our group toasted each other with the syrupy red wine that tasted like black cherries, and my ear tuned in to the conversations around me. The place was fermenting with ideas, often about subjects that were taboo: anarchism, socialism, free love, birth control. 'Women are too reliant on men for their survival,' I heard one woman say to another. 'Sex should be as pleasurable for them as it is for men.'

An older woman wearing a turban plonked herself down next to me. She had a triangular-shaped face like a Siamese cat and stared at me with searching eyes. 'You're new,' she said above the din. 'I haven't seen you with the Confirmed Bachelor Girls before.'

'I'm not quite a bachelor girl,' I told her. 'I have a beau.'

She let out a husky laugh. 'And I suppose you believe your beau is going to love you forever, although the evidence is all around you that marital bliss doesn't last. You think you and he will be different, right?'

Her words pierced my mind and numbed my thoughts. What she'd said was exactly what I believed: Claude and I *would* love each other forever.

Her words flowed endlessly on despite my lack of a response. 'Those heady early days won't last. If that's all you believe in, you'll be yearning for those times for the rest of your life and inventing ways to recapture them. But when they're gone they're gone. Your beau will be free to spend your inheritance, and you'll be trapped by limited resources, limited interests and limited opportunities because you handed over your fate to a man.'

I did not like my treasured beliefs being challenged by a stranger. 'What's the alternative?' I asked, trying to deflect the conversation away from me. 'What's your philosophy?' Then I realised she had manoeuvred me into getting her to explain the direction she had intended to take all along.

'My philosophy?' She squinted at me. 'Why, I'm experimenting with a completely different type of womanhood. I don't belong to a man as his wife or mistress, and I'm certainly not the mother of some holy terror. I am enjoying a life lived for me and only for me.'

I regarded her with a mixture of trepidation and wonderment. I couldn't imagine a life of not belonging to anybody. To belong to a husband and a family was what I wanted more than anything else in the world.

'But what about loneliness?' I asked her. 'Isn't that a high price to pay for freedom? And what about your natural maternal urges? Don't you have any at all?'

The woman regarded me as one might a very dull child. 'You think loneliness is a high price to pay for freedom? I'll tell you what real loneliness is. It's to be trapped in marriage with a man who continuously finds fault with you, makes demands of you, and claims superiority over you.' Satisfied from my silence that she had unsettled me, she added, 'The trouble with young women like you is that you're too earnest. Give up your earnestness and put your effort into being great. Live your life outside a cage.'

Having had the final word on the subject, she moved on to talk to somebody else, leaving me feeling like a bottle of milk that had been shaken violently. My skin was hot, and my head was light and full of bubbles.

Florence touched my arm. 'I see you've been speaking to Berenice. She has a gift: whatever your greatest insecurity, she homes right in on it and stirs up a hornets' nest in your mind. After a while you get used to it and start to appreciate it. It's good to be challenged sometimes. It prevents complacency.'

'I suppose so,' I replied. 'Perhaps if I came here every night I would never be sure of anything again.'

Later, when we all took a stroll to relieve our full stomachs, Florence walked next to me. 'So Claude is coming to New York? That will be exciting. He'll need you, no doubt — he doesn't speak a word of English, does he?'

I shook my head. 'No, but Claude is Claude — he always manages on his own somehow.'

'Men are encouraged to be self-sufficient,' Florence replied. 'But from the moment a girl can talk she's taught to always see herself in relation to others — what they're thinking, what they're feeling, what they need. We are trained to be servants from the cradle.'

Was that true of me? I thought Grand-maman had raised me to be self-sufficient, but also to be loving and kind. Yet I did question sometimes why I gave in to Claude's views on marriage when they conflicted so strongly with my own.

Although it was late, the street was filled with vendors selling buttons, cloth, olives and cheese. The accents were predominantly Italian.

'New York has more Italians than Rome,' Cecilia said, catching up with us. 'Twice as many Irish as Dublin, and it's home to the largest Jewish community in the world. Right here in the Village we're a mix of all those cultures, plus a large number of working and middle-class Negroes who came up here after the war.'

'Until tonight, almost everybody I've met in New York has been of Dutch or British descent,' I said.

Cecilia glanced at me curiously and I reminded myself not to say too much to her.

'Over the past thirty or so years New York's population has increased two hundred and fifty per cent, mainly because of immigration,' Florence explained. 'The old-stock Americans aren't too happy about it. The editor of the *Saturday Evening Post* claims that New York has become a foreign city with "an American Quarter".'

We turned into a street where the old row houses had been replaced by factories producing everything from artificial flowers to chocolate tins.

'Very few of us like change,' I said. 'When things have been a certain way for a long time, we feel safe with that. We usually only change when we are forced to, or when it becomes too painful not to.'

Cecilia smiled. 'So true, Emma. And succinctly put. You're a perfect addition to the Confirmed Bachelor Girls' Club.'

A 'confirmed bachelor girl' I definitely was not. But later, travelling home in the plush interior of Caroline's carriage, I reflected on the conversations I'd had that evening. I'd been challenged, informed and shaken, and my mind was buzzing with ideas. For the first time I felt I was participating in the world around me rather than simply plotting a course.

My hand slipped into the large interior pocket of my cloak and fingered the silky material hidden there. I hadn't put my corset back on after we'd returned to Cecilia's apartment. I laughed to myself that such a simple thing as not wearing a piece of clothing should take on the proportions of a delicious secret.

SEVENTEEN

Since my reply to Claude telling him how excited I was that he might be coming to New York, I hadn't heard anything further. Every day I checked with Woodford but no letters arrived. Was he frantically painting for the New York exhibition? But even if that was the case, it wasn't like him not to write at all.

I sent him an elaborately gilded Christmas card with a two-fold door on the front that opened to reveal some rabbits singing by a fireside. I thought he would find it amusing enough to respond with a similar card of his own. But the only correspondence I received from Paris was a letter from Paulette.

Dear Emma,
In your last letter you asked me if Mrs Nettleton and her
daughter were good tenants. I must say your question
made me chuckle. When Mrs Nettleton wasn't harrying
her daughter, she was scolding and criticising me. Then
one week she developed such terrible headaches she
was sure she had caught the plague from washing her
face with Parisian water. Doctor Sourzac was called.
He examined Mrs Nettleton, then glanced at me and
her poor put-upon daughter. 'You must drink no less
than one bottle of French champagne per day, Madame

*Nettleton,' he told her. 'It is the only thing that will cure
you.' After that, the daughter had a wonderful time in
Paris and Mrs Nettleton and I got along well!*

I burst into laughter at Paulette's story of Doctor Sourzac's very
French prescription for all ills. I wrote back saying that I hoped
the new boarders, two young women from San Francisco, would
be pleasant company for her. I pictured Paulette laying out a
delicious supper of *salade niçoise* and *gratin dauphinois* for the
Americans and hoped they would appreciate her kindness and
warmth.

I was tempted to ask her if she had heard from Claude, as he
had promised to check on her while I was in New York. But I
didn't want to worry her.

Instead, after I'd finished my letter to Paulette, I wrote
another one to Claude.

Dearest Claude,
*I haven't heard from you in a while. Please send me even
a short note to let me know you are all right.*
*I await impatiently for news of when you are coming
to New York ...*

~~~~~~

I could only imagine what the Confirmed Bachelor Girls would
have thought of the way I spent the weeks before Christmas.
My days were swallowed up by a round of formal dinners,
parties and daily afternoon parading in Central Park, which
was more about being seen than getting fresh air. It involved
Caroline, Lucy, Isadora and myself being driven out in an open
carriage by a coachman. We drove along a carriageway through
the park, waving — or not, depending on the passengers — to
the other paraders in their barouches, phaetons and landaus.

One afternoon we passed Augusta Van der Heyden and her granddaughters several times and each time we all looked in the opposite direction.

'When it starts snowing, we'll ride in a sleigh with bells and red aigrettes on the horses' heads,' said Caroline. 'How I love the Christmas season!'

One afternoon, something whooshed past us at lightning speed, whipping up chunks of dirt and sending it flying into our faces and over our coats. Our horses whinnied and reared. The vehicle that had overtaken us was a Russian troika with three white horses; it came to a halt and waited for us to catch up with it. There was no coachman in the troika, and as we got closer I saw that it was driven by a woman wearing a white ermine coat and a matching bonnet decorated with beads and ostrich feathers from under which a few curls of blonde hair dangled.

She turned and flashed us a smile. She was very beautiful, with crystal blue eyes and a sharp chin with a cleft in it.

'What is she doing here?' hissed Caroline.

The woman flicked the reins and the horses took off again.

'The gall!' said Lucy. 'How dare that upstart overtake *us*?'

Our afternoon ride came to an abrupt end when Caroline ordered the coachman to take us home. She and Lucy disappeared to the library, telling Isadora and me to amuse ourselves. We went to Isadora's sitting room and had Jennie bring us some hot tea and a jar of lanolin for our chapped cheeks and lips.

'No doubt battle plans are being drawn up downstairs,' Isadora said, dabbing her finger into the lanolin.

'Who was that woman? An actress?'

Isadora shook her head. 'But she may as well be. Her name is Permelia Frances and she's married to Father's fiercest competitor. He recently swindled Father on a business deal worth ten million dollars so clearly she wanted to show off.'

'Oh,' I said, now understanding Caroline's indignation.

'Apparently she's vulgar too,' added Isadora. 'Rebecca's aunt heard that Permelia has a gold chandelier in her bedroom that releases twenty-five thousand dollars' worth of rose perfume each time she pulls a cord.'

I dropped the glob of lanolin I had balanced on my fingertip. It was a sum of money too enormous for me to fathom. One puff of Permelia's chandelier and not only would I have been out of debt to Roche & Associates, I could have bought two other apartments as well.

❦

The following Monday evening we went to the opera. I was surprised when Oliver joined us, and even more surprised when he sat next to me in the private box and not with Caroline. I'd got the impression that he didn't enjoy social activities.

While everyone else chatted, Oliver studied the program book with great interest, not only the main cast but the members of the orchestra. He took out a fountain pen from his pocket and made notations next to several of the names.

'So you are an opera aficionado?' I asked in astonishment.

He shrugged. 'I'm one of the odd few who prefer to stay until the end of the performance instead of rushing off to dinners and balls.'

Although I'd been in New York nearly three months, I still didn't know what to make of Oliver. I couldn't put out of my mind his ill-temper with Caroline or the room that displayed the animals he'd shot. Yet, the concern he showed for Isadora and his politeness to me made it impossible to dismiss him entirely. The man was a puzzle.

'Do you know the story of *Faust*?' he asked me.

'I do. An ageing scholar sells his soul to the Devil in return for renewed youth and a second chance.'

Oliver nodded, and studied me for a moment. 'What would you sell your soul for, Emma? I'd sell mine for a second chance — I'd do everything differently if I could go back to being the man you first met in Paris. But it's too late now. My course has been set and there is nothing I can do but hold to it.'

What was it that troubled Oliver so? A bad business decision? The loss of his mother and sister? His marriage to Caroline?

He peered into my face, waiting for my answer.

I frowned. 'What would I sell my soul for? Nothing! I don't think there is anything that is worth burning in hell for.'

His pitying expression reminded me of the look Berenice had given me in the Italian restaurant in the Village, as if to say that one day my naïve optimism would desert me and I would see life as it really was.

Before we could say more, the orchestra began to play and the curtain rose. Normally I would have lost myself in the lush, elegant music and the sentimentality of the story, but Oliver's question and my answer haunted me. What about Grand-maman? Wouldn't I have sold my soul to spare her the agony of her last few months, or to find a cure for her cancer? The memory of that time sliced my heart like a cold, hard knife. I'd mortgaged our home to try to help her. Yes, I probably would have sold my soul too if I could have. I blinked my tears away and glanced with compassion at Oliver. Perhaps we all had a price.

During the interval, Caroline took Oliver and Isadora to visit the Harpers' box, while Grace came to sit with me.

'So Caroline brought you here at last,' she said, fanning herself against the stuffy heat.

Now the interval lights were up I spotted Augusta Van der Heyden seated in the box opposite us. She was staring in our direction, ignoring Mrs Williamson next to her who was desperately trying to gain her attention.

'Augusta is glaring at us,' I said to Grace.

'I'm not surprised. This ball your sister is organising has the whole town talking. Is she really planning it for the third Thursday in January?'

'I believe so.'

'Tch-tch,' Grace said, gesturing towards the auditorium. 'All these people are faced with such a conundrum should they be invited. Should they go to the Hoppers' exciting ball, or stay faithful to Augusta and sit through another of her wearisome dinners?' A smile came to her face. 'But you know, the dilemma will even be worse for those not invited to Isadora's ball. How will they deal with the humiliation of being excluded from the biggest event of the new century? They will have to pretend they received an invitation but pressing events mean they can't attend. Just think how many mysterious illnesses, ailing aunts and dying grandmothers will have to be invented!'

'So Caroline has set a cat among the pigeons?' I said, imagining how pleased my sister would be by that. The old elite would have to come calling on her now. She was as ruthless in her tactics as Napoleon.

❧❧❧❧

On Christmas Eve, Caroline, Isadora and I, helped by two footmen, set about decorating the tree in the dining room. It had taken ten servants to raise the twenty-foot fir tree the previous day and now the room was filled with the alpine scent of balsam. While the others added lights and filigreed glass ornaments to the tree, I decorated the table and mantelpiece with garlands of pine and pomander balls, which gave off a delicious citrus, clove and cinnamon fragrance.

The following morning, as we got into the carriage to drive to church, I thought of Claude and his family. They would have already been to the Christmas Eve midnight Mass and would now be gathered for *le réveillon* of stuffed goose. I still hadn't had any reply from Claude to my recent letters. Surely he could understand I would be worried until I heard from him? Equally as strange, I hadn't heard from Madame Tremblay. Claude's mother had made a tradition of sending me a hand-painted floral bookmark each Christmas with a line from one of her favourite poems written on the back. If she had done that when I had been close by in Paris, surely she would have understood how much I would appreciate the gift now I was far away in New York?

Luncheon was a light meal of broiled oysters and *consommé royal* in anticipation of the larger meal we were to have that evening. Grace and Harland arrived at seven o'clock, along with the Grahams, the Harpers, the Potters and the Bishops. It was the first time I had met the husbands of Caroline's friends and I found it as difficult to distinguish between them as I had their wives. They were all grey-bearded, stooping men dressed in tailcoats and expensive patent shoes, and all appearing worn out by life. Harland, with his glowing skin, vitality and gaiety in his eyes, stood out among them like the star on top of the Christmas tree.

'Did you hear the Millers are divorcing?' he offered, once the soup had been served. He said it as cheerily as if he were talking about the post-Christmas sales.

'No!' said Bessie Graham, putting down her wine glass. 'Why?'

'Apparently Buford wants his favourite horse to sleep in the bed with them,' answered Harland.

Franklin Harper nearly choked on his bread. 'Did I hear you correctly? He wants his favourite whore to sleep with them?'

His mishearing of the word brought peals of laughter from the others. But I didn't laugh, and neither did Isadora, nor Grace, who stared at her lap.

'Another woman would be better,' said Caroline, dabbing at her eyes. 'A horse, for goodness sake! The man is mad. He loves those thoroughbreds more than he does his wife and children.'

'Having met his wife and children, I fully understand,' said Newton Graham. 'Natica is quite obsessed with Eastern philosophy — she has the children meditating and practising yoga!'

His comment elicited more laughter.

'It seems Buford is done with the company of people altogether,' continued Harland. 'He's approached me to build him a castle in North Carolina where, instead of reception and drawing rooms, he will have luxurious stables for his horses, with ceilings of moulded plaster and Louis XV fireplaces to keep them warm in winter.'

Isadora spoke up. 'I can understand that some people might prefer the company of animals to humans. I know I prefer to sculpt them.'

'Don't be ridiculous!' Caroline scolded her.

Isadora turned pale and stared at her plate. I wished my sister wouldn't be so harsh; it didn't do Isadora's confidence any good.

'If the tombstones in Le Cimetière des Chiens in Paris are anything to go by, Isadora has a good point,' I said. 'Sometimes a person's bond with an animal is much closer than with any human.'

Caroline ignored my comment. 'Well, if Natica is seeking a divorce I will have no choice but to strike her off my invitation lists,' she said. 'And I imagine others will do the same.'

Grace's eyes flashed. 'Why her and not him? It sounds as if it's Buford's behaviour that's caused the trouble. Surely Natica will win her case based on insanity or mental cruelty?'

'Divorce is bad for everyone, Grace,' Elsie Bishop said with a sigh. 'But it's a woman's duty to keep the marriage and home together no matter what. Men get on with things, but every married woman will be suspicious that Natica is after her husband. It's simply the way things are.'

Charlotte nodded in agreement. 'Natica's divorce will ostracise her, no doubt. It's a pity because I've always found her rather interesting company.'

'I couldn't agree more,' said Harland, glancing at Grace. He was smiling, but I saw malevolence in his eyes. 'Divorce always reflects badly on the woman.'

The jangle of clattering metal brought the conversation to a halt. Grace had accidentally knocked her cutlery to the floor. One of the footmen rushed in to retrieve it.

'I'm terribly sorry,' she said as Woodford placed a new set down for her.

'I'm always telling Grace not to wave her hands about like an Italian,' Harland said with an odd note of triumph in his voice. 'But when she's excited by something there's no stopping her.'

'Yes,' said Grace, with a carefree air that I could tell was false, 'I do get clumsy sometimes.'

Something was upsetting her, and I attempted to catch her eye. But she turned her face away from me, as if everything Bessie was telling her was highly interesting. Whatever was troubling Grace, she didn't want me to know.

The second course of Spanish mackerel and cucumber salad arrived and the conversation turned to Christmas.

'What a blessing it is to spend this evening with you all,' said Helen. 'We've been with the family all day, and I tell you: my daughters are the most ungrateful women I have ever met. Gideon gave them two hundred thousand dollars each for Christmas this year and do you know what they said? "Is that all? The Perrys gave each of their children one million!"'

'When I was a child,' chimed in Bessie, 'we were lucky if we got candy for Christmas. I saw how hard my parents worked for every little thing. Our children don't know that struggle.'

'My grandfather had a policy whereby no matter how successful our family business became, each one of his children and grandchildren had to spend a month working in the factory when they came of age,' Franklin Harper said, 'or they would be cut out of their inheritance. It's a good policy and Charlotte and I have kept it up. It prevents young men and women from becoming spoiled better than any other method I know.'

'What a marvellous idea,' said Caroline, glancing in Isadora's direction. 'Sometimes our children have no idea how lucky they are.'

'We are very fortunate with our daughter,' cut in Oliver. 'She is naturally unspoiled. I'm very proud of her.'

Isadora's face lit up at her father's compliment. They exchanged a brief glance of mutual sympathy that thankfully Caroline didn't notice. A secret thrill stirred up in my heart. Was this the beginning of Oliver standing up for his daughter at last?

⁂

The following day, after breakfast, Oliver called me into his study. 'I hope your first Christmas in New York has been a pleasant one?' he asked.

'Yes,' I told him, but I was stretching the truth. Christmas dinner had been a disappointment: the intimate family celebration I'd anticipated had been shared with a group of Caroline's friends who had nothing better to do than gossip.

The hesitation in my voice brought an expression of commiseration to Oliver's face and he made no further mention of the evening. Instead, his eyes drifted to the notepaper and pen on his desk.

'I would appreciate it if you could do something for me,' he said. 'My mother and sister were simple women. They disliked the fuss around Christmas and spent the season volunteering at the Salvation Army Christmas dinner and making visits to the hospitals for the poor. Since Anne passed away, I've regretted not keeping up donations to those organisations in their memory.' He sighed. 'But here's my problem: with those reporters hounding me all the time, I'm damned if I do and damned if I don't. If I make a donation myself, they always suggest I have some ulterior motive.'

He wrote on a piece of notepaper, reread it, then handed it to me. 'I'd like you to take that to my banker, Mr Howell, tomorrow. He'll arrange the payments anonymously.'

I glanced at the paper. Each charity was to receive one hundred thousand dollars. It was incredibly generous. But why wasn't he entrusting Caroline with the task?

He must have guessed what I was thinking because he quickly added, 'I would appreciate it if we could keep this between ourselves. Caroline ... isn't particularly altruistic.'

Although he was asking me to deceive my sister, something about Oliver's earnest manner compelled me to help him. 'It would be my honour,' I said.

I thought that would be all to the conversation, but Oliver stood up, opened a cupboard and took out a large roll of paper. He spread it out on his desk and indicated for me to join him.

'Look at this,' he said.

On the paper was an architectural drawing for a colossal house. There were forty-five bedrooms, thirty bathrooms and over eighty fireplaces! Included in the plan were an indoor swimming pool, and a bowling alley in the basement; and all the rooms were double the size of those in this house on Fifth Avenue.

'Is it a resort or something?' I asked, knowing that Oliver had some interests in commercial property.

He gave a dry laugh. 'It may as well be. Four acres of floor space! It's the new house Harland Hunter and Caroline have dreamed up for Newport.'

My mind was stilled by shock. Nobody, not even Caroline, needed a house as big as the one on the plan.

'Sometimes I admire Caroline's relentless ambition,' Oliver continued. 'And sometimes I think I should be reining it in, protecting us from the tyranny of excess. What do you think, Emma?'

I thought it was insanity and Caroline should be restrained. But it was my sister, not Oliver, who was going to repay my debts to Roche & Associates. For that reason I could not side with him against her. I recalled Oliver's question at the opera about what I might sell my soul for, and realised that since I had come to New York I'd compromised myself right and left. But what choice did I have?

'Caroline understands the rules of society here far better than I do,' I said diplomatically. 'Perhaps this is all to increase your prestige as a man of business.'

His eyes sought mine and he smiled bitterly. 'You're right. I have become very successful with Caroline by my side — which is why I've never hesitated to give her what she wants. Even to the point that —' He stopped and looked away. 'But this?' He indicated the plan and shook his head. 'There is a danger in drawing too much attention to ourselves. The newspaper headlines this Christmas were all about the widening gap between the rich and the poor. At the moment the wealthiest businessmen of New York have been given a free rein by the government, but those kinds of articles turn public opinion against us.'

I got the impression that Oliver was asking me a deeper question, as if he wanted me to absolve him of a burden he was carrying. But of course I couldn't do that. No one could, except his own conscience, or God.

EIGHTEEN

On New Year's Eve we attended a glittering ball at the Grahams' mansion. The gilded dining room and ballroom were aglow with strings of electric lights. But even though we were on the cusp of a fresh epoch where it was predicted that buildings would reach the sky and women would get the vote, the talk of the guests when we sat down to the eight-course dinner wasn't about what exciting developments the new century might bring, but about Isadora's debutante ball.

Helen Potter leaned towards me. 'I believe twelve hundred invitations are to be sent out this week, Emma. Caroline will remember her old friends, won't she?'

'Is it true six thousand orchids are to be brought up from the south for it?' asked another woman.

After the dessert course, the dancing commenced but the questions didn't cease.

'Will the party favours really be black pearls and gold cigarette cases?' one man asked me.

'Is it true you are going to wear a ruby necklace that once belonged to Marie Antoinette?' his dance partner enquired, her keen eyes searching my face.

If I'd thought the interrogations about Isadora's ball would end at midnight, I was wrong. New Year's Day was the traditional time for making visits and Caroline told me to be prepared for 'a few guests' to call during her open house between eleven o'clock and five.

A steady procession of visitors streamed through the house. No sooner had we farewelled one caller than another arrived. And it wasn't only Caroline's usual set who called, but members of the old elite too.

Mrs Schorer, a black-clad dowager with sharp eyes and a walking stick, arrived at the same time as Helen Potter, who was beautifully attired in a steel blue dress decorated with rosettes and bows. Her hat had so many flowers on the crown it looked as though she was carrying a miniature garden on her head. Mrs Schorer's toque hat was very plain by comparison.

Although Woodford brought tea for both women, Mrs Schorer refused to acknowledge Helen's presence in the room. It put Caroline in a difficult position: she did her best to be cordial with both guests while conducting a conversation that gave her the air of a spiritualist rather than a society hostess.

'Mrs Schorer, I believe you have the most splendid greenhouses that keep you well supplied with vegetables and flowers all year. My friend Mrs Helen Potter has created a beautiful Italian garden at her villa in Newport and even has some rare plants that were used in the past for medieval medicine. May I introduce her to you?'

The old dowager sipped her tea, then pursed her mouth resolutely. 'Mrs Hopper, I cannot grant that request no matter how kindly you express it. In our world, introductions can never be made at open homes. And while I understand that you would prefer people you know to know each other, unfortunately there are some people I could never receive into my home. Therefore introducing me to them burdens me with a duty I simply cannot fulfil.'

Helen turned bright red at the cut. Her mouth tightened and she appeared on the verge of giving Mrs Schorer a piece of her mind, but Caroline signalled with a slight lift of her hand that she would handle the matter.

'But my dear Mrs Schorer,' she said, sweetly but firmly, '*we* had not been introduced to each other until you came this afternoon to my open home. So we have, in effect, already broken convention. I am so glad to have made your acquaintance because now I will be able to invite you to Isadora's ball. But I fear there may be a great many guests whom you would not be able to receive in your home. If you would prefer I did not put you in such a difficult situation by inviting you to the ball, I perfectly understand.'

Mrs Schorer's face froze like a chess player who has been checkmated. Her eyes darted from left to right, trying to find a way out. Seeing there was none, she sighed in surrender. 'I see you are quite right, Mrs Hopper. If you should like to bring your friend to my home tomorrow afternoon, I would be happy for you to introduce us then.'

When Mrs Schorer had departed, Helen grasped Caroline's hands and said in astonishment, 'Did I understand her correctly? Am I to go with you tomorrow to the *Schorer* residence? Don't they have a very eligible grandson who would be perfect for my Louise?'

'Don't get carried away,' said Caroline, sitting back down on the sofa and smiling triumphantly. 'I hope Mrs Schorer won't expect me to introduce all of my "*parvenu*" friends to her personally before the ball,' she added. 'There won't be time!'

'Who are you calling a *parvenu*,' said Helen with a laugh, checking her elaborate hat in the mantelpiece mirror.

Half an hour later, we had another visitor: Mrs Warburg, who I had met at Augusta's formal dinner and hadn't liked. I remembered her insult to my family but she was all smiles now.

'Oh, Miss Lacasse,' she said, in a tone that suggested we were on the friendliest terms, 'please forgive me for not calling on you sooner after I had a chance to make your delightful acquaintance at Mrs Van der Heyden's dinner. Unfortunately family matters detained me.'

She sent me a glance of entreaty that she didn't intend Caroline to see. But my sister caught it and stifled a smile. 'The Blumenthal ball was the first costume ball I ever attended,' Mrs Warburg said, her eyes misting at the memory. 'I went as a Venetian princess in a beautifully embroidered gown and a cap encrusted with jewels. My sister, who was always more daring than me, went as a bumble bee. She wore a gown of yellow and black stripes and had gauze wings and diamond-encrusted antennae. Ah, to be young again.' Isadora and I exchanged a glance before Mrs Warburg came to her point. 'A magnificent ball like that is the most magical night of a debutante's first season, Mrs Hopper. Being excluded could lower a young woman's prestige and see her left out of other important events.'

'Yes, indeed,' said Caroline. 'That has always been my concern with Isadora.'

Mrs Warburg hesitated. 'Then you understand the situation? You see, I've come on a rather delicate matter.'

'Go on,' said Caroline, tilting her head and raising her eyebrows.

'Mrs Van der Heyden ... well, she has two very beautiful granddaughters, Georgia and Minerva. They are twins. Augusta has been like a mother to them since their own mother passed away.'

'Yes, I've seen them parading with their grandmother in the park,' said Caroline. 'They do seem like lovely girls. We have never been introduced, of course.'

'Both young women are out in society,' Mrs Warburg continued.

'Are they?' said Caroline, taking a sip of tea. 'I had no idea.'

Mrs Warburg swallowed and seemed on the verge of faltering. But then she gathered her courage. 'As it is their first season it would be frightfully ... well, it would be humiliating if they weren't invited to your ball.'

Caroline put down her teacup and turned to me as if she had finally grasped Mrs Warburg's point. 'Oh, my dear Mrs Warburg, now I understand.'

Our guest relaxed and gave a short laugh. 'I'm sure Georgia and Minerva would make very good friends for Isadora. Perhaps I could introduce them to you before the ball and then all the young ladies could practise their dancing together?'

'Isadora would be delighted to make their acquaintance, I'm sure,' Caroline said, giving Mrs Warburg a look of sympathy. 'But I'm afraid that inviting them is quite out of the question.'

Mrs Warburg turned as white as a sheet. 'Out of the question?'

'Well, you see, here is the problem,' said Caroline, her voice full of false regret. 'As Mrs Schorer kindly reminded me, you simply cannot invite people into your home when you haven't been properly introduced. And no member of the Van der Heyden family has ever called on *me*, or indeed even received me.'

Mrs Warburg's shoulders slumped and she stood up like a person who had been condemned to the gallows. I could imagine how furious Augusta Van der Heyden would be when she heard that Caroline was snubbing her granddaughters.

'I tell you, it absolutely breaks my heart,' said Caroline, shaking her head as we walked with Mrs Warburg to the front door. 'But Augusta Van der Heyden knows the rules. In fact, I believe she made them.'

'What now?' I asked Caroline after Mrs Warburg had left.

'We wait,' she said with a cunning smile. 'Money trumps old values every time. But do you know what trumps money?'

I shook my head.

'Vanity. It's the folly that brings all of us — even the most moral — to our knees.'

୧୦୨୧୬ ୧୭୬ ୧

The following day I gave Isadora her harp lesson as usual, but we were all on high alert, and Caroline had instructed us to wear receiving dresses.

'Do you suppose Augusta Van der Heyden will pay a call today?' Isadora asked me, then added, 'Look, it's starting to snow.'

The music room had a view of the street, and I joined her at the window to watch the flakes drifting from the sky and covering the trees in the park in a layer of white. Caroline had a sixth sense for such matters, I thought. She had known that Oliver was coming to our apartment in Paris to propose to her. If she predicted Augusta was coming today, I was sure she would.

As if by magic, a sleek black brougham appeared through the veil of white. It came to a halt outside the house, and a footman dressed in an olive-green uniform with gold piping climbed the front steps in a stately manner despite the snow.

'I wonder if Augusta is in the carriage?' I said. 'Perhaps the footman is simply delivering a message.'

The answer came a minute later when Jennie arrived with instructions from Caroline to go to the reception room. 'Mrs Augusta Van der Heyden is paying a call.'

I glanced outside again. The footman and the coachman were holding a cloth awning over the carriage door. Woodford was laying down a carpet so Augusta could make her way to our front door without soiling her shoes. What a production! I remembered all the times I'd got soaked to the skin in a sudden Paris shower and had simply had to live with it.

Caroline was dressed in a burgundy wool suit. The tight-fitting jacket had a stand-up collar and black braiding on the front and shoulders and made her look like a military general.

When Woodford announced Augusta's arrival, we all rose.

She was dressed in head-to-toe black silk, and if not for the gold lace around her cuffs and collar could have been going to a funeral. The symbolism wasn't lost on me. Augusta knew that her minions, whom she had ruled over for decades, were deserting her in favour of Caroline and her spectacular ball. Augusta had kept my sister out of old New York society for almost twenty years, and now Caroline had brought her to her knees.

To her credit, my sister didn't gloat. 'Mrs Van der Heyden, how good it is to see you. You have already met my sister, Miss Lacasse; and this is my daughter, Isadora.'

Augusta nodded at each of us in turn.

'Won't you please sit down?' Caroline said, gesturing to a gilded Louis XV chair that resembled a throne. Now she was sure of her victory, she could afford to be generous. 'It is very kind of you to come through the snow to see us.'

Augusta relaxed her defiant pose. 'I assumed I ought to call as my nephew, Douglas Hardenbergh, speaks so highly of you all.'

'He certainly has a splendid art collection, and is a fine musician too,' said Caroline.

'Yes, his late wife was an accomplished pianist,' Augusta replied, glancing in my direction. 'They used to entertain us with their beautiful flute and piano duets.' I wasn't sure if she was taking a stab at me, but then she added in a kind tone, 'Douglas praised Miss Lacasse's ability with the harp, which is high praise indeed. He is very particular when it comes to music.'

'Our grandparents were talented musicians,' offered Caroline. 'I believe that's where my sister inherited her talent. I am more like our mother, consumed with the practicalities of life.'

'Practicalities are important too,' said Augusta.

The conversation continued in this odd, polite way, covering topics as broad as Macy's Christmas window display, the Boer

War, and the debate over whether the new century had already begun or would not begin until January 1901.

When the traditional quarter-hour for a first visit was up, Woodford was summoned to lay the carpet down the front steps again so Augusta could return to her carriage.

'I will have invitations to Isadora's debutante ball delivered to your granddaughters this afternoon,' Caroline told Augusta in a reassuring tone. 'I do hope you will grace us with your presence too?'

Augusta gave a little laugh. 'I'm afraid it's many years since I attended a costume ball.'

'But so many of your friends are coming. They will be disappointed if you are not there.'

Augusta regarded Caroline for a moment. Her eyes moistened and her lips trembled, but then the sternness returned to her face and she nodded. 'I will await your invitation.'

At the door, she paused before looking back to Caroline. 'I don't live in a fairyland. I know that one day other women will rise in my place to guide the society I have so carefully constructed. My entire life has been given to creating beauty, elegance, refinement and culture, but I see now that I should not have excluded people of quality whose husbands have been busy building up this great country of ours. I was too harsh on you, Mrs Hopper.'

Caroline's mouth dropped open and she had to make a quick effort to compose herself. 'It is time for us to put down our weapons and make an alliance, Mrs Van der Heyden,' she said. 'There are women far worse than I, or Helen Potter or Bessie Graham. Crass women who would make fools of us all.'

Augusta's eyes narrowed and she turned in the direction of Central Park. 'I quite agree, Mrs Hopper. I have seen Permelia Frances in that ridiculous troika.' She shuddered. 'I don't know what the world is coming to.'

꧁꧂

Caroline was in high spirits after her triumph with Augusta Van der Heyden. I took the opportunity to suggest I visit Grace, but when I asked Woodford to organise a carriage, Caroline said, 'I'll take you! Go change into an afternoon dress and get a scarf.'

I had assumed we would take a detour on the way to parade in Central Park and was surprised when Caroline led me to the carriage house, where Teddy was polishing a white motor car with red leather seats and pneumatic tyres. He stood to attention when we approached.

'Do you like it?' Caroline asked me, admiring the nickel-plated mudguards. 'It was my Christmas present to myself. It's got a steering wheel, a pram hood and a reverse gear!'

The automobile was larger and more solid-looking than the one I had seen last time, with a double seat at the front and a long passenger seat in the rear.

'But you don't drive it yourself, do you?' I asked, glancing at Teddy who shifted his feet. 'Not when you have such a capable chauffeur?'

'There is no sport in forever being driven around, Emma,' Caroline said sharply. 'If Permelia Frances can manage her own troika, I can certainly drive my own motor car.'

Now I understood the reason for the new motor car. It was to outdo Permelia Frances's bold display.

'Mrs Hopper, excuse me for speaking up, but it's been snowing,' Teddy said with a nervous edge to his voice. 'The roads are wet and slippery. It's not the best day to try driving the new motor car.'

I didn't like the idea either, especially if Caroline wasn't familiar with the vehicle. 'Perhaps you should wait for better weather,' I suggested.

'Oh, Emma, stop being such a sensible bore!' Caroline scolded me. 'And don't lecture me on something you know nothing about. I raced my other motor car at Bessie Graham's property in

Newport last summer and won first place, and that automobile has a tiller and is much more difficult to drive than this one.'

I bit down on my bottom lip, cut by Caroline's words. I recalled the night the Confirmed Bachelor Girls had taken off their corsets and how self-conscious I had been. Maybe I was a sensible bore.

I allowed Teddy to help me into the passenger seat beside Caroline, who climbed in the motor car herself. She produced a round hand mirror from under her seat.

'Bessie's daughter showed me this trick,' she said, holding the mirror up and to the side. 'You use it to check behind you while you're driving.'

A groom opened the carriage house doors, while Teddy primed the engine before crank-starting it. The noise was deafening and it set the horses in the stables whinnying.

While Caroline was working out the controls, Teddy walked around to my side of the vehicle and spoke into my ear. 'The speed limit is eight miles per hour, four miles per hour around corners, but this motor car can do up to thirty-five. Make sure Mrs Hopper keeps to a low speed.'

Caroline released the brake and the motor car lurched forward. A groom stood out on the pavement to make sure no pedestrians got in the way as Caroline drove onto the street. The vibration, the noise and the gasoline fumes combined to give me a throbbing pain in my head. How could anyone prefer a motor car to the elegant clip-clop of a horse carriage? But I was still stinging from Caroline's rebuke so I sat up straight and pretended to enjoy the ride.

As we progressed up Fifth Avenue in the noisy, noxious-smelling machine, spectators gathered on the pavements to watch us, their expressions a mix of wonder, adulation and horror.

'Look at the two fine ladies in a motor car!' a newspaper boy cried out.

Shopkeepers stood in their doorways, and children peered out of windows. We were a greater novelty than two men might have been, and Caroline lit up at the attention. She winked at some of the children and waved to the people who opened their windows and leaned out to get a closer look. Even I started to relax and enjoy myself when I saw that there were only a few clumps of snow left on the sides of the street. I stopped gripping my seat and became brave enough to wave to people also.

Caroline turned the motor car back towards the park, and took the way we would have used to parade in the carriage. Many of our usual acquaintances were there and looked astonished by our mode of transport.

Helen Potter cried out from her carriage, forgetting all decorum and waving wildly. Even the women from the old elite who would normally have snubbed us applauded as if it was all good fun.

'What absolute dash!' called Mrs Warburg, even though the horse pulling her victoria jerked nervously at the noise when Caroline passed her. The poor animal seemed on the verge of bolting.

'I have set the fashion!' Caroline said to me, her face glowing with triumph. 'You'll see: all the ladies will be taking driving lessons now.'

We did the circuit a few times, each time seeming to pick up speed. I glanced at the controls but couldn't make sense of them. Teddy had said not to let Caroline go over eight miles per hour, but how fast was that?

Caroline's elation had turned to disappointment. 'Let's drive past her house,' she said, heading back out onto Fifth Avenue.

'Grace's house?' I asked.

'No, Permelia Frances's house. She's built a mansion with substantial grounds on the West Side,' Caroline said with a sneer. 'She says she refuses to follow the "old" crowd, and in the future the West Side will be more "cosmopolitan" than the East Side. As if that is a good thing!'

The more Caroline spoke about Permelia the harder she gripped the steering wheel and the faster we seemed to go.

'What speed are we doing now?' I asked her.

She ignored me and said in a high squeaky voice, obviously imitating Permelia: 'I must have trees, darling! I can't live in a cement block without trees and flowers! On the West Side you can have a garden, you know. You can have your own railroad under the house to deliver coal and even your own private chapel!'

I'd forgotten how worked up Caroline got about people she viewed as competitors. If she'd been a dragon, she would have been breathing fire.

Thud! It happened so quickly. A man stepped off the pavement right in front of us, distracted by a piece of paper in his hand. I felt the bump as he disappeared beneath the motor car.

I screamed, and Caroline braked and looked over her shoulder. I looked too. The man was lying on the road.

'Where did he come from?' she said. 'There's no one else around!'

For a terrifying moment I thought she was going to drive on and leave the man there.

'We have to go back to help him!' I cried.

I was about to climb out of the motor car and run to the man when Caroline reversed. The man was just lifting himself up when we struck him again. By some miracle, the wheels hadn't gone over him and, although his coat was torn and dirty, he didn't appear to be badly injured. He climbed to his feet, swaying from shock.

'Goodness me!' Caroline shouted to him. 'I'm so sorry!'

I thought she might offer to take him to a doctor or to pay for his ruined coat. Instead, she put the motor car into forward gear and sped away.

'We could have killed him!' I said, barely able to get my words out. My throat was taut like an over-tightened harp string.

'If people are going to be stupid enough to step out in front of us, I can't be responsible for their early demise,' Caroline said matter-of-factly.

Her callousness left me angry and shaking. I had always known it was part of her but had chosen to forget it.

'Caroline, could you please drop me off at Grace's house. I will find my own way home.'

She regarded me with disgust. 'Really, Emma, he should have heard us coming. And we couldn't have been going very fast or we would have killed him.'

Nevertheless, she stopped in front of Grace's house. I climbed out of the motor car with trembling legs and watched her drive off, honking her horn at pedestrians and cyclists. I tried to wipe the image of the pedestrian we had run over from my mind, but I couldn't. A sudden vertigo overtook me and I leaned against a lamppost for support. When Caroline was obsessed with something, she was terrifying.

A disturbing thought edged at my mind and I shivered. What if Isadora should reject the suitor Caroline chose for her? What would happen then?

NINETEEN

The invitations to the ball were written out by a stern-faced woman named Maria de Amaragi. Despite the air of grimness about her the calligraphy she produced was beautiful. The lines were perfectly straight, the letters well-spaced, and her embellishments were complex and well-executed. I could understand why Caroline used her.

When Isadora and I were in her studio, my niece startled me by saying, 'You know Madame de Amaragi has spent time in gaol?'

'Really? What for?'

'Forgery. Apparently she signed paintings to make it seem as if they were by famous artists, and forged cheques. She even wrote a false confession to convict someone who was most certainly innocent.'

'Why on earth would your mother use someone like that for your ball invitations?' I asked, astonished.

Isadora laughed. 'Because she's the best, of course. And people like intrigue. She was an aristocrat in Argentina but now lives in genteel poverty. Besides, she would never dare to cheat Mother. No one would be foolish enough to do that.'

Once the invitations had been sent out, our days were filled with planning for the 'Ball of the New Century' as the press termed it. After poring over history books, Caroline wrote out a list of notable personalities from the Versailles era and presented it to us when Harland was visiting for afternoon tea. Caroline had decided she would be Catherine the Great, and Harland would be Napoleon, 'a victorious conqueror'. Isadora and I were delegated Madame du Barry and Marie Antoinette, both of whom had gone to the guillotine during the French Revolution — Madame du Barry crying and protesting; and Marie Antoinette calm and fatalistic.

I thought of La Conciergerie in Paris and shivered. Dressing up as someone whose life had ended so brutally was anathema to me. All the writers I knew were highly superstitious about something and I was no exception. I rarely wrote anything in first person unless it was based on something that had actually happened to me or something I didn't mind happening. Otherwise, I was fearful of manifesting a terrible occurrence into existence.

'If you don't mind, I'd rather go as a different character,' I said. 'I don't want to be someone who was executed by guillotine.'

'Don't be such a child!' Caroline said, in the same tone she'd used when I'd suggested Teddy should drive the motor car for her. 'Would you rather be some silly court underling? While she lived, Marie Antoinette lived brilliantly! Who cares how she died?'

Harland rolled his eyes. 'Death is never pretty, Emma, even if you go in your bed. Instead of focusing on how Marie Antoinette died, you ought to aspire to how she lived. Like a firework!'

I glanced at Isadora; her fists were clenched in her lap. It was her debutante ball and Caroline had given her a character like Madame du Barry? It was bad enough that my sister diminished me, but I had a reason to keep my mouth shut and stay the course. I imagined my apartment in Paris and Paulette safe, warm and well-fed in old age. But now I knew how much

Isadora loathed herself, her mother's condescending attitude was harder to bear.

I took my niece's hand to show my solidarity and said, 'All right. Both of us will symbolically lose our heads for the night.'

Isadora flashed me a grateful smile and her shoulders relaxed.

'And who am I to be?' asked Oliver, stopping in the doorway for a moment on his way to the great hall.

'Ivan the Terrible,' said Harland, turning away so Oliver wouldn't see his smirk.

Oliver caught the sarcasm but didn't react to it. 'Very good. Go ahead and organise my costume, Caroline. I'll need a sword, I imagine?'

'Ivan the Terrible didn't carry a sword,' she told him. 'He didn't need to. He was a Tsar — other people carried swords for him.'

Oliver drew in a slow breath, then said, 'I'm returning to the office. I won't be home in time for dinner.'

But neither Caroline nor Harland appeared to have heard him. They flipped through more books and admired the pictures as if Oliver hadn't spoken at all.

What had happened to the Oliver I had first met in Paris? That bold and brash man wouldn't have tolerated insolence from anyone, let alone his wife and someone who relied on him for his income. He would have put both of them in their place.

I wondered what he thought now of his hurried proposal to Caroline. Perhaps he wished he had listened to Grand-maman and got to know my sister better first.

If Oliver had learned anything from his mistakes, I hoped he would recall it when it came time for Isadora to choose a husband.

❧❦❧ ❦❧❦

The ball had sent New York society into a whirl. According to the *New York Times* every costumier-dressmaker, seamstress, wigmaker, dancing master, milliner and jeweller was working around the clock to have their customers ready for the ball.

Those privileged enough to be invited are determined to outshine the other guests. Bank vaults will be emptied as family heirloom jewellery that hasn't seen the light of day for decades will be put on display. Mrs Herman Fishburn will be adorned in $200,000 worth of jewels; and Mrs Floyd Dumonceau intends to don a diamond tiara that once belonged to the French empress Marie Louise. Mr Gilbert Chaser, on the other hand, is keeping Tiffany & Co. in business by commissioning an $8000 ruby-encrusted sword to accompany his costume ...

Caroline came to see me one afternoon when I was practising my harp in the music room. 'I've brought you something,' she said, holding out a red jewellery box with a royal insignia on it.

I took it from her and unfastened the clasp. The box opened five ways to reveal a sparkling diamond and ruby parure inside: a tiara, a necklace, a pair of earrings and a brooch. I gasped at the beauty of them.

'They are for you to wear at the ball,' she told me. 'They were part of Marie Antoinette's personal collection.'

My fingers hovered over the pieces — they seemed too precious to touch. The tiara had seven spikes, the largest in the middle, each composed of an oval-shaped ruby surrounded by rose-cut diamonds. The lower semicircular band was a single row of diamonds over a layer of spherical pearls. The other pieces were equally magnificent. I couldn't even guess how much Caroline had paid for the collection, but in terms of their historical value they were priceless.

'For me to wear? But I can't ...'

'Emma, you are not telling me that they're too good for you?'

Caroline said with a trace of irritation in her voice. 'You are my sister! Don't you believe you deserve glorious things?'

Her gaze fixed on me as if she was offering me a challenge. I thought back to my childhood and remembered how Caroline had always believed that she deserved the fine things we saw in the shop windows on Rue de la Paix. Whereas for me they had been a fantasy — something I could only daydream about.

The realisation of my inferior opinion of myself was confronting and I lowered my eyes. 'I will enjoy wearing them at the ball, thank you. They will be a happy part of my time in New York. Something to remember when I go home.'

'You aren't thinking of leaving, are you?'

I looked up at her. 'When Isadora has found a suitable husband, as we agreed.'

A change came over Caroline, revealed by the subtlest repositioning of her shoulders, and she shifted her gaze away from me. 'You know, Emma, the Hardenbergh family own so much real estate that Douglas Hardenbergh's life is extremely comfortable. I believe he spends most of his time improving his mind: reading, playing music, travelling. Think of it: you would stay near us in New York and be a permanent part of our family. No one is as particular about second marriages as they are about first ones.'

I was unnerved by her insinuation but managed to rally myself. 'Caroline, Douglas Hardenbergh is a very nice and well-educated man, but I have someone in Paris. I'm engaged to him.'

The lie sent my pulse racing. But how else could I explain my arrangement with Claude to her?

She waved her hand dismissively as if I had told her something she already knew. 'Oh, not the artist? They are such fickle people — always flitting from one lover to another. No wonder you didn't have any money for the apartment. A *good* man would have paid off your debts. You wouldn't have had to come begging to me.'

My hand flew to my chest. It was not the slight that shocked me, but her knowledge of Claude. How had she found out? Isadora must have told her. My niece would not have divulged my secret vindictively, but I'd have to be careful what I confided to her in the future.

'Of course, you are an adult and in charge of your own life,' continued Caroline, 'but Douglas Hardenbergh seems keen to know you better. Imagine what it would be like to be mistress of a fine household, Emma. To have a wealthy, respectable husband, and to be stepmother to those delightful children — and perhaps even mother to one or two of your own. Isn't that what you always wanted — *a family*?'

My heart was beating so fast I thought I might faint. Of course my sister was manipulating me, but it was diabolical how cleverly she managed it. It terrified me that she knew my desires so well when I had never confided anything of the sort to her.

Her voice flowed hypnotically on. 'With Douglas, you could have a home and a family of your own. An artist could never offer you anything as stable.'

I stood and stepped back from her as if trying to break the spell she was casting over me. 'You've forgotten one thing,' I said. 'Douglas Hardenbergh is still very much in love with his late wife. He hasn't asked me to marry him.'

Caroline smiled mysteriously. 'Nothing lasts forever, not even grief. It's untrue that love is eternal. Love can be willed to appear or disappear any time you want. You'll see.'

ळ

The following day, I received by post the French edition of *A Tale of a Lonely House* and a note from Monsieur Plamondon saying that he had forwarded it to an American publisher who claimed to be very interested in the translation rights.

I mulled over the premise of the novella while I was supervising Isadora's lesson with Mr Gadley. I had originally written it in third person, but Monsieur Plamondon had convinced me it would be more powerful and immediate in first person and I had given in to his logic. In the story, Genevieve, a wealthy spinster, married a man who she believed would be a good companion for her in her isolated hilltop house. But he estranged her from her friends and slowly gained control of her life. Genevieve became sicker and sicker with a mysterious illness, eventually coming to the realisation that the husband she adored and trusted was poisoning her.

A laugh from Mr Gadley brought my attention back to the present. 'What a splendid outcome, Miss Hopper! You might even say it was therapeutic.'

'Indeed,' said Isadora, smiling.

'What are you two talking about?' I asked.

Isadora turned to me. 'You've been off in your own world for some time, Aunt Emma. Have you been thinking of a new story?'

'Daydreaming is often discouraged and even ridiculed,' said Mr Gadley. 'But to an artist it is as vital as air and water. What glories do we pluck from the invisible realm of ideas!'

'I couldn't agree more, Mr Gadley.' I moved over to the bench to see what Isadora had been sculpting and found a clay head of a sloe-eyed woman with an enchanting smile. The hair was shaped into ringlet curls swept to the side. 'What's so amusing about this?' I asked.

Isadora grinned. 'It's Madame du Barry's severed head. I'm going to hold it in my hands instead of a bouquet at the ball. It will be my revenge for never getting a say in anything, not even my own debut.'

I laughed too. 'I like it. But you know you can do nothing of the sort.'

Isadora covered the head with a cloth. 'Of course I do. But why do we have to dress up as characters we don't want to be? Marie Antoinette and Madame du Barry didn't even like each other! Besides, poor Madame du Barry didn't become a courtesan by choice.'

'I don't believe your mother is thinking that deeply about it, and most of the guests won't either,' I told her. 'It's more about the sumptuous costume and wig you will get to wear.'

Mr Gadley bounced on his toes and a wide grin lifted his lips. 'You do share some of Madame du Barry's good qualities, Miss Hopper. She led an extravagant life at Versailles but by all reports her good nature wasn't spoiled. She was generous, fun-loving and above all kind.'

Isadora blushed. 'Thank you, Mr Gadley. You also are very kind.'

She opened the drawer in her bench and gave him the envelope with his payment, and he in return passed her an envelope with the receipt.

'Till next week,' he told us and left.

Isadora went to the window overlooking the courtyard, as if to catch every last glimpse she could of her beloved teacher. 'Before you came, Aunt Emma, Mr Gadley and Rebecca were the only people I had to talk to. But after I'm married ...' Her eyes filled with tears.

'After you're married, what?' I asked, concern pinching my chest.

'Mother told me that you're going to stay in New York until I'm married. You know that might mean you'll be in New York forever?'

She was trying to make a joke, but it was clear she was upset. 'Why do you say that?'

'Even before her official debut, Rebecca was sought as a tennis partner or walked home by some young man or another after church. Although she hasn't been proposed to yet, people are interested in her. Nobody in society wants to be with me because they find me strange — except for the three of you.'

'Nonsense, Isadora. You are shy, that's all. Unfortunately shyness is often mistaken for aloofness. After the ball you will find many young men calling on you. Perhaps that's why your mother chose to make your debut a costume ball rather than a *bal blanc*. It will take some of the pressure off you.'

Isadora held my gaze for a moment and I sensed I'd missed some important point in what she had been trying to tell me.

She turned away and shook her head. 'Oh, that stupid ball! Mother is spending half a million dollars on it, but it's all about her — so she can show off to everyone. The only thing it will do for me is attract men who want me for my dowry!' She picked up her current art notebook and flicked through it absent-mindedly. 'My life could have been so different. If only my brother had lived! Mother would have placed all her hopes and ambitions on his shoulders, and perhaps I could have been left alone to live my life as I please.'

The world rocked around me, as if I was standing on a ship that had been lifted by a wave and put back down again.

'Your brother?'

'You don't know about William?' Isadora put her notebook back down on the bench. 'No, of course you wouldn't. Mother forbids us to speak about him, and there isn't a photograph of him anywhere in the house. It's as if one day he existed and the next day vanished into thin air. It's Mother's particular way of surviving her grief.'

A chasm opened beneath my feet. 'You've shocked me,' I said, leaning against the bench for support. I had never imagined that Caroline had borne another child. Why had she never mentioned him to Grand-maman or myself? But then I had only discovered Isadora by accident, I remembered, so it was unlikely Caroline would have told us about her son.

'I was eight when he died,' Isadora said. 'William was the long-awaited boy and nothing was too good for him. Mother spent all her time with him, while I was put into the care of a nursemaid. A few days after his second birthday he got the fever. Mother was by his bedside day and night, and when he died she still wouldn't leave him or permit anyone else to see him. Father had to slip her a sleeping draught so that the funeral director could take his body away.' Isadora took a handkerchief from her sleeve and dabbed at her eyes. 'But not once since his funeral has she gone to visit the family mausoleum, although Father and I go several times a year. Mother hates cemeteries of any kind.'

Now I understood that queer expression on Caroline's face in Paris when she had said she didn't like cemeteries. I couldn't fathom why my sister hadn't shared her grief with me. Any closeness I hoped we had been developing during my time in New York was an illusion.

'I'm a stranger to your mother,' I said to Isadora. 'Sometimes I think we are becoming better acquainted, but then I realise I barely know her.'

'That's what Mother is like with everyone, Aunt Emma. She's a closed book. You can never know what she's thinking or feeling — or whether she actually feels anything.'

That evening at dinner, I watched my sister as if I were seeing her for the first time. As she talked excitedly about her plans for the ball, I kept picturing her bent over her dying child. How was it that she showed no signs of that terrible grief?

I watched Oliver, his head bowed as he cut up his food. Was it William's death that had destroyed the goodwill in their marriage? It would have been enough to put a strain on any couple.

When the evening was over and we made our way upstairs, Caroline stopped me and studied me with her piercing gaze. 'Truly, Emma, you have been staring at me strangely all evening. What on earth is the matter with you? I have enough on my hands with Isadora's moody sentimentality. Don't you start too. I don't need two artists moping around while I have a ball to plan.'

Tears stung my eyes, but I was at a loss how to reply. Caroline would not tolerate me feeling sorry for her. Instead I squeezed her arm and promised myself that I would be less judgemental of her. Who knew what secret agony she carried in her heart? Perhaps her constant demands for attention were an expression of that grief.

TWENTY

The ball was set to begin at half-past eleven at night, but spectators started gathering early in the evening to stake their claim behind the velvet rope to watch the guests arrive. The police came to keep everything under control; and soon there was a group of reporters too, waiting to describe the city notables and their costumes for their readers the following day.

At half-past ten, as Jennie was helping me with the finishing touches to my costume, Woodford summoned me to join the rest of the family downstairs for the receiving line.

'Some of the guests have arrived earlier than expected,' he explained.

I guessed why. They were hoping to see as much of the house as they could before the ball officially commenced.

'I respect people who arrive punctually,' Lucy whispered to me as we hurried down the stairs together. 'But I can't abide people who arrive early!'

It was hard to take Lucy seriously, dressed as she was as the famous letter-writing Marquise de Sévigné with her hair in two high bunches of ringlets on either side of her head. Apparently the men of Versailles had found the hairstyle hilarious when their women started wearing it.

Oliver had trouble keeping a straight face when he saw her. 'You look like you have a cabbage on either side of your head.'

'Don't make fun of me,' she mock-scolded him. 'This is all my own hair and I had to sleep with a hundred rollers last night, which nearly killed me. Besides, have you seen yourself?'

Oliver did look ridiculous with his fake pointed beard, fur hat and boyar-style brocade coat. But so did the rest of us. My embroidered gold silk gown was sumptuous with its U-shaped neckline and elbow-length sleeves ending in frills, but the pannier undergarment gave me such enormous hips that I had to turn sideways to get through doorways. Tender bruises were developing on my thighs from when I'd bumped against the balustrade on my way down the stairs.

Isadora had cleverly eschewed court dress and her Madame du Barry was outfitted in a riding habit consisting of a grey silk jacket over an open waistcoat, and a plumed hat. Although her skirt was padded it was infinitely more practical than mine.

Our guests had spared no expense on their outfits either. They arrived as famous painters and composers of the period, explorers, and even well-known Americans such as Benjamin Franklin and Thomas Jefferson. There were legendary generals, Indian kings and Chinese emperors. Helen Potter came as Marie Antoinette's loyal spaniel, Thisbe, and kept yapping around me. Harland and Grace arrived as Napoleon and Empress Joséphine; while the Grahams, in a spirit of black humour, came as the royal executioner and one of the knitting women who watched heads roll during the Revolution. The waiting staff, who had been especially hired for the evening, were all dressed as courtiers in breeches, frilled shirts and powdered wigs; and the female servants were dressed as French maids.

Caroline, however, outshone us all. Wearing a copy of Catherine the Great's silver silk coronation gown with embroidered golden eagles on the skirt and a blue sash across her torso, she sat on a gilded throne. In her left hand she grasped a golden orb, and in the right, a sceptre; and the crown on her head was two half-spheres joined by rows of pearls and a garland of oak leaves and acorns, and encrusted with diamonds and topped with a giant ruby. It was as well Caroline had a strong, short neck, I thought. Holding my head straight under the weight of my pouf-style wig was already giving me a sharp pain in my shoulder.

There was a hushed moment when Augusta Van der Heyden arrived as Maria Theresa of Austria and two of the most powerful women in history came face to face with each other.

But Caroline's expression broke into a smile when she saw Augusta and she rose to greet her. 'My dear Archduchess,' she said, taking her arm, 'which of our rivals shall we rid ourselves of today?'

My eyes eagerly followed Augusta to see if she and Harland would greet each other, but they both looked away as if pretending the other didn't exist. What must it be like to see someone you had once loved and know you would never again be together? I couldn't imagine feeling that way with Claude. A familiar ache dragged at my heart. Why hadn't he written to me?

Douglas Hardenbergh arrived wearing a frock coat of grey and blue striped silk with an ivory waistcoat, black silk breeches and a curled white wig. When he was announced as the Swedish count Hans Axel von Fersen, I stood stock still. Von Fersen had been Marie Antoinette's lover and the reputed father of her children. Was his costume a coincidence — or had Caroline had some hand in it?

He bowed to me, and indicated the vases of pink and white roses, orchids, lilacs and lilies that the florists had placed around the house. 'The flowers are spectacular, Your Highness. Are they from the palace garden?'

'Indeed, Count, they are,' I replied, hoping to defuse an awkward situation with humour. 'But the violets on the dining tables are from an exotic place called the Hudson Valley.'

Douglas nodded knowingly. 'A mysterious place, Your Highness. Yet to be fully explored, I believe.'

Lucy took my arm as the maids began to guide the female guests upstairs. 'Please excuse us, Douglas,' she said. 'This will be fun and I'm sure Emma doesn't want to miss it.'

Caroline had planned that her own bedroom and boudoir on the first floor would be available for the ladies to leave their coats and wraps and to complete their toilettes. This way the doyennes of the old elite would be treated to a view of her magnificent rococo-style bed and her gold and mirrored bathroom with its solid marble tub.

'I can't imagine what this staircase alone must have cost,' one female guest whispered to Mrs Schorer as Lucy and I followed them upstairs. At the top, we almost bumped into Mrs Warburg, who had stopped to stare at the ornate ceiling.

Some of the older women acted as if the French silks that decorated Caroline's bedroom were nothing new to them, but the younger women gasped over the gilded columns that surrounded the canopied bed.

'What do you think that's for?' one of them asked, pointing to the ceremonial railing around the bed. 'Is it to keep her husband out, or to keep him in?'

After adjusting their costumes and fixing their hair in Caroline's boudoir with its frieze depicting the triumph of Cupid and its cabinets inlaid with gold and ivory, the ladies joined the gentlemen again for a parade of costumes up to the third floor and the ballroom.

The ballroom had been spectacularly decorated to simulate the Hall of Mirrors in the Palace of Versailles. Cascades of pink and white orchids and roses dangled over the walls and bowers of them flanked the doorways. The guests gasped at the mirrored arches reflecting the trompe l'oeil windows opposite that depicted scenes of parterre gardens. The gilded sculptured gueridons holding crystal lights showed how far Caroline had gone for authenticity, while the barrel-vaulted ceiling with paintings that glorified the reign of Louis XIV had everyone staring upwards. Large and small solid silver chandeliers dangling from the ceiling set off everything to sparkling effect.

A forty-piece orchestra borrowed from the Metropolitan Opera played the overture from André Ernest Modeste Grétry's opera *Le Magnifique*. The music was so elegant that it sent shivers of pleasure through me. Spectacular music always evoked deep emotions in me. An unexpected harmony, a sudden change in rhythm, or the moment when a soloist entered a piece could send me into a state of euphoria.

'You know that Marie Antoinette fell in love with Grétry's music?' Grace said, standing at my side. 'She appointed him her personal music director. Even the new regime was enamoured of him. When he died, Napoleon gave him the most opulent funeral ever held for a creative artist. The story goes that half of Paris turned out to follow the funeral cortege.'

'I didn't know what to expect when Caroline planned this ball,' I said. 'I was anticipating something showy ... but this ... this is beautiful.'

The ball began with a *quadrille d'honneur*: Oliver led Isadora down the length of the parquet floor, which the servants had scrubbed with milk to a high shine the day before. I was happy to see father and daughter together, and wished Oliver would make more time for Isadora. Then I recalled what he'd said to me about Isadora being Caroline's domain. I could well imagine that it might be Caroline who kept them apart.

Isadora and Oliver were joined in the courtly dance by the other debutantes of the season and their partners. I noticed Lucy slip a piece of paper from her sleeve and peruse it. She had compiled a list of gentlemen known to be good dancers who would come to the aid of any young woman who should find herself without a partner. 'There will be no tears at this ball,' Lucy had confided in me. 'I will make sure of that.'

After several more quadrilles, the rest of the guests were invited to dance. Douglas, as my dinner partner, led me onto the floor.

'Did you know that Count von Fersen wanted to rescue Marie Antoinette?' he asked me. 'He planned to ride into Paris with some cavalry officers.'

Now I was sure Caroline was putting ideas in his head. Fortunately I was prevented from answering by a burst of laughter from the direction of the punch table. We both turned to look. Augusta was engaged in a lively conversation with Franklin and Charlotte Harper. Even though Caroline and Harland danced past together several times, she didn't glance in her former lover's direction once.

'I can't imagine your aunt being in love with Harland Hunter,' I told Douglas. 'She has dignity and pride, whereas he is crass and self-seeking.'

'I'm glad you haven't succumbed to that man's charms, Miss Lacasse. He knows instinctively what people need to hear and how to manipulate them through their vulnerabilities. The more esteemed and respectable the woman, the more he enjoys breaking her heart.'

'He sounds like a villain! Still, your aunt seems to be handling him the best way — by ignoring him.'

Douglas arched his eyebrows. 'Don't be fooled that my aunt will give you a clue as to what she is truly thinking. From the time she can walk, a society woman is taught to smile even if she wants to murder the person she is smiling at.'

'I'll keep that in mind. I am used to artists who wear their hearts on their sleeves.'

'Do they?' He gazed at me with a fascinated expression. 'Yes, I suppose they must in order to create art. But in society, the truth is never articulated. Everything is indicated through signs. You have to be able to read those signs.'

'I'm not sure I will master the signs,' I said. 'I'm like a foreigner who will forever speak English with their native accent.'

He laughed. 'I believe you will do very well, Miss Lacasse. And I'm pleased to know you aren't fooled by men like Harland Hunter.'

'We all have our blind spots,' I told him. 'Although none of us likes to admit it.'

Newton Graham asked me to join him for the next dance, a waltz. The program continued with gallops, more waltzes and a sprightly mazurka that I had to withdraw from after my wide skirt knocked over Gideon Potter.

Eventually, a footman blew a trumpet and Oliver announced that supper was to be served in the dining room in quarter of an hour.

The women retired to Caroline's boudoir so their lady's maids could dab their perspiring faces, straighten their wigs and fix stockings that had fallen down. The scene reminded me of the dressing room at the Théâtre de l'Oeuvre during interval. The chit-chat of the women tinkled like a thousand bells.

'This ball is a heavenly dream!' said Mrs Warburg to Mrs Schorer. 'An event that happens once in a generation.'

Retouched and repinned, the ladies joined their partners again for a stately procession down the staircase into the dining room, which Harland and his assistants had transformed into the Garden of Versailles. The internal doors to the salon, library and music room had been opened up to extend the dining room and create one huge, grand space, and the walls were a solid mass of roses, lilies of the valley and evergreen boughs. The mirrors were framed with garlands of ivy wired with glowing electric lights. Pots of orange trees lined the room, while a fountain with rose-scented water bubbled in its centre. The overall effect was so evocative of a spring garden that I could almost hear birds twittering and see butterflies flitting between the leaves.

'This is incredible!' said one of the old elite guests, Mrs Dumonceau.

As well as the long table, which was now covered in white damask cloths, wreaths of lilacs tied with gold ribbons and bowls of sweet-smelling violets, twenty smaller tables, as beautifully decorated, had been added.

'Lilacs are my favourite flowers,' I told Grace, breathing in the richly floral scent. 'They evoke a dewy garden full of nymphs and fairies.'

Caroline's French chef had brought ten chefs from Paris to help him with the evening's menu, which included chestnut soup with truffles, caviar-stuffed oysters, lobster, canvasback duck and suckling pig.

'Is it true Caroline spent thirty thousand dollars on the flowers alone?' Bessie Graham asked me. 'She has certainly thrown down the gauntlet for Permelia Frances to dare to outdo her.'

'I heard that Permelia tried to bribe the Duchess of Dorset with twenty thousand dollars to get her an invitation,' said Charlotte Harper.

'There was no chance of that,' replied Helen Potter, chewing on a piece of pork in imitation of a little dog for my entertainment.

'That was the other side of Versailles,' Grace whispered to me. 'Intrigues, gossip, excess and eccentricity.'

'Perhaps humans can't stand too much beauty before they feel compelled to somehow pollute it,' I replied.

She nodded. 'You may well be right.'

After consuming three thousand bottles of Moët et Chandon champagne, which had been especially shipped from France for the occasion, and a dessert of *bombe glacée*, chocolate mousse, *petits fours* and fruit, the guests returned to the ballroom in an enlivened mood. The dancing recommenced with a cotillion that should have been majestic but yelps rang out as toes were stepped on by unsteady dancers.

Afterwards, Lucy oversaw the passing out of party favours. Instead of the usual antique coins, reticules, tiepins and card cases, the guests were given gold cufflinks and shirt studs, pearl brooches, sapphire earrings, silver desk sets and jewelled table clocks.

Isadora, flushed from all the attention she was getting, touched my arm. 'Please could you find Father for me, Aunt Emma? I've been dancing non-stop and I'd like to do the gavotte with someone who doesn't scare me half to death.'

'Where is your mother?' I asked. 'And Harland for that matter?'

'Mother's having a nap so she can be fresh when she sees off the guests. I don't know where Harland is.'

'I don't blame her, she's been working hard. I'll find your father.'

Oliver's smoking room had been turned into a men's cloak depository, and so he was sitting with some of the male guests in an enclosed colonnade adjacent to the ballroom. Through the glass door, I saw that he was handing out one-hundred dollar bills for the men to use to roll their tobacco.

'Despite all the doom and gloom in the press, business has been splendid,' he said in his booming voice. 'It's time for us to celebrate!'

I was about to tap on the glass to get his attention when I noticed one of the hired staff in courtier dress behaving oddly on the other side of the colonnade. He was hiding behind a palm plant so he could observe the men without them noticing. I waved to the men and knocked to get their attention, but they were engrossed in conversation and didn't hear me above the music from the ballroom. It would have been unseemly for me to walk into a group of men smoking, so I went to find Woodford.

'What's the matter?' Grace asked when I re-entered the ballroom.

I described what I'd seen to her. 'I'm looking for Woodford so he can inform Oliver.'

'Let's find one of the detectives instead,' she suggested. 'Caroline said they're wearing purple rose boutonnières.'

'Detectives?' I said, astonished. 'Did Caroline anticipate the hired staff would be thieves?'

'She's not worried about the staff — they're carefully checked by the agency. No, it's the guests. Just because they're the wealthiest people in New York, don't be deceived they're above going home with "souvenirs". Dear Mrs Sommer is a known kleptomaniac, for example. There's been a female police agent stationed in Caroline's boudoir all night to make sure nothing goes missing.'

'You can't possibly be serious, Grace! Are you playing a joke on me?'

Her eyes flashed with amusement. 'My dear Marie Antoinette, I've read in history books that you were quite innocent and now I see that you are! At my debutante ball there wasn't a cigarette case, bath soap or silver teaspoon left in the house after the guests left, and there wasn't anybody there who wasn't worth at least ten million.'

We found one of the detectives and alerted him to what I'd seen, but when we returned to the colonnade the mysterious courtier had disappeared. Oliver came out and asked what was the matter. When I explained it to him, he gave the detective orders to search the house and sent Grace and me back to the ball.

The dancing continued until six in the morning, when a buffet breakfast of sausages, eggs, ham and fishcakes was served. But after all the champagne and the chocolate mousse I had eaten only a few hours ago, the greasy odour turned my stomach.

Caroline and Harland entered the dining room looking refreshed. Caroline's hair had been redone and her dress had been ironed, while everyone else resembled survivors of shipwreck, with wigs askew and powder settling in the creases of their faces. Oliver, Isadora, Lucy and I lined up with Caroline and Harland in the great hall to farewell the guests.

'This has been the most stupendous, the most beautiful, the most entertaining ball I have ever attended in my life!' Mrs Warburg exclaimed, taking Caroline's hand. Then, noticing Augusta standing within hearing distance, she quickly added, 'Except for Augusta's annual balls, of course. They are very elegant affairs too.'

I was glad that at least one of Augusta's devotees had maintained her loyalty.

Then I noticed that Augusta was chatting with Grace. 'I have missed our conversations,' I heard her say. 'Please do call on me, Grace.' It seemed they were mending their friendship, and I wondered what had brought about Augusta's change of heart.

The other guests voiced similar views — 'Magical!'; 'Unequalled!'; 'Never to be forgotten!' — as we waved them off, and their footmen, valets and lady's maids guided them down the red carpet to their carriages.

The early morning light gave the glistening snow a golden hue. Soon the city would spring to life: shop shutters would open, workers would head to their offices and street vendors would be calling out their wares. But I was sure the ball guests would all be going straight to bed.

'This is my favourite time of day,' Douglas said to me as he bid his farewells. 'Fresh with new possibilities.' He hesitated then added, 'I'm off to California for a while to attend to some business matters there. I would like to call on you when I get back.'

'We will be so pleased to see you,' Caroline said, before I could respond. 'You are welcome in our home any time.'

Douglas bowed in the manner of the French court before getting into his carriage.

'Honestly, Caroline,' I said, 'you are creating an awkward situation for that poor man. I told you that I'm engaged.'

'Really?' She lifted my left hand. 'Where is your ring? Or can't he afford one?'

Despite being surrounded by guests, I was tempted to tell Caroline to mind her own business and stay out of mine. But then I remembered my promise to myself about being more patient with her.

After the last of the guests had left, Isadora, Caroline, Oliver and Lucy retired to their rooms. Isadora was swaying on her feet with fatigue, but I was too full of music and food to contemplate going to bed. I sat in the library, watching the male servants taking down the decorations and putting the furniture back in position, and the maids beginning to clean the house. When would the staff get a chance to rest?

Finally succumbing to a yawn, I went into the great hall to make my way upstairs. The door to Oliver's office opened and the suspicious courtier I had seen earlier sneaked out and slipped into the ladies' reception room, closing the door behind him.

My mind snapped to alertness. 'Stop, thief!' I cried and, without thinking, ran after him. I entered the reception room in time to see him open the window and put his foot to the sill. 'Stop!' I cried again, this time much louder.

The courtier hesitated and turned around, his mouth open in an expression of surprise. 'Emma!' he said in a feminine voice. 'What are you doing here?'

I stumbled back a step. The features under the white powder became suddenly familiar. 'Cecilia! I live here! What are *you* doing?'

Footsteps pounded outside in the great hall. Some servants had heard my cries and were running to my aid.

Cecilia gave me another puzzled glance before climbing out the window and dropping the short distance to the pavement below. I shook my head, unable to believe what had happened. I ran to the window and peered out, but a snow storm had begun to blow and Cecilia had vanished into the whiteness.

Woodford burst into the room accompanied by two footmen and a maid. 'Where is the thief, Miss Lacasse? Where did he go?'

I pointed out the window but they would never catch up with Cecilia now.

'Did you get a glimpse of the scoundrel's face?' Woodford asked.

I paused, then shook my head. 'No, he was too fast.'

Whatever Cecilia West was doing, no good would come of it, of that I was sure. I was also certain that my association with her would make whatever she had discovered ten times worse.

TWENTY-ONE

While Caroline basked in the success of her magnificent ball the following day, and Isadora received bouquets of American Beauty roses from potential suitors, I twisted at the emerald ring on my finger and fretted over the chance of something going terribly wrong. Why had Cecilia been at the ball? She was a 'muckraker', so what dark secret was she endeavouring to reveal? As I ruminated over the possible scenarios, I realised how terrible it would be if she revealed a connection to me. Caroline would view me as a traitor. And the consequences of that were too ghastly to imagine.

After luncheon, Caroline called me, Isadora and Lucy to her so we could review the newspaper reports together. Each time one of them discovered another article, a creeping dread stirred in me.

'Look, here's a comment in the *New York Times*,' said Caroline. She smiled as she read the words aloud: '*Mrs Hopper is no doubt the new leader of New York society, and so she should be. Her taste is irreproachable. One only has to take in the lavish details of her home on Fifth Avenue to see that.*'

'Oh, wonderful!' cried Lucy. She read from a piece in the *New York World*: '*Mrs Hopper's ball in honour of her daughter was an event without equal in the social annals of this city. She*

*spared no expense to create a brilliancy of dress and decoration
that far outdoes anything that has come before it.'*

Caroline and the ball were likewise praised in the *New
York Herald* and other smaller publications. I racked my brain
to remember the publication Cecilia had said she was writing
for — *McClure's Magazine*, wasn't it? I had never come across
a copy in the house, so it was unlikely that Caroline read it, but
if it did carry a scandalous story, the daily papers were likely
to pick it up too. Cecilia had said she was writing an exposé
of wealthy men who exploited foreign labour. I remembered
Florence's reaction when she'd first found out I was related
to the Hopper family. Was there some wrongdoing I didn't
know about? If so, what would be the effect of its revelation
on Isadora? Caroline had warned me that my niece had already
suffered two nervous collapses.

My fear only grew worse when I received a note from
Florence in the last post of the day: *Please come and see me
tomorrow at ten o'clock on a matter of urgent importance. Plan
to spend the whole day.*

༺ೋ෴ೋ༻

It was with trepidation that I arrived at Aunt Theda's house
the following morning at the appointed time. My fears weren't
allayed by the serious expression on Florence's face when she
greeted me at the door instead of Nora.

'Come in, Emma,' she said in a weary tone. 'Cecilia is waiting
for you.'

Cecilia? I hadn't expected her. Was she going to grill me
for information? I could counter that she had trespassed in my
family's home, and if I identified her to Oliver he would press
charges.

Cecilia must have realised that too from the wary way she
regarded me when I followed Florence into the drawing room.

How different the mood was from the last time we'd been together for the Confirmed Bachelor Girls' social night.

'Well, Emma, you certainly surprised me,' she said. 'I knew you and Florence were hiding something, but I didn't imagine for one second that it was the fact that you're related to the Hopper family.'

I didn't answer. When I'd first arrived in New York I might have launched into an explanation about how Caroline and I had been estranged for years. Now I had too much invested in Isadora's welfare to dissociate myself from Caroline and Oliver.

Cecilia pressed harder. 'As you know, I've been writing stories on the robber barons of New York. Oliver Hopper, being one of the wealthiest, is of particular fascination to our readers. I've gathered quite a bit of information on the Hopper family and none of it is good, I'm afraid. But out of respect for Florence and her friendship with you, I've agreed to keep your name out of it — on one condition. That you spend the day with me and Florence and keep an open mind to the circumstances we present to you.'

I didn't like being cornered, but I had to tread carefully. My first priority was that Cecilia didn't write anything about Isadora that would hurt her or ruin her chances of a happy marriage. Caroline and Oliver were robust, but my niece was sensitive.

'You'll have to change into something plainer,' Florence told me. 'I've laid out a suitable outfit for you in my bedroom. Please leave your jewellery with Nora. I'll let your coachman know that we'll take you home at the end of the day so he's free to go.'

Upstairs I found a grey woollen suit-dress on Florence's bed, along with a black coat, scarf and lace-up boots. Where on earth were we going?

I had become so used to the beautiful garments that Caroline had bought for me that putting on the grey skirt and jacket made me feel as if I was going to prison. But I had done nothing wrong. I removed my emerald earrings and ring and put them in the box that had been left for me.

Despite the cold and the snow, which was hardening and turning slippery, we didn't take a carriage or sleigh to our destination. Rather we walked for some distance in silence before coming to a junction of the elevated railway. I had to cover my ears against the deafening rattle of a train passing overhead. Florence bought our tickets and we climbed the slippery iron steps to the platform. A transit officer, bundled in a coat with only his eyes showing through the scarf wrapped around his face, took our tickets and we pushed our way through the stiff turnstile. The wind stabbed at me like icicles and I was glad when a train screeched to a halt next to us.

The musty stink of damp clothes lingered in the carriage, which reeked of soot, and the floor was littered with discarded tickets. I was glad I wasn't wearing my good coat when we sat down on the grimy wooden bench. I peered out the grease-smeared windows, but the only view was straight into the apartments of the buildings that lined the track. After catching sight of too many men in their underwear and women cooking in tiny kitchens, I gave up and stared at my hands.

'At least there are no men exposing themselves or women caught in amorous activities today,' said Florence in an attempt at humour.

We alighted from the train and descended another set of slippery steps to the street. I grabbed the railing but it was so chilly I was afraid that I might stick to it and let it go. We walked past a butcher in a bloody apron skinning a goat, a pawnbroker and a baker with grime under his nails sorting bread.

'He's the only baker who doesn't add sawdust to his flour,' Florence told me. 'Everyone else does, or waters down their milk. That's why so many children starve no matter what their parents feed them.'

We stopped at a German delicatessen where Cecilia bought liverwurst sandwiches, pickled vegetables and cooked sausages. Surely she didn't intend for us to eat those things? We turned down a side street and the stench of urine and faeces was so overpowering, I had to stop.

'It's worse in summer,' said Cecilia letting out a loud breath that steamed in the air.

Something touched my leg and I glanced down to see a pile of rags moving. Then a craggy, sallow-skinned face popped up and the pile became a woman. 'Penny to save someone starving?' she asked, holding out a hand blackened with dirt.

Florence reached into her pocket and gave her some coins before we walked on.

The street was lined with ramshackle houses. One might have once been as handsome as Douglas Hardenbergh's charming Georgian mansion, but now its front steps were worn and cracked, the ironwork was missing and the windows were caked in a brown crust. The dwellings on either side of it were rickety wooden houses; two of them nothing more than burned shells on the verge of collapse. Oversized rats scurried between the piles of rotting garbage that were stacked in the gutters with seemingly no expectation of collection.

'These homes were built to house a single family,' Florence explained, 'but as the wealthy moved further uptown, they were divided into smaller and smaller apartments. Now there could be as many as twenty people living in each apartment, sometimes more.' She nodded towards one of the burned-out buildings. 'That caught fire last year. One hundred adults and eighty children were killed.'

We all stood in silence imagining what that terrible catastrophe must have been like. I remembered the grisly accounts of the Bazar de la Charité fire in Paris a few years previously, in which one hundred and twenty-six people had perished, including children. I couldn't imagine a more terrifying way to die than to be trapped in a burning building.

'Of course there are many poor areas in Paris,' I said. 'But since Haussmann remodelled it, there aren't slums quite as bad as this in the city.'

Cecilia gave a grunt. 'Two-thirds of New York's population live in tenements. That's nearly two and a half million people, Emma.'

'Two-thirds? How could that be possible?'

Neither Cecilia nor Florence answered me. Instead, to my horror, they walked up the steps of the Georgian house and gestured for me to follow them. Surely we weren't going inside?

I steeled myself. I had to go through with this for Isadora's sake.

The hallway was dim with a tomb-like chill that sank into my bones. Every kind of human odour assaulted my nostrils — faeces, urine, vomit, blood, sweat — mixed with the stench of rotting food and mud. In the gloom I glimpsed sacks of rubbish everywhere, as if we had entered a rag-and-bone merchant's. A rat scurried between us with a piece of bloody meat in its mouth and I stifled a scream.

At the end of the hall stood a staircase with some of the steps missing. 'Be careful,' Cecilia warned us as we climbed. 'Last time I was here the railing gave way and hundreds of bugs scurried out of it.'

We stopped on the third-floor landing and Cecilia knocked on the first door we came to. 'Mrs Dempsy, it's Cecilia West and Florence Garrett. We've brought some food for you and the children.'

A woman in a threadbare dress and torn apron opened the door. She couldn't have been more than twenty-five but her face was drawn like an old woman's and her hands were red and raw. She showed us into a dingy apartment, no bigger than the ironing room in Caroline's mansion, where two small children were lying on a pile of dirty straw. There was only one window, and the ceiling above the coal stove was black with grime. The stink of cabbage and fried onion seemed to have sunk into the peeling wallpaper.

'This is our friend Miss Emma Lacasse,' Cecilia said, holding out the food package to Mrs Dempsy. 'I'm showing her the ropes today. She's a cadet.'

'Thank you,' Mrs Dempsy said, taking the package. 'I was wondering how I was going to stretch things. Mrs O'Brien has measles at her place and I couldn't leave the little ones with her to go to work. The rent's due tomorrow, and the collector says it'll go up to nine dollars next month. When I told him that was too much and the window seals and stove pipe still hadn't been fixed, he said there are ten other people waiting to take the place if I don't want it.'

Mrs Dempsy's tone was that of a woman resigned to bad luck and frustrations. Cecilia took out a pencil and notebook and wrote down what she'd said.

One of the children had a wheeze to his breathing that didn't sound healthy. Florence bent down and touched his forehead.

'He has a temperature,' she said. 'Make sure you send for Doctor Johnson, and let him know I'll fix up the bill.'

'Thank you, Miss Garrett,' Mrs Dempsy replied. She glanced at me with a look of apology. 'I'm sorry I don't have anything to offer you. Things have been much harder since Angus was killed. It must be exciting being a cadet and all. You must be smart.'

I wasn't sure what to say to this woman who was being kind to me while she was trapped in a nightmare.

'Not as smart as I'd like to be, Mrs Dempsy,' I replied eventually. 'But I'm always learning.'

We visited some of the other apartments in the building. In one of them, an old man was crouched by a stove trying to keep warm. He was drinking hot water from an empty can and my eyes fell to his hands, painfully swollen with rheumatism.

'Tell us how many people live here, Mr Sauer,' Cecilia asked him.

'In the evening, when everybody comes home from the factory, there are fourteen of us. My son and his wife and her two sisters, six children, and three boarders.'

'Where do they sleep?' asked Florence.

I had been wondering the same thing. The room was barely twelve feet across.

The old man pointed to a pile of dirty rags. 'We spread them out so everybody has something.'

'How old are the children?' I asked. 'Do they go to school?'

He shook his head. 'There's no time to worry about school when everyone's hungry. The children only bring in a few cents making artificial flowers but it's something.'

On our way out, Cecilia gave some money to a new mother who only had newspaper to wrap her newborn child in.

'Thank you, miss,' she said, with tears in her eyes. 'But I don't think he's long for this world. I saw that look in the eyes of my last two. They took one glance around them and decided not to stay.'

Back on the street, the open air I had thought so foul was much fresher than inside the house. I couldn't wait to scrub the stench of dirty rags and foul straw off my skin, but I didn't believe anything would wash away those images of poverty from my mind.

'You're shocked, aren't you, Emma?' said Florence. 'You've never seen anything like that before?'

I shook my head, ashamed of what I and the rest of my family would look like to a woman in Mrs Dempsy's situation, or to Mr Sauer, or the new mother whose baby would probably die. One of those hundred dollar bills Oliver had handed out at the ball for the men to roll into cigarettes would have kept these families housed for a year. What Caroline had spent on my costume and jewellery would have provided amply for a lifetime. If Lucy had handed out the party favours to the people in these slums, it could have changed the course of a whole neighbourhood's history.

'How do these people end up living like this?' I asked. 'I don't understand.'

Cecilia studied me for a moment, then pointed to the brownstone across the street. 'The tenants in that building pay their rent to a collector, but do you know who owns the building? The landlord who refuses to spend any money on repairs; who orders the collector to extract the maximum rent possible?'

'A criminal perhaps?' I said.

'That house is the property of Augusta Van der Heyden, along with the two beside it. Those further down the street have been in the Schorer family for years. The two that burned down were owned by the Warburgs.'

I was stunned and couldn't do anything but stare at her. I thought back to Augusta's elegant formal dinner, to the night at the opera, to the showy parades in Central Park. Those people acted so civilised, so cultured, so superior, but this was where their money came from. My mind blurred.

'Two streets down, the entire area is owned by Douglas Hardenbergh,' Cecilia added.

A buzzing started in my head. I had the sensation of staring down a dark tunnel.

'I admit he is one of the better landlords,' Cecilia went on. 'He has at least complied with regulations to provide adequate ventilation, plumbing and fire escapes, but the tenements are still how he makes his money. The other supposedly elite families have point blank refused to make improvements of any kind that would cost them money.'

'Every day more and more immigrants flood into New York — from Ireland, Germany, Italy, Russia, China, and even from the south,' Florence said. 'They're all hoping for a better life, but instead they find this.' She grimaced, looking around her. 'And their sheer number means the landlords can afford to exploit them.'

'My family don't own any tenements, do they?' I asked. 'I've only heard that Oliver invests in some commercial property.'

Florence shook her head. 'But he does own railroads and factories and in that way he contributes greatly to the terrible position these people are in. The low wages he pays means these families can never escape the cycle of poverty. You heard what Mr Sauer said: the adults' wages are so low, the children have to work too. They'll never learn to read.'

Cecilia's eyes narrowed. 'It's Oliver Hopper's sheer arrogance that most angers me,' she said. 'Would you like to know how Mrs Dempsy's husband was killed?'

I shivered, knowing that she was going to tell me something terrible. For a moment none of us said anything, then Cecilia spoke slowly and deliberately.

'Oliver Hopper loves his European automobile so much he makes a game of it when he speeds down Fifth Avenue, forcing pedestrians to jump out of the way. Vendors throw fruit at him in an attempt to make him slow down. Late one afternoon, he struck Angus Dempsy as he was getting off a streetcar. Angus's head was crushed like a cantaloupe. The police arrived, but Oliver was never charged because of who he is. Afterwards, he didn't even offer any compensation to Mrs Dempsy. Angus's funeral was paid for by what the other tenants of the building could scrape together. He's buried in the potter's field on Hart Island.'

Her words ran through me like a bolt of lightning. I stumbled as the image of Teddy cleaning gore from the tyre of Oliver's automobile rose in my memory. My brother-in-law had killed a man? I wanted to argue with Cecilia and tell her that she must be wrong, but I couldn't get any air into my lungs. My vision turned white and my legs gave way beneath me.

Florence grabbed my arm. 'All right, Emma, let's get you somewhere warm.'

❧❧❧

Aunt Theda ladled pea soup from the tureen and placed the bowl in front of me. The fire in her dining room was blazing but nothing could take away the chill in my bones. Tears burned in my eyes when I recalled destitute Mrs Dempsy in her rat-infested apartment, trying to support her starving children.

'That can't be what happened,' I said again. 'Oliver is selfish and ambitious but he's not completely without morals. He gives money to charities anonymously —'

'He *is* completely without morals,' snapped Cecilia. 'All of them are.'

My mind swam with anger and confusion. I'd thought that Oliver's distant and sometimes harsh manner was due to his unhappy marriage. But I should have seen him for the callous brute he was when I came across his trophy room with its slaughtered animals. Then another idea scratched at my brain: did Caroline know about it? I recalled the evening of the accident and remembered that she and Oliver had fought fiercely. Out of all the awful discoveries I had made that day, at least I could take comfort that my sister hadn't condoned Oliver's atrocious behaviour.

'How does it feel to be a member of the Hopper family now?' asked Cecilia.

I could not bring myself to look at the women, ashamed of how they must view me. But Oliver's behaviour did not change my love for Isadora. She was faultless in my eyes. Being born into the Hopper family was not something she had chosen for herself.

'Will my brother-in-law be arrested?' I asked. 'I can't understand how he got away with killing someone, intentionally or not.'

Aunt Theda sighed. 'Unfortunately New York is corrupt from the police to the politicians. Those with money can get away with practically anything, including killing an innocent man and leaving his wife and children with no support.'

I shook my head. 'If I could help, I would — but I'm not rich. I'm in New York to assist with my niece's debut in return for my sister paying off debts I owe in Paris. Perhaps I can persuade my brother-in-law to pay Mrs Dempsy some compensation ... Well, she can never be truly compensated, but it will help with her children.'

'He won't agree to that,' said Cecilia. 'It would be as good as admitting guilt.'

Florence touched my arm. 'We're not expecting you to make amends. We only wanted to let you know what the Hoppers and the people you associate with in New York are really like.'

'My niece isn't like that,' I said, turning to Cecilia with a plea in my voice. 'I realise you need to write the truth, but please leave Isadora out of it. If she had a choice she would be your most enthusiastic member of the Confirmed Bachelor Girls' Club, and I believe she does try to contribute positively to the world through her art.'

Cecilia let out a breath. 'I'll only mention it was her debutante's ball. But in return you must do something for us.'

'What?' I asked.

The three women exchanged glances.

'Meet me at my apartment this time next week and I'll show you,' Cecilia said.

⁂

Cecilia's article describing the tenements of the Lower East Side and how the 'robber barons' were exploiting poor immigrant workers appeared in *McClure's Magazine*'s next issue. She mentioned Oliver handing out one-hundred dollar bills to his fellow businessmen at the ball:

> *These men are well-known subscribers to the theory of*
> *'social Darwinism', which allows only the fittest and*
> *best-adapted individuals to survive. They, and others*
> *like them, have opposed welfare systems, compulsory*
> *sanitation and free schools, arguing that society can only*
> *progress and prosperity and personal liberty flourish*
> *when competition is given free rein. Supply and demand*
> *must determine prices and wages — no other factor. But*
> *doesn't their 'dog-eat-dog' philosophy put them only a*
> *little above common criminals?*

The daily papers were quick to take up Cecilia's points, and soon the publications that had praised Isadora's debutante ball only a short while ago were now condemning the Hoppers.

Three thousand bottles of French champagne! Such a wanton display of wealth when so many in the city are suffering is simply outrageous, said the *New York Times*.

The *New York World* followed suit: *Like the royalty of Versailles, these people have sunk to the level of debauched parasites and ought to be condemned to death. Heads must roll!*

Even politicians and preachers denounced us. Caroline received death threats, and Oliver hired private detectives to guard the house. Both of them stopped driving their motor cars, and whenever Caroline went out in the carriage she always had a bodyguard to accompany her.

Since I'd seen the horrors of the Lower East Side, I'd been unable to look Oliver in the eye. I made an effort to control myself but it took all my willpower not to visibly cringe whenever he approached me. He had killed Angus Dempsy and the knowledge played on my mind every day. If I wasn't so concerned about Isadora, I would have left the house and returned to Paris, even if it meant my debts went unpaid.

Isadora was shocked by what was written about her ball. 'Perhaps we really are nothing more than parasites,' she told me. 'Mother spent half a million dollars on that farce! The guests combined would have spent thousands on their costumes. Imagine how that money could have changed the lives of the people in the tenements.'

Caroline came to speak to us one afternoon when we were in the music room.

'I know these articles in the papers have upset the both of you,' she said, sitting down on the piano stool and brushing her hand absently over the keyboard. 'But you're overreacting. Oliver and I went through something similar during the Pullman Strike a few years ago. People condemn us, then they forget and life goes on.'

'But so many people live in terrible conditions,' I said. I hadn't told anyone that I'd seen the tenement houses and their pitiful inhabitants, but the images were firmly imprinted in my mind. 'I hadn't imagined that such slums could exist in New York. Maybe somewhere like Calcutta ...'

'That muckraker exaggerated the situation for her own purpose,' Caroline said firmly. 'Of course not everyone lives as splendidly as we do, but most people in the city have nice apartments and comfortable lives. This is the wealth capital of the United States after all! Cecilia West wants to make a name for herself by playing on the jealousy people feel towards the rich. What she failed to mention is these people wouldn't have work at all if it wasn't for men like Oliver or Franklin Harper or Newton Graham. They're the ones who take all the risks to start an enterprise; the ones who suffer sleepless nights because they've put everything they have on the line. Oliver started out with nothing, but he was industrious, diligent and ingenious. Life has simply rewarded him for those qualities.'

'But, Mother,' protested Isadora, 'that *was* an excessive amount to spend on my debut. We could have had a nice affair with much less than that and given the rest to charity.'

Caroline visibly bristled at the word 'charity'. 'I don't believe people should get something for nothing,' she said. 'Your ball generated a lot of money for the seamstresses who made the costumes, as well as the hairdressers, wigmakers, caterers and florists.'

Isadora seemed about to say something else, but pursed her lips. She and I both knew we'd never win this argument with her mother.

'As for the condition of the housing on the Lower East Side, the tenants themselves are to blame for that,' Caroline continued. 'Mrs Warburg told me that she's forever paying for repairs because of the slovenly way those people choose to live.' I must have had a dubious look on my face because she became insistent. 'It *is* a choice, Emma, believe me. I'll give you an example. Oliver's sister, Anne, was one of those women forever trying to do good for others. It came to her attention that one of the workers at the textile factory had developed gout so painfully that he could no longer stand, and several of his children had rickets. She took it upon herself to find the family a home in the countryside where both the husband and wife could do light work on a farm and have plenty of healthy food and fresh air for their children. Within three weeks they were all back in their hovel in the Bowery. When Anne asked the wife about this, she replied: "It was too quiet for us in the country. We like to be where the activity is."' Caroline threw up her hands. 'You can't help those people if you try! They are used to living in slums and ghettos!'

Caroline's arrogant attitude angered me and I couldn't resist challenging her. 'But what about Douglas Hardenbergh? According to the papers he owns hundreds of tenement properties in New York.'

Caroline rolled her eyes. 'Dragging Douglas Hardenbergh into it only shows how little proper investigation was done. He of all people has been extremely generous with his tenants, only to find that the fire escapes he had installed into all his properties at great expense are so packed with refuse they would be no use at all in an emergency.'

'I can't help feeling sorry for the children who live in the tenements,' Isadora said. 'Whatever their parents do or don't do isn't the children's fault.'

Caroline rose, bringing the discussion to an end. 'We all choose our destinies. Now, you two go and get dressed for dinner. We are going with the Harpers to Delmonico's. We'll hold our heads high and show the world that the Hopper family won't be daunted.'

TWENTY-TWO

Imet Cecilia at her apartment in Greenwich Village as requested the following week. From there, we walked in the direction of Bleecker Street through a neighbourhood where so many different accents rang out from the shops, wagons and beer halls that if everyone was dressed in suits instead of overalls and aprons we could have been at the Hague Convention. We turned a corner past a barber shop and a coffee house where the tables and chairs had been fashioned from upturned beer barrels, and then into a street where the tenement houses were as bleak and dilapidated as those I'd seen on the Lower East Side. With less than a foot of space between them, the buildings rose five to seven storeys high and many of them had makeshift wooden buildings attached where the poorest of the poor lived. But what was exceptional about this street was that in the middle of the squalid block stood an elegant mansion with tidy black shutters and gleaming white columns. In the late evening light I could see that the windows were clean and the roof in good repair.

Cecilia led me towards the front door. 'Welcome to Charles Garrett House,' she said. 'It's named after Florence's father who purchased the building for us.'

The entrance was beautifully appointed, with water-silk floral wallpaper and parquet flooring. A fireplace kept it warm and inviting, and above the mantelpiece hung a painting of two women playing the guitar. I stepped towards it to examine it. The signature showed that it was an original Marguerite Gérard. Through a set of double doors I glimpsed a drawing room with damask-covered chairs and more fine art. The house was an elegant oasis from the grim world outside its walls, and could have easily belonged on Fifth Avenue, although less grand in size. It was only after I had taken in the pleasant surroundings that I became aware of the patter of light but active footsteps reverberating from the upper floor.

'Is there a dance school upstairs?' I asked Cecilia.

She laughed. 'On Saturday afternoons we do have social dancing in the ballroom, but that's not the sound you're hearing.' She glanced at the grandfather clock in the corner of the entry hall. 'Wait a moment and see happens next.'

Before long the chatter of women's voices came from outside. They were mostly Italian accents but I heard some Hungarian and Russian accents too. The door opened and in walked a group of women in woollen coats and felt hats. At the same time the footsteps from upstairs grew louder and dozens of small children appeared, walking in pairs down the staircase, led by Violet and Edna from the Confirmed Bachelor Girls' Club.

'Hold on to the banisters,' Violet told the children. 'Don't hurry now. Watch your step.'

But there was no containing the children's excitement once they had spotted their mothers. They rushed straight into the women's outstretched arms, each child keen to tell what had happened that day.

'So this house is a kindergarten?' I asked Cecilia.

'During the day it is,' she said, guiding me up the now free staircase. 'We started the program so working women with children can avoid the situation you saw Mrs Dempsy in last week — not having a safe place to leave their children when they go to work. Here the women can be certain their children will be fed and well looked after, and bathed if necessary. The older children are taught basic reading and arithmetic skills.'

We reached the first-floor landing and Cecilia opened a door to reveal a room lined with bookshelves where several people were reading at tables with banker's lamps. 'We also have this library for adults, and an art gallery. And on the third floor is an artists' studio where we teach drawing and sculpting.'

'What is this place?' I asked as Cecilia ushered me into a room filled with cabinets displaying silverware and fine china. I sat down in the leather armchair she offered me.

'It's a settlement house. Do you know what that is?' she asked, taking the armchair opposite me.

I shook my head.

'They're a social experiment that's been tried with great success in the United Kingdom and some cities here in the United States. We have a few of them starting up in New York. Young college-educated people — or in the case of Charles Garrett House, young college-educated *women* — leave their comfortable homes to come live among the working classes. The gap between the rich and the poor in this country has become so wide that there are many in the upper classes who no longer view the less wealthy as human beings. That's why they have no compunction about treating them appallingly.'

Cecilia had described my sister perfectly. I doubted Caroline truly believed all she had said to me and Isadora about the poor creating their own conditions. But perhaps she had told the story so many times to justify herself that it had come to be true in her mind.

'This house is a place where we can get together to better understand each other,' Cecilia continued. 'We have a social club on Sunday afternoons where the community's most pressing problems are discussed. That allows the people living in the neighbourhood to come up with solutions for themselves.

Florence and I and the other volunteers here then use that information to write articles, lobby politicians and campaign for change in other ways.'

'Is the house a charity?'

Cecilia shook her head. 'No, not as such, although we do have some emergency supplies like soap and blankets we can give out, and we host a free spaghetti night twice a week. But our main function is to give people back their humanity. That's why we offer classes in art and dancing and frequently hold theatre or musical evenings.'

A silver and ivory Asprey teapot in one of the cabinets caught my eye. It must have cost a small fortune. Considering the living conditions outside, weren't Cecilia and Florence afraid the house would be robbed?

'I know what you're thinking,' Cecilia said. 'You're asking yourself why we don't sell all these things to help the poor?'

I blushed, ashamed that I hadn't been pondering anything as generous as that.

Cecilia rose and took the luxurious teapot out of the cabinet and handed it to me as if to make her point. 'Many of the immigrants living in squalor in New York were intellectuals and professional people in their home countries, but political or economic circumstances forced them to flee. Instead of paying them fairly, the factory owners use their numbers to drive down their wages and conditions.'

I handed the teapot back to her and she placed it on the low table next to her before sitting down again.

'You mentioned last week that you want me to do something. What is it?' I asked.

'Well, that's up to you, Emma. We always need well-educated volunteers: we have newsletters that require editing, and conversational English classes where you could be very helpful. But most of all I thought you might like to play the harp or perhaps give readings of your stories.'

I was puzzled by her request. 'I would be happy to do that, but don't these people have more pressing needs than to listen to music or a mystery story?'

Cecilia formed a steeple with her hands. 'The most pressing need these people have is hope. Music, beauty, kindness and understanding provide that.'

'Well, of course I will help,' I told her. 'I would be glad to.'

'Good,' she said, rising to put the teapot back in the cabinet. We walked down the staircase together and to the front door.

'I'll be in touch soon,' she said. 'Do you know your way back to Washington Square? Or do you need me to accompany you?'

Her eyes flashed and I recognised that the question was a challenge: she wanted to determine if I was afraid of walking through the neighbourhood on my own.

'I'll find my way,' I told her. Then I took a deep breath and met her gaze. 'I'm not as selfish or as frivolous as you may believe I am.'

She seemed amused by my accusation. Gripping my hand lightly, she shook it. 'What I think of you doesn't matter, Emma. What matters is what you think of yourself.'

ᦂᦂᦂ

Before meeting Teddy at the appointed time at Washington Square, I ate dinner in a Romanian bistro. I was excited about the idea of helping at Charles Garrett House but uneasy too. I anticipated my commitment was going to incur Caroline's disapproval, or maybe she would even forbid it. In the carriage on the way back to Fifth Avenue, I deliberated whether to tell her the truth or not, although it would be difficult to discreetly leave the house lugging my harp with me. Perhaps I could say I was practising a duet with Grace; or I'd been asked to give a series of recitals and readings for select groups at the New York Public Library.

Then I recalled Cecilia's parting words: *What I think of you doesn't matter, Emma. What matters is what you think of yourself.* There was nothing to do but to tell Caroline the truth. Although I needed her to pay my debts, I couldn't let her control every decision I made in New York.

By the time Teddy brought the carriage to a stop in front of the house, I'd made up my mind that I would tell Caroline straight away. I was brave about the decision until Woodford opened the door for me.

'Is my sister home yet?' I asked, my heart racing. 'I wish to speak to her.'

Woodford's gaze shifted in a way that made me uneasy. 'Mrs Hopper returned some time ago, but she retired to her room. She won't want to be disturbed. Is it a matter of urgency?'

I was both relieved and disappointed I wouldn't be able to speak to my sister until the morning. 'No, it can wait. Thank you, Woodford. I assume my niece has gone to bed too? If you could give me one of your oil lamps, I can find my way to my room without you having to turn on all the lights again.'

He lit a miniature oil lamp and handed it to me. 'Thank you, Miss Lacasse. Goodnight.'

The tiny lamp created a comforting circle of light around me as I climbed the stairs. The shooting pains of panic in my muscles disappeared and my breathing relaxed. Why did the threat of Caroline's anger fill me with such terror? It wasn't as though her displeasure could kill me. Hopefully after a good night's rest I would be able to discuss the matter rationally with her in the morning. But when I reached the landing, I heard a burst of laughter from the wing where Caroline had her bedroom and boudoir. Had she not gone to bed after all and was entertaining a guest in her sitting room? She had done that before with Lucy when she'd stayed overnight after a late dinner or ball.

It fell quiet again, and I turned in the direction of my own room. Then the door to Caroline's room squeaked open.

I slipped into a doorway and turned down my lamp as if I were a thief about to be caught. Caroline's silhouette, attired in a lace dressing gown, appeared in the doorway with another figure. But it wasn't Lucy. It was a man — and not Oliver.

The stranger bent his face to Caroline's and kissed her passionately. I drew back further and stifled a cry. They said something to each other but the words were indistinct, and then the man turned to walk down the hall towards the stairs. In the sliver of light coming from Caroline's room I recognised him. It was Harland!

Caroline closed the door to her bedroom and the hall was dark again. I stayed where I was, too shocked to move. My heart which had only returned to a regular rhythm a few minutes ago was now beating in a frenzy again. What I had seen couldn't be real. I had to be dreaming.

Finally, some instinct that I should move lest a maid or servant discover me took over. Bewildered and not thinking to turn up my lamp again, I put one trembling foot in front of the other and returned to my room. I shut the door behind me and stared into the darkness until my eyes ached. A grim sense of foreboding swept over me and I collapsed on the bed.

The following morning, as I dressed for breakfast, I tried to contrive some mistake in my observation to explain the tryst I had witnessed between Caroline and Harland. But in the end I had to face the upsetting truth that my sister was having an affair with her architect.

When I arrived in the dining room, Isadora was already seated at the table.

'You look tired, Aunt Emma,' she said, concern wrinkling her forehead. 'Is everything all right?'

Poor Isadora! I was sure she didn't know about her mother's affair. I placed my hand on her arm, feeling more protective of her now than ever. She was on the cusp of womanhood and becoming the mistress of her own house, and instead of supporting her Caroline was running around with Harland!

'I was up late writing, that's all,' I told her.

'How exciting,' she said, turning back to her omelette. 'The best nights are when I wake up with an idea and can pour it out into a notebook, then start work on it the next day. Despite the lack of sleep, those are the days I feel most alive.'

'Indeed,' I replied, willing myself not to let my weariness or my anger show.

I carried on as best I could through our lessons together that day, but my mind kept turning to Grace. My sister had betrayed not only her husband but her friend. I had grown fond of Grace but how could I carry on seeing her with such a terrible lie between us? Yet if I told her the truth, I feared Caroline would have me thrown out of the house.

My new dilemma far outweighed my worry about telling my sister I intended to volunteer at the settlement house. It played over and over in my mind until I couldn't stand it any more. After our harp lesson, I told Isadora that I wanted to visit Grace as she had lent me a book I wished to discuss with her. In fact, I had no idea what I would say to Grace when I saw her.

'Of course,' replied Isadora. 'I'm so glad that you two have become friends. I will take the opportunity to pay a call on Rebecca.'

The butler, Aston, showed me into the Hunters' reception room, and I came to an abrupt stop when I found Augusta Van der Heyden sitting with Grace. They were drinking tea and talking intently together.

'I'm sorry to intrude,' I told them with an apologetic smile. 'I was excited to play Grace a difficult harp piece I've mastered.'

'You're not intruding at all,' said Grace, rising to greet me. 'We were discussing the opera last night. The costumes and sets for this season's *Aida* are superb. The pageantry is impressive,

particularly the triumphal return of Radamès. You must go to
see it as soon as you can.'

Grace's grasp of my hand was affectionate but the skin
around her eyes was pinched and I caught the note of strain in
her voice. I glanced at Augusta, who smiled at me through tight
lips and absently brushed the folds of her skirt. It didn't look to
me as if they'd been discussing the opera.

A maid arrived with more tea, and after she'd left Augusta
turned to me. 'The harp accompaniment in the consecration
scene was most effective. I would be interested in your thoughts
after you have heard it.'

I glimpsed Grace's copy of *Laelius De Amicitia* on a side
table: *A true friend is honest, outspoken and caring.* When I
picked up my teacup my hand trembled, and as much as I tried
to control myself, tears burned my eyes.

Grace peered at me. 'You know, don't you, Emma? You've
found out about Caroline and Harland and you came here
to tell me?' Hearing the gentle tone of her voice, someone
witnessing the scene might have believed that it was my
husband who was being unfaithful and that Grace was
comforting *me*.

'You already know about them?' I asked her.

The slightest frown flickered across her forehead. She averted
her eyes.

Augusta tutted. 'I told you they were becoming reckless,
Grace. Until now, only a select few were aware of their liaison,
but last night even May Satterfield asked me if the rumours
were true. And who tells *her* anything?'

Grace nodded. 'Oliver has noticed their lack of discretion as
well. He is worried about what it means for Isadora. Instead
of admiring her entry into society, everyone will be gossiping
about her mother's behaviour.'

'Oliver knows?' I asked. I was feeling increasingly foolish.
I had thought I'd stumbled across some terrible secret, but

it was apparent that I was one of the last to know about my sister's affair.

Augusta raised her eyebrows. 'Of course he knows. But such affairs can be accepted as long as everything is arranged quietly and no one oversteps the rules of good taste. I'm afraid Caroline is losing her head.'

She sounded as if she was quoting from a rule book — perhaps one she'd written herself. I remembered the bleak tenement buildings she owned on the Lower East Side and wondered how she reconciled her mightier-than-thou attitude with her exploitation of desperate people.

Grace took my hand. 'You are a good friend, Emma. It was a risk for you to come here today to tell me.'

I stared at my lap. 'I don't know what to say,' I whispered. 'I'm so ashamed of Caroline.'

'I don't blame Caroline,' Grace said with a shrug. 'She's a victim to Harland's diabolical charm, as I was, and all the other women he's broken over the years. And believe me, there have been many.'

'Many?' I echoed, horrified.

Grace's expression was fatalistic. 'Emma, my marriage to Harland was a sham from the beginning. He was the most adoring suitor any woman could hope for, but on our wedding night, after the guests had left, he turned into a different person. He announced that I was not his type and he had never loved me. Then, not even waiting for me to recover from the shock of that declaration, he went on to say that while he was prepared to play the part of a loving husband publicly, he intended to continue to see whoever he wished.'

Grace was beautiful and elegant. What did Harland mean that she wasn't his type? Then again, she was also educated, gentle, moral and cultured, so perhaps there was truth in the statement.

'Why did he marry you?' I asked her.

'For her name and her money,' Augusta answered on Grace's behalf. 'Both could open doors for him. It was the same with me. He uses people.'

'I'm living with a stranger,' Grace added. 'The man I thought I'd married never existed. He was a fabrication created by Harland to snare me.'

'So why not divorce him?' I asked.

Grace shook her head. 'It would kill my mother; she's already in frail health. She's also a strict Catholic and turned away her own sister along with her two young nephews after her sister got a divorce from a violent man. My mother would feel compelled to disown me, and I'm all she has left. I don't care what Harland and Caroline do as long as the rumours don't reach my mother's ears. She thinks Harland is the perfect son-in-law.'

I imagined him turning on the charm for the elderly lady, bringing her flowers and books while appearing devoted to Grace.

'I was young and desirable when I met Harland,' she went on, 'and I had many richer suitors. But I thought he was fun and carefree and life with him would be a merry affair. How wrong I was.'

'Life can still be merry,' I prompted gently. 'It's not too late. Surely your mother would come to understand.'

'The only way I'll ever be rid of Harland,' Grace said, meeting my gaze, 'is if he dies. If I try to imagine the future I can't see anything. He has destroyed me inside.'

'Harland is like a vampire who sucks the life blood out of you and discards you when he's finished,' Augusta added. 'Yet we go on, as the living dead.'

'You are both well-educated and cultured women with positions in society,' I protested. 'How could you be the living dead? It's only that Harland has convinced you of it. At least Caroline is strong enough to stand up to him. She will destroy him before she'll let him destroy her.'

'Nobody can outsmart Harland,' Augusta replied. 'He studies people for a long time. Believe me, he will be aware of Caroline's Achilles heel, whatever it may be. People assumed I would swat Harland away like an annoying mosquito once I saw him for the upstart he was. But he swatted *me* aside.'

'Why is he so intent on destroying people?' I asked. 'It's one thing to be a careless cad, quite another to be a predator.'

'After his father lost the family's fortune, Harland was snubbed by society,' Grace explained. 'He had to take a job in a men's suit store to put food on the table and felt enormous humiliation. He's been intent on revenge ever since.'

'Much of this is my fault,' said Augusta. 'I raised him up from the dust. I should have left him there.'

'If it wasn't you, he would have found somebody else to do it,' Grace told her. 'But I'm worried for Caroline — she might be his most ambitious target yet. He's pleased with the idea of making a cuckold of one of the most powerful men in the country.'

But it wasn't for Caroline that I feared. My sister was indomitable. Taking her on would be like attacking an iron-clad warship. But her 'Achilles heel' might be her sweet and sensitive daughter.

TWENTY-THREE

When I was worried about something, reading with intense concentration was often a good way to restore my calm. While Isadora and Mr Gadley worked on a sculpture, I absorbed myself in an article in *New York City Magazine* about Newport, Rhode Island, the seaside town where New York's rich went in summer to escape the city's oppressive humidity.

During summer the atmosphere is soft, balmy and refreshingly tinged with salt. The prevailing breeze is southerly and brings with it air cooled by leagues of water. The natural beauty of the town gives way to artifice as one travels along Bellevue Avenue. Stone walls and tall gates open onto sweeping driveways lined with beech and pine trees that artistically frame the mansions beyond them. It's Fifth Avenue by the sea, with an array of European-style palazzos, chateaux and manor houses.

Seacliff, the Hopper family's 'holiday cottage', is the most astonishing in terms of grandeur. A shimmering white Italianate palace on eleven acres of lawn with the sapphire waters of the Atlantic as its backdrop, it is set on the highest point of Bellevue Avenue. The cliffs that edge the perfect lawns drop dangerously to the ocean below. The gardens are bordered by carefully clipped

privet hedges and exotic trees and shrubs, and the air is
heady with the sweet fragrance of the hundreds of roses
that line the drive.

After passing through a grand porte-cochère, *and*
entering the glass and wrought-iron doors of the great
hall, one is immediately taken by the marble walls
and Ionic pilasters adorned with sculptured reliefs of
mermaids and fish. A twin staircase of Caen stone leads
up to a landing, where a tall arched window reveals a
view of the ocean.

From there one's gaze travels up to the immense
ormolu and crystal chandelier and white coffered ceiling,
its entire expanse dotted with silver stars. The effect is
light and airy and one can almost hear the strains of
heavenly harps ...

I breathed in sharply. The house sounded magnificent. Was
Caroline truly intending to abandon it for an even grander one?
Where would her excess and ambition stop?

The foul odours and horrors I'd seen in the tenements on the
Lower East Side rose in my mind. The glory that was Seacliff
had been built on the suffering of New York's poor.

Woodford entered the studio, rousing me from my musing.
'Miss Lacasse, Her Grace, the Duchess of Dorset has come to
call. Mrs Hopper requests that you join them.'

Lucy came to the house regularly, and Caroline only asked
me to take part in their conversations when she wanted
something of me. What was it now? Or was I being summoned
because Caroline had found out I'd gone to see Grace to tell her
about Harland?

Both women smiled at me as I entered the room, so I knew
the reason for the summons couldn't be my visit to Grace.

'We're having an *English* afternoon tea,' said Caroline,
gesturing towards the table. 'Lucy brought everything.'

An array of silver platters were adorned with sandwiches, shortbread, tiny meringues and preserved ginger. Lucy herself measured out the tea leaves and added them to the pot. After a few minutes she nodded to Woodford to pour the tea into rosebud-patterned cups that were so fine they were almost translucent.

Caroline watched the operation with fascination. 'I do like the way the English do things. It's as if everything is a ritual that has been practised to perfection.'

I shifted in my seat. What had brought about this sudden fascination with England? Now that I had discovered my sister was having an affair, I found myself questioning everything she said.

She smiled at me. 'Things have taken an exciting turn! A remarkable opportunity has presented itself for Isadora's happiness.' She nodded to Lucy to explain.

'The Duke of Bridgewater is here in New York,' Lucy said. 'I've had my eye on him for some time, and now that he's out of mourning for his father and has inherited the title, he has written to ask me to assist in finding him a suitable American wife. He was very keen when I wrote to him about Isadora. For a long time it was expected that he would marry his childhood friend Lady Mariam, daughter of the Earl of Essex, but now the Duke is responsible for his various estates and the beautiful Lyndale Palace, he will be pressed financially. Lyndale is held in entail, which means he cannot sell or mortgage any part of it, so he will need to marry a bride with a substantial dowry — and of course he is eager to produce a son and heir.'

I waited for Lucy to describe why this young man would be a good match for Isadora in temperament or interests, but she had finished speaking. I glanced at Caroline, expecting her to baulk at the idea of someone whose only interest in Isadora was her money.

But my sister nodded enthusiastically. 'Quite understandable. His family heritage is at stake.' She turned to me. 'The Duke is coming here for dinner tomorrow night. Before word gets out about his visit, we must make sure he is impressed by Isadora. I will seat her next to him, but I need you nearby to supervise, Emma. I don't want her to say anything silly and she's more confident in your presence.'

I eyed her levelly, rankled by her comment. In the last few months Isadora had matured beautifully. All it had taken was for her to be able to express herself and have someone take an interest in her.

'I don't think there's any risk of that,' I said. 'Her poise at her debutante ball was much admired.'

Lucy waved her hand as if to dismiss my comment. 'That's true, but she can still be a little … *odd*. The American heiresses who successfully break into English society are those who can adapt quickly to the British way of life. We don't want Isadora doing anything to ruin her chances.'

'The right suitor will recognise Isadora's good qualities,' I protested. 'She is honest, kind, intelligent and witty.'

Caroline flicked her eyes upward. 'Oh, Emma! We can't let this opportunity pass us by. The London season is fiercely competitive, much more so than New York. Isadora wouldn't be able to compete in that environment. Here we have a chance for the Duke to meet her before all the other mothers find out he is available. Tomorrow night is of great importance for Isadora's future happiness. Simply nothing can go wrong!'

'But there were so many nice young men at Isadora's ball,' I said. 'If the Duke doesn't find her to his liking, I'm certain there will be someone among them more suited to her.'

Caroline raised an eyebrow. 'Who do you mean?' she asked testily. 'One of the frivolous Potter or Graham boys? No one from any of the important old families has shown any interest in her. The Duke has a title, a name and a history. No one in New York can offer Isadora that.'

I suspected the reason none of the old New York families were putting their sons forward to court Isadora had more to do with rumours about Caroline's behaviour than my niece's personality.

'There are only twenty-seven dukes in the entire United Kingdom,' Lucy added. 'Isadora would be doing so much better than a lowly viscount or lord.'

'A title and a grand country house in England is the stuff of dreams,' said Caroline. 'And we need you to help make Isadora ready to take up her role as a duchess.'

The stuff of Caroline's dreams perhaps, but not my niece's. I remembered Isadora telling me how doors that had been shut to Lucy because of her background had been flung wide open when she became a duchess. Was this evaluation of the Duke about Isadora's marital happiness at all, or purely my sister's ambition?

❧❦❧

As I dressed for dinner the following evening, I tried to allay my fears that Isadora might be forced into a marriage that was unsuited to her; and also resolved to reserve any judgements about the Duke until I met him. He might turn out to be an amiable man, and the headaches, nausea and anxiety I had suffered all day would have been for nothing.

Isadora had simply been told we had an aristocratic guest for dinner. I hadn't wanted to make her nervous by revealing the true purpose of the evening. When I met her at the door to her room, I was filled with pride: she was more beautiful than ever. She wore a white crêpe de Chine Empire-style gown trimmed with fringed ruching. Her hair was styled in elegant waves on top of her head and decorated with a pearl headband. Caroline and Lucy had implied Isadora was odd and awkward, but if anything went wrong tonight it would not be my niece's doing.

We arrived in the salon to find, as well as Caroline, Lucy and Oliver, three young men and a slim girl with auburn hair. I hoped the blond gentleman with the warm brown eyes was the Duke of Bridgewater, or perhaps the distinguished young man with the high cheekbones and dimpled chin, but to my dismay it was the gauntest and palest of the three who carried the title. The blond man was Lord Randolph, the Duke's younger brother, and the other man was his friend, Charles Whitlock. The young woman was the Duke's sixteen-year-old sister, Lady Clara.

The Duke's nose was long and straight above a wispy moustache, and his thin lips formed only the barest of smiles when Lucy introduced Isadora and me to him.

'Welcome to New York,' said Isadora cheerfully. 'What brings you to the city at this time of year? It must be as cold here as it is in England, and just as foggy too.'

'We've come for the Madison Square Garden automobile parade,' answered Lord Randolph. 'We are all motor car enthusiasts, including Lady Clara here.'

'Well, I've only mastered a small gasoline runabout so far, but I'm learning,' the young woman said, smiling shyly at Isadora.

While Clara was pretty, she wasn't wearing an expensive gown by Worth like my niece. Her silk voile dinner dress wasn't the latest fashion and the lace around the neckline was slightly worn, but it wasn't in Isadora's nature to care about such things.

Instead, she sat down next to Lady Clara and said, 'I should very much like to learn to drive a motor car. Is it difficult?'

'Not at all,' replied Lady Clara.

From the way the two young women chatted together, I sensed a friendship had sprung up between them.

After a pre-dinner sherry, during which Lord Randolph and Mr Whitlock regarded Isadora with admiration, while the Duke studied her with a cooler, more appraising eye, we moved to the dining room. A twelve-course dinner of hare soup, plovers' eggs, roast beef, turkey in aspic, pigeon pie, grouse, snipe, partridge, pheasant and woodcock was served. They were all English dishes and I wondered why Caroline hadn't given the guests a typical Manhattan society dinner of turtle soup and lobster. Was the Duke one of those people who refused to eat 'foreign food'?

I studied him, desperate to find something admirable that would reassure me he would be a good match for Isadora. Did he have a steady and constant heart beneath that cool exterior? Was he well-educated? Did he appreciate art and especially sculpture? Was he a model landlord, known for his goodness to his tenants? But try as I might I found nothing outstanding or charismatic about him. All I could discern was a tremendous air of entitlement.

It was Lord Randolph who kept up the conversation. 'All three of us have De Dion-Boutons,' he said, indicating his brother and Mr Whitlock. 'But we're hoping to purchase an American racing car while we're here.'

'The American car industry is gaining momentum,' Oliver told him, 'but the few people who are driving here have European cars. My wife and I both have Daimlers now. In my opinion, they are the finest cars manufactured yet.'

I thought of Angus Dempsy and shivered. How could Oliver speak so easily of motor cars after what he'd done? Did he truly feel no remorse at all for killing a man?

'We competed in the Hudson Valley obstacle course last year and enjoyed ourselves immensely,' Caroline told the guests. 'The Daimlers are easier to manoeuvre than the De Dion-Boutons.'

'You see, Charles,' Lord Randolph said with a wink to Mr Whitlock, 'this is a civilised and modern country!' Turning to us he explained, 'My dear friend imagined all Americans lived on plantations and spent their time fighting off Red Indians and stampeding buffaloes.'

Mr Whitlock took a sip of wine. 'Perhaps it was the terrifying painting my aunt had in her library of Major Patrick Ferguson being shot from his horse during the American Revolution.'

Lucy threw back her head and laughed. 'Well, I can assure you we are not savages, Mr Whitlock.'

'That is obvious from the present company,' he replied, glancing at Isadora. 'But it is astounding what impressions we carry from childhood.'

'My ancestors fought the French, but that doesn't stop me enjoying champagne,' said the Duke, cutting into his partridge pie.

It could have been an amusing comment but it was delivered with a note of irritation that instantly dampened Lord Randolph's and Mr Whitlock's high mood, which I sensed it was intended to do.

Turning to Isadora, the Duke asked her in French if she knew much about the conflicts between England and France. Although she wasn't as fluent in French as she was in Italian, she answered that she had read some interesting books on the Norman Conquest and the Anglo-French Wars, but knew much more about English art and greatly admired Gainsborough.

It was quite a complicated subject and I beamed with pride at how much Isadora's French had improved from our lessons together. It was near perfect — but not perfect enough for the Duke.

'You pronounce French very well,' he told her in English, 'but your vocabulary is rather basic. You should read more books in French. That would help.'

Isadora's gaze dropped to her dinner plate. She was crestfallen. I wanted to kick the Duke under the table. He was no better than Caroline and Lucy in his patronising superiority towards her.

'I've never been good at foreign languages,' Lord Randolph told her cheerfully. 'I'm as thick as a plank. That little exchange sounded most impressive to me.'

'Randolph is very modest,' Lady Clara said, smiling at her brother. 'He excelled in his studies in law at Oxford rather than wasting his time there as many other young gentlemen do.' Turning to me, she asked, 'Is it true you are a writer, Miss Lacasse? That sounds terribly exciting.'

'I write mainly mystery and fantasy stories,' I told her. 'I'm currently working on a novel.'

Lord Randolph put down his fork. 'I should very much like to read your stories, Miss Lacasse. Are you published in English?'

It was impossible not to like Lord Randolph, I thought, as I answered his question. I would be much happier if Caroline and Lucy were trying to match him with Isadora rather than his sullen brother, but as a second son Lord Randolph had no title, and wouldn't as long as his brother remained alive. A title was what Caroline wanted most.

After the guests had left, and Oliver and Isadora had retired to bed, Caroline and Lucy called me into the library.

'Well, what's your impression of the Duke?' Caroline asked me, her eyes shining.

I was sure she'd already made up her mind, but for Isadora's sake I was compelled to speak up. 'His brother and sister are nice. But the Duke himself is rather dour.'

'Dour?' repeated Caroline, pulling at her earlobe. 'No, I think he is merely serious. And a bit of seriousness in a young man isn't a terrible fault.'

'He has a lot of responsibility on his shoulders,' added Lucy. 'He's only twenty-five and yet he's inherited one of the largest duchies in the United Kingdom. Lord Randolph can be carefree because he has none of his brother's burdens.'

Caroline nodded as if Lucy's observation should assuage any misgivings I had about the Duke's personality.

'It also pays to remember that Englishmen don't *need* women the way American men do,' Lucy continued. 'They are self-reliant and often not expressive in their emotions. It's best to compare them to a solid rock: a person who can be relied upon.'

Caroline clapped her hands together. 'The Duke is sounding more suitable for Isadora by the minute.'

By contrast, I was growing more afraid for Isadora by the minute. Later, when Caroline and I were making our way up to our rooms, I tried again.

'Caroline, have you consulted with Isadora about any of this? Do you know what *she* wants from her marriage?'

She stopped walking and stared at me. 'Isadora is too young to know what she wants. If I asked her, she would say it was to make sculptures all day with Mr Gadley!' She shook her head. 'It is a mother's role to make these decisions for her daughter. You don't know that because you don't have a daughter for whom you are responsible.'

She kissed me goodnight and turned along the corridor towards her room, leaving me stunned at the top of the stairs. Had Caroline intended her comment to sting as badly as it had?

I puzzled over her lost son, William, and how she had grieved over his death. Isadora was Caroline's only child now. Didn't she want to keep her daughter — and her future grandchildren — near to her? Once again, I was at a loss to understand my sister.

❧❧❧

The next day, I confided my worries to Grace while we walked in Central Park.

'Well, unless Caroline gets that marriage announcement out soon, the Duke might indeed be snapped up by somebody else,' she said with a wry smile. 'Young American heiresses are crazy about European titles in a way my generation never was. If you have worries about the Duke's personality, take comfort in the knowledge that a pushier girl than Isadora might snatch him.'

'Caroline is pushy enough for the both of them.'

'That's true,' she said. 'But many of the transatlantic marriages are organised by skilled brokers in London. One of them may already have someone in mind for the Duke.'

We stopped to watch a pair of squirrels scamper across the snow and race up a tree.

'The English mothers can't be happy about all these American women coming to steal the titled men they had marked out for their daughters from birth,' I said.

'Not happy at all, I imagine. But what can they do? The decline in England's rural economy has left most of the landed gentry on the verge of ruin. They view cashed-up American heiresses hungering for the status of a British title as an opportunity to save their beloved estates and preserve their family names.' Grace linked her arm with mine to guide me out of the way of two small children gliding down the slope on a toboggan. 'While the Duke may be dour, at least there are no rumours to suggest he's a degenerate — unlike the Prince of Wales and the Marlborough set.' She cast her eyes down. 'Besides, it's often said that arranged marriages work out better in the long run than those made for love. The couple involved have much more realistic expectations of each other.'

I knew she was referring to her own marriage and put my hand on her shoulder to console her.

She drew a measured breath and continued. 'You could consider it as an opportunity for Isadora: she would be closer to you in Paris and far away from Caroline's control. And the women in England aren't idle like we are here. They're expected to be involved in philanthropic activities and to assist the political responsibilities of their husbands. Isadora might come into her own.'

Perhaps England would give Isadora a chance to be independent. But I couldn't shake my fears that the Duke might make her miserable.

'I get the impression that he's one of those people who can't be questioned,' I told Grace. 'And if you disagree with him, he'll get up and leave the room.'

Her good humour returned and she winked at me. 'That could work out well for Isadora if ever she wanted to rid herself of him for a while!'

The idea of Isadora manipulating the Duke that way amused me. 'She's smart, but she's not that ruthless.'

Grace's expression turned dark again. 'None of us are at that age. Ruthlessness is something marriage teaches us.'

TWENTY-FOUR

My first harp recital at Charles Garrett House was for a gathering of deserted wives. After Florence had set me up with a chair and Cecilia had introduced me, I commenced Debussy's *Rêverie*. As I played, I glanced up now and then at the careworn faces of my audience. Some of the women's hands were blistered and raw from their work in factories and as cleaners. One woman looked like her nose had been broken in two places; a parting gift from her husband perhaps? I was moved to see how the music gradually transformed the women's demeanours: their shoulders relaxed and smiles came to their lips. I now understood what Cecilia had been trying to explain to me: that these downtrodden people *needed* beauty to make them feel alive again after their spirits had been deadened by drudgery and the horror of their surroundings.

My mind flashed to Cecilia's latest article on the exploitation of workers in New York City, which I'd read on my way to the recital:

> *After the sacrifice of the Civil War, it seems that all that*
> *has been achieved is a new type of slavery. The hostility of*
> *unions towards female workers makes their burden even*
> *more onerous and puts them completely at the mercy of*
> *men like Oliver Hopper, the richest man in America ...*

That my family was contributing to the suffering of the women in front of me filled me with shame. How was it that Caroline was so unconflicted about her obscene wealth and the source of it? Why couldn't she look beyond herself and feel empathy for others?

'That was sublime,' said Florence when I'd finished. 'It's so often overlooked how a simple act of kindness can transform the life of someone in need. I haven't seen joy in some of these women's eyes for months, and you stirred it in them, Emma.'

I was touched by Florence's kind words but still felt my contribution to have been inadequate. It was Caroline who had the real power to change these women's lives, yet she would never do it.

While Florence and Cecilia laid out a supper of fruit cake and custard, I spoke to some of the women.

'It would have been better if he'd divorced me,' a mother with a baby in her arms told me. 'Then at least I'd be free to find myself another man. I can't get any help from the charities — too many people take advantage of them, lying that they've been deserted when their husband's still at home.'

Although it was a dishonest thing to do, I couldn't blame people for it when they were desperate and couldn't make enough money to feed themselves and their children.

The other women told similar stories, but it was Hadassah's situation that disturbed me the most. She was younger than me, but her hair was grey and her skin was as wrinkled as a walnut. She worked in a factory during the day and finished blouses for another factory when she returned home at night. Astonishingly, her husband still lived with her. She openly admitted it, and none of the other women reproved her for claiming to have been deserted. I wondered why.

'Hadassah's husband is an idler,' Florence explained to me later. 'He is happy for Hadassah to work herself into nervous exhaustion while he sits in a café reading newspapers. He says it was her decision to come to the United States, and it was a bad one, so she's the one who has to make things better.'

'But they're Russian Jews, aren't they?' I asked. 'They *had* to flee for their lives. They had no choice.'

Cecilia shrugged. 'There is no logic to the arguments given by an abusive husband.'

'Can't she throw him out?'

'Unfortunately not. Jewish divorce law is stacked in his favour.'

At the end of the evening, while Florence, Cecilia and I were cleaning the dishes, Florence asked me what I thought of the women I'd met.

'It makes me appreciate how fortunate I am to have Claude,' I told them. 'I can't imagine being trapped by a man who abuses you then deserts you.'

'By the way, you must be proud of Claude,' said Florence, handing me a plate to dry. 'I haven't been to his exhibition yet because I've been preparing for my own, but do tell him I'll see him early next week. The review in the *New York Times* was very enthusiastic.'

I stared at the plate in my hand. A strange numbness started in my toes and spread up the backs of my legs, locking me in the moment so I couldn't move. Claude was here in New York and hadn't told me? Florence must be wrong. She had to be. I couldn't fathom that Claude could have come to New York and not written to me.

'Are you all right, Emma?'

I looked Florence in the eyes. She didn't believe it was possible either. That's why she'd assumed I knew.

'Claude didn't tell me,' I began.

'About the review?' she said with a grin. 'It's not like him to be so shy.' She walked into the pantry and came out with a newspaper. 'I've got a copy here. Take it.'

❦❦❦❦

My heart pounded as I approached the art gallery on Lexington Avenue where the exhibition was being held. Through the glass doors I saw dozens of paintings set against red-ochre walls.

A bell tinkled as I entered, and a man with white hair stood up from behind a desk to welcome me. He was an American, not Claude's dealer, Maignat.

'You have an interest in French paintings?' he asked. 'This is a special exhibition of France's younger, more progressive artists.'

'I am a friend of Claude Tremblay,' I told him.

I immediately recognised some of Claude's paintings and moved towards them. The open-air landscapes, the social scenes, the detailed portraits with their intriguing facial expressions — everything brimmed with life.

'There are more here,' said the dealer, leading me to another wall.

Claude had been prolific! And now I had an explanation for his silence, for this amount of work would have taken intense concentration.

My eyes moved from a painting of two men in a rowing boat to one of a young woman with clear blue eyes, dark straight eyebrows and a well-defined chin. The portrait was exceptional for its immediate impression of freshness and the purity of its colours, but it was the radiance of the subject that was most captivating. The girl looked directly out of the painting at the viewer. She was somebody who knew what she wanted.

'Who is she?' I asked the gallery owner. 'She's very pretty.'

'She's a milliner who wants to be a painter. Her name is Lise. She models in return for lessons.'

I nodded. 'Did some of the artists come to New York for the exhibition?'

His answer sent a sharp pain through me. 'Yes, they are all here. They arrived a fortnight ago.' He indicated a staircase at the back of the gallery. 'Would you like to meet some of them?'

At first I hardly understood what he had said. A fortnight ago? Why hadn't Claude told me he was coming to New York? Why hadn't he invited me to the opening? Was he hoping to surprise me?

I went upstairs, but didn't recognise any of the artists who were sitting around a table drinking coffee. They were eager to have the opportunity to discuss New York with another French person.

'American collectors are different to Europeans,' said a dark-haired artist with a pencil moustache. 'Americans buy because something appeals to them, not because they expect the painting will appreciate in value.'

'They're happy to purchase something and consider it a loss,' agreed one of his colleagues. 'I like that attitude. They appreciate art for what it really is.'

I tried to follow their excited chatter but my mind was foggy. 'Do you know where Claude is this afternoon?' I finally managed to ask.

'He and some of the others went to the Metropolitan Museum of Art,' answered the artist with the moustache.

'What time will he be back?'

'Everybody will be here for the evening exhibition, which begins at eight o'clock. You are welcome to return then, or I can leave him a message.'

'I'll return,' I replied.

When I walked out into the winter sunshine, the streets were full of New Yorkers rushing here and there in a purposeful manner but my whole world had turned to slow motion. I deliberated over going to the Metropolitan Museum of Art myself, and trying to find Claude there.

At that moment, I heard his laugh. 'One day our art will be in that museum too!' he said.

I spun around to see him approaching the gallery. Our gazes met in instant recognition. The beauty of those eyes was deeply familiar to me, but something in their expression had shifted. My body turned rigid, as if girding itself to face some ill.

I glanced at the girl who was clinging to his arm, not in a friendly way but as a lover. She was the girl from the picture: Lise.

'Emma!' Claude cried. 'What are you doing here? I didn't expect to see you.'

His voice was high and tight; not the warm voice that used to send tingles down my spine. It was the voice of a man speaking to a distant acquaintance rather than his beloved.

My voice too seemed to be coming from far away. 'You didn't tell me you were in New York. I read about the exhibition in the newspaper.'

My palms were sweating, drenching my gloves. All the plans, hopes and dreams I'd held for years were pouring out of me through my skin.

'I'm Lise,' the girl said, giving me a vivacious smile. She was even prettier in real life than in the painting. Everything about her was vivid, from her sparkling eyes to the big red bow she wore around her neck. She was young too, no more than eighteen.

'You must be the Emma they talk about in the café in Montmartre,' she went on. 'You've been here in New York a while, haven't you? You must love it here. It's so exciting!'

You stopped writing, Claude. Why did you stop writing? I wanted to say the words aloud but my lips wouldn't open. I had been shocked into silence. The answer was standing in front of me, wearing a red bow and chatting incessantly.

In *A Tale of a Lonely House*, when my character Genevieve succumbs to the poison her husband has given her, she sees her body being taken away by the undertaker, and is surprised to find herself still sitting in an armchair by the fire. That was the sensation I experienced now: I was observing a scene I was strangely no longer part of.

'Your paintings are superb, Claude,' I managed to get out, as if we were neighbours having a friendly exchange on the street.

Lise kissed Claude's cheek. 'I'm very proud of him. He's been working hard.'

My mind was jumping all over the place. It went from watching Lise kiss Claude's cheek and trying to interpret the meaning of it, to thinking about *A Tale of a Lonely House*. I should never have written that story in first person. Genevieve had welcomed Theron into her life and held nothing back from him, not her heart, not her home, not her fortune. And she had paid for that mistake with her life. Theron wasn't a man to be trusted, but how could she have known that? He had been so loving. So kind. So *perfect*.

Claude swallowed. 'And you, Emma ... have you been well? Is everything going to plan for your life here in New York?'

He stared at me as if expecting an answer to a question I didn't understand. I had no idea how to answer. Nothing was going to plan. It was all chaos. My brother-in-law was a murderer more or less, my sister an adulteress, and my niece a pawn in a terrible game. And the one person I had trusted as my rock had dissolved into sand.

The world came crashing down on me like an enormous wave. I turned and hurried away. Claude called after me but I couldn't hear what he said through the blood thumping in my ears.

I had written about betrayal in my stories many times, but had never managed to describe it as precisely as I now felt it. A fog of hopelessness? A river of tears? Hands desperately digging into the dirt to try to stop yourself falling off a cliff? None of those metaphors came close to capturing it. I only knew that betrayal wasn't something I had ever expected to feel with Claude. I had been faithful to him for five years, and now he had found someone else.

It took all my courage even to sit up in bed the following morning. All I could see before me was emptiness.

If I'd had a choice I would have stayed in my room all day, trying to determine when my relationship with Claude had come to an end and why. There had been no harsh words in our letters, no ill feeling between us. It was true that we couldn't agree on the question of marriage, but if that were the reason surely Claude would have had the decency to write and explain his change of heart?

Maybe this is how a man deserts one woman for another, I thought. He simply picks up his coat and hat and walks out the door. No explanation, no letter, nothing.

I turned to the photograph of Grand-maman on the escritoire. 'What shall I do?' I asked her. 'Something inside me has died.'

My heart was broken, but I couldn't let my grandmother down. She wouldn't want me to give in to despair. She'd always said: 'God is more interested in our character than our comfort.' I knew she would want me to take my heartache and use it to improve myself in some way.

When Jennie came into the room half an hour later to help me into my first glorious outfit for the day, I put on a brave face and smiled cheerfully. The maid would have had no idea of the utter despair in my heart. I was alive and breathing, but I was crushed. Yet I was determined that nobody should know it.

Two days later, I was again summoned to join Caroline and Lucy in the drawing room.

Caroline was aglow with excitement. 'Lucy, tell Emma what has taken place!'

'I have the most pleasing news,' Lucy said, clasping her hands. 'Lady Clara called on me to say the Duke has invited us all to Lyndale. It seems Isadora has quite charmed him.'

'The Duke is very proud of his home,' Caroline explained for my benefit. 'He must want to find out whether Isadora will fit in there.' She stood and paced the room, her delight turning to ambition. 'This London season must be the most spectacular of all. I will write immediately to Worth in Paris and arrange some fittings. Isadora has to look glorious.'

She came to a stop in front of me. 'You must come with us, Emma. The Duke wasn't very impressed with Isadora's French — you must make her try harder. Speaking French fluently is important among the English aristocracy.'

I suspected the Duke would have found fault with Isadora's French even if it had been her native language. Still, I was keen to know what life on a grand English estate was like and to help my niece in any way I could. And perhaps seeing England for the first time would help me forget what had happened with Claude. I needed to keep moving. Every pause, every moment of reflection was a blade jabbing into my heart.

Lucy shook her head. 'We can't wait until the London season, Caroline. The Duke and his companions are sailing back to England tomorrow. We must follow as soon as possible *before* the season begins. You forget that there are only two dukes in the United Kingdom currently eligible for marriage — and the other one is sixty years old!'

'But the season here isn't quite finished, and we must have time to prepare,' said Caroline, twisting the rings on her fingers anxiously. 'Isadora only has her gowns from last year. She needs an entire new wardrobe.'

'I wouldn't be worried about her clothes,' replied Lucy. 'An English father would never spend thousands of dollars at Worth or Paquin on a daughter. It's not English girls we have to be concerned about. It's Permelia Frances.'

Caroline's eyebrows knitted into a frown. 'What has she got to do with anything?'

'A friend of mine in London has informed me that Permelia Frances has been making enquiries about the Duke through a famous society matchmaker. Apparently her younger sister Vivien is exceptionally beautiful and witty to match. Darling Isadora may not be able to outshine her.'

Caroline's entire body stiffened. 'Then I will summon Woodford now and tell him to arrange our passage.'

TWENTY-FIVE

The steamship we travelled on to Europe was luxuriously appointed. There was a Viennese-style café on the bridge deck where we ate apple strudel and drank black coffee served in glasses with whipped cream. In the ladies' parlour, we sat on velvet divans under an enormous oil painting of Princess Margaret of Prussia. My cabin suite was decorated in carved walnut with leaf motifs, and big enough to allow my harp to travel with me.

When we arrived in London, I was surprised to find it very different from Paris or New York. The air was smoky and dirty, and the houses along the railway line were drab, but when we reached Victoria Station there was no doubt we had entered the heart of the greatest empire in the world. The whole place seemed to be bustling with people from the four corners of the world: Australia and New Zealand, Canada, Africa, India and China.

Not long after our train had pulled into the platform and its passengers were disembarking, another train arrived — a private one. From it emerged an Indian maharajah wearing a turban decorated with pearls and sapphires. Five wives came after him, bedecked in chiffon saris and tikas with jewelled drops. A small army of servants busied themselves unloading at least one hundred pieces of Louis Vuitton luggage.

A stately carriage with a coachman, a footman and a pair of Cleveland Bay horses was waiting for us at the station entrance. The footman took our luggage and then helped us into the carriage. The rest of our things would arrive later with Caroline's and Lucy's lady's maids.

On our way to Mayfair we drove past Buckingham Palace and its gardens. I was awe-struck by the grandeur of the neoclassical building; and also by the Georgian magnificence of Apsley House, which Lucy informed us had been the London home of the first Duke of Wellington. Layers of history and tradition seemed to emanate from the buildings and streets, as if they were living things. Paris was the more beautiful and feminine city, I decided, while London was stately, imposing and masculine.

The sombre brown exterior of Lucy's residence belied the luxurious décor inside. A butler ushered us into a great hall that must have been at least a hundred and twenty feet high from floor to ceiling. A grand stone stairway occupied the centre of the hall and opened up to a gallery on the first floor. My eyes drank in the velvet-covered walls, the Brussels and Flemish tapestries and the magnificent eighteenth-century painting of a woman playing a harp.

A maid accompanied me to my room, unpacked my bag and informed me that afternoon tea would be served in the drawing room at five o'clock. She curtsied and left, and the room fell into an eerie quiet.

I stared at the walnut bed with its elaborate cornice and scrollwork and its flame finials. 'This is England,' I said, sitting down in a tapestry-upholstered chair.

It should have been a thrilling moment for a writer, but for some reason, I was filled with dread.

We met for pre-dinner drinks that evening in an L-shaped drawing room where the sideboard was covered with photographs in silver frames surmounted by coronets. I recognised the portraits of the Prince and Princess of Wales.

An elderly man tottered in, and Lucy introduced him as her husband, the Duke of Dorset. With his stooped posture and balding pate he wasn't at all what I had pictured. I'd imagined Lucy had been swept off her feet by a dashing aristocrat like the smouldering, romantic figures Adriaen Hanneman painted. The Duke of Dorset was at least twenty years older than his wife, and his red-rimmed eyes and pouched cheeks gave him a startling resemblance to a basset hound. I thanked God that at least the Duke of Bridgewater was much closer in age to Isadora than Lucy was to her husband.

'It is a pleasure to meet you, Miss Lacasse,' the Duke said, covering me in his stale breath. 'Should I drop off to sleep during dinner, I hope you will kindly nudge me. The preliminary parliamentary meetings were particularly tedious today.'

'Where do you think Lucy's children are?' Isadora whispered to me as we mounted the stairs to our rooms afterwards, behind Caroline and Lucy. 'I was hoping to meet them.'

I had wondered that myself. 'Perhaps the English truly do believe that children should be seen and not heard,' I whispered back.

Isadora rolled her eyes. 'But in this case we haven't even seen them. Have you heard the saying "An heir and a spare"? Apparently that's all English nobles want wives for: to produce an heir and another son in case the first one dies. After that, they leave their wives alone.'

Our eyes met and I knew for certain now that Isadora had guessed what this trip was about.

Caroline turned to look at us, suspicious of our whispering. When I entered my room, she followed me, wandering around and examining the bed and chairs as if she were there merely to admire the decoration.

Finally, she said, 'You remember our agreement, don't you, Emma?' She was smiling, but the menacing tone was unmistakable. 'When Isadora is married, I will pay off your debts so you may keep Grand-maman's apartment and look after Paulette. Don't let anything go wrong now. The debt collectors won't be kept at bay forever.'

Caroline wasn't one for mincing words and I knew her threat was real. I had managed to forget my money worries while living in her world, but unless I obeyed my sister's wishes, they would be waiting for me exactly where I'd left them.

I shuddered when I recalled Monsieur Ferat, so gentlemanly, so proper — and so truly frightening. I would have been less scared of a thug.

∽◦◦∽◦◦∽

The Duke of Bridgewater sent a carriage to meet our train from London and transport us to his estate. I had heard that the countryside of England was picturesque and it turned out to be true. The quaint rural village with its thatched-roof cottages and the Tudor inn that came into view at the first bend was like something from a fairytale. From the market square to the old stone church, it looked as though nothing had changed for centuries in this part of the world.

We drove alongside a meandering river bordered by willow trees, and passed through a wood where the branches of the oak, ash and hazel trees were laden with snow, before coming to a stop outside the entrance gates to the Lyndale Estate. The coachman called out and a porter came out of the lodge house to open the gates for us. He was dressed in livery and carrying a staff topped by a silver knob.

The long driveway wound through a vast parkland with a lake at its centre. Swans glided over its silvery surface, and the banks were brimming with birds that hadn't flown south for winter: pheasants, cormorants and snow geese. A herd of deer swept past us, their hooves silent in the deep snow.

'I love deer,' said Isadora. 'For me they are as mystical as the fabled unicorn. They are heavenly messengers: angels in disguise.'

'A good omen for our visit then,' said Lucy.

The coachman caught our conversation and raised his voice so we could hear him inside the carriage. 'His Grace will release whole herds of deer this spring, along with thousands of pheasants and other game, in time for the shooting parties in autumn. The hunting is always good at Lyndale.'

Isadora recoiled and brought her hand to her mouth. 'I can't understand men who hunt. I'm glad that Father —'

Caroline stopped her with a sharp kick and said loudly, 'The ladies join in sometimes too, I should imagine?'

'Some of them,' the coachman agreed. 'Lady Clara is afraid to ride after a bad fall as a child, but her mother was known for her great prowess in stalking. If there was a hunt on, she was sure to be in it.'

The carriage approached a stone bridge over the lake and glimpses of Lyndale came into view, teasing us with flashes of turrets and minarets between the trees. Then, as we crossed the bridge, we were treated to a full view of the building's baroque grandeur. The central block and wings were Corinthian in style, and the columns of the portico and the pilasters on either flank resembled the entrance to a pantheon, while the towers at each corner were suggestive of the pylons of an Egyptian temple. It was far more dramatic and imposing than Buckingham Palace, and perhaps even Versailles. I was sure that Caroline had stopped breathing.

'The palace building and its courtyards alone cover seven acres,' the coachman told us. 'It was designed by the architect Sir Christopher Wren, who is famous for Saint Paul's Cathedral.'

'I wish Harland was here with us,' Caroline whispered to Lucy.

I suspected that the planned new house in Newport might suddenly become English baroque in flavour instead of French. Caroline's admiration increased when we passed under a stone arch with a statue of a coroneted lion on top of it savaging a rooster.

'There is such power here,' she remarked. 'You can feel the command of it all.'

The carriage came to a stop in an arcaded quadrangle where the Duke waited for us, along with a butler, housekeeper, three footmen and four glum-looking maids.

'Welcome to Lyndale,' he said with a smile. He seemed more relaxed than he had been in New York and even had a polite comment for each of us.

To me he said that he hoped the train journey had given me some time to conjure up new stories. 'I find that the scenery and the steady rhythm of the wheels on the tracks help to solve a myriad of problems that require the use of one's imagination.'

His comment to Isadora was that he hoped she found the beauty of the parkland to her liking. 'Even though it couldn't be more different from the bustle and hurry of New York, or London for that matter.'

'The air is so fresh,' she replied. 'Even in winter it is alive with the fragrance of pine and the icy crispness of the lake.'

The Duke's eyes crinkled as if he was amused by Isadora's observations.

He introduced us to the maids who would be attending each of us. The maid assigned to me was a young, rake-thin girl named Patsy.

We entered the immense hall, which was more like a guardroom than a welcoming space. The lofty ceiling was supported by fluted Corinthian columns, while smaller columns created an arched corridor that spanned a minstrels' gallery. On the keystone was carved a coat of arms. Long vaulted corridors ran to the north and south wings. Paintings of hunting and battle scenes covered the walls, and the wainscoting was embellished with pistols and bayonets. In each corner stood a suit of armour. The hall had clearly been designed to impress — and subdue — guests rather than to please them.

Tea was served in the library, which the Duke informed us was one hundred and eighty feet long. The fine stucco of the ceiling was beautiful, but the size of the room and the height of the ceiling only made it chillier. Lucy discreetly wiggled her toes to warm them up. I wrapped my hands around my teacup to relieve my frozen fingers but the heat had already vanished from the drink. The Duke seemed oblivious to our discomfort. He was probably used to the cold. Portraits of the previous dukes stared down at us as we nibbled on raspberry jam sandwiches cut into circles the size of an English penny and honey cakes.

'Everything we eat comes from either the kitchen garden or the nearby farms,' the Duke explained. 'It's rare to find food as fresh in London. We dine well at Lyndale.'

The windows of the library overlooked an enormous area of ground interspersed with broken low walls. A statue of a mermaid surrounded by fish stood in the middle of it.

'It used to be a water garden,' the Duke explained. 'It was my father's dream to restore it to its former glory but there were other priorities during his time, such as repairing the roof and the bridge.'

Restoring a water garden of that size would be a large financial undertaking. In fact, it would take an enormous amount of money to keep this house going at all. I glanced around: although the library furniture was glorious, the upholstery was frayed, the walls were showing signs of damp and the stone floor had some cracks in it. I understood now why the Duke was forgoing his childhood love in order to marry a wealthy heiress. I only hoped he had more than his ancestry and this museum of a house to offer Isadora.

After we had finished our tea, the Duke gave us a tour of the staterooms, which, rather ironically I thought, were decorated in Louis XVI gilded style. In each of them hung tapestries of the first duke's military victories over the French.

When the Duke noticed the intense way that Isadora studied them, he told her, 'The English and the French were often bitter enemies, but over time we have come to appreciate each other.'

As we moved from room to room, we followed a path set out by a crimson carpet.

'The main rooms are open to public tours on Tuesdays and Thursdays,' explained the Duke. Glancing in Caroline's direction, he added, 'It is not for myself alone that I desire to restore Lyndale, but for everyone. I believe Lyndale could become the finest estate in the whole of England.'

I thought it curious that he should direct so many of his comments to Caroline rather than Isadora. He must have understood who it was he really had to charm.

The palace had over three hundred rooms and we weren't going to cover all of them in one afternoon. After showing us the drawing room with its Roman marble busts, and the chapel, the Duke asked the butler to summon the four maids to escort us to our rooms.

'I'm sure you would like to rest before dinner,' he told us.

Despite the magnificence of the palace's public rooms, the bedroom assigned to me had a low ceiling and was furnished only with a plain wrought-iron bed and a large, shabby wardrobe. The walls were covered in faded china-rose paper that was peeling at the seams. A musty stink like swamp water pervaded the air although the room looked as though it had been cleaned and dusted.

I had become so used to the modern plumbing in Caroline's New York house that it was a surprise when Patsy and three housemaids brought in a copper bath, and proceeded to fill it with buckets of water that must have been coming from the kitchen given the time it took them.

'Better get in before the water gets cold, miss,' advised Patsy, squeezing out her sodden apron before helping me undress.

I had washed this way in my Paris apartment, but the source of the water had been much closer to the bathtub then — and I hadn't had a small audience of women ready to hand me soap, washcloths and brushes.

After my bath, the maids removed the tub and left me on my own. I wrapped myself in several blankets, trying to get warm again. If the house was this cold on the cusp of spring, what was it like in the dead of winter? I wondered if the housekeeper had assigned me this draughty room because the Duke considered me of lower status than the others.

However, when I went to see Isadora after Patsy had helped me dress for dinner, I found that her room was as frayed and faded as mine. Isadora was used to the best of everything and had grown up with thick carpets, luxurious bedding and flush toilets. Would she languish away if she had to live permanently in this cold and damp house?

'I won't be able to sleep here,' she whispered to me after her maid had finished doing her hair and left the room. 'It feels haunted. No wonder Lady Clara and Lord Randolph spend as much time in London as possible.' She nodded in the direction of the fireplace. Above it was a stuffed pike with a carp in its mouth. 'Look at that hideous thing. Why are the English so ghoulish?'

Isadora's love of animals didn't bode well for life on an English estate. The pictures in the great hall of men and women fox-hunting had sent a shudder down my spine. I'd read that the foxes were often ripped apart while still alive, and the hounds put to death when they were no longer considered good for hunting. But it wasn't my role to encourage my niece to reject the possibility of marriage to an English aristocrat; at least, not unless she expressed complete disgust at the idea. Caroline's warning to me rang in my mind: *Don't let anything go wrong now.*

'Your father's trophy room is ghoulish too,' I reminded her.

She touched her throat and looked at me askance. 'Father? He hates hunting. He's only interested in business, his motor cars and playing cards at his club. Those poor animals were shot by Mother. She put them in Father's wing of the house to mock him.'

'Your mother? But I've never heard of a woman hunting big game.'

'Big game is the only type of animal Mother's interested in killing,' Isadora replied. 'She thinks women who only shoot at birds are pathetic. I feel that way about people who shoot at anything.'

An odd tingling disturbed my stomach, as if I'd been given the first piece of a puzzle but didn't know quite what to do with it yet.

I placed my hand on Isadora's. 'What do you think of the Duke? Seriously.'

She lowered her eyes. 'What does it matter what I think? I can tell Mother is determined I shall marry him.'

Her words rang in my head. 'What does it matter? It matters a lot! If you object to him, you must tell your mother that. My opinion of him won't sway her. It must come from you.'

Isadora turned away. Her shoulders were shaking, but I couldn't tell if she was laughing or crying. 'You would think, wouldn't you, that when you tell someone who is supposed to love you that they are hurting you, they would stop.'

'Of course! Nobody wants to deliberately hurt somebody they love.'

Isadora shook her head. 'Each time I've tried to stand up to Mother, she has destroyed me. She doesn't care; she knows all our deepest fears and how to use them against us. She does it to Father, she does it to me, and she does it to you too, Aunt Emma. Once, when I asked for a kitten, she ripped into me, ridiculing everything I loved — from Aunt Anne, to my art, to my friendship with Rebecca. She twisted my mind so much that I held a knife to my heart and threatened to kill myself. But did that stop her? No. She smiled a smile I will never forget, because she knew then that she had absolute power over me. So don't ask me to stand up to my mother.'

Even as a writer, I would never be able to express the horror Isadora's story roused in me. Now I knew the real reason for those 'nervous collapses'. Caroline herself had driven her daughter to them.

I put my arm around Isadora and drew her close. 'I'm here with you now. I won't let her hurt you like that again.'

She turned to me, her face very pale. 'Mother told me that you're only here because you need money from her. She said I shouldn't get too close to you.'

Any semblance of regard I still held for Caroline vanished. It was horrific the way she played people off against each other. Divide and conquer seemed to be her motto.

'Isadora! It's true that your mother agreed to pay my debts in return for me tutoring you. But I would have come regardless. When I met you in Paris I was enchanted by you.'

She smiled. 'And I with you. Don't think I believe her lies about you. She slanders everyone I love, but it's only when she attacks me directly that she has any effect. You have shown me nothing but kindness, Aunt Emma. That's why I want to ask you to do something for me now.'

'Of course. What is it?'

'Don't oppose Mother about the Duke. She'll destroy you if you try to stand between her and something she wants. Go along with this engagement, please — for my sake. You will be much more help to me if you are still in one piece and Mother doesn't forbid me from seeing you. Once I'm here in England I won't have Mr Gadley or Rebecca any more for comfort, but perhaps I will be allowed to visit you in Paris and invite you here. That is the best I can hope for.'

A sense of helplessness swept over me, a feeling that Isadora and I were facing insurmountable odds, and all because of my sister's unappeasable ambition. Yet I had to stay calm for Isadora's sake.

I clutched my niece to my chest and kissed her head. 'I'll do anything for you, my sweet Isadora. Anything!'

 broadcast

We ate supper in the dining room under a ceiling frescoed with cupids. From the rapture on Caroline's face when the Duke informed her that the baroque paintings on the walls were by Rubens and Caravaggio it was apparent that even a dingy bedroom and a cold bath couldn't dampen her enthusiasm for the English aristocracy.

'I should imagine that installing plumbing and electricity will be next on your list,' she said to the Duke, cutting into a lamb cutlet that had turned rubbery with cold. 'And to move the kitchen closer to the dining room.'

He lifted his eyebrows, surprised. 'But it is much more dignified to have servants wait on your bath than to have water spurting from a tap. And electricity might be acceptable for a London house but it is too harsh for the ambience of Lyndale. As for the kitchen, it was built so far from the dining room to avoid unpleasant cooking odours.'

Caroline's face pinched, but she replied as if his remarks had been made in jest. 'How delightful!'

Isadora's story of Caroline nearly driving her to take her own life had enraged me so much that it took all my effort during dinner to pretend everything was normal. As for the Duke, I comforted myself by thinking that if the marriage went ahead at least I could be satisfied that Caroline would make his life miserable. She wouldn't stand for an English palace that wasn't comfortable *for her*.

The evening concluded with a recital in the library by Lyndale's own organist. I was glad I'd brought a shawl with me because the temperature was dropping by the minute. Yet I forgot my discomfort as the majestic music of Wagner burst from the grand pipe organ and flooded the room. The library's acoustics were near perfect. Perhaps there were things that could make living at Lyndale if not joyful then at least bearable. I promised myself that I would come as often as I was invited to help Isadora, and I would write to her every day. I would be her lifeline.

The following morning, the Duke took us around the estate's gardens, including the rose garden where tiny buds were starting to form on the bare shrubs.

'The garden contains sixteen hundred specimens of roses,' he told us. 'But not yet the American Beauty rose.'

'We can arrange that,' Lucy whispered to me.

The grounds were spectacular, but the pergola in the rose garden was in need of repair, and the temple of Diana near the lake had fallen into ruin. In summer, it would take dozens of gardeners to scythe the vast lawns. The cost of upkeep of the grounds must surely be almost as high as the house, I thought.

In the afternoon we travelled by open carriage into the village, where we were the subject of curiosity. Faces popped up in windows, shopkeepers rushed out to see us, men tipped their hats and women curtsied. A group of children hurried out of a house to hand us each a hastily assembled posy of whatever flowers and greenery could be found in the frosty garden.

I found the villagers' reverence for the Duke rather quaint, but, from the gleam in Caroline's eye and her self-satisfied smile, it was obvious the attention was appealing to her sense of vanity. As she looked about her, I wondered if she was imagining herself as the Duchess of Bridgewater rather than her daughter.

❦

On our last evening at Lyndale, Caroline and the Duke had a lengthy discussion in his study after dinner. Later, after Isadora had gone to bed, my sister called me to go with her to Lucy's bedroom.

'Well?' Lucy asked as soon as we were all seated.

'He is very pleased with Isadora's manners,' Caroline said, unable to keep the satisfaction from her voice. 'He feels that she will come to understand the running of Lyndale in time, and he is willing to help her. His lawyer will begin negotiations with Oliver's London lawyer. If all is agreeable, he will propose to Isadora before we leave England.'

'Has he agreed that they will marry in New York?' Lucy asked.

'Of course. The wedding will be at Saint Thomas's. Everyone will marvel at the fine duke we've captured for Isadora!'

'Then you have triumphed!' said Lucy, clasping her hands together. 'All has gone splendidly!'

Neither woman said anything to me. I was too insignificant for them to worry about.

TWENTY-SIX

Back in London, Caroline indulged any request Isadora asked for, including going to see Shakespeare's *Macbeth* at the Lyceum Theatre and visiting Madame Tussaud's waxwork exhibition. I didn't know which was worse: Caroline's false generosity born of her elation at having got what she'd wanted from the Duke; or the way Isadora found means to distract herself from her sorrow, as if doing so was habitual.

During a visit to the Victoria and Albert Museum, Isadora was captivated by a marble bust of Thucydides. 'The secret to happiness is freedom ... and the secret to freedom is courage,' she said, quoting the Greek philosopher. 'Mr Gadley is always saying that. Perhaps I haven't chosen freedom strongly enough.'

That evening, Caroline called us all into the parlour for 'a chat'. I quailed at what was coming, even though I was prepared for it and Isadora seemed to have resigned herself to marriage to the Duke.

'Isadora, when we were visiting Lyndale Palace you must have noticed that the Duke of Bridgewater couldn't take his eyes off you,' Caroline said, watching her daughter closely. 'He has asked for your hand in marriage.'

I squeezed my palms together, feeling all the angst and helplessness of someone hearing that their loved one has been condemned to death. What happened next caught me by surprise.

Isadora pursed her lips, then lifted her eyes to meet her mother's. 'I know you have arranged this proposal with the best of intentions, Mother. But I'm not going to marry the Duke.'

At first I thought I must be hearing things. I leaned forward in my chair, intrigued by the sudden turn of events. What had made Isadora change her mind and decide to assert herself?

Caroline's mouth twitched and her brow furrowed. 'But you've hardly got to know him,' she said with a merry laugh at odds with the hard expression in her eyes. 'How can you decide that?'

'It's true that we haven't spent a lot of time together,' Isadora answered calmly, 'but it's enough to know that we aren't compatible.'

Caroline's fingers kneaded the armrest of her chair. 'What do you know of compatibility? You are only a child. Compatibility is more than the silly chit-chat young people make these days. It's a deeper understanding and sympathy with one another.'

Isadora's eyes flashed at the word 'child' but she continued in a firm, even voice. 'Well, I don't think we have those either. He doesn't listen when I speak so how could we develop any understanding?'

'You're being absurd, Isadora,' Lucy said. She looked as perturbed as Caroline by the turn of the conversation. Usually she and my sister made a formidable team when they wanted something. 'You know nothing of life. Your mother has your best interests at heart. You have to trust her to make decisions for you.'

'How will marrying a man who is only after my money benefit me?' Isadora said. 'The Duke has no fortune to offer *me*. By your logic, I should marry one of the New York wealthy heirs; at least then I would know that my husband is marrying me for myself and not my money.'

'The Duke has a title, a position in parliament and a history,' Caroline said. 'No one in New York can offer you that.'

Her voice was getting louder and more agitated. My pulse was racing, but Isadora remained resolute.

'A title means something to you, Mother. It means nothing to me. I respect that a title might have helped Lucy, but since my debut I am accepted wherever I go.'

Caroline's eyes narrowed. 'You are so ignorant, Isadora — I could slap you! A title is something that can never be taken away from you. Why do you think in London society the peers aren't threatened by new money as the Van der Heydens, Schorers or Warburgs are in New York? Because in England they have positions that can never be taken away. If a man is a duke or an earl, he will be a duke or an earl until the day he dies.' Her voice trembled with emotion and tears welled in her eyes. 'I know what it is to struggle, and how terrible it is to be poor. Your Aunt Emma and I were born into one of the most prominent families in Louisiana; we had a grand plantation on the Mississippi. But everything was lost in the war. You can have money and lose it, but you can never lose a title!'

Isadora blinked, taken aback by her mother's distress. I was unsettled too. The only strong emotions I had witnessed Caroline display before were rage and triumph.

'I didn't mean to upset you,' Isadora began.

It was her first stumble. I willed her to keep going, to stay strong. But it was too late.

'Well, you have!' Caroline shouted, her voice hoarse. 'If you continue in this vein, you will force me to take action I don't wish to. If you refuse to marry the Duke, I will no longer consider you as my daughter.'

Isadora flinched as if her mother had struck her.

My stomach pitched. I turned to Lucy, hoping she might intervene, but she only lowered her eyes.

'Are you saying you will disown me if I don't marry the Duke?' Isadora asked, her gaze never leaving her mother's face.

Caroline lifted her chin but still wouldn't look at Isadora. 'I have to take a firm hand to stop my daughter foolishly throwing away an opportunity she doesn't realise the value of.'

Isadora rose from her chair, her face contorted with disbelief. 'Is your ambition so great that you're prepared to sacrifice my happiness? Are you glad for me to live in a dreary, cold and isolated place in a far-away country just so you can say you have a duchess for a daughter?'

Lucy finally spoke up. 'Of course not! My husband understands that I need to visit friends and family in the United States, and travel in Europe to refresh myself. And your mother will see you in London every season.'

Isadora's mouth set into a grim line. 'So you are prepared for me to have a loveless marriage.'

Caroline glared at her. 'How dare you insinuate that I am thinking only of myself,' she hissed. 'When I recall how I suffered to bring a spoiled, ungrateful girl into this world, I curse God that it was William who perished and not —'

She stopped, but not before Isadora had gasped and stepped backwards. 'Me?' she said.

She staggered as if she had been stabbed.

My hand flew to my throat in sympathy. It was as Isadora had described it: Caroline knew all our worst fears and turned them into weapons against us.

I jumped to my feet and wrapped my arm around Isadora's shoulders. 'Stop it, Caroline! Calm yourself!'

My sister glared at us. 'Get out!' she screamed. 'Get out, the both of you!'

'We're all tired,' I said, endeavouring to stay composed but quivering from head to foot. 'Let's talk rationally about this tomorrow.'

I took Isadora's hand and led her out of the room. She didn't resist me. I guided her upstairs to her room, and with the assistance of a maid helped her out of her gown and into bed.

'Miss Hopper must have caught a chill,' the maid said kindly.

I was grateful for her discretion. She and all the other servants had surely heard Caroline's raised voice.

'Is there anything I can get you, Miss Hopper?' she asked.

Isadora didn't respond. She rested her head on the pillow and closed her eyes as if all energy had been drained from her.

The maid left and I sat on the bed, rubbing Isadora's arm. 'You are brave and courageous,' I told her. 'You are a survivor. You will survive this.'

Eventually her breathing steadied and she fell asleep. I returned to my own room and changed into a nightdress, before going back to Isadora's room and climbing onto the bed next to her.

I did believe she was strong, but I also knew from experience the devastating effect of Caroline's maliciousness. I stared into the darkness. How could Caroline say such terrible things to her own daughter?

I thought of Oliver with anger. Why didn't he stand up for Isadora, for God's sake, instead of sneaking around his home like the pathetic ghost of the man he used to be?

❧❧❧

Sometime before dawn, I fell asleep too, curled up on top of the covers next to Isadora. I was woken by a knock on the door just as light began to peep through the curtains. I slipped off the bed to answer it.

Lucy stood there, still wearing her dinner gown from the previous evening, her hair hanging about her face in dishevelled whorls. 'I couldn't find you in your room,' she said. 'I thought you might be here.' Her trembling voice had an edge of hysteria to it.

'What's happened?' I asked.

Isadora stirred.

Lucy glanced at her before turning back to me. 'I had to call Doctor Ashby last night. Caroline had a heart attack.'

Lack of sleep caused my mind to move slowly. 'Are you sure? It's not merely tiredness or indigestion?'

Lucy sneered at me. 'Of course Doctor Ashby is sure. She nearly died!'

'Mother?' said Isadora, getting out of bed so fast she knocked over the table lamp next to it. 'Is she going to be all right?'

Lucy ignored her. 'She's asking for you, Emma.'

Isadora grabbed her dressing gown and searched under the bed for her slippers. 'We must go to her,' she said, her voice tight with fear.

'Doctor Ashby has given strict orders that you're not to go near her,' Lucy told Isadora. 'You triggered this crisis. She was as strong as an ox yesterday.'

Whatever colour sleep had brought to Isadora's face drained away. She swallowed and looked at her feet.

'That's not fair, Lucy,' I said.

'I have strict orders Isadora is not to come,' she repeated.

Seeing that I couldn't persuade her, I touched Isadora's arm. 'Let me go and see her first,' I told her.

I followed Lucy to the other side of the house where Caroline's room was located. The situation seemed unreal. My sister was the last person in the world I'd thought could suffer a heart attack. Interspersed with my apprehension about her health was the nagging suspicion that she might be faking this sudden illness to manipulate Isadora. But surely even my sister wouldn't go that far?

Lucy knocked on the door of Caroline's bedroom and a nurse opened it. A grey-bearded man I assumed must be Doctor Ashby was packing medicine bottles into a leather bag.

'Mrs Hopper must have absolute rest,' he said, turning to look at us. 'Don't discuss anything with her that might add to her distress.'

As soon as I caught sight of Caroline lying in bed, her complexion ashen and her hair damp with perspiration, I was ashamed of my suspicions that she might be pretending to be ill. Her eyelids fluttered as if she was drifting from wakefulness to unconsciousness then back again.

'Oh, Caroline,' I said, seating myself beside her and taking her hand. The icy chill of her skin shocked me. All the vitality I associated with her had vanished. With her greying hair spread out on the pillow and her lips a frightening shade of blue, she had become a frail old woman overnight. Tears welled in my eyes. The tender feelings I believed had vanished after learning of her abuse of Isadora rose in me again. 'Caroline, please don't upset yourself so much. Everything will be all right.'

She opened her eyes and stared at me. Her lips moved but no sound came out.

I became truly panicked then. If Caroline died, Isadora would blame herself. For my niece's sake I had to remain calm and do everything I could to help my sister.

'Do what Nurse Derby instructs you,' Doctor Ashby said to Lucy. 'I will come back in the afternoon.' Then he added ominously, 'Unless I am sent for sooner.'

Lucy and I sat with Caroline for an hour while she dozed. When Lucy's own head began to nod I told her to go to her room for some rest.

'It won't do Caroline any good if you get sick too,' I said. 'I'll send a maid if I need you.'

Later, a maid brought me a tray with tea and some eggs and bacon, but I turned her away. I had no appetite, but I was also concerned that the greasy smell might upset Caroline. When she was awake, my sister was lost in her thoughts and I didn't want to disturb her.

Doctor Ashby returned in the afternoon, and Lucy came downstairs to join me for his verdict.

'Mrs Hopper isn't completely out of danger,' he said. 'But she is showing slight signs of improvement.'

I let out a deep sigh and thanked God.

A relieved smile came to Lucy's face. 'Thank you, Doctor Ashby,' she said. 'If you hadn't come so quickly, we might have lost her.'

We accompanied the doctor to the front door, where the butler handed him his hat.

'She must not have any more shocks or upsets,' Doctor Ashby warned us before leaving. 'The next attack could be fatal.'

We turned to go back inside and found Isadora waiting at the bottom of the staircase, her shoulders drooped and her head bowed.

'Is Mother all right?' she asked. 'Can I see her now?'

Lucy regarded her with contempt. 'You must have heard the doctor just now — she's not to have any more shocks or upsets or the next attack could be fatal.'

Isadora looked up, blinking back tears. 'I have some news that might raise her spirits. The Duke of Bridgewater's footman has delivered a note informing me that the Duke is to visit us tomorrow afternoon. I assume he intends to propose.' She faltered, before gathering strength and adding, 'Tell Mother that I will accept his proposal. Tell her I agree to be the Duchess of Bridgewater.'

I shuddered. After witnessing Isadora's brave attempt to carve her own destiny, her forced acquiescence now was even more crushing. It was as if I had heard gaol bars clanging shut around my niece. She was a prisoner and I was unable to free her.

TWENTY-SEVEN

We remained in London for a few weeks after the Duke's proposal as Caroline decided that Isadora's wedding dress would be made by the designers who created gowns for the British royal family. The Duke would be impressed by the dress no doubt, for it cost fifteen thousand American dollars. But I would have preferred that he appreciated the beautiful woman who would be wearing it.

The afternoon of Isadora's final fitting, I broke down in tears. The dress was white silk satin with gold thread woven through so it sparkled and shimmered. It was trimmed with silk orange blossoms and finished with a silver moiré train that would require eight bridesmaids to carry it. Isadora looked beautiful, yet my tears were of grief not joy. How happy I would have been if she was marrying someone she loved and who loved her.

'I feel like I'm split into two people,' I told her that evening when we were alone together. 'One who is helping your mother to entrap you; and the other who longs to set you free.'

Isadora's eyes fastened on me. 'You must go along with her, Aunt Emma. If I lose you, I will die.'

We returned to New York as an early spring was touching the city. The air was still frigid, but the snow had vanished and the gusty winter winds had transformed into soft breezes. Buds were emerging on the trees in Central Park, and the warblers, swallows and thrushes reappeared.

As soon as Caroline returned to her position as the queen of New York society, she ensured everyone was aware of her near brush with death. She sat in the drawing room each afternoon with her feet propped on a stool, ready to have a fuss made over her by the women who called.

'Oh my Lord!' exclaimed Bessie Graham, arriving with an enormous bouquet of lilies. 'I couldn't believe it when I heard it, Caroline — a heart attack!'

Caroline lowered her eyes. 'I know. I nearly died, Bessie. I even glimpsed heaven — the angels were blowing their trumpets and Saint Peter was welcoming me through the gates. And what gates they were! Pure gold and encrusted with pearls and diamonds. But it wasn't my time.'

If my sister ever did get to heaven, God would have a hard time holding on to his throne, I thought. Then I chastised myself. Caroline had nearly died and I shouldn't make light of it.

Charlotte Harper arrived with a tincture of hawthorn berries. 'This helped my sister when she had trouble with her heart,' she told Caroline. 'She swears it saved her life. But don't let anybody without heart problems touch it. It can *cause* palpitations otherwise. Take it. You only need two drops in a glass of water.'

Charlotte went to pour Caroline some water from the crystal decanter on the table, but my sister waved her away. 'Not now, my dear. I take all my medicines before bed. Doctor's instructions.'

'Very well,' said Charlotte, putting the decanter back down.

Helen Potter arrived next. She was carrying a book and placed it on Caroline's lap. The title read *Science and Health* by Mary Baker Eddy.

'It's a marvellous book,' gushed Helen. 'It says that sickness is an illusion that can be healed by prayer alone. You must read it, and follow the instructions exactly.'

Caroline opened the book and perused a few pages as if she'd been given a splendid gift. 'I certainly will, Helen. I'll start on it tonight.'

Later, when her guests had left and Woodford had cleared away the tea things, Caroline opened the book again and glanced at the flyleaf where Helen had written a note wishing her good health.

'What a load of nonsense,' she said. 'As if prayer can heal anything.' And she threw the book in the fire.

Witnessing my sister, with her rosy cheeks and bright eyes, receiving the adoration of her subjects made me wonder again about the truth of her heart attack. But hadn't I seen her myself, lying in bed ill and grey in the face? Besides, although Lucy was Caroline's best friend, I doubted she would have colluded in a fake heart attack. I shook the doubt from my mind.

I was thankful that Caroline was distracted by the constant stream of visitors, because it left Isadora free to work on her sculptures in the afternoons and soothe her mind before she had to listen to her mother's chatter about the wedding over dinner.

Mr Gadley must have sensed Isadora's downcast mood for he was especially gentle and encouraging of her.

'I've decided that you are ready to work in bronze,' he told her. 'It is the perfect material for your subject.'

They chose to create a series of the animals that Isadora had sketched at the zoo. She threw herself into the work with enthusiasm, but one day her nerves got the better of her and she dropped one of the clay pieces.

Mr Gadley picked it up and remoulded it for her. 'Don't try to think of the whole picture at once, Miss Hopper,' he said kindly. 'I want you to close your eyes and imagine each piece separately. When you have a grasp of the parts, then slowly start putting them together, a piece at a time.'

Isadora's breathing steadied and her body became still. Even the colour that so rarely visited her face these days filled her cheeks again.

'Better?' asked Mr Gadley.

Isadora opened her eyes. 'Much better, thank you.'

He handed the piece back to her. 'Sometimes, when you surrender yourself to the subject, all sorts of answers and possibilities come to mind. Life always has possibilities, and as artists we must be constantly on the lookout for them.'

Isadora smiled for the first time in a long time. I smiled too, convinced that Mr Gadley was the last decent man left on earth.

The Duke wouldn't be arriving in New York for another fortnight, which gave me time to strengthen Isadora for the lonely life ahead of her. And perhaps for the lonely life ahead of me too, I thought, without Claude.

Rebecca came regularly to call on Isadora. She had avoided coming to the house before, but now she sensed her friend's need. I told Caroline I was giving both the young women French lessons. In reality, I would sit in an armchair writing and let Rebecca and Isadora play cards, sketch, read to each other or whatever else they wished to do in the short time they had left together.

'Do we really have to have that insufferable Rebecca Clark here every day?' Caroline asked me one morning. 'I'm sure she's got wind that Isadora is engaged to a very important man and she's hoping to be a bridesmaid. Not a chance! Not a dumpy girl like that. Isadora's bridesmaids must be beautiful.'

I had long ceased to be amazed by Caroline's cold-bloodedness, and for the past few weeks had adopted the role of a skilled diplomat negotiating a fragile peace with a volatile despot, but I had to take a deep breath before answering her this time.

'Rebecca's French is far superior to Isadora's and the competition is making Isadora work harder. You do want

Isadora to be above the English girls she'll be associating with after she's married, don't you? You told me that you want her to outshine them in every way.'

Competition was something Caroline understood and appreciated.

'Very well,' she agreed. 'But only until the Duke arrives. Then I never want to see the girl again. She has been out for a season and hasn't received a single proposal yet. I don't want her failure bringing down Isadora by association.'

⁂

Caroline's preoccupation with the forthcoming wedding and the ball at which Isadora's engagement would be announced gave me some free time. I took advantage of it to visit Florence while she was working on the mural she had been commissioned to paint for a women's college. The institution had been set up by female philanthropists, for girls from poor families to pursue higher education.

I walked into the great hall and stopped a moment to enjoy the scene before me. Florence, wearing a smock, was standing on a ladder and adding finishing touches to the leaves of a tree. Her painting spanned the length of the wall and showed women in a lush green orchard with a backdrop of mountains and rivers. Some of the women were picking apples from the trees and handing them down to others. Scattered around the women were cats, dogs, sheep, chickens and pigs. The colour palette was blues and greens with touches of pink, and the brushwork was loose and flowing. My heart stirred joyously to see it.

'Florence — you have nearly finished. It's magnificent!'

'You're back from England!' she cried, climbing down from the ladder to embrace me. Then she nodded towards the painting. 'Do you like it?'

'I do. It's brimming with life!'

'It's bound to cause a scandal,' she said with a wink. 'The women are picking the fruit of knowledge for themselves.'

'That's a theme of yours,' I said, smiling. 'Before we left Paris I remember you telling me that for centuries men have been terrified of what might happen to women if they gain the knowledge that comes with freedom.'

Florence cleaned her brush and wiped her hands. 'Tell me what happened with Claude,' she said, offering me a stool to sit on while she plonked herself down, cross-legged, on the floor. 'I went to see his exhibition and he was there with a girl, Lise.'

Tears filled my eyes. I hadn't confided in anyone what had happened, not even Isadora or Grace. I shook my head. 'I feel like such a fool ...'

I didn't want to continue, but the earnest expression on Florence's face had me pouring out all the pain in my heart like a great flood.

When I'd finished, she tapped her finger against her lip. 'But, Emma, I confronted him about it and he told me that *you* broke things off with *him*.'

I stared at her, stunned. 'That's not true. I wrote to him constantly for weeks but received no reply at all. I wrote to his parents as well. When I saw him with Lise at the exhibition I suddenly understood why he hadn't written back.'

'But that doesn't sound like Claude. I can't believe he would treat you like that.'

'I can't either! That's what's broken my heart most of all. Perhaps if he had written I would have been upset but I'd have understood. The way I found out was humiliating.'

Florence rubbed her cheek, mulling over what I had told her. 'No, that wasn't a kind thing to do. Nothing is more distressing than being betrayed by someone you've trusted. It's as if they've taken off a mask and the person you loved never existed at all. Claude probably told me that you'd broken it off so I wouldn't give him a piece of my mind.'

Her words scorched me. If that was what Claude had done, then I hadn't known him at all. I thought we had shared everything, even our honest opinions about marriage. But perhaps Lise had the same views of life as he did and he felt less pressure from her. That didn't explain why he hadn't had the decency to tell me though. I would never have believed Claude capable of such cruelty if I hadn't experienced it myself.

∽∾∽∾∽∾∽

On my way home, I called in on Grace. The Hunters' usually unflappable butler, Aston, looked agitated when he greeted me at the door. A muscle was twitching in his face and he avoided meeting my eyes as he led me to the reception room.

'I will inform Mrs Hunter that you are here, Miss Lacasse,' he said, glancing over his shoulder as though nervous about something.

A door slammed and I glimpsed Harland rushing down the stairs into the great hall. A servant ran after him. 'Your watch, sir,' he called.

Harland snatched the watch from the man without a word, then looked about the hall and shouted the butler's name. 'Aston! Where is the damn carriage?'

The butler glanced at me, clearly humiliated that a guest was witnessing such a scene. 'I am coming, sir,' he called back. 'The carriage is only around the corner. We had to move it for the street sweepers.'

Harland dashed out the door without saying any more. Aston returned to the reception room and cleared his throat, again promising to inform Grace I was there. A sheen of sweat had broken out on his forehead and he kept patting his pocket and shaking his head as if he had forgotten something. Poor man, to have Harland as a master. It would break anyone's nerves.

He disappeared and a few minutes later, Grace arrived. She was shaking like a leaf and there was a red welt on her cheek.

'Grace!' I cried, standing.

She threw herself into my arms. 'Emma, thank goodness you are here.'

We sat down together and I took her trembling hand in mine. 'Tell me what's happened. What was that all about?' I brushed my fingers against her cheek. The skin was burning hot. 'Shall I tell Aston to get some ice?'

She grasped my hand harder and began to cry. 'I don't know if I can stand this any longer. For years I've avoided Harland's temper by not doing anything to upset him. I've let him lead his life, and I've led mine as best I can. But this morning he stormed into my bedroom, sent my maid away and shut all the doors, then raged at me for over an hour, listing all my character flaws. I hoped if I kept quiet and let him rant he would run out of steam. But when I didn't respond, he slapped me across the cheek.' She paused for breath. 'He's never struck me before, Emma. The abuse has always been verbal. Things are getting worse. Dear Aston knocked at the door to tell him the carriage was ready, but really to get Harland away from me. Poor Aston. He was originally my late husband's butler — he must be appalled at what's become of me.'

My head throbbed. I was burning with anger that Harland had hit Grace, but I controlled myself. My adding fuel to the fire wouldn't help.

'What set him off?' I asked.

Grace dabbed her eyes with a handkerchief and sighed. 'An article in the *Journal of American Architecture*. It accused him of turning New York into a replica of Europe, and praised instead the younger architects who are creating original buildings that reflect a modern city.'

'And you were unfortunate enough to be close at hand — an object Harland could unleash his anger on instead of the people he really wants to rage at?' I said.

Grace lowered her eyes and nodded.

'Caroline is getting worse too,' I told her. 'I wonder if people like my sister and Harland regress with age. Perhaps they sense they're losing their youthful charm and so they resort to intimidation.'

Grace considered what I said, then nodded. 'That's a keen observation. And perhaps now your sister is back, she and Harland can spend their time intimidating each other and leave the rest of us alone.'

I could tell that Grace was using her characteristic wry humour to soothe her fear, but I was worried that things were escalating between her and Harland. I made up my mind to introduce her to the women of Charles Garrett House. She was intelligent and good-natured and I was sure Florence and Cecilia would like her. Grace needed friends like them, and I wouldn't be in New York for much longer.

As I made my way home after sharing some tea with Grace, I wondered what would happen if Caroline and Harland did turn on each other. My sister's anger was a bottomless pit — Isadora had warned me of that. Harland was probably the same. It would be a savage battle.

◌◌◌◌◌◌◌

The following morning, I received in the post my first piece of good news in weeks. *The American Literary Journal* had accepted my short story about the bear that escaped from the Bronx Zoo. The editor was full of praise for it: *I found the story a rare combination of the whimsical and the powerful and I'm sure our readers will enjoy it. We hope to receive more of your stories.*

The payment was to be on publication. I turned to the accounts slip enclosed with the letter and saw that it was for thirty dollars. I had been expecting no more than ten if it ever got published at all!

Later, when Rebecca arrived for her and Isadora's supposed French lesson, I told the young women I was taking them to the zoo instead. 'It will be fresh air and more inspiration for us all!' I said.

When we arrived at the bear enclosure, I left the two friends alone to sketch and chat and went off for a stroll around the other exhibits. At least Isadora was more confident in herself now and might find it easier to make friends in England — if the Duke didn't keep her isolated at Lyndale.

I was on the path to the aviary when I heard a voice call out, 'Miss Lacasse! What are you doing here on your own?'

I turned to see Douglas Hardenbergh with his children. Auberon was eating cotton candy. Mabel was riding a hobby horse.

'Good afternoon,' I replied. 'I'm not here on my own. I came with my niece and her friend, but I've left them to spend some time together on their own.'

Douglas straightened his shoulders. 'Then allow me to accompany you. Unfortunately the zoo sometimes attracts unsavoury types. I'm not looking forward to the day the new subway reaches here — then we will get mobs of every description.'

By 'mobs of every description' I understood he was referring to the kinds of people who lived in his tenement buildings. I wanted to say something, but decided not to upset his children.

Auberon took my hand in his sticky one. 'My cousin Edwina has a rocking horse that becomes a real pony at night,' he told me.

Mabel glanced at him and I thought she was about to scold him for being silly. Instead she elaborated the story further. 'I think Edwina said it became a unicorn. In fact, I'm quite sure it was a unicorn.'

Douglas and I exchanged a smile.

'When I write fantasy stories the child in me comes alive,' I told him. 'It's a pity that we lose our sense of magic when we reach adulthood.'

'I believe that magic is simply a higher understanding of life,' he replied.

An artist with a sketchpad beckoned to us. 'What a handsome family! Let me sketch you all. Only one dollar for a fine memento of the day!'

Douglas pretended not to have heard. From the way he kept his attention strictly ahead I could tell he was as acutely embarrassed as I was.

When Mabel and Auberon ran ahead of us to look at a sloth, he cleared his throat. 'When I married Nancy, I expected we would grow old together.' He glanced fondly towards his children and shook his head. 'It shouldn't be this way. Mabel and Auberon shouldn't be growing up without their mother.'

'She sounds like an exceptional woman,' I said, uncomfortable with the intimate turn of the conversation. I had an inkling Caroline had spoken to him about me again and he was letting me know that there were high expectations to live up to.

'That's what gives me comfort,' he said, 'that we made the most of every day. We never held grudges. We forgave each other everything.'

'You were fortunate to have loved like that,' I said. 'Not many people experience that kind of love.'

He nodded, as if satisfied he had conveyed his point clearly. 'How are you progressing with your writing?' he asked.

'I've just had a story accepted by *The American Literary Journal*.'

'That's quite prestigious! Congratulations!'

Mabel and Auberon rejoined us, and we came full circle to the bear enclosure.

Rebecca picked up Auberon. 'Goodness me, this little fellow is solid,' she said. 'He's as heavy as a sack of potatoes!'

'Indeed,' laughed Douglas.

'I'm solid too,' said Mabel, standing on her tiptoes.

'You have grown since I last saw you,' Isadora told her. 'Soon you will be taller than me!'

The zoo was about to close, so we made our way to the entrance and parted ways to take our separate carriages. Douglas helped his children into the brougham and waved to us as it moved off. I realised how much my perception of him had changed. He was by all accounts a chivalrous and pleasant man, yet I wondered how he could feel so deeply for his lost wife and his own children while at the same time showing such lack of compassion for the people who lived in his tenements. Spouses dying, children being orphaned and starvation were daily occurrences on the Lower East Side. While Cecilia had said Douglas was one of the better landlords, he was still squeezing people for maximum rent.

The words of the French writer Michel de Montaigne came back to me: *I write to keep from going mad from the contradictions I find among mankind — and to work some of those contradictions out for myself.* That Caroline considered I could ever be happy married to someone like Douglas only showed how little she knew me. But then my sister's main criterion for marriage was not happiness.

My heart was heavy as I sat down in the carriage next to Isadora. I wished she were like the bear in my story and I could whisk her away in a private railcar. But that was a fantasy story too far-fetched for even me to conceive.

TWENTY-EIGHT

Whatever courage Mr Gadley, Rebecca and I had tried to instil in Isadora vanished when the Duke arrived in New York. Who could blame her? When I saw him standing in the great hall with his twenty-five trunks of clothes and sporting attire that Caroline had paid for, a chill ran through me. He was a dark cloud looming on an otherwise beautiful day.

'Good morning, Isadora,' he said, taking her hand.

His cool eyes appraised the furnishings and paintings with a keen interest that he didn't show in his soon-to-be bride, who was pale and trembling.

The Duke's Christian name was Mervyn, and now that he and Isadora were engaged we, as her family, were free to use it. But I couldn't bring myself to think of him as anything other than 'the Duke'. He had brought Mr Whitlock with him, but his brother and sister wouldn't be arriving until a few days before the wedding so we didn't even have those two cheerful spirits to lift the mood.

'Oh God,' Grace whispered to me after meeting him that evening, 'he's like an undertaker. Doesn't the man have any sense of humour at all?'

The ball in honour of the Duke and to announce his and Isadora's engagement had been organised for the week after Easter. To build the anticipation, Caroline made sure that everyone in society had a chance to view him. He and Isadora were paraded in a carriage in Central Park, with Isadora dressed romantically in an organdie gown, and the Duke in a top hat and day suit and carrying a walking stick that he didn't need. They could have been wax figures on top of a wedding cake: smartly dressed, attractive and totally devoid of expression.

'For God's sake, Caroline, you're making them look old-fashioned,' Harland told my sister one day when we were riding with him and Grace in the carriage behind Isadora, the Duke and Lucy. 'Why not do something more modern, like a motor car parade?'

It wasn't the usual tone Harland used when he spoke to Caroline but she was so enthusiastic about the idea of a motor car parade that she didn't notice. But I did. Was he still out of sorts because of the article in the architecture journal? I glanced at Grace, but she was staring off into the distance. She had a way of drifting into her own world whenever she was forced by circumstances to be with Harland and Caroline. 'That's brilliant, Harland,' Caroline said. 'That way the whole city can admire the Duke. I'll organise it with Lucy for Palm Sunday, before the Easter Parade can steal the show.'

'Isn't the commemoration of Jesus's triumphal entry into Jerusalem an odd date to choose for the motor car parade?' I said to Grace afterwards when we were having afternoon tea together. 'Is Caroline expecting the public to lay down palm branches before the Duke?'

The idea appealed to her sense of humour. 'Well, with any luck they'll crucify him the following week!'

Later, on my way to my room to dress for dinner, I was surprised to hear Oliver speaking in a raised voice to Caroline in the drawing room.

'I don't want some uppity noble with an aversion to hard work as a husband for Isadora! If you're so determined for her to marry an Englishman, why not that affable Lord Randolph?

He studied law, didn't he? I could set him up in his own business in New York. That would be preferable to sending our only child to live on the other side of the Atlantic!'

Oliver was finally standing up for his daughter.

I stood still, my whole body tense, waiting for Caroline's response. I didn't hear it, but whatever she said it must have been the final word. The next day the preparations for the ball and the wedding continued with no change. Oliver's stand had made no difference.

❦

On the day of the motor car parade, the participants assembled in Central Park after the morning church service. Teddy supervised an army of white-aproned maids putting the finishing touches to the Hopper family's automobiles. Oliver's car was so heavily decorated with blue hydrangeas, cornflowers and clematis that it was barely recognisable as a vehicle. Caroline had bought the Duke a Daimler too, and the maids had adorned it with red roses as befitted a young couple 'in love'. But it was Caroline's touring car that was the *pièce de résistance*. Attached to either side were two metal and tulle butterfly wings. From the windscreen sprang a pair of wire antennae embellished with tiny lights, while two upturned bowls served as the butterfly's eyes.

The other participants arrived in their De Dion-Boutons, Renaults, Panhards and Fiats, all the cars elaborately decorated with garlands of flowers and vines twisted around arbours. Together, they resembled a postcard I'd seen of the Mardi Gras parade in New Orleans.

Those who didn't come in automobiles arrived in their elegant carriages. To many in society, motor cars were a novelty that would never replace the horse. Among those in the carriages were Harland and Grace, although Harland was going to ride with Caroline in her motor car, while Grace would travel with Oliver in his.

'Is that such a good idea?' I overheard Lucy ask Caroline. 'You don't want any whiff of a scandal now the Duke's here. The attention must be on him and Isadora.'

'It's very fashionable for couples to mix at these events in America,' Caroline assured her. 'No one will think anything of it.'

Alarm flashed in Lucy's eyes but she quickly covered her concern with a smile. 'Yes, I'm sure you are right,' she said, sounding unconvinced of her own statement.

Did Caroline believe that the rules of society no longer applied to her, I wondered.

Newton and Bessie Graham arrived in a motor car covered in yellow and white daisies. Lucy was to ride with them, while I had been assigned to Douglas Hardenbergh's vehicle. My heart turned over when I saw his automobile was lavishly decorated in lilac blooms.

'Oh, look at that!' said Caroline. 'He's chosen your favourite flower, Emma. It must be a sign.' Giving me a wink, she added, 'Perhaps after Isadora and the Duke are married there will be another society wedding to plan!'

I knew perfectly well that Caroline had told Douglas that lilacs were my favourite flower. The fact that he'd gone along with her was what concerned me. Up until then, Douglas had been dallying with me but remained distant. But as he helped me into the passenger seat the twinkle in his eye confirmed a change in his demeanour towards me. My stomach tensed when I noticed that the wedding ring he always wore on his right hand to signify his widowhood had gone.

Once everyone had arrived, we proceeded along Fifth Avenue towards Bryant Park in order according to Teddy's instructions, which Caroline had dictated to him the previous evening. This was no casual affair and the order was purely hierarchical. Only the top fifty people in society had been invited.

Dozens of policemen had been assigned to the route to stop people crossing the road in front of the automobiles, but children slipped between the adults' legs and darted in front of us to wave. Although we were driving slowly, my imagination conjured an image of Angus Dempsy being crushed under the wheels of Oliver's motor car.

'Be careful of the children!' I said to Douglas. 'Can't we go slower?'

He seized the occasion to display his manly calm. 'I assure you that you are in safe hands, Miss Lacasse. We are not travelling above five miles per hour.'

The rumble of the engines, the gasoline fumes and the crowds were making the horses jittery. Some of them stepped backwards, trying to turn and bolt. I forced myself not to imagine the carnage that would result from a stampede, or if one of the drivers put their motor car into the wrong gear and ploughed into the crowd.

To add to my unease, Douglas took the opportunity to spout his philosophy on men, women and marriage.

'It's all very well for a woman to have a career when she is young and free,' he said, giving me a significant look. 'But matrimony is the sweet surrender of a woman's mind and body to one who, with his greater knowledge and wisdom, is most fit to determine what is best for her. Don't you agree?'

I wasn't sure which of my preferred responses would plunge me deeper into the hole Caroline had dug for me: to refute him or to ignore him. So I merely smiled and changed the subject.

'There's a definite touch of spring in the air today. The gentle transition between seasons is my favourite time of year.'

❧❧❧❧❧❧

At the conclusion of the parade, there was a picnic in Central Park. I was glad when the gathering finally dispersed and I could escape back to the house. An afternoon of intense writing would be required to clear my head of Douglas and his platitudes.

When I sat down at the escritoire in my room, I discovered to my horror that the picture of Grand-maman had disappeared. I searched behind the desk and in every corner of the room, but couldn't find it. Where could it have gone?

It was Jennie's day off, but it occurred to me that the frame might have been broken when the maids were cleaning and taken to the housekeeper for repair. I rushed downstairs to find her.

'I haven't seen it,' said Mrs Green. 'Have you looked everywhere in your room, Miss Lacasse?'

'Everywhere,' I told her. 'It was on my desk yesterday.'

'But not this morning?'

'I didn't notice it this morning because I was rushing to get ready for the motor car parade.'

'Well, we'll have to ask Jennie about it when she returns tomorrow.'

I couldn't see any way that Grand-maman's picture could have vanished unless someone had taken it. But why? The frame was silver, but there were much more valuable items in the house to steal if one of the servants was a thief. Then my mind turned to Caroline. I had gone to speak to her in the morning room before the parade and she had slammed the drawer of her desk shut as if there was something in it she didn't want me to see. For what perverse reason she would have taken the picture I couldn't say, and I certainly couldn't confront her outright. I would have to look in her desk drawer when she wasn't home.

I'd lost the urge to write and headed to the library to comfort myself with a book. I had only been in the room less than a minute when Caroline burst in, followed by Oliver. He slammed the door after him, his face as red as his hair and his eyes narrow with fury.

Caroline wheeled to confront him. 'What's the meaning of this behaviour, Oliver?' she asked imperiously. Then noticing me she said, 'Emma, you had better leave the room.'

'Stay where you are, Emma!' Oliver said, standing between me and the door. 'I want you to hear this too. I want you to know the truth about your sister.'

The blood pumped in my ears. I had never seen Oliver this angry.

'Tell that maggot you are finished with him,' he shouted at Caroline. 'And find another architect to build the house in Newport or don't build it at all! I'm not paying a man to make a fool of me!'

'I don't know what you're talking about,' replied Caroline.

'You don't, do you? Explain to me then why Colonel Mann approached me today at the picnic and knew all about you and Harland.'

'If any of the servants have been gossiping, I'll dismiss them immediately,' said Caroline, her voice rising indignantly.

I was astounded that she showed no remorse about the affair or fear of being exposed publicly.

'Mann wants ten thousand dollars to keep the story out of *Town Topics*,' Oliver said. 'God knows what's making you behave so stupidly over that fool, Caroline. I've turned a blind eye until now but it seems you haven't got the sense to be discreet. If it wasn't for Isadora and Grace, I'd tell Mann to go ahead and print the damn story!'

'Well, what else was I supposed to do?' Caroline said coldly. 'You're always working. You're not interested in the new house. You're not interested in *me*. And you're not exactly perfect yourself. What about Cora Branson? I didn't make a fuss about her.'

It was horrifying to witness Caroline turning the blame onto Oliver and making herself the injured party. Oliver's face took on a tortured expression and he sank into an armchair, wincing as if he was remembering something painful.

'That was years ago,' he said. 'After William … And I never brought her into our house. There was never a hint of gossip.'

Caroline straightened, pleased that she'd delivered an effective strike. 'If you're so worried about gossip, I can hardly fire Harland now and hire another architect. You're going to have to carry on as if everything is normal. The Duke is here now and we have to think of Isadora.'

Oliver's eyes screwed tight. 'Do *you* think of Isadora?'

'What do you mean?' Caroline shot back. 'How dare you imply I don't think about my daughter. Sometimes it seems like I'm the only one who thinks of her! You don't care any more about Isadora than you did about William. *You* brought that fever home from the factory floor — the doctor was sure of it. And where were you when our son was dying? I was the only one by his side.'

Oliver looked stricken. 'You know I was in San Francisco when I heard he was ill. I got on a train immediately!'

'But you were too late,' Caroline hissed at him. 'You've never been there for us. Never!'

Oliver sank his head into his hands. He was still and tense. I expected him to respond, but he said nothing. I realised how accurate Isadora had been about her mother's ability to attack people where it would hurt most.

'So you will turn me into a cuckold for a man who'll flit off to someone else the first chance he gets?' Oliver said quietly. 'After all I've done for you?'

'All you've done for me?' Caroline regarded him with contempt. 'You'd still be floundering around like a backwoodsman if it wasn't for me. It was I who made you great!'

Oliver lifted his face and stared at her stonily, as if he was finally seeing the real person he'd married. 'I took the blame for you over that poor Dempsy fellow after you callously left him lying in the street. I paid the witnesses to say that I was behind the wheel of my motor car that day, and then paid more money still to the press so they didn't report the death.'

My mind blurred with shock. *Caroline* had killed Angus Dempsy, not Oliver? A picture of Mrs Dempsy and her children in that dingy room rose up in my memory. My sister had done that to them! I wanted to rise to my feet and flee the room, so overwhelming was my horror at the revelation. But I couldn't move. I had turned to stone.

'You did it because having a wife in gaol would have been bad for your business,' Caroline replied without a note of remorse. 'A man could get away with such a thing but not a woman.'

Oliver cast his eyes over her. 'If you continue this ridiculous affair with Harland,' he said, 'I will be forced to shoot him. I will hang for it and my death will be on your head.'

It should have sounded like an impassioned threat, but Oliver's calm tone made the warning all the more menacing.

'Don't overreact,' Caroline said. 'You always overreact —'

But before she could finish, Oliver had left the room. We heard him shout to Woodford to have the carriage brought around, and then he was gone.

Caroline turned to me, expecting me to offer some words of support. But I couldn't speak.

She considered me with a curious expression, as if thinking about how much to tell me. 'The man I hit was a known drunkard. He stepped out right in front of me.'

'He had a family, Caroline. A wife and children.' I couldn't continue.

She lifted her eyebrows, no doubt wondering how I knew anything about Angus Dempsy. 'If that man had a family who needed him, why was he spending his money on drink? Ask yourself that before you look at me that way. And remember: you still have debts. I can very quickly write to Monsieur Depaul to tell Roche & Associates that I have withdrawn my support. Paulette will be out on the street before you even get back to Paris.'

I should have expected the threat but it still drew me up short. I was under my sister's thumb, and she not only knew it but *relished* it. I had no choice but to comply with her if I wanted to protect Paulette.

I stood, locked eyes with Caroline for a brief moment, then left the library, burning with impotent anger.

⚮⚮⚮

When my cheque arrived for the three stories that had been published in *New York City Magazine*, I forwarded it to Cecilia with a note: *Please make sure this money goes to Mrs Dempsy and her children.*

The amount would help for a month or two, but it wasn't going to change that family's life. It was merely my pathetic attempt to make amends for having a monster for a sister.

TWENTY-NINE

Lucy brought news of Oliver the following day. Caroline had commanded me to join them in the drawing room, but it was impossible for me to look my sister in the face after finding out it was she who had killed Angus Dempsy.

'Oliver's staying at the Hotel Chelsea,' Lucy told Caroline. 'Fortunately that's also where the Duke and Mr Whitlock have suites so it merely looks as though you've cleared the house of men so you can concentrate on the rumoured wedding preparations.' She paused, looking unsure of herself for the first time since I'd known her. 'But given the gossip that was circulating at the motor car parade, you'd better invite the Hunters for afternoon tea today to put on a show of unity. This is a very sensitive time for there to be any suggestion of things being less than harmonious in the Hopper family.'

When Grace and Harland arrived later that afternoon, Grace was as beautiful as ever in a pastel blue chiffon and lace dress. With her dark hair and fine features she resembled a pretty bellflower. But her eyes were full of despair. I wondered how this woman who could do anything with her life that she chose remained caught in an empty and abusive marriage.

Then I remembered Caroline's threat to me the evening before. *She's got us all trapped*, I thought, as I watched her pour tea for Harland and Grace and share some private joke with

Lucy. *She's got each of us exactly where she wants us. We are entangled in her web, unable to break free.*

It was a welcome relief when Isadora burst into the room. She looked flushed and excited. 'My sculptures have come back from the founding firm. I want you all to come see them.'

We followed Isadora to her studio where Mr Gadley was waiting. He had dressed for the occasion in a grey suit with a bowtie and winged collar shirt, and his normally unruly hair was combed to the side.

'Good afternoon, ladies and gentleman,' he said, leading us towards a bench where several sculptures each about fifty inches high had been arranged. There were deer, foxes, horses, bears and various species of birds. 'I present to you the magnificent work of Miss Isadora Hopper!'

I gazed at the sculptures in amazement. They had been formed in a dark brown bronze and were so beautifully observed and composed it was as if the animals were alive. A doe nudged her fawn with tenderness. Two horses rubbed their heads together in friendship. A bear stood on its hind legs and sniffed the air for danger.

'Isadora,' said Grace, astonishment in her voice, 'you are exceptionally gifted!'

'The patina and the texture are perfect for the forms,' I told her. 'Much better even than marble.'

Isadora sent a look of gratitude to her teacher. 'The founding firm Mr Gadley took them to hire some of the best mould-makers, casters, chasers and patineurs.'

Harland was staring at the sculptures with his hand on his chin. Why hadn't he said anything? He worked with sculptors all the time; surely he could recognise talent when he saw it.

Caroline stepped towards the bench and cast her eye over Isadora's work. She appreciated enough about art to judge these weren't ordinary pieces. I could see her mind ticking over and understood my sister well enough to guess that she was trying to gauge what this meant for her. How would having a brilliant artist for a daughter work in her favour?

Mr Gadley caught her expression too and seized his opportunity. 'Mrs Hopper, I assure you that your daughter is a sculptor of the very first rank. The market for private sculpture has exploded in the city, and she could easily be selling her work for twenty-five to three hundred dollars a piece through Tiffany & Co or the emporium of Shreve, Crump & Low. But as she is an artist who has no need to earn an income, she could concentrate on important commissions. The United States wants to make its mark and there are sculpture committees springing up all over the city. The Metropolitan Museum of Art would be interested in a great work by an American artist, for example.'

'There are no public monuments in New York City created by a woman,' Lucy said dismissively.

'Not yet,' I replied. Everyone turned to me but I kept my eyes on Caroline, trying to measure her reaction. I could see what Mr Gadley and Isadora were attempting to do, and I wanted to support them. 'There are no heroic statues of women in the city. Who better to sculpt those statues than a woman herself?'

Caroline's eyes gleamed and I knew I was hitting my mark. Who was she picturing herself as the model for? Jeanne d'Arc?

'But first …' said Isadora.

Caroline woke from her dream and turned to her daughter. 'But first … what?'

Mr Gadley cleared his throat. 'But first Miss Hopper must study in Paris for at least a year under a master at the École des Beaux-Arts. It will give her great prestige. Then she must enter a significant work in the Paris Salon. She is more than capable of achieving such success. I will tell you again, Mrs Hopper: your daughter is exceptional.'

Grace grasped my fingers and squeezed them. We waited for Caroline's response.

'Paris?' Caroline shook her head. 'But Isadora is to marry the Duke. He wouldn't want his young bride to spend a year in Paris.'

He wouldn't care, I thought. As long as she produced an heir and put on a good show when required, he wouldn't care if she lived at the North Pole as long as he had her dowry to spend.

'She could stay with me in Paris,' I said. 'I would go with her to her classes every day. There would be nothing unseemly about that.'

Isadora mouthed 'Thank you' to me.

Caroline was always so sure of her own opinions that I expected her to give her verdict straight away. But to my surprise she turned to Harland.

'What do you think?' she asked him. 'This is very risky. But then if Isadora is exceptional ...'

Harland removed his hand from his chin. 'What do I think? I think I've never heard such drivel in my life! These sculptures are good enough for a department store, but they are not brilliant.'

Caroline's face froze while the rest of us were shocked into silence.

'You are being hoodwinked by this teacher,' Harland continued. 'He wants to make a name for himself and he wants Isadora's money to do it.'

Mr Gadley's complexion turned a greenish-white. 'Why would you accuse me of such a terrible thing, sir? I am a teacher at the renowned Art Students League of New York. I know brilliance when I see it!'

'Do you?' Harland said with a laugh. 'More than I do? Look at this house, Gadley. I designed it as well as other monumental houses and buildings all over New York City. Where is your work? Do you have some obscure piece in a park in Louisville with pigeon shit all over it?'

Poor Mr Gadley. His polite, gentlemanly manner was no match for Harland. Now I understood what Grace lived with every day.

Harland turned to Isadora. 'Even if you were very talented, which you're not, it's near impossible for a woman to succeed as an artist. Have some sense, you silly girl! Marry your duke and be a duchess. Produce babies, not art. That is the life for you.'

Isadora's whole body had turned rigid. She looked as though she had stopped breathing.

'Will you stop it, Harland!' Grace cried. It was the first time I'd ever heard her raise her voice. 'Just stop it!'

Harland flashed her a look that was potent with violence and Grace withdrew into herself.

'I leave it up to you, Caroline,' he said. 'Isadora is your daughter. But Lucy has set up everything so well with the Duke. You should consider the consequences carefully. Isadora will fail in her endeavour to be an artist and then where will you be? Permelia's sister will marry the Duke, and you will be the laughing stock of New York.'

Mr Gadley rallied himself. 'If you won't believe me, Mrs Hopper, I will bring the great Augustus Saint-Gaudens himself here to view the work. Please don't destroy Isadora's ... Miss Hopper's spirit.'

Caroline glared at Mr Gadley's slip. I too realised something that I hadn't before. The exchange of envelopes at the end of each lesson — what had they been? Letters? Oh, poor Isadora! She and Mr Gadley were in love.

Caroline's mouth hardened and a steely look came to her eyes. 'Mr Gadley, you have deceived me and broken my trust. I allowed you into my home and you have led my daughter astray. You will leave this house immediately, and if you ever try to return I shall have you arrested.'

'Send me away,' he said, his voice hoarse and broken, 'but don't destroy your daughter —'

'I am the best judge of what's good for my daughter,' snapped Caroline. 'Now go!'

Mr Gadley gave Isadora one last adoring glance before he left the room. Isadora burst into tears.

'Why would you do such a thing?' she asked Harland. 'What have I ever done to you?'

'Enough, Isadora!' said Caroline. 'You've made fools of us. Imagine if word of this got out? I have enough to worry about.' She squinted at the sculptures and shook her head. 'If I hear any more of this, I will have those silly animals destroyed and banish you from using this room.'

Caroline left with Harland and Lucy, but I couldn't abandon Isadora. Grace stayed with us too.

'Why did Harland do that?' Isadora asked, sobbing pitifully. 'He knows how much Mother values his opinion. Surely he could see how unique the sculptures are?'

Grace clenched her fists. 'Because my husband is a terrible man! He enjoys destroying people. I hate him and I wish him —'

Her voice cracked and she stopped herself, but I knew what she had been about to say because I was thinking the same thing.

We both wished Harland Hunter dead.

⊙⊙⊙ ⊙⊙⊙

I stopped writing and tapped my pen. It was two in the morning and silence reigned over the house and the street outside. Only the clock on the mantelpiece ticked monotonously.

After the events of today I had been too agitated to sleep. I had tried to relax by reading, but a story was brewing in my head and the only way to calm myself was to spill it out into my notebook.

Ralph Richards was the most envied man in New York City. Coming from Swedish stock, his golden Nordic looks and tall stature were striking. The finest suits and shoes were given to him by the best tailors and cobblers

*on Sixth Avenue with gladness. He ate at Delmonico's
and Sherry's for free, because whatever Ralph Richards
wore or wherever he went, New York society was sure
to follow. He was married to a great beauty who was
both cultured and charming; and he designed houses
and interiors for the wealthiest families in the city. His
life was a whirlwind of invitations to fabulous balls,
exclusive dinners, elite clubs and luxurious estates. Men
admired him and women desired him. Ralph Richards
seemed pre-destined for glory — which made the ghastly
nature of his death all the more horrific.*

I tried to continue writing in third person, but it was like
wrestling an alligator. I poised my pen over my notebook and
switched to first person.

*One of New York's richest society matrons, Carrie
Weppler, organised a motor car obstacle course at
her family's summer mansion, Waverly. I watched the
participants arrive in their shiny De Dion-Boutons,
Renaults, Panhards and Fiats. The motor cars were
elaborately decorated with garlands of flowers and vines.*

*Among the guests were Ralph and Fannie Richards.
Always ahead of everyone else in fashion, Ralph wore
a white flannel long-roll sack suit with a striped shirt
and bowtie. Fannie was stunning in a pastel blue chiffon
and lace dress with a monobosom bodice. She held a
matching parasol, and with her dark hair and her fine
features she looked like a pretty bellflower.*

*Beulah and Alvin Dipple arrived in a motor car
covered in yellow and white daisies. From the arbour
frame dangled dozens of taxidermied canaries.*

*'I had to have Beulah's entire aviary gassed for this
display,' Alvin said, helping his wife out of the car.*

'Their songs became annoying after a while anyway,'
said Beulah.

I was about to strike out the part about the taxidermied canaries, but then I remembered the hummingbird on Oliver's mother's hat. It had obviously left an impression on me as a child. Besides, New York society *was* terribly callous towards animals and nature. I would leave the canaries in.

I picked up the copy of *New York City Magazine* where I'd seen the description of Oliver and Caroline's Newport estate and knew exactly how I was going to dispose of Ralph Richards. A smile came to my face. People really shouldn't upset writers. We might put them in our stories ... and kill them.

Before the obstacle course, the guests picnicked on the
beach at the foot of the steep craggy cliff for which
Waverly was famous. It was the largest drop from any of
the properties along Bellevue Avenue. Afterwards, tipsy
from all the champagne we had consumed, we made our
way back up the cliff stairs to the obstacle course.

Golf flags marked the path the contestants would take.
The obstacles included carriage tyres, potted shrubs and
bales of hay, but also wooden cut-outs fashioned into
the life-sized forms of pedestrians: policemen, newspaper
boys, old men, ladies with their arms full of packages,
nursemaids pushing prams, and tramps. The artists had
given each cut-out a lifelike expression of terror.

A stand with a striped canvas roof had been erected to
one side of the course for the spectators. We applauded
as the contestants approached their automobiles and
were assisted into them by Jake, the Wepplers' chauffeur,
and some footmen.

Jake had lined up the motor cars in the order the
driver was to compete. More glasses of champagne were

offered around and Carrie Weppler proposed a toast:
'May the best man — or woman — win!'

Wallace Gartside was the first driver onto the course.
He drove so slowly and carefully that the guests playfully
jeered him.

'It's an obstacle course not a parade!' Unwin
Langsdorf shouted at him. 'The pedestrians aren't real!'

Wallace's wife, Evelyn, who was riding as his
passenger alternately pulled faces or blew kisses at the
spectators.

Lester Weppler was next. He drove his Panhard
skilfully but at speed, taking risks just as he did in
business. While his timing was good, he misjudged a turn
and drove straight into a bale of hay.

Lulu Kinkle drove so recklessly that when she swerved
to avoid hitting a tramp cut-out, her pet cheetah leaped
out of the motor car and ran down the course. Footmen
fled in all directions in terror.

'He won't hurt you!' Lulu called. She stopped the
motor car and chased after her pet. 'Zishe! Zishe! Come
back to Mommy!'

A footman who had been raised in Texas tried to lasso
the cheetah. The spinning rope spooked Zishe and he ran
straight back into Lulu's arms.

'Oh, my baby,' she said, cuddling him to her. 'Did
those men frighten you?'

The next contestant was Ralph. He handed his glass
of champagne to Jake and lifted his arms in the air to stir
up the crowd.

I hesitated. Writing was more than merely putting words
on paper. It was about imbuing those words with emotions,
desires ... Should I really be pouring out my anger and thirst for
revenge through this story?

I remembered a conversation I'd once had with Belda about a matador who had been gored to death by a bull in the south of France.

'I couldn't feel any pity for that man,' she'd told me. 'I was happy for the bull — although of course he was slaughtered anyway. It's a one-way fight and the bull never wins.'

'You're identifying with the helpless animal,' I'd replied. 'You're hoping fate will intervene on its behalf.'

I turned back to my story. Perhaps it was time to stop waiting for fate.

The butterfly wings attached to the sides of the motor car made it difficult to access the driver's seat, so Jake had removed the wing on that side. He said something to Ralph, who nodded and climbed into the seat. Jake and a footman reattached the wing and locked it into position.

Ralph waved to us spectators as he passed, and headed down the slight slope towards the obstacle course.
The first part was straight, but at the first curve Ralph drove right past the flags, narrowly missing a clump of shrubbery that would have brought him to a halt.

We clapped, amused by his antics. Ralph Richards, it was commonly said, could always be relied on to enliven even the most boring party.

But a cry of surprise rose up when Ralph ploughed straight into the wooden cut-out of a policeman, knocking it flat, then proceeded to knock down a tramp and a lady carrying parcels in fast succession.

From there, the slope got steeper and Ralph continued to gather speed.

'Slow down, sir!' one of the footmen shouted after him.

The horse and carriage cut-out splintered as Ralph drove straight through it.

Jake ran down the course after the motor car, waving
his arms. 'Turn to the left, Mr Richards! Turn to the left!'

The real inkling that something was wrong came
when Ralph struggled with the butterfly wing attached to
the driver's side of the motor car.

'He's trying to get out,' said Margaret Altherr.

'He's getting faster!' her elderly husband observed.

'My God, the man is heading straight for the cliff!'
cried the Duke of Surrey, rising to his feet.

Everything seemed to slow down. Except for Ralph's
motor car, which was speeding towards the edge of the
lawn where the terrain roughened to rocky soil and low
shrubs.

Now everyone was on their feet. Jake and several
footmen ran after the car, throwing off their jackets as
they went.

Ralph's car hit a bump. It dipped, then rose into
the air as if it were a butterfly taking flight. For a few
seconds it seemed to hover in the sky, before it turned
nose down and plunged off the cliff. The silence was
broken by the bone-chilling sound of smashing metal.

'Oh my God!' cried Beulah, bringing both hands to
her face.

Suddenly all of us were running towards the cliff edge,
stumbling and tripping in shock.

My stomach lurched when I saw the rocks below.
The motor car had landed upside down. One of the back
wheels was spinning, while the two front ones had come
off and were bobbing in the waves. The chassis was
dented and crumpled as if the motor car had hit the rocks
nose down then flipped over. Blood dripped into the
ocean, turning the water red. It was impossible to believe
that oozing mess had only moments ago been handsome
Ralph Richards.

Too sickened to look any more, my gaze travelled to Carrie Weppler. The dispassionate expression on her face was even more chilling than the carnage below.

Carrie, I thought, how quickly you can turn against someone when they have crossed you ...

⚜

I was still feeling my way with the narrative and had intended for it only to be a short story. But my ideas were expanding and I wondered if I had the bones for a full-length novel at last. I'd never written a story so close to my own life before. My other stories were complete fantasies that had come from who knew where. Although it was only a first draft, I'd found writing it entrancing. It was allowing me to make sense of all that had happened since I'd arrived in New York, to see things more clearly. Through writing about those events, I was able to step out of the drama and become the observer again.

It was what Claude had said I would need to do in order to survive my sister. It finally dawned on me how wise his words had been.

THIRTY

I slept late the following morning and nobody disturbed me. When I woke, I squinted at the sunlight that was bright through the gap in the curtains and rubbed my head. A feeling that I had forgotten something floated in my mind. I sat up as I remembered dinner the previous evening with the Duke and Mr Whitlock. It had been another miserable affair. Isadora's face had been swollen from crying at Harland's cruel rejection of her work. Despite her obvious distress, the Duke didn't make one reassuring gesture towards her. Damn that man!

I quickly dressed and went in search of Isadora. I wondered why she hadn't sent Jennie for me when I didn't come down to breakfast.

I couldn't find her in the sitting room off her bedroom or the music room. I was on my way to her studio when I heard Caroline scream. I had a terrible vision of Isadora hanging from her wedding veil — and ran to the salon, which was where the cry had come from.

When I burst into the room, Caroline was holding her hand to her chest. 'I don't believe it!' she said to Harland and Lucy, her voice shaking.

She was pale, but not as distressed as she would have been if she'd discovered her daughter dead. Something else must have happened. Excitement flooded my mind. Had Isadora run away? Or perhaps the Duke had decided that marrying into the Hopper family wasn't worth the money.

'What's happened?' I asked.

Caroline turned to me. 'It's dreadful, Emma! Permelia Frances has bought a yacht!'

It took me a moment to be sure that I'd heard her correctly. It was all I could do not to show my disgust as I said, 'Do you know where Isadora is? I can't find her.'

Caroline waved her hand dismissively. 'Rebecca Clark has taken her for a carriage ride. I couldn't stand to see Isadora's long face any more. The last thing I need is for the Duke to start viewing her as a melancholic.'

There was no point expressing my concern for Isadora to Caroline. I turned to leave the room but she caught my arm.

'Didn't you hear what I said, Emma? Permelia Frances has bought a yacht!'

'And not just any yacht,' Harland added. 'It's a 323-foot steam-powered vessel. According to *Town Topics* no expense has been spared: the whole ship is decorated in the Art Nouveau style, with stained-glass interior doors and light fittings in the shape of exotic flowers. The petals conceal the electric light bulbs apparently.'

'It sounds perfectly dreadful,' said Lucy.

That wasn't the impression I was getting from Harland. Rather, he sounded envious of the yacht's design.

'It's called *The Blue Blazer*,' said Caroline. 'Who names a boat after a cocktail? And she's launching it the same night as the ball for the Duke and Isadora. She's invited all my close friends to an exclusive dinner on board — the Grahams, the Potters, the Harpers!'

So there was the real problem. Permelia Frances was doing to Caroline exactly what she had done to Augusta Van der Heyden.

At that moment, I heard Isadora return from her carriage ride. 'Excuse me,' I said to Caroline and the others, and hurried out to catch my niece as she made her way upstairs.

She turned when I called her name and it saddened me to see her dispirited face. Even the beautiful magenta dress she was wearing couldn't lift her pallor.

'Let's have a chat,' I said, inviting her to come to my room. I wished I could comfort her by taking her to the studio where she would be able to transform a lump of clay into something beautiful. But that pleasure was gone now. It had been destroyed by Harland and her mother.

We sat together by the window and held hands. 'Are you all right?' I asked, knowing as soon as the words left my lips that it was a foolish question.

She blinked away tears, and I promised myself I wouldn't pursue the subject of the sculptures — or Mr Gadley — while they were too raw for her.

'The Duke's got a headache so he won't be coming here until later,' she said. 'He gets more headaches than anyone I know.'

'Hopefully they'll get worse after you are married, and he'll leave you alone.'

She half-smiled, then shook her head. 'You've changed, Aunt Emma. New York has made you harder. I'm sorry for that. I hope you will be happy again when you return to France.'

I doubted that I would be happy in France or anywhere else for a long time without Claude. But Isadora had too many griefs of her own to burden her with mine.

'I needed to become harder,' I told her. 'Being too soft only makes you a target for liars and manipulators. I'm sorry you've had to learn that lesson too.'

'I only pretend to be soft in order to protect myself,' she said. 'I'm more conniving than you think.'

'You, conniving — I can't see that.' I remembered the inventive way she and Mr Gadley had exchanged love notes right before my eyes. 'Clever maybe, but not conniving.'

She nodded sadly and turned to my desk. 'Where is your photograph of Great-Grand-maman Sylvie?'

'I think your mother took it,' I said. 'For what reason I have no idea. I asked Jennie about it and she swore it wasn't her or one of the other maids. I suspect it's in Caroline's desk drawer in the morning room because when I went to see her there, she closed the drawer as if there was something she didn't want me to see in it. I haven't had a chance to look. Every time I try to sneak in there, Woodford or one of the other servants appears.'

'No wonder you write such good mystery stories, Aunt Emma, because your suspicions are right. It will be in that drawer along with the photographs she took away of Grandmother Hopper and Aunt Anne ... and William. Mother won't have pictures of departed family members in the house.'

'Do they make her sad?'

'They're not reminders to *her*,' explained Isadora. 'They're reminders to *us*. Mother doesn't want us feeling loyalty to anyone but her. The drawer is locked, by the way. The key is in the majolica urn on the mantelpiece.'

'How do you know that?' I asked.

She lowered her eyes. 'When I was younger I used to go in there to look at photographs of William. I wanted to etch him so clearly in my mind that I wouldn't forget a single detail. One day, when I'm away from here, I will make a sculpture of him so he can always be with me.'

I marvelled at how clever Isadora had been at circumventing her mother. Much cleverer than me!

Until now, when it seemed there was no way out of her marrying the Duke.

❧❦❧❦❧

The *New York Times* report on the 'Under the Sea' ball described it as the most exquisite event Manhattan had ever seen:

> *Forty tables were arranged in the dining room, each decorated with engraved scallop shells instead of place cards and a centrepiece of a glass tray of sand in which sat candles, cockle shells, and silver-painted starfish. Party favours were hidden in the sand too — Tiffany sapphire bracelets for the ladies and Cartier pearl cufflinks for the men. Miniature spades were provided along with the cutlery and the guests had a delightful time performing their own treasure hunts.*
>
> *The footmen were dressed as sailors; and in the ballroom a fishing net spanned the ceiling and was decorated with hanging artificial jellyfish, sea fish of all kinds and even a whale. Three orchestras played, and three sumptuous suppers were served. But perhaps the most exciting moment was when Mr Oliver Hopper announced the engagement of his daughter, Miss Isadora Rosamund Hopper, to the Duke of Bridgewater ...*

On the surface the ball was indeed stunning, but each of us carried a burden in our heart.

The Duke did his best to maintain his act of the adoring fiancé while sneaking glances at the other beautiful women in the room. Oliver, who had agreed to return to the house for formal occasions, looked grim, no doubt contemplating the farce his life had become.

Isadora stood dutifully between her parents and the Duke, smiling for the guests, but her sunken shoulders and grief-stricken pallor suggested one attending her own funeral. I did my best to support her, but my own heart ached to know that soon she would be off to England and I would return to Paris, to begin a new life without Claude. I had come to New York to discover my family, and now I felt more alone than ever.

Caroline stood rigid, her eyes glued to each arriving guest, desperate to discover who would stay loyal to her and who had decamped to Permelia's dinner on her yacht. She visibly relaxed when the carriages of the Grahams and the Harpers arrived.

But when Lucy and Grace appeared without Harland, Caroline was put out.

'He has a terrible fever,' explained Lucy. 'The thermometer went up to one hundred and three. After he left here today, he collapsed into bed utterly exhausted and Doctor Mitford has ordered complete rest. Harland sends his deepest apologies.'

'It's a great pity,' said Caroline testily. 'You know how popular he is, and the decoration is all his work. But it can't be helped.'

I knew she was worried about how Harland's absence would be perceived. Nothing short of death should have kept him away from Caroline's side tonight, especially as the stakes were so high.

Lucy recognised it too. 'He exhausted himself creating all this beauty,' she said. 'I'm sure people will understand when we tell them that. They know that Harland never does anything by halves. He completely throws himself into his work.'

As the evening progressed it became clear that not all of Caroline's friends had remained loyal. When the Potters and the Bishops hadn't arrived by midnight, Woodford discreetly removed their places at the tables that had been assigned to them.

❦

The following morning, Caroline ordered her florist to send Harland an enormous arrangement of royal purple and magenta roses set among ferns and ivy. Perhaps she wouldn't have acted

so hastily if she had waited for the arrival of *Town Topics* a day
later.

Lucy and I were with her in the drawing room when
Woodford brought the newspaper on a tray. Caroline read
the announcement of Isadora and the Duke's engagement with
satisfaction, then her eyes moved to the article below it. She
blanched and the paper slipped from her fingers to the floor.
'Impossible!'

Lucy and I exchanged glances and bent for the paper at the
same time. We read the article together.

> *It seems New York society has a new star hostess in*
> *Permelia Frances. For what she lacks in background and*
> *education, she certainly makes up for in beauty, charm*
> *and wit. While she ignores the rules of convention and*
> *leaves a party soon after arriving if she considers it 'a*
> *bore', her sparkling dinner upon her yacht, in honour*
> *of the Grand Duke Boris Vladimirovich of Russia, was*
> *definitely the most exciting event of the season, even*
> *eclipsing a certain debutante's costume ball. Guests were*
> *served an extraordinary meal of Lobster Newburg and*
> *baked alaska by footmen dressed as cupids, and danced*
> *to the stirring music of a Hungarian tzigane band.*
>
> *As well as the glittering array of wealthy guests from*
> *around the globe, the invitees included artists, writers*
> *and actors — a mix regularly found in London society*
> *but rarely in New York. The most surprising guest of all*
> *was a certain architect who, it seems, will be designing*
> *the Franceses' new homes in Manhattan and Newport in*
> *a modern style unlike anything that has been seen among*
> *the city's elite before.*

Our eyes went immediately to the article below to confirm who
Colonel Mann was writing about. Lucy let out a gasp at the

drawing of Harland arriving at the Potters' musical evening the previous week.

'But he was so sick!' she cried. 'He must have been pretending! I can't believe he could feign a fever like that.'

Caroline's mouth set in a grim line. 'It's easy to feign a fever. All he had to do was put his thermometer in hot tea when the doctor wasn't looking.'

'This is utter betrayal,' said Lucy. 'I will write to all our friends immediately to tell them that Harland is never to enter their houses again. But what about Grace?'

Caroline stuck out her chin and squared her shoulders like a general going into battle. 'Don't do that,' she said. 'It's best not to acknowledge the betrayal. Instead we will act as if we pity him. We'll make a joke of it, as if we don't care. I will engage another architect for my house in Newport and people will assume that Harland had to run to Permelia because *I* discarded him.'

I recalled Carrie Weppler in my story, peering over the cliff and cold-bloodedly viewing the crushed remains of Ralph Richards. Harland had been Caroline's lover. Was she so obsessed with being superior to everyone that she couldn't feel anything else at all?

Then I realised that the terrible suspicion that had been stirring in the back of my mind was true. Caroline had faked her heart attack as surely as Harland had feigned his fever. They were people who stopped at nothing to get what they wanted.

∽∾∽

The unease in the house drove me to seek solitude and I spent the next few afternoons in my room developing my story, which I had titled *Death at Waverly*.

I could no longer deny the truth of Caroline's immoral nature. She had manipulated Isadora into a marriage that was in every way unsuited to her. She held me prisoner by my debts and had even threatened to have Paulette thrown out of our apartment and onto the street. Yet despite all this, the ties that bound us were too strong to break completely; I could not bring myself to emotionally disown her as much as I desired to. Some part of me was waiting for Caroline to show a glimmer of the fine person Grand-maman had believed she could be.

One afternoon while Isadora and the Duke were out making calls on society matrons, and I was hard at work on a scene in which the chauffeur reveals to the narrator that the brakes on Ralph Richards' motor car have been tampered with, there was a loud knock at my door, which caused my pen to skid across the page.

Jennie burst into the room. 'Miss Lacasse, please come quickly! Mr Hunter is here demanding to see Mrs Hopper. He's drunk and I can't find Woodford, and none of the other servants have the authority to order him to leave. Please come down and tell the footmen they have your permission.'

'Where is my sister?'

'Mrs Hopper is visiting Her Grace, the Duchess of Dorset. I don't know when she'll return.'

Harland was waiting at the bottom of the staircase. His eyes were bloodshot and he was swaying on his feet. But I could see he wasn't drunk. It was pure rage that was driving him. The whites of his eyes were showing and his teeth were bared.

I'd been happy to do away with him fictionally, but coming face to face with him, I faltered. I wanted nothing more than to get him out of the house, but I didn't want to send him home to Grace in his current state.

'Harland, you aren't well,' I said. 'Would you like to sit in the drawing room a while? I will call a doctor.'

'I'm perfectly well,' he said, sneering. 'Where is Caroline?'

At that moment my sister swept through the front door. She didn't look surprised when she saw Harland.

'Hello, Harland, what are you doing here?'

'I know what you've done, Caroline,' he spat. 'All my contracts in New York have been cancelled.'

Caroline stared down her nose at him, as if she were a schoolmistress dealing with an insolent child. 'It was my understanding that you quit being our architect without notice. I've hired a new firm now — and so have all my friends.'

He lurched towards her. 'You vengeful bitch! Yes, I went to Permelia's dinner — is that a crime? It was a darn sight more exciting than one of yours! If one wants to be fashionable, one must mix with fashionable people — not passé ones.'

The veins popped out on Caroline's neck. She glared at Harland, her hands clenched into fists by her sides. I tensed, waiting for her to unleash her fury. She thought she had groomed Harland like the rest of us to be wholly in her power. Instead he was proving himself her match.

'You're the one who is passé, Harland,' she said, stepping up close to him although she was half his size. 'I will always be rich. I will always be powerful. But what will you do when all your commissions dry up? Because they will. Permelia Frances doesn't have the status that I do. She's a novelty at present — like you. But neither of you have staying power. You'll soon be finished, with only Grace's humble fortune to get you by.'

Two footmen opened a door and peered into the hall. I was about to signal to them to throw Harland out — more alarmed now by Caroline's potential for violence than Harland's own — when Woodford turned up with Jennie by his side.

'How dare you insult Mrs Hopper in her home!' His booming voice echoed around the great hall. 'If you think you can come here and behave so outrageously you are greatly mistaken, Mr Hunter. If you don't leave immediately I will summon the police and have you arrested.'

'Are you threatening me?' Harland said.

'I'm just giving you the facts,' the butler replied with heroic calm.

Harland's nostrils flared. He rolled his shoulders as if preparing for a fight, then thought better of it. He stormed out of the house, sending the pigeons that were foraging on the front steps into flight.

Caroline lifted her chin and narrowed her eyes. 'Harland made a mistake thinking he could crush me like he did the others,' she told me. 'A lot worse could happen than having his contracts cancelled. He'll see.'

THIRTY-ONE

When I had finished my story, I rewrote it in French and sent it to Monsieur Plamondon with a note.

> *The story still needs some reworking, of course,*
> *but I thought I would send it in this form for your*
> *opinion to see if it is worth expanding into a novel.*
> *The novel would be a murder mystery. With so many*
> *people having something against Ralph Richards, it*
> *will be a guessing game as to who the murderer — or*
> *murderess — is …*

I longed for fresh air and sunshine so I took my package to the post office myself rather than giving it to Woodford.

When I returned to the house, Caroline intercepted me in the great hall and told me to go into the drawing room. Woodford was already there. She was shaking with anger and I wondered if there had been another encounter with Harland.

'The Duchess has given me some shocking news,' she said, looking from Woodford to me. 'Those bronze sculptures Isadora made have somehow found their way to an exhibition at Shreve, Crump & Low. I don't know who helped her, but I know it wasn't the Duke.' She turned to Woodford. 'I would like you to question the staff. Anyone who has any knowledge of the matter is to be brought to me.' Then she regarded me. 'Do you know anything about this, Emma?'

I didn't, but I admired Isadora's determination. Yet I had to be careful; I didn't want to lose Caroline's trust lest she separate me from my niece at a time when Isadora needed me more than ever.

'Absolutely nothing,' I said. 'I thought Isadora was out in the afternoons with the Duke so I've been working on my novel.'

Caroline glanced at Woodford, who nodded.

A chill ran down my back. *I am being watched.* That's why Woodford or a servant appeared whenever I ventured near the morning room.

'It was Rebecca Clark then, I'm sure of it,' Caroline said. 'She's jealous of Isadora's successful match and is trying to sabotage it. Her name is to be struck off the guest list,' she told Woodford, 'and she's never to set foot in this house again. And I will make sure the gallery destroys those sculptures before anybody else sees them.'

As the wedding date grew closer, Caroline became more despotic. Two footmen were stationed outside Isadora's bedroom day and night, preventing me from visiting her to find out more about the exhibition of her sculptures; and a bodyguard accompanied her and the Duke whenever they went out. Caroline spread a rumour that there had been kidnap threats, but we all knew she was keeping Isadora a virtual prisoner until she was joined in matrimony to the Duke. As for me, whenever I asked Caroline about arranging my passage back to Paris after the wedding she was deliberately vague about the dates, although she did inform me she had requested Monsieur Depaul to make another instalment to Roche & Associates.

'Why don't you join us for the Newport season?' she said to me. 'There is no need to hurry back to France after Isadora and the Duke's wedding.'

My mind went into turmoil with the sickening realisation that Caroline was attempting to steer me into marrying Douglas Hardenbergh.

I was glad when I received a note from Florence asking me to visit her at her studio in the Village: *I thought you might like an advance viewing of my exhibition before you return to France.* Florence's father was a congressman and a lawyer: perhaps he would be able to intervene on my behalf so that Caroline couldn't break the contract she had made with me before I'd left France? I would ask Florence's advice straight away.

I was about to request Woodford to arrange a carriage for me when the sight of the afternoon's newspaper on his desk stopped me in my tracks. The headline read: *Genius Architect Meets Grisly Death.* Before I even read the first line, I knew it was referring to Harland Hunter.

◦◦◦◦◦◦◦◦

Black crêpe tied with a white ribbon was pinned to the front door of the Hunters' house. I rapped the knocker softly. Aston answered, wearing a black armband. He showed me into the reception room, where Grace was sitting with two elderly women, all three of them in mourning clothes. Through another door I glimpsed a coffin with candles placed around it.

Grace stood and led me to the drawing room. 'I'm so glad you came, Emma,' she whispered.

'What happened?' I asked, taking her hands. 'The newspaper gave very few details except there was an accident at a construction site?'

'Harland got into an argument with the new architect for the Westbay building on Park Row. They were on the roof and Harland went to take a swing at the man. He slipped on a tile and slid straight off the roof and plunged to the pavement below. A section of scaffolding fell with him and crushed his body.'

My blood tingled as I remembered Ralph Richards' gruesome end in my story. I vowed never again to write in the first person.

'We had to have a closed coffin,' Grace added. 'His remains don't resemble anything human.' She began to cry and I put my hand on her arm.

'I'm still keeping up appearances even though Harland is dead,' she went on. 'I've had to pay actors from a Broadway theatre to pose as pallbearers for the funeral. Nobody I asked was prepared to do it. I've given them each a story about how they knew Harland.'

'But he had so many friends,' I said. 'He was society's darling!'

Grace flashed me a look. 'Society loves a sensation but it has to be the *right* sensation. Everyone is shying away because they know about the rift between him and Caroline. There's even a rumour that she paid someone to push him and silenced the witnesses.'

'Do you think that's true?'

Grace held my gaze for a moment, then shook her head. 'No, I don't think so. Harland was always impetuous. It was exactly the sort of accident he would have.' She rubbed her arms. 'The only person I'm expecting at the funeral to support me is you, Emma. And honestly, if it wasn't for the sake of our mothers, I wouldn't be going through with this farce at all. His remains will be placed in the Hunter family mausoleum, but I'm specifying in my will that I'm not to be buried anywhere near him. I'm building a new mausoleum for myself and my mother.' Her voice trembled. 'I was still a young woman when I met Harland. He took my best years from me. Now I must wear black for a man I couldn't stand, who subjected me to the greatest humiliations and loneliness.'

I remembered the portrait I had seen of Grace, the one by Boldini. 'That young woman is still there inside you,' I assured her. 'Step by step you will discover her again.'

She lifted her eyes and looked me in the face. 'One thing is for sure,' she said with bitterness. 'I will *never* marry again.'

❦

Harland's funeral was a sobering affair. There were more spectators and press reporters outside the church than there were mourners inside. And most of the mourners had been hired by the funeral parlour. Grace had tactfully explained to her elderly and frail mother, who attended with a nurse, that she'd thought it best to keep the funeral private. Harland had told me before Isadora's debutante ball that Marie Antoinette had lived so brilliantly it didn't matter how she'd died. Was that true? Apart from his mother and Grace's, there was nobody in the church who truly loved him.

Caroline was unmoved by the news of her former lover's demise. She went on with the wedding preparations as if Harland had been nothing more than a pesky fly that had finally been swatted away. However, there was another problem that could not be so easily dismissed: Caroline's reputation. Nothing was more important to my sister than how people viewed her. She had clawed her way to the top of New York society and she did not intend to lose her position.

She no longer took me into her confidence, but one day I was passing the morning room when I overheard her and Lucy talking. There were no servants about and I stopped by the door to listen.

'Whether or not to accept the invitation to Isadora and the Duke's wedding is the subject of every conversation in every drawing room I have visited this week,' Lucy said. 'Society is in a dilemma because many people think you had Harland disposed of.'

There was a silence before Caroline answered. 'I don't understand what the fuss is about. Harland was nothing more than a dead mouse the cat brought in. Isadora is the wealthiest heiress in the United States and the Duke descends from one of the most important families in England.'

'That may be so, Caroline, but the Schorers and the Warburgs already intend to use the excuse of needing to get away early for the London season in order to decline.'

I rubbed my throat. It didn't matter to me if Caroline's plans were coming undone, but what would be the implications for Isadora? I still hadn't had a chance to speak to her alone since the incident with her sculptures. Caroline's maid was always by Isadora's side wherever she went in the house, and even joined us at breakfast. It made private conversation impossible.

'Why are they rushing to the London season when all the aristocrats will be here, including the Prince and Princess of Wales?' Caroline asked.

Lucy gasped. 'But, Caroline, the only notable guests coming from England are the Duke's brother and sister. Even the rest of the Duke's family aren't going to inconvenience themselves for a foreign wedding.'

'The Schorers and the Warburgs don't know that,' said Caroline. 'And can't your husband encourage a few of his associates to attend? They need money, don't they? I will offer them generous sums. We will also spread the rumour that you are acting as an official matchmaker for titled Englishmen to find suitable brides in New York. The Schorers' granddaughters are almost spinsters, but a large dowry as an enticement to an impoverished earl or lord could fix that.'

Woodford was coming down the stairs with two maids in his trail, ending my eavesdropping. I headed towards the music room, closed the door behind me and leaned against it, shivering. Isadora's wedding was either going to be Caroline's greatest triumph — or her Waterloo.

THIRTY-TWO

Caroline threw herself into the final preparations for the wedding with a zeal that was terrifying. A crew of sixty workmen were hired to decorate the church under the instruction of New York's best florists. The floral display itself would be spectacular, with garlands of orchids hanging from the gallery, vines wound around the columns, and floral gates of pink roses. The walls of the church were to be covered in palm foliage, roses and chrysanthemums so the overall effect would be like sitting in an enchanted garden. Besides the organist, the choir, and a soprano and tenor from the Metropolitan Opera, a sixty-man symphony orchestra was to be brought in from Vienna. As well as playing the Bridal Chorus from *Lohengrin*, they would entertain the guests with stirring pieces by Beethoven and Tchaikovsky.

Isadora listened to all these plans with a subdued expression. Each day she became more and more like a ghost until I feared she might fade away completely.

The afternoon before the wedding was my only chance to visit Florence at last at her studio in the Village.

'I'm sorry I couldn't come earlier,' I told her when she answered my knock. 'A dear friend's husband died — and that, along with the wedding preparations, have turned my life into chaos.'

The studio was cluttered with paint-splattered tables and the familiar washing line of notes strung across the room, but there wasn't a single painting anywhere.

'I've already hung everything at the gallery,' Florence explained. 'The opening is next week.'

The air went out of me. 'I'm so sorry. But it seems I will still be here for the exhibition after all because —'

I was about to launch into my explanation of virtually being Caroline's prisoner and to ask Florence's advice on the legal matter of the contract regarding my debts, but before I could continue she went to her desk and pulled a sheet of paper out of its drawer.

'I didn't invite you here only to see the paintings,' she said. 'I received this letter from Claude.'

I was tense with expectation. From the agonised expression on Florence's face, the letter clearly contained something of momentous importance.

'When you told me that you hadn't broken things off with him, as he'd said to me, I was furious but also suspicious. Both of you were telling vastly different stories with absolute sincerity. I wrote to him and explained you seemed at a loss as to why the relationship had ended. He replied, and enclosed this letter. It is from you to him, Emma.'

I took the paper from her. The letter was written on my blue stationery.

Dearest Claude,
I have composed this letter to you in my heart over and over again, but now that I sit here with a pen in my hand, words fail me. If I did not love you so much, I might be able to explain all this with platitudes and pithy phrases, but all I have to offer is stark honesty.

When I came to New York, I missed you even more than I would have believed. We always shared everything that was in our heads — but perhaps, I see now, not

*what was deeply in our hearts. Something wonderful has
happened to me — suddenly and unexpectedly. I have
met someone: a widower with adorable young children.
He is a very good man — honest, clever, intelligent and
loyal. I feel that with him I can have what I have always
most wanted: a home where I feel safe with people I
belong to and who belong to me.*

He has asked me to marry him and I have accepted.

*I am both happy and bitterly unhappy with my
decision. Happy because he is such a good person who
cares deeply for me; and bitterly unhappy because I must
say goodbye to you when I still cherish you and always
will. But we want different things, Claude.*

So I set you free, and I set myself free too ...

I dropped the letter to the floor as if it were evil. The handwriting
was most certainly mine, right down to the loopy l's and p's.
Had I gone mad? Had I written this letter in some delirious
fever-induced state?

'This can't be real! It just can't be real!' I said.

Florence frowned. 'What do you mean? It's your handwriting,
isn't it?'

I shook my head. 'The only part of that letter that's true is that
I love Claude, and always will. I never had the slightest interest
in Douglas Hardenbergh. Ever! That was all Caroline's —'

The words caught in my throat as an image came to me: a
swarthy woman, beautifully dressed but hard in the face, holding
an ivory fountain pen. The writing was a perfect imitation, but
it was the phrasing, tone and content that was most disturbing.
It sounded exactly as if I had written it.

I sat down quickly lest I fainted. Florence was watching me
with wide eyes.

'Maria de Amaragi wrote this letter,' I told her. 'And Caroline
dictated it!'

I stormed into the great hall and straight towards the morning room, not caring that a maid was in there cleaning the mirrors. My eyes locked on Caroline's desk. The maid hurried out — to alert Caroline or Woodford most likely — so I only had a few minutes to find what I was looking for.

I shook the key from the majolica jar on the mantelpiece and pressed it into the drawer lock. On top of a pile of photographs was my silver frame containing the picture of Grand-maman.

'Stall them, please, Grand-maman,' I prayed, slipping the frame into the bodice of my dress.

I lifted the photographs and discovered a pile of envelopes underneath. All the letters I had written to Claude since November. Below them were the letters Claude had written to me.

Isadora had not told Caroline about Claude; my sister had learned about him by reading our letters. How else could she have known my writing style and tone, the kinds of words I would choose? She even deduced that I would never have mentioned to Claude that Douglas Hardenbergh was very rich.

I pulled out the last letter Claude had written to me.

Dearest Emma,
You have given me a shock and broken my heart at once.
You have also shown me what a fool I was not to marry
you when I had the chance. But what can I say now?
You have found someone who will give you what you
want. I put too much faith in love and trust, and not
enough in an official commitment, and now I have paid
the price.
But, sweet Emma, although I have bitter tears pouring
down my cheeks, I only have goodwill towards you.
I wish you every happiness, and only happiness, in your

new life. Your widower and his children are very lucky to
have you. I hope they will always appreciate —

'What are you doing?' I spun around to see Caroline standing in the doorway, the maid hovering behind her. 'How dare you go through my private things?'

'Your private things?' I choked on the words. If Caroline thought she was going to turn this around and make herself the victim, she was in for a surprise. 'These are *my* personal letters. You read them. But worse than that, you forged a letter to Claude!'

My voice cracked at the full realisation that Caroline had purposely destroyed the most precious thing in my life. But why did that surprise me? My sister knew no boundaries. Perhaps she *had* engineered Harland's death. At that moment I could believe anything of my sister if it was evil enough.

'Do you know what you've done?' I told her. 'You've broken the heart of someone I love, and broken my heart too in the process.'

'Pffft,' she said, as if I was crying over something trivial like a broken doll. 'That artist! You don't know what's good for you, Emma. You never did. I was always the one who had to think about practicalities. You exist with your head in the clouds.'

'How dare you —'

She raised her voice over mine. 'How dare I? You were the one who came begging to me for money, Emma. You had debts.' She waved her arm around the beautiful room. 'Do you see any debts here? I don't. I see wealth and luxury. *My* wealth and luxury! I was smart about who I chose to marry.'

'I was in debt because I tried to help Grand-maman. As for your marriage to Oliver, I'd hardly describe that as a match made in heaven!'

Caroline ignored me. 'I've done you a favour and you don't appreciate it! Douglas Hardenbergh wouldn't have looked twice at you if it wasn't for me.' She flicked one of the emerald earrings I was wearing with her finger. 'I've dressed you in exquisite clothes and jewellery, taken you into the finest homes, showered you with nothing but the best.' She brought her face close to mine. 'What have you ever done for me, Emma? What single thing have you ever given me? Nothing! But I have done everything for you!'

It was what Caroline was best at: taking a grain of truth and twisting it and twisting it until you felt the only way to stop the torture was to open a window and jump out. But her attempt strangely calmed me.

I lifted my eyes to hers. 'It doesn't work any more, Caroline. The manipulation has lost its power. I'm leaving this house now. I shall return tomorrow to accompany Isadora to the church as I have promised. After that you will never see me again.'

Caroline's mouth moved but she said nothing. She had expected me to argue with her, but I knew better than that. I had seen how she defeated Oliver that way. He tried to fight with her to make a point or reach an understanding, but Caroline never argued for that purpose. Trying to reason with Caroline was like throwing yourself into a net, and the more she attacked and the more you countered, the more entangled you became in its mesh. I wasn't playing that game with her.

I swept past her and ran up the staircase. My heart was throbbing in my chest when I reached my room. I didn't have any of my old clothes from Paris, but my trunk was still in the bottom of the wardrobe. I dragged it out and filled it with linens, but when I turned to the dresses in the wardrobe they all looked ridiculously showy. Florence could lend me something until I had a chance to buy some new clothes. I packed only my books, papers and Grand-maman's picture into the trunk.

My harp was still in the music room. I turned to walk out the door — but it slammed shut and clicked.

I rushed towards it. The key was no longer in the lock. I turned the knob. The door was secured from the outside.

'Open this door now!' I shouted, banging my fist on the wood. 'You can't keep me in this room! Caroline! Open this door!'

But there was no answer. I turned around and leaned my back against the door. Now I truly was her prisoner.

My mind turned to Claude and his letter. At least there was one thing I could do to try to remedy my sister's evil.

Dearest Claude,
The contents of this letter may sound too fantastical to
believe. I wouldn't blame you for thinking I have gone
mad and lost myself in some fictional world, but I have
to know for myself that I have told you the truth about
the terrible thing that has been done to us ...

Tears fell down my cheeks as I told him about the forged letter and Caroline's machinations to marry me off to Douglas Hardenbergh for her own ambition, just as she was forcing her daughter to marry a duke.

I also wrote about all that had happened in New York since he'd last heard from me.

That I managed to overlook so many things that
Caroline did and said disturbs me. Perhaps I didn't want
to believe what was always glaringly obvious: my sister is
wicked.

  I can no longer excuse her behaviour. She has
absolutely no compassion for any human being, not even
those who, with all their hearts, have tried to love her:
her husband, her daughter and me. All we are to her are
objects for her use. But that is all in the past now. The
damage has been done and cannot be repaired.

  I discovered your last letter to me in Caroline's desk
drawer. She caught me before I could finish it but I did

get to read your words: 'I wish you every happiness, and only happiness, in your new life.' Those are the words I wish to express to you as well, dearest Claude. For although our precious, beautiful life together came to an abrupt and unanticipated end, you have left me with invaluable gifts. You gave me the gift to be myself.

Strangely, as I sit here locked in a room in Caroline's mansion, I have come to terms with myself. There will be times when I must face challenges by myself and trust in my own resourcefulness.

I let you go with love, Claude, and wish you every happiness with Lise. Perhaps one day I shall meet someone as wonderful as you — although I very much doubt it. But should that happen, I hope it brings a smile to your face to know that I will not be pestering him to marry me. What I want more than anything now is to be free. Perhaps being locked in a room has finally made me see that!

Without this heartbreak between us, I may never have discovered that desire. I would have clung to you and never gained the clarity of self-determination. I want to be free, Claude: to own no one and to not be owned either.

Your truthful friend,
Emma

THIRTY-THREE

The next day I woke with the dread of someone who would be attending a funeral rather than a wedding. I stared out at the street. The pavements and the park were filling with spectators. Ever since the engagement, Caroline had been feeding information to the press to whip the city into a state of excitement.

Jennie arrived with my breakfast on a tray, and it was only then that I realised there had been two footmen posted outside my door overnight. I was sure nothing Caroline did could shock me again.

I got ready, slipped the letter to Claude into the bodice of my dress and went downstairs. I could barely bring myself to look at Caroline, although in her queenly gold gown with the Medici-style collar and ermine trimmings she was hard to miss. I wanted to attack her, if not physically then with a barrage of bitter words, but I controlled myself. This day might be the last time for me to give Isadora all the love I could before we were separated forever.

The bridesmaids, beautiful in gowns of ivory satin, fidgeted nervously, while Oliver leaned against a windowsill as if he was on the verge of being sick.

The first carriage was brought to the door and Caroline gathered the bridesmaids around her. I was to travel with

Oliver and Isadora. Before Caroline departed, she whispered some instructions to Woodford, who glanced in my direction. The spectators weren't the only ones who would be watching me today.

After Caroline and the bridesmaids had departed, Oliver turned to me. 'We'd best go see to the bride.'

The footmen outside Isadora's room stood aside for us with slight bows. Oliver knocked on the door and Isadora's maid opened it.

'Thank you, Lizzie,' Oliver said. 'We would like a few moments alone with my daughter now.'

Lizzie cast a pitying glance back at Isadora, who was sitting at her dressing table. In her magnificent dress and veil she should have been a beautiful bride, but when she lifted her eyes to look at us they were full of sorrow. She had the air of a condemned woman.

'Is it time?' she asked in a barely audible voice. It was as if the Isadora we knew was gone and only a thin, pale shell sat before us.

A swelling of love and self-sacrifice rose in my chest. And something else too: anger. It started as a tingle in my legs, then caught fire and burned in my veins. My blood pumped furiously. Then I practically roared with it, as if I had turned into a fierce mother bear ready to defend her cub. All this time I had failed to intervene because I was convinced that by complying with Caroline I was protecting Isadora. Now I viewed the situation differently. Caroline had trapped us all by using our own fear against us. For who was my sister anyway? She wasn't particularly beautiful, talented or clever. She could never have built up a business the way Oliver did, or created sculptures like Isadora, or written books like me. She was a parasite, sucking the lifeblood out of her victims. How could I have expected Grace to leave Harland if I couldn't break away from my own sister?

I turned to Oliver. 'I'm through with this, aren't you?'

His eyebrows knitted together and he gave a shake of his head. 'Through with this?'

'We have been avoiding the consequences of what might happen if we go against Caroline. But what will *really* happen to us if we do? Especially if we do it together?'

His eyes opened wide and he rubbed the back of his neck. 'The consequences would be disastrous. Caroline's anger knows no bounds. You know what she did to Harland Hunter. She won't be content until she has utterly destroyed anyone who opposes her. I don't think she had Harland killed as some people suggest, but I believe she could have if she'd wanted to.'

'But the consequences for whom?' I asked him. 'You're one of the most powerful men in the United States. Or has she convinced you otherwise?'

'Me? No! I'm thinking of Isadora. What Caroline could do to our daughter if this wedding doesn't go ahead.'

We both turned to Isadora. Her wasted figure and sunken cheeks gave her the appearance of someone who hadn't eaten for days.

'More than she has already done to her?' I said, looking back to Oliver.

He held my gaze until it was clear that we understood each other perfectly.

I glanced at the door. 'What will we do about Woodford and the footmen?'

Oliver drew himself to his full height. 'I pay their wages, for God's sake. I am the master of this house.' Then turning to his daughter, he said, 'Get out of that dress, Isadora. We're going away.'

❦

The spectators cheered for me as I was driven along in an open carriage to the church. Most of them wouldn't know who I was, but the Hopper crest on the carriage door signalled I must be someone important. Every window of every building I passed was filled with faces of those enjoying their own private parties. Hundreds of pairs of eyes stared at me through opera glasses, scrutinising my silk damask dress and the sapphire and diamond brooch that embellished it. I watched their excited expressions with a sense of my writer's curiosity. *How strange human beings are,* I thought. *How we love spectacle! We project all our hopes and dreams onto people we consider perfect, instead of concentrating on making our own lives flourish.*

Although my circumstances couldn't have been more different to Marie Antoinette's, a sudden image of her came into my mind: wearing a simple muslin dress and cap, her hands bound behind her, being taken to the guillotine in a trundle cart. Did the shouts and cheers of the spectators who watched her journey become only distant sounds as a sense of sublime indifference enveloped her and she surrendered to what must be? She had fallen from great heights. I, on the other hand, was stepping up.

The crowds were even thicker near the church: mostly women, struggling and quarrelling with each other to get a better view of the wedding party. The policemen were having trouble holding them back. When they saw my carriage they pushed harder and I cringed at the sight of the policemen shoving them back or threatening them with their clubs.

The coachman had to stop the carriage some distance from the church steps, and I was protected by a column of policemen as I squeezed my way to the door. The bridesmaids, who were waiting on the porch, peered at the crowd with terrified faces.

I walked past the bridesmaids and into the church. Someone must have signalled the bellringer because the bells pealed out in anticipation of the appearance of the bride and her father.

My courage almost failed me as the guests rose to their feet. Grace turned and blinked at me in surprise, but everyone else melded into a sea of silks, brocades, linens, feathers and pearls — until I spotted Caroline in the front pew. She was frowning, probably thinking I had entered the church out of order due to nerves. She would never have anticipated what her downtrodden little sister was about to do.

Mistakenly believing the bridal procession had begun, the organist commenced the Bridal Chorus and the choir began singing. But they were abruptly stopped by the orchestra's conductor when he saw I was alone.

Stunned silence reigned as I walked down the aisle, before hushed whispers began running through the gathering. I didn't dare look in the direction of the Duke and his groomsmen, or the Bishop of New York and his clergymen who were waiting in their places on the chancel. I could have cursed Oliver for leaving me to walk into enemy territory on my own, but because we'd had to act quickly there had been no other choice.

When I came to a stop in front of Caroline, I was David facing Goliath. My stomach sank to my feet.

'Caroline, I need to speak to you and the bishop, alone, in the vestry.'

Her face froze. 'What is it? What has Isadora done?'

When I realised that she was more concerned about the murmurs going around the church than Isadora's wellbeing, my courage returned.

'There isn't going to be a wedding,' I said.

Lucy, standing beside Caroline, gasped. The bishop stepped towards us to find out what was happening.

'I'll fetch my daughter myself if you and Oliver can't manage to bring her here!' Caroline shot back.

'Isadora's not at the house.'

'We had best speak in the vestry,' the bishop whispered, nodding in the direction of a side door.

The murmurs grew louder as Caroline and I, followed by

Lucy, made our way to the vestry. The guests now understood that there was a serious problem.

'The bride has been kidnapped!' I heard Mrs Warburg say to another guest. 'The unions must be behind it. They don't want so much money leaving the country.'

The bishop shut the vestry door behind us and waited for me to speak. I opened and closed my fists as if I could somehow speed Oliver and Isadora on their way in Oliver's private railcar. Isadora had already packed for a long trip so all they had to do was get to their secret location.

'Where is Isadora?' Caroline demanded.

'She's gone. Oliver has taken her away. I don't know where.'

It was the truth. Perhaps at the time Oliver had left the house with Isadora he hadn't been certain himself where they were going. He had told me only that he would have a room booked at the Waldorf-Astoria for me, and had ordered Jennie to have my clothes and personal items sent there.

'I will arrange for your passage back to Paris,' he'd assured me. 'And a bodyguard if you need it.'

I had thought he was joking, but perhaps not from the fierce way Caroline was glaring at me now. It was as well Oliver hadn't told me where he was taking Isadora: Caroline might try to torture it out of me.

'This is an outrage!' Lucy hissed at me. 'How am I supposed to explain this to the Duke? You have made us the laughing stock of society! Not just here but in England too!' She fixed me with that condescending look I knew so well. 'You ungrateful, pitiful woman. How could you do this to Caroline after all she has done for you?'

Caroline glowered as if a demon had possessed her. Her eyes were narrowed and she bared her teeth at me. 'Of course she can do it!' she spat. 'I invited her here believing I could trust her: my peculiar little sister and her strange books. But she couldn't make anything of her own life so she came here to destroy mine out of jealousy. I should have known she wouldn't be loyal to me. She's treacherous! She was born with an evil soul.'

I flinched at Caroline's attack. Born with an evil soul? I had been an innocent child who had adored her. And I'd come to New York out of a strong desire to help my niece and a secret hope that Caroline and I could be sisters again.

Lucy was taken aback by Caroline's outburst. She glanced at the bishop, who was watching the exchange with his mouth open.

'We must stay calm, Caroline,' Lucy said, touching my sister's arm. 'We must keep our heads and think of something to tell the guests. We can say that Isadora has come down with some terrible illness. Or she's been poisoned. We must buy ourselves time to fix this.'

Caroline turned cold, hard eyes on her friend. 'Why don't we tell them she's dead? Because that's what she is to me.'

Lucy's hand flew to her mouth. For once she was lost for words. Obviously she had never seen this side of Caroline's nature.

'Mrs Hopper,' the bishop intervened, 'we are in the house of God.'

Caroline paid him no heed. Her eyes fixed on me with a fierce stare. 'I should have finished what I tried on the plantation.'

Her words baffled me. I began to unravel, and wanted to turn and run, but my feet were glued to the spot. 'What do you mean? What did you try on the plantation?'

Suddenly I was overcome by a deep primal fear. It chilled me like ice down my back. For some odd reason I remembered Monsieur Plamondon remarking that Louisiana had a darkness to it, and although I'd been very young when I left there, such things could remain in the unconscious mind.

'When you were a few weeks old, I snuck into the nursery and saw your pale form,' Caroline said. 'No human could be that white and I knew you were a bad omen. I picked up a pillow and tried to smother you, but I was caught by your nursemaid. After that, they kept me away from you.'

'Caroline! You don't know what you are saying!' Lucy cried. 'You have been under enormous strain. I will call for Doctor Mitford and he will give you something to calm you. Please don't worry. We will sort this out together as we always do.'

If Caroline heard her friend's pleas she showed no sign of it. She just kept her eyes on me and I saw their deep emptiness. I had suspected well before now that I was nothing to my sister; merely someone to be summoned and used. What I hadn't fully understood was that Caroline actually hated me. But I also saw that it wasn't my fault. She was someone devoid of love. Perhaps even devoid of a soul.

If she had spoken those words to me as a child, I might have thrown myself in the Seine. Even if she had said them only a few months ago, I would have been shattered. Now all I experienced was the severing of any final attachment towards her: it tore like a thin, worn-out rope.

'She does know what she's saying, Lucy,' I said calmly. 'And she means every word of it.'

But she couldn't destroy me because I finally knew who I was, and it was someone infinitely better than her.

I turned and walked out of the vestry, down the aisle past the gaping guests, and out of Caroline's life forever.

THIRTY-FOUR

Paris, 1900

Dear Grace,

*I am very sorry to hear that your mother has passed
away. I know she was precious to you, and she couldn't
have had a more caring daughter.*

*It does give me great pleasure, however, to know you
will soon be joining us in Paris and also on our planned
trip to Italy. Our initial stay there after the debacle in
New York was soothing for us all, and Isadora and
Thomas (I'm finding it difficult to stop calling him 'Mr
Gadley') were married in Rome.*

*Our little 'artists' village' here in Rue Jacob is a happy
and productive place. We spend our mornings working: I
write, while Isadora and Thomas study, model, cast and
carve together. In the afternoons we visit the museums or
walk the streets for inspiration. Isadora is working on a
large-scale sculpture of a mother bear defending her cubs.
It will be superb when she finishes it.*

*Oliver continues to be very generous to us, offering
to pay for a grand apartment and for Isadora's tuition
at the École des Beaux-Arts, but my niece is determined*

to make it on her own. She has told me that she can feel Grand-maman's presence in this apartment, helping her with her work, and wouldn't want to be anywhere else.

She is barely recognisable as the Isadora we knew in New York. She is strong, calm and confident — and not easily fooled by anyone. She and Paulette have formed a solid bond, and like to go to the market together. Sometimes the vendors try to cheat them, but nobody can pull the wool over Isadora's eyes. She can argue and bargain as well as any fishwife. She has become as vibrant and lively as I always sensed she could be.

I have received very generous advances for my novella The Mysterious Cat *and my novel set in New York, so I am now without debts and determined to be a self-made woman too. We have instead asked Oliver to be a generous patron to Charles Garrett House in Greenwich Village and their subsidiary projects, which he has been doing with some zeal I believe.*

I was pleased to learn from you that Oliver and Mrs Natica Miller have come to an understanding. Oliver was never particularly interested in New York society, and as Mrs Miller was shunned after her divorce from her horse-loving husband, they should make quite a pair. Oliver was very generous in his divorce arrangements with Caroline — even going so far as to allow himself to be 'caught' with a woman of ill-repute so the blame would fall on him. He deserves to be happy now that he has escaped my sister's clutches.

I stopped writing and turned to the newspaper articles Florence had sent me. All of them were about how Caroline had become a champion for women's rights and a defender of the poor tenement dwellers of New York. I picked up the one from the *New York Times.*

Since journalist Cecilia West exposed Permelia
Frances's ill-advised 'hobo party', where the guests
came dressed in rags and ate their dinner off garbage
lids, New York society has been held in contempt by the
general public who once venerated it. People are now
demanding laws to make sure the wealthy contribute
their share of taxes and to establish better and fairer
labour practices.

Nobody in society has listened to the public's cries
better than Mrs Caroline Hopper. 'As a society leader I
consider it my duty to set high standards of behaviour
and to pave the way for other women in less fortunate
positions,' she said. 'That is why I decided to divorce
from my husband despite the risk of being shunned for it.
I don't believe any woman should be forced to stay with
a cruel and neglectful man.'

The article went on to say that after 'Mrs Hopper's courageous
decision' other women of note had divorced their husbands.

'I have always been the first to do anything,' Mrs Hopper
said. 'I have always been a natural leader.'

I shook my head in amazement. Never mind that it was Oliver
who had wanted the divorce! But that was Caroline. She could
rise like a phoenix from the ashes of the worst scandal and
somehow turn the situation around to appear in her favour.

I knew my sister didn't care about working women or New
York's poor. She only cared about herself and how she appeared
to others. As soon as social reform went out of fashion, she
would drop it like a hot potato and find something else she
could use to aggrandise herself. Still, I had to admire her ability
to survive.

I sighed and returned to my letter to Grace.

You asked if I ever think of Caroline. The answer is that it gives me more peace not to do so. But during those moments my mind does drift to her, I try to picture her keeping vigil over her dying son, or as a child terrified by the destruction of her home during the Civil War. When I do that, I am able to see her as human. Otherwise, the story of my sister and my relationship with her is too tragic to contemplate.

Oliver, Isadora and I were the people who loved her most. We would have been there for her. But Caroline cannot really love herself and therefore she could never love us. And she didn't want our love anyway; all she wanted was our blind obedience.

Maybe one day some very clever scholar of the mind will devise a theory to explain personalities like Caroline's and Harland's. For myself, although I often yearn to find an explanation for the inexplicable, I have learned to let things be.

After I'd finished my letter, I took out the typeset pages for my novel, *Death at Waverly*, to mark up my corrections before the final version went to the printer. I was making annotations in the margin when I heard Isadora and Thomas burst into laughter. I smiled. They laughed so much together I didn't know how they managed to produce such good work — but perhaps that was their secret.

The mirth continued for some time and my curiosity got the better of me. I winked at Grand-maman's photograph and put the pages aside. 'Let's go and find out what they're up to.'

I entered the sculpting studio — formerly Grand-maman's bedroom — expecting to find Isadora and Thomas with their heads bent over a clay model. What I witnessed instead was Isadora sitting in a chair sketching while Thomas reclined on a couch as naked as the day he was born. At the sight of me he grabbed a handkerchief to cover his nether regions.

'Oh my goodness!' I cried, trying to make a hasty retreat but getting my sleeve caught on the door catch.

Isadora cackled with laughter. 'Aunt Emma! I never expected you to be a prude! Thomas is posing for me. Come and see the miniature clay models I've made of him. I'm working on a bigger one now.'

'I'd rather not,' I said, having trouble freeing my sleeve. My face was burning. 'I must finish the final editing of *Death at Waverly* today.'

Thomas stood and tugged on a robe. 'Emma,' he said, trying to calm me, 'you know that women artists aren't allowed to work with life models as men are. That puts them at a distinct disadvantage when it comes to public commissions. I'm merely offering my humble form so my wife can create the art she's capable of. There can't be a scandal if she uses her husband for her studies.'

I remembered Douglas Hardenbergh's extensive collection of female nudes. Thomas was right: there was a reason female artists had been limited to painting fruit and flowers.

'Very true,' I said, finally freeing my sleeve and escaping out the door. 'I won't keep you.'

I was returning to my room when the ringer on the front door tinkled. Paulette was out on errands so I went to answer it. My heart stopped when I found Claude on the doorstep. Under his arm he held a painting covered in cloth and tied with string. He must have been on his way to his art dealer.

The surprise slowed my responses and I stared at him for a long moment before coming to my senses.

'Claude! Come in!' I stammered.

He was as beautiful as ever with his handsome olive-skinned face and mop of wavy hair. An ache welled inside me, just like the day I'd left Le Havre on the ship to New York. Only this time it was worse because of how things had changed so significantly between us and why.

'I knew you were in Italy for a while,' he said, following me into the drawing room, 'but I didn't find out until yesterday that you'd returned to Paris. Belda told me.' He looked at me directly. 'Why haven't you come to see everyone at the café? They're all asking after you.'

I indicated for him to sit down and took a seat too. For the first time since he had arrived, I managed to lift my eyes to his. From the perplexity in them I realised he was finding this visit as difficult as I was. It gave me the courage to be honest.

'I wasn't ready, Claude. It would have been too hard for me to see you with Lise.'

He stared at me unblinking. 'Lise and I haven't been together since I received your letter from New York. It wasn't a serious liaison on her part or mine.'

'Oh.' I turned away, my mind racing as my sense of reality shifted. When I'd seen them together in New York I'd thought they were in love. But perhaps my deep hurt had exaggerated things in my imagination. I squeezed my hands together so tightly they throbbed. Was it possible I had been acting on a wrong conclusion these months past?

A burst of laughter came from the studio. Claude glanced in that direction.

'My niece and nephew-in-law,' I explained. 'They enjoy working together ... a lot.'

He nodded and glanced around the room. His eyes rested on the bronze bust Isadora had sculpted of me, and he stood up to examine it.

'This is a superb piece. It captures your natural radiance and poise.'

I liked the bust for those reasons too, and gazed at it whenever I felt my courage failing. It was failing now. Claude was watching me, but I kept my eyes averted.

'She did a lot of damage, didn't she? Caroline, I mean,' he said.

I nodded. 'I'm sorry, Claude. The worst thing was how much she hurt you. I will never forgive her for that.'

'What about you, Emma? Aren't you angry about what she did to you?'

Tears rose in my eyes so I squeezed them shut, then opened them again. 'I can't. If I feel rage, it ties me to her … and I've set myself free.'

He listened intently, absorbing every word. I'd forgotten how good Claude was at listening; it was one of his many endearing qualities.

'I liked what you wrote in your last letter,' he said. 'I admire your determination and self-reliance. I've heard that your career is soaring too?'

'I'm certainly enjoying more success than I did in the past. But it's my life that I'm thinking about now — I treat it as a piece of art that will never be finished. And I've learned that it's full of surprises. I longed for a family, and now I've got one with my niece and her husband. I'm very happy even though it isn't the family I'd pictured.'

Claude drew a breath and picked up the painting he'd brought with him. 'I too have been doing a lot of thinking,' he said, tugging the string off. 'I finally bought that property in the country I was always dreaming about. It's in Grez-sur-Loing — there's a large artists' colony there. I've been spending a few days at a time in the house to carry out repairs. One day I sat down and asked myself: who am I doing this for? What is the point of all this if I don't have Emma?' He lifted those beautiful smoky eyes to mine. 'I was foolish. Why did I refuse joy when it was offered to me? I should have married you and trusted that nothing would change for the worse. I should have had more faith in us — and especially in you.'

He removed the cloth and turned the painting towards me. It was of an old wooden house surrounded by a garden of peach trees and flowers gone wild. It was painted with thick brushstrokes and bright with colours: lilac, pink and gold. In the doorway of the house stood a blonde woman — me — holding a child in her arms.

'The house is fixed now, but I left the garden for you. You always dreamed of a garden, Emma.'

I stared at the painting, unable to believe that something I had once fantasised about had been depicted so beautifully.

'Emma, will you marry me now?' Claude asked.

Tears filled my eyes. I had longed to hear those words for years, and now that Claude was saying them I saw how easy it would be to return to my former self: the needy, unsure person I'd once been. I had yearned to belong to someone then because I hadn't known how to belong to myself.

I took a deep breath. 'I need more time, Claude. I faced the person I'd feared most of my life and lived to tell the tale. But it wasn't Caroline; it was me. I'm just starting to grow into the real Emma Lacasse, and I like her. I want to fill her empty spaces myself. I want to be free of shackles and insecurities.'

Claude stared at me open-mouthed. Then a slow smile broke over his face and he laughed. 'Well, that wasn't the "yes" I was hoping for, but it wasn't exactly a "no" either. The irony of the situation is too good. I can hear Belda and the others laughing at me now.'

I took his hand. He squeezed mine and stared lovingly into my eyes.

'The house in Grez-sur-Loing has been there for a long time. It can wait a while longer — until Emma Lacasse is good and ready.'

I smiled and kissed his soft lips. My lessons had been hard-earned, but they had been worth the pain and tears. Once I'd stopped wishing that things could be other than they were, a whole world had opened up to me. I was ready to embrace it.

Author's Note

'The Gilded Age' refers to a period in the history of the United States that coincides approximately with the Victorian era in Britain and the Belle Époque in France. It was a time of rapid economic growth, when great fortunes were made and millions of immigrants flooded into the country. It was also a period of extreme wealth for some and destitution and abject poverty for others. The term was first coined by Mark Twain in his novel *The Gilded Age: A Tale of Today*. 'Gilded' is not the same as 'golden'. It implies a thin, shiny patina that covers something less attractive underneath.

In writing this story I was influenced by the colourful characters of this time — Caroline Astor, Alva and Consuelo Vanderbilt, Diamond Jim Brady, Harry Lehr and Stanford White among others. However, while their stories and personalities inspired some of the events in the novel, it is still a work of fiction and none of the main characters represents a real person in temperament or life history.

Acknowledgements

I am indebted to the team at HarperCollins Australia for their enthusiasm and support while I was writing *The Invitation*. I would like to make special mention of Kathy Hassett and Anna Valdinger, Fiction Publishers, and Scott Forbes, Senior Editor, for their professionalism and the time they devoted to helping me make *The Invitation* shine. I would also like to give thanks to editor Nicola O'Shea, whose extraordinary grasp of character and structure makes working with her feel like magic. Special mention should also be made of the wonderful Roslyn McGechan, who helped me check the final pages.

Writing is often a solitary activity and the support of my family and friends and their eagerness to see me succeed is the wind beneath my wings. I am so appreciative of them all, especially my father, Stan, and my friends Tracey, Melinda, Lily and Halina, as well as my three cats, Valentino, Versace and Gucci, who share my writing space and lend their own special energy to the task at hand!

Thank you so much to you all for contributing your own unique touch to this book!

With love and appreciation,
Belinda Alexandra

Discover the world of Belinda Alexandra …

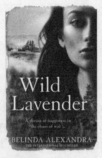

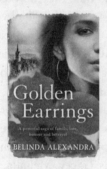

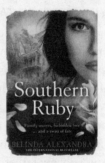